FUGO

TERROR FROM THE SKY

ELIZABETH L. YOUNG

DIVERTIR
PUBLISHING
Salem, NH

Second Edition

Elizabeth L. Young

Copyright © 2016 Elizabeth L. Young

Cover design by Kenneth Tupper

Published by Divertir Publishing LLC
PO Box 232
North Salem, NH 03073
http://www.divertirpublishing.com/

ISBN-13: 978-1-938888-15-1
ISBN-10: 1-938888-15-4

Library of Congress Control Number: 2016948981

Printed in the United States of America

Dedication

*For my husband, Robert,
and in memory of my parents,
Maude and Louis Young.*

Acknowledgments

This book could not have been written without the help of several people. First, my thanks to Dr. Thomas M. Harris, who provided valuable guidance on many details concerning chemicals and epidemics. At Divertir Publishing, my editor, Elisa, gave suggestions that have made the book much better. Mary Pettigrew has been my guide for my web site and creative details. Finally, my most sincere thanks to Dr. Robert Lovell, my husband, who collaborated on the original idea, helped with research, and provided technical guidance concerning the balloons and satellites. Any errors of detail are mine alone and not the fault of any of the friends or family who so generously helped me.

CONTENTS

PROLOGUE
June 22

In November, 1944, the Japanese began launching 9,300 unmanned bomb-carrying balloons (Fugo) that were carried east over the Pacific Ocean by the jet stream. The balloons were made of paper and tree parts; they were filled with hydrogen gas. The bombs were intended to drop over America and explode, causing forest fires, general panic and deaths. However, without a reliable guidance system, most of the balloons did not reach North America. The US Government suppressed information about the project, and fortunately most of the bombs fell into the ocean or exploded harmlessly. Only six deaths occurred. Japan stopped the launches in 1945.

§ § §

Melissa, a golden lab, did not notice the cloudless, blue Wisconsin sky that enveloped the farm. She was trotting from the house to the haystack by the barn. She had seen something drop into it a few days before. She was going back there since nobody was taking her hunting today. She liked retrieving for her master, but she was young and happy to think about discovering a small animal that she could chase or corner on her own.

The three boys had made a big hole in the haystack when they were playing in the yard, and the oldest one had thrown the youngest one's jacket into it, but then they had all been distracted and left the haystack. Later that day, during a loud thunderstorm, Melissa had seen something fall into the hole. She put a paw down as far as she could. The hay felt soft and dry. Nothing. But she knew she had seen something—and there was this hole...

CHAPTER ONE

December 5, the preceding year

Farley McDonald had secretly missed the long hours. When he sold his original company, FM Craft, to AeroProducts, a mid-sized company in Dallas, he and his wife traveled and visited their grown children. After a year of this, Farley was bored and contacted the owners of AeroProducts, offering to consult. They immediately accepted. They gave Farley a choice of where in the business he would like to help out, and he chose the research balloons.

FM Craft had started out in the business of making small boats for the inland lakes that dot Kansas, but Farley had seen a market in weather balloons. He won his first NOAA contract and more followed. So, for fifteen years, FM Craft had successfully manufactured balloons. When Farley became a consultant, he felt like he was building a start-up all over again. Maybe it was a coincidence or good luck, but three months after he went back to work, a man from the FBI showed up.

"Mr. McDonald," his secretary said, poking her head around the door of Farley's new office at the front of the balloon factory, "Mr. Ricotti is here to see you."

"Bring him in, please," Farley answered, closing out his computer screen.

"Mr. Ricotti, it's a pleasure," Farley said, shaking the hand of the powerful looking, dark complexioned man in the gray suit who stood before him. Without being asked, Mr. Ricotti closed the door and sat down in the chair facing Farley's desk.

"Mr. Farley, my agency has done its background checking on AeroProducts and on you. We have a classified program we would like to begin, and we need your expertise and your balloons. I cannot tell you the nature of the program, but I am here to ask if you are interested. If so, we will continue. If not, I will wish you success in your very fine business here." Farley could not quite place the faint accent. French Canadian, maybe. The man had shown all the proper credentials and it was true that the factory had done classified work in the past.

Mr. Ricotti continued. "I have, as you know, had two meetings with Mr.

Steelman and Mr. Goldberg at AeroProducts in Dallas. Last week, they told me that they will be pleased to accept the contract, but neither of them has a clearance, although you do, so I could not tell them anything other than the business details. They said they would take on the contract only if you personally accept working on it."

"Can you give me an idea of what we would be doing?" Farley inquired, without committing himself.

"Yes. We need a relatively large number of constant altitude helium balloons that will have a seven to ten day lifetime when operating at 55,000 feet, plus or minus ten percent. They must be able to attain a minimum nighttime altitude of 45,000 feet. The balloons must have a payload lift capability of slightly less than seven pounds, including a simple payload attach ring."

Farley, who had designed hundreds of balloons, began to move his hands in ball-shaped patterns as he spoke. "If we assume a balloon weight roughly equal to the payload weight, then it would take about fifty cubic meters of helium. That would give you a 15-foot diameter inflated pressure vessel. We could use Stratofilm-420 resin film like I used on one of NASA's research balloons to withstand the overpressure required to hold the upper atmosphere altitude limit you are specifying. This doesn't sound too hard, Mr. Ricotti. How many balloons do you need?"

"We need 600 balloons and we need delivery within six months. But there are some other requirements that may make this more difficult. I have included a complete list of them in the contract for your detailed review, but there are a couple of specific issues that I want you to understand. Your design must take into account that there will be a launch system that allows a maximum of three men to launch each balloon in a 10 mile per hour wind in no more than two minutes from out of the crate to release. And, because of payload sensitivities, the balloons must not have any metal parts or metalized fabric and should preferably be optically transparent."

"You are right—those are significant requirements. The quick launch specification may be difficult to achieve. The lightweight material that I would choose to withstand the overpressure is also quite fragile, but the smaller size is an advantage. Unfortunately, until I do some preliminary design work, I won't know how to price this job."

"I've negotiated a cost plus fixed fee contract with Mr. Goldberg, and a copy of that contract is here for you to look at." Mr. Ricotti pulled out the document and spread it in front of Farley. "It also contains more detailed requirements. Why don't I give you a day or so to review this and decide and then let me know if you can meet our requirements? Time is of the essence here and we do have other options."

"That's fine," Farley replied, as both men rose from their chairs. "I'll be back to you tomorrow. Is using the phone to talk about this all right?"

"We prefer that you send a fax to this number," replied Mr. Ricotti, circling a number on his business card, "and simply refer to this contract as 'Party Favors'. Indicate that either 'Party Favors' can be delivered on time or that the project cannot be undertaken. If you need to speak to me, however, you may call this number—it is my 'hello' phone."

Farley escorted Mr. Ricotti to the outside door, smiling at his secretary as he passed her desk. It was already after 5 p.m., but no way was she leaving before he did.

After "Mr. Ricotti" got into his black sedan and drove out of the parking lot, he stopped and shed his suit coat. He pulled a cell phone out of the glove compartment and turned it on. He dialed and waited a minute. No need to identify himself as Georges Labadie; the party on the other end knew his voice. "I think 'Party Favors' will be just fine for our children," he said into the phone as soon as someone answered. "I'll know tomorrow." He hung up. Driving in Kansas reminded him of the desert where he had spent so many days and nights. "In another life," he thought to himself.

CHAPTER TWO
The following April, first week

Rafik Muhaimin had flown to Los Angeles from Vancouver and rented a red Mazda. Known as "the chauffer" within the organization, his skills included desert driving. He loved going fast. He had two stops to make in the morning, both north of LA, and one later in the day in the San Francisco area.

He drove north from LAX for thirty minutes and then took an exit that led him to a squat, gray cinder block building with a sign saying "Electronic Parts and Supplies." Checking himself in the driver's mirror, he was pleased at how Canadian he looked—clean-shaven, wearing a conventional dark suit, white shirt and tie.

Inside the wholesale electronics store, a middle-aged woman with gray braids sat at the counter, working on her computer. "Good morning," Rafik said to the woman. "I have an appointment with your owner. I am Silvio Franchetti from Vancouver."

The woman looked up and smiled. "He's in his office in the back. Let me be sure he's in and I'll show you back there." She activated an intercom and a moment later came out from behind the counter to walk to the back of the building with Rafik.

The owner was half way out of his door when Rafik saw him. "Come in, come in! I'm so glad you decided to come down here and see our place," the owner added, showing Rafik to a straight-backed chair in his neat but modest office. Rafik did not tell him that his trip had nothing to do with "seeing the place" since they had researched over 50 such places on the Internet and had decided on this one, along with a few others, because they offered the right products.

"Have you decided which brands of GPS's you wish to carry and which models?" He had previously asked "Silvio" on the phone why an office supply store would be interested in ordering GPS units for retail sale. "Silvio" had explained that an increasing number of their clients had company vehicles, aircraft, and even boats, while some also wanted small hand-held units for personal use. So, Vancouver Office Supply and Service Company was branching out into electronics.

"I'd like to see the Magellan Mite 300 if you have it in stock," Rafik replied. It was a new product on the market and they had not been able to see it until now.

"We have it—I'll ask my assistant to bring one in along with the product specs."

When an assistant came back with the Magellan, Rafik turned it over in his hands. It was the smallest GPS unit they had seen. It looked rugged. "How many of these can you get to us immediately?" he asked, and then added, "We want to begin our new retail lines as soon as possible—certainly before the summer season."

"Well, we can ship 100 this week and up to three hundred more by the end of the month."

"Good!" Rafik said and pulled out a checkbook. "I'll write you a check for the first one hundred today. After you check our credit, you can ship another hundred if that is convenient."

"Very convenient," the owner replied, surprised at the offer of the check for the first order—but cash was cash. "I'll have the warehouse package the first hundred immediately." They moved on to the necessary paperwork and in fifteen minutes had concluded their business.

When Rafik returned to his car, he programmed his GPS for his next stop, about an hour away. Rafik's second visit went much as his first. The factory manager was eager to show him the new products he had asked about, and this time, Rafik expressed interest in the Garmin AP Mini. "Our company will take 100 now and possibly more next month," he told the young proprietor who, with his sister, owned and ran the factory.

"It's the best!" he assured Rafik and happily took the check.

After the second purchase, Rafik sent a short progress message to Ahmed and then sped up to see how fast he could make the Mazda go, providing no highway cops interfered with him. It was mid-afternoon when he reached the third factory store, Bay Electronics, located in an industrial park in Palo Alto and selling to the public as well as to the trade.

Rafik was ushered to the back of the building and through to a smaller office where business customers were met. The head of sales, a short woman of ample build with bright red hair, smiled broadly at Rafik when they shook hands.

"I know you wanted to look at the Navigon-2G, but I can highly recommend the Magellan Mite 300 and the Garmin AP Mini also," she began bringing out units for Rafik to handle. Rafik refrained from saying anything about his other purchases. "Thank you, but my boss has specified the Navigon-2G, and we need two hundred of them immediately; we might need more later," Rafik replied graciously. The check signing and paperwork followed smoothly.

Rafik drove to the modest motel near the San Francisco airport where he planned to spend the night. He would fly back to Vancouver early the next day. He sent one more text to Ahmed and included Georges. It said simply, "Mission accomplished."

§ § §

After Rafik had left Bay Electronics, the head of sales pulled a chair up to her assistant's desk. "Carmen, I want you to do something—not urgent but best done this week if you can. We just signed up a new customer: Vancouver Office Supply and Service Company. I've left the paperwork in your in-box, along with their check. But I want to know more about them."

"You mean their credit rating?" Carmen asked. She had worked for Bay Electronics for ten years, learning many things and bringing them some of her skills from her former life in Colombia.

"Well, yes, check the credit rating, of course, but get me some background on the owners, the management, how long they've been in business, who else they buy from—in fact, see if you can tap into their customer data base. There's something about this one that seems a bit strange, although I can't put my finger on it."

Carmen made a mental note to call her brother to ask for some help with her boss's request. She could find many things on the Internet, and, of course, through the Agency, but Raul was better placed to tap those resources. And he might find the Vancouver company interesting as well.

CHAPTER THREE
April 21

Carmen had to wait three weeks to see Raul, as he was traveling on one of his missions. She wanted to see Raul in person for several reasons—and what better way than to enjoy an opera together? So since the San Francisco Opera was mounting a new production of "Carmen" that was where she asked Raul to meet her.

They made a handsome couple, Carmen with her black hair piled high on her head and Raul in a tux, a foot taller than she but with the same olive complexion and slender good looks. The Caballeros. Most people thought them to be husband and wife, but they were not. Carmen lived alone although she had many admirers. Raul was also unmarried. Privately, Carmen wondered if he would ever take a wife as he could do most things well for himself, including cook and entertain. His work also made lasting relationships difficult. He traveled often, and then, of course, there were aspects of his work that he could not discuss with anyone. Raul was a specialist on Latin America, working for the CIA.

Carmen, too, worked for the Agency, but only as a part-time consultant. Her fulltime job, with Bay Electronics, gave her access to the business world, which was valuable to them both. Raul maintained a cover as a consulting architect, and he had earned a degree in the subject from the University of Washington.

As soon as the curtain went down on the first act, Carmen said, "Come on, I'll buy the champagne!" They went to the elegant bar in the south lobby and then found a relatively quiet corner where they could talk.

"Raul, we have a new client that my boss wants to know more about. They are called Vancouver Office Supply and Service Company. I have a copy of some paperwork from them in my purse. I'll give it to you at supper."

"All right," said Raul, looking around the foyer. Perhaps for beautiful women, Carmen thought. "What is so special about them?" he asked, still letting his eyes roam.

"I'm not sure. My boss sensed something and she has good instincts. They want to start selling GPS equipment and made a large order from us, and, of course, we may not be the only ones they are buying from." Carmen paused, thinking back on the brief encounter with Rafik. "They sent a man—I think he may originally have been Algerian—as their buyer."

"Algerian?" Raul asked, casually, still casing the lobby. "Why would that arouse any suspicions?"

"I don't think it was the man himself," Carmen replied, "but it may just be that we've never heard of this company before—and our marketing people are pretty good at finding prospects. Are you going to be home for a while, or traveling?"

"Not sure until tomorrow. There's word of a special mission coming up. I'll do some research on your Vancouver company as soon as I can and call you or send you an email.

Carmen smiled. "And what lovely lady will you be leaving in the lurch if you have to go off again suddenly?" She expected Raul to joke about this, but he did not.

"I'm not seeing anyone regularly now, but there is someone I could become more interested in." Then he flashed his customary grin. "She's about your size and height—must be I've always been in love with my sister!"

Carmen groaned. They would have no more serious talk tonight. "Come on," she said, just as the intermission bell rang. "Let's see if the second act lives up to your high standards."

CHAPTER FOUR
May 3

Gerard parked his rusting blue Camaro at the back of the small parking lot outside the Vancouver seafood restaurant, which was closed. It faced the boat yard. He was still smarting from the lecture Luc had given him. "Rahmid knows nothing, nothing!" Gerard had angrily told his older brother. "He's not a spy—he is just looking for work, and I like him and thought maybe we could use him."

"He cannot be trusted," Luc replied, in that even voice that meant he was mad. "I will take care of him." So, Gerard had shrugged and decided to get on with his main task—lining up the boats.

The captain in charge of the fleet of the five boats Gerard was chartering stood on the dock waiting for Gerard. "I'm Gerard Dufee from the university," the young man said, "and I have all the paperwork here for you."

The captain, who had white hair and deep-set eyes in a surprisingly unlined face, took the clipboard from Gerard and examined it. "This all seems to be in order, except I don't see the part about paying me more if we are out more than ten hours," the older man asked.

"It's here, on the next page—we pay you double for every hour beyond the ten," Gerard replied, "but I don't think the research team will need more than about eight hours unless we have unfavorable winds, in which case we will have to postpone the trip." The captain continued reading. "Let's go on board the *Filly* and I'll sign," he said, leading the way.

As they boarded the 50-foot fishing boat, which was clean and freshly painted, he turned back to Gerard. "You go with the students or are you just arranging this?"

"Sometimes both," Gerard replied, "I assist in teaching the course. I am responsible for the observation equipment that we will deploy to measure the effects of photoelectric emissions. The information is needed to develop lightning protection on aircraft."

The captain merely nodded.

Once the contract was signed, the deposit changed hands. "All five boats will be here at the dock and ready to go out early June 2nd," the captain said. "I'll have two of my best men ready to work with your men and to assist the captains on each boat."

"Thank you for all your assistance," Gerard said politely, folding his copy of the contract. After they got off the *Filly* he looked back. Maybe a life of fishing would not be so bad, but this boat would not be going out in a few weeks to find fish.

After he left the parking lot, he drove a few miles further north to another boat yard. Again he met a captain who operated a fleet of five boats. Again Gerard presented himself as working for the university. The preliminary conversations, all conducted over the telephone, went well. This captain, too, was happy to sign the contract and seemed incurious about the purpose of the lease of his boats, all of which looked as if they spent considerable hours in the rough seas of the coastal Pacific.

Tomorrow he would conclude the leasing of five more boats at still a different boat yard from the first two. These last boats were part of their reserve fleet, in case something went wrong with any of the other vessels. He hoped they would not be needed, but the mission was meticulously planned. He knew that in addition to the boats he was leasing, five more would be leaving a port in Los Angeles for the same purpose on Saturday, June 2nd.

Gerard believed in the cause, but he also liked the money he was making. If it were not for Luc's constant suspicions and frequent anger at everybody in the group, including Gerard, things would have to be said to be going quite well. "I need to find Luc a girlfriend," Gerard muttered to himself the next afternoon, when all the leases were signed and filed. He thought about treating himself to a beer at the Bar Blu but feared he might run into Rahmid. "I hope I have not lost him as a friend," Gerard thought. His only friends these days were part of the cell, and most of them were humorless and intense.

CHAPTER FIVE
May 4

Rahmid Shalif, code name "Playboy," had hoped to learn more from Gerard about the boats so he could pass on information to Colonel Diep. But when Rahmid went to Bar Blu the next night, Gerard was absent and his cousin, Luc, was waiting instead. Rahmid's guard immediately went up when Luc said he could offer him a job with his garbage removal service. Rahmid's cover story with Gerard had been that he needed work. Now, worried that Luc knew that he was an informant, Rahmid kept trying to turn the conversation back to working on the boats. Luc, however, was insistent that Rahmid visit the "garbage removal" company for a job interview, so Rahmid agreed and excused himself after he finished a coke.

In his car, Rahmid activated his mobile phone. "It's me," he said when someone at the other end answered. "Remember when I talked to you last night about sailing? I think the subject is more important than I thought. I will pursue it." He clicked the power off. He checked his rear-view mirror. He was not being followed. Still, he would have to make good on his "looking for work" story. Just not today.

Colonel Po "Johnny" Diep weighed his options. Meeting Rahmid in person always involved risk, but he was feeling more and more that Rahmid needed guidance, maybe even protection. Johnny had a healthy estimate of his own abilities and value. He also believed the luck that first helped him survive as a young Vietnamese refugee in a new country still followed him. He could assume many guises and even worked once undercover as a cook for six months to infiltrate the Vancouver Chinese community. At least his wife, who was also in Military Intelligence, appreciated his vegetable chopping skills now! He reactivated his phone and dialed Rahmid's number. He got voice mail. "Call me back, please, before you make any more dates—my sister may be interested." It was one of the codes to alert Rahmid to call back immediately.

They met in a small park, frequented by mothers, children and dogs the next morning. Rahmid was dressed as a construction worker, in a blue jump suit. Col. Diep wore a baseball cap and tinted glasses. He carried a newspaper and a book and sat on one of the most remote park benches, drinking coffee. Gerard sat down at the other end of the bench, also with a coffee.

"Who did you meet with yesterday? Was it Gerard again?" Col. Diep asked.

"I met him the night before at the Bar Blu; got him a little bit drunk. He talked again about his great responsibility to rent boats, and maybe I could get temporary work on one, but he doesn't know what they are going to be used for. He said there would be a fleet going out in early June. Then, yesterday when we were supposed to meet again, his brother, Luc, came instead. He seemed very interested in offering me a job." Rahmid gave Col. Diep all the details of the conversation. "I did not plan on seeing him, at least not until I talked with you. Do you think I should go to this company where he works so I can keep my story about wanting work?"

"No. Do not go. Do not see this Luc again, if you can help it, and if you encounter him try not to be alone with him. He has a reputation, and it is not good. We need you to keep in touch with Gerard. You are giving us valuable information. You can contact Gerard after a day or two; that would be natural, wouldn't it?

Rahmid left first. Johnny Diep read his paper for a few minutes, threw away his empty coffee cup, and left the park. His wife would be surprised to see him home again so soon, but he had some research to do—he hoped his contacts in Washington were up to delving into their databases.

CHAPTER SIX
May 5

The day after Johnny met Rahmid in the park, he became "Ming Lew." "Ming" had a solid resume as a kitchen helper, but he was out of work. Just after noon on Friday, Johnny rang the bell at the modest-looking building on Front Street that had a small plaque reading Best Removal Company. He patted his right leg. He felt good about the "job interview" to come.

A tall, lanky man with black hair answered the bell after a few minutes. "Yes?" he glanced down at the short Oriental man with unusually broad shoulders. Johnny noticed no obvious bulge in Luc's clothing, no scabbard on his belt.

"Pardon me, sir, but I am Ming Lew, it's my day off, and I'm looking for work. I'm going to all the businesses in this neighborhood. I used to work in the kitchen at Chan Palace two streets over, but they had to lay two of us off. Do you have anything? I can carry heavy loads."

Luc frowned; he did not appreciate this distraction as he had to be prepared if Rahmid showed up today.

"No, no we have nothing. We are not hiring." Luc started to close the door.

Ming looked down at his feet. "Then may I ask a favor—to use your bathroom for just a minute? I am sorry—I have been out all morning and all this afternoon." Saying this, Ming inched a few steps into the doorway.

"This is not a public place!" Luc answered harshly, looking up and down the street, worried that if Rahmid came, there would be complications. He looked squarely at the Chinaman—or whatever he was—and decided it might be better to let him in and get rid of him quickly. "All right, the bathroom is just there," Luc motioned down a dark hallway, "but hurry up. I have work to do."

He let Johnny in, closing the door behind him. Johnny took a few steps down the hall; when he heard Luc begin to follow him, he turned back swiftly, with his right hand already inside the highest pocket of his cargo pants. He pulled out the long, curved-blade knife with one motion and aimed it at Luc's neck.

Luc did not cry out, but the look of surprise on his face gave Johnny much satisfaction as the knife sank into his skin. Luc collapsed to the ground. Johnny returned the knife to a heavy plastic pouch he carried in another pocket. He bent over Luc and retrieved a small ring of keys from Luc's side pocket. Johnny immediately went back to the front door and found the two that fit the two door locks. Stepping back inside, he dialed a number on his cell phone. "The cargo is ready for pick up," he said and hung up. It was tempting to search the building, but he suspected he would find little. He had his small revolver ready in his left pocket in case Luc had any friends on the premises, but he heard nothing.

A final search of Luc's pockets extracted some loose pieces of paper, a wallet, and a cell phone. These Johnny dropped into his ample side pockets. Then he reopened the front door, locked it, and checked the street. He moved quickly to the corner and walked the two blocks to his rendezvous with the minivan. When he saw it parked just behind a taxi stand, he went up to the driver's side. A middle-aged woman in a white uniform lowered the window. Johnny handed her the keys. "In the lobby," he said, and kept on walking.

The minivan pulled carefully into the thin stream of traffic. In a few minutes, two women medics entered a building on a side street in an industrial area and removed a body. They brought credentials in case anyone asked, and guns in case anyone interfered. But they were able to accomplish their work uninterrupted. They chuckled at the "Best Removal" sign. "We should have been the ones applying for jobs here!" said Mrs. Diep, the shorter one. Her friend, one of US Military Intelligence's best operatives for more than twenty-five years, smiled. It was all in a day's work.

CHAPTER SEVEN
May 7, in Washington, DC

President Elliott Bradley scrolled down to the newest "urgent" report that had appeared on his computer during lunch. In thirty minutes, he would convene the afternoon briefing with his National Security Advisor, Jeff Sanchez. The Secretary of Defense, Maya Tchernov, would accompany Jeff. President Bradley had requested this because of the report that Jeff had promised to send him. He began to read.

The essence of the report described a situation with which they had previously been threatened. Terrorists, nationality unclear, were up to something having to do with spreading deadly viruses and possibly poison gasses, this time staging the attempt from Canada. The information had passed through to military intelligence from an informant.

The report did not make it clear how the poisons were to reach the US or be spread. What gave the report urgency was the speculation that a key figure was Ahmed al-Kodari, who had escaped from Iraq after that country had emerged from its civil war and who had seldom been heard from in the past several years. The western world had assumed that during those years al-Kodari had been behind the bombings of US and British interests in Latin America and the minor disturbances at military bases in Australia and Norway, but nothing had ever been proved.

Elliott, in the third year of his first term as President after a successful career as a physicist and CEO of Markham Controls, continued to be grateful—both to the predecessor governments and to civilian leaders as well as to the military that no significant attacks had occurred on American soil since September 11, 2001. In the world at large, terrorism continued and al-Qaida still claimed responsibility for some attacks, but no single group seemed to have much central cohesion. More governments in developing countries were now democratic or at least less despotic. Elliott continued to support initiatives that would make the US safe and also help countries trying to rid themselves of terror and dictators. So far, the opinion polls showed the American people believed he was succeeding.

Promptly at three o'clock, Elliott's personal aide came through the door. "Sir," he announced, "Secretary Tchernov and Dr. Sanchez are here to see you."

"Thank you. We may take a little longer today, although I'll try to keep to my schedule."

The Secretary of Defense walked in and grasped the President's hand warmly. "How are you, Mr. President?" she asked in her deep voice. As always, the President heard the slight inflection that hinted at her growing up as a child of Russian immigrants in Manhattan. She stood a few inches taller than the President, and if anyone had ever thought that the first female Secretary of Defense would look like a dull gray retired soldier, they would have been wrong. Maya was tall, straight-backed and blond with large blue eyes, still youthful at 65. Her credentials included not only twenty-five years of military service, retiring as a four-star general, but a successful law practice on top of serving as Baltimore's mayor for eight years.

Elliott had appointed her shortly after his own inauguration; neither Democrats nor Republicans had opposed her. Toward the end of her career in the military, Maya had been responsible for overseeing US troops in several trouble spots in the world where no further serious disruptions took place. She had worked closely on the detente with North Korea that finally eased tensions in that part of the world. She shared with Elliott a keen intellect. He greatly appreciated Maya's skills and the two felt shared mutual admiration.

"Jeff," the President began, motioning Maya and Jeff to the chairs near his desk, "I've just finished the report about the possible poison attack. Can we calibrate the authenticity of this and possible timing?"

Dr. Jeffrey Sanchez's informal appearance, even in the White House, belied an exceptionally sharp mind, great wit, genuine respect for the Presidency, and a surprising ability to manage people, situations and—on occasion—the President's three dogs. He wore his trademark corduroy trousers—forest green today, but his beard was neatly trimmed and his loafers shined.

"Mr. President," he began, "I've brought Maya along to address the authenticity issue since her staff uncovered this, but I think we have to assume the timing of this possible attack could be very soon, perhaps in the next month or six weeks. If they're going to try something with some kind of poisonous substance, we have to assume there is no development involved, and they may have a plan to move into the country both by land and sea—that's where we are concentrating our efforts now."

Elliott nodded and turned without speaking to the Secretary of Defense. Maya adjusted her notes.

"We have an Army colonel in Seattle who frequently has liaisons with Canadian military officials in British Colombia. Two years ago, the CIA recruited a Canadian national, who has Middle Eastern ties, as an informant. They requested that our colonel be the 'handler' for this informant, and we agreed. He now maintains residences in Canada and the US.

Maya got up to pour herself a glass of ice water, sat down and continued.

"We believe the informant has tried to ingratiate himself with a variety of groups who may be working with al-Kodari, because apparently he has some kind of grudge against al-Kodari. It's because of this that he came across information that one group—he says they are in Vancouver—now wants to mount a major attack on the US. Our colonel questioned him closely as to why this would be happening now and he was vague on this. But he hinted that al-Kodari may be getting set to mount several major offensives around the world to show 'moderate' leaders in Arab and Middle Eastern countries that the US and Britain are still vulnerable and should not be thought of as models or allowed to further influence politics in the Middle East and other Muslim countries."

"How sure are you of this informant's motives?" Elliott asked, thinking about other similar reports he had seen over the past thirty months.

"We pay him, of course," Maya responded, "but his information has been accurate about much more minor events in the past two years."

The President nodded and turned back to Sanchez. "Jeff, unless you think we should take a different approach, let's go to 'Red Alert' at all airports and to level three security on all our ports. We must activate 'Code Cobra' for all immigration officers along the Canadian and Mexican borders. I'd like you to brief the Homeland Security people but make it clear that Defense and the CIA are to be involved—Maya, it's your decision how many resources you can put on this."

The Secretary of Defense nodded. "Mr. President, I'll coordinate with Jeff. Since I know you have other matters to discuss, I will excuse myself now. But, if it's all right, I will personally direct that the colonel be asked to stay involved as he may be able to extract more information from the informant."

When she was gone, Jeff remained standing and walked over to the window overlooking the spring green leaves on the maple and oak trees overhanging Pennsylvania Avenue. When he turned around again, he said, "Something about this worries me—it seems too pat. We get a report, arguably from a good source, but with information that sounds as if this particular group of terrorists is composed of amateurs. Either they are, or they wanted the information leaked, or they are up to something quite different and that means this may be a smoke screen."

The President was accustomed to Jeff's thinking out loud and waited without interrupting. Jeff sat down again and faced the President. "We've had threats of bioterrorism over the last three years. With your concurrence, I'd like convene a special team on this one." The President nodded his agreement, and with that, they turned to the next item on the afternoon briefing agenda.

CHAPTER EIGHT
May 7, in Colorado

Two women in white labs coats were bending over a stainless steel sink at the first lab station Ahmed al-Kodari visited. One of them reminded him of his sister, Saleeth. They smiled, recognizing his face although they did not know his name. They thought he was a senior lab official who visited every few months. They knew their work was important and highly classified. It was enough. There had been confusion when they had moved all their operations out of Denver, but now they were working as a team again. All the secret work for the US part of the operation was now being done in this lab under Kamal Telal's direction, with its two separate sections, close enough to a major US city for convenience but quite camouflaged as to its real purpose. "What are you working on?" he asked in his soft, melodic voice as they both looked up.

"We have most of the material harvested, and now we are coating it for packaging," the more senior woman, who was tall and had penetrating dark eyes, replied to Ahmed. "See—when one of these breaks open, the material will be released and spread."

"Indeed," replied Ahmed, feeling a slight increase in his pulse rate. They were so close. So much to manage but so close. The lab outside Calgary, disguised as a metal parts shop, was completing work with the spores that had arrived in Canada one month ago. Ahmed had visited that lab, also, and determined they were also on schedule.

"Do not let me disturb you, then, and stay safe," he added as he and his companion, a smaller man with thinning hair and a preoccupied look moved down the aisle. "Can we go into the other section where the microorganisms have been harvested?" he asked Kamal.

"Certainly," Kamal replied as he led the way down a long corridor and through double doors, although he knew that Ahmed already memorized every inch of the laboratory.

Kamal never worried that his technicians were not doing their jobs properly. They were all well educated and committed to the cause. He was secretly pleased that women were allowed equal status; that was very French and very right, and Ahmed agreed. "You see," he told Ahmed once, "they misjudge us because of our religion but we are not all fanatics or bigots or wedded to the old ways. We come from many countries and many of us are enlightened." Ahmed had again agreed, although with a sense of irony as he thought about how the results of the work at this factory would be perceived.

He and Kamal were still in the most secure part of the building and Kamal was saying, "We are very careful here with the packaging, and there have been no accidents."

"Nor must there be any—none!" Ahmed replied firmly. "We must have the substances packaged and ready in three weeks. The Canadian lab is on schedule," he continued, although he knew that Kamal was efficient and knew the schedule by heart.

As a manager, Ahmed knew that he should give Kamal some insight, some understanding so that Kamal would be even more vested in the mission. Ahmed had thought about this for some time, so he said, "We are going to use these substances very carefully, very specifically against people who have hurt us and who hate us. Some of them are in this country, some of them are not, but we must not let anyone know yet that we have this power."

Kamal nodded gravely. "I will do everything to ensure that we meet our schedules," he replied simply, not questioning beyond what he was being told.

"Thank you, Kamal, you have good people here and good processes," Ahmed told him warmly, and meant it.

CHAPTER NINE

The long drive from Kamal's lab back to the Denver airport should have given Ahmed time to think about the mission. But today all he could see in his mind was the young female lab technician—slight, dark-haired, intense—who reminded him so much of his sister. It was not just that he missed Saleeth or that his guilt for ever having let her go to the West grew with each passing month. No, the worst of it was that most of the time he actually hoped she was dead. "If you had come back right after graduate school, if you had not gone to work in their corrupt society, you would be alive still," he spoke to her silently many times a day. The man who had jilted her seemed almost incidental. To be sure, Ahmed was taking great care that this man's death would be assured if the man was found.

"Oh my sister, why did you not confide in me?" he asked himself for the thousandth time. They were twins, born to a wealthy family, liberal in its views but traditional in many ways. Because Saleeth was every bit as brilliant as Ahmed, their parents had seen to it that they both received the best educations possible. In Ahmed's case, that had involved universities in Paris and London. In Saleeth's, it was the US. She had always wanted to be a chemist. She graduated first in her class at The American University, and then she was Phi Beta Kappa getting her doctorate at the University of Southern California, so she had many job offers. By this time, Ahmed was resigned to her not returning to the Middle East. Ahmed worked in industrial planning in Syria as a cover, but he had early on joined the movement and grew more and more suspicious of the corruption of the West and especially America.

Ahmed and Saleeth communicated constantly—by email, phone, on Facebook and even by letters, although she was a better writer than he was. Her long letter about dating a fellow chemist had shocked him. Even though he knew she was not living as women did in their home country, he found it impossible to think of her as possibly marrying an American. He did not know the man's religion or background, but Ahmed knew he must meet him.

Just before planning his first trip to see his sister in two years, he received a terse email from her, telling him not to come—that she would not see him as planned. He could not reach her by phone, although he tried off and on for days. Finally, a letter came—long, somewhat rambling, but with a very clear message: her friend had rejected her. Her romance was over, and she was distraught. Perhaps she also felt guilty, he assumed at the time, and perhaps she also felt she could not go back to her family disgraced, for undoubtedly she had slept with the bastard.

He had decided that he must find her and convince her to return with him. Women worked in many countries in the Middle East, and he was not without friends who would be good to Saleeth. So, he made the trip anyway—and could not find her anywhere. At her laboratory they told him she had resigned with two weeks notice. Her apartment lease had four months to run but she had apparently moved out; it was almost empty. Ahmed made discreet inquiries about the man she had been seeing, but no one seemed to know anything about him. Ahmed found this odd as he assumed women confided in one another, but then again she had not seemed to have any really close friends at the lab, and he had little idea how she spent her time off work, although she often wrote about going to the theatre and to concerts.

After two frustrating weeks in San Francisco, he flew back to Syria, where a letter from Saleeth waited for him. It was short. She wrote: "Do not grieve for me. You have been the best brother anyone could have. My life as I would have had it is over. May Allah be with you." There was no return address, and the postmark was smudged. There were no emails from her, and when he tried sending one his server bounced it back as "address unknown." Her apartment phone and cell phone numbers were disconnected. Even her Facebook page was deleted. Much as he feared it, he gradually convinced himself that she committed suicide. Maybe the man had been married. Maybe she had become pregnant. Saleeth was a strong person, but she had been so alone. "If only I had been near her, if only I had gotten there sooner," he told himself for weeks, and then recognized that his own guilt and despair were overwhelming him.

It was at this point that Ahmed sought out Abu and offered his services on a more direct basis. When he met the man in a nondescript café in Paris, Abu greeted him warmly. "We know what you did for us in Iraq and what you are doing in Syria and elsewhere. We know that you are working to defeat the great Infidel. So, I understand you would perhaps like to do more, yes?"

After some more conversation with Abu, Ahmed found himself volunteering for whatever would fit his background in physics, chemistry and engineering—but most of all in management, for he knew how to motivate people.

Finally, Abu told him, "We have a mission for you. It is in North America and it will not take place right away, but you are needed to prepare the work and if that goes well to oversee this mission. Can you leave soon?"

"In a week's time," Ahmed answered with enthusiasm and then hesitated—he wanted to ask many questions but he only said, "Who will be my contacts when I am there and am I to know what the mission is?"

Abu sat back in his chair, crossed his legs, sipped his strong coffee and smiled broadly. "I will be your contact, and in time you will have two people to work with you who will also know almost everything about the mission—as will you. There is also a man, a good man, Kamal, who runs one part of this project for us. He is in the United States. His cousin runs a similar operation in Canada. However, even they do not know the details of the mission. No one other than you and the two others I am assigning must know all the details about this mission or why we do it. I will give you the code procedures in six days—just before you leave, along with a letter, telling you more about this project. And you will have plenty of money. I have arranged for five million dollars to be deposited in a Swiss bank account for you. Both you and Kamal will have access to it, and I do this because I trust him. If any of the three of you gets in trouble, Kamal can help." He paused, expecting a question; Ahmed was silent. He was not sure Abu trusted him yet, and he was skeptical of the motives behind the assignment.

As if sensing Ahmed's thoughts Abu continued, "We want to show the Americans that their government, their entire country is vulnerable and can be brought to its knees by us, even though they murdered *him*. Then, when we have made them realize this, we will make them do certain things for which we have waited a long time—and give us money as well to finance our cause."

"You mean blackmail them?" Ahmed asked with some surprise.

"If you want to call it that, yes, but we prefer to believe that we are exerting our holy purposes and making their power work for us," Abu replied, still smiling. "Killing some of them is not enough; as we have seen, they are defiant. They have to learn to be afraid—that we have the power, we are in the right. We want them to get out of our countries. We want them to listen to us in the future and do as we say. If you can conclude our mission, you will not be in any danger, and you can help us in the next phase."

"Please tell me where to contact you in six days," Ahmed said respectfully, and Abu stood to embrace Ahmed. A surprising knot of tension crept into Ahmed's stomach. "I am honored and excited," he thought to himself. He refused to acknowledge that he was also afraid.

The Denver Airport signs brought Ahmed back to the present. "And so, now, we begin," he told himself, and, strangely, all feelings of fear had vanished.

CHAPTER TEN
May 9

On Wednesday, Maya was in Jeff Sanchez's office in the Executive Office Building ten minutes early. She admired Jeff for his keen intellect, having graduated first in his class at Stanford, and his loyalty to the President made him stand out in an already distinguished administration. She enjoyed collaborating with him and shared his occasional impatience with the bureaucracy that had grown up in the NIA.

"Maya, before the others come, I want to tell you that I think we should get more assets on this Canadian business. If I go to NIA, it will take them days if not weeks to sort out whether it should be the CIA or some other division that should field the people. I have a few people in my stable I can tap directly, and I'm wondering if you do?"

"Do you think Col. Diep is not doing his job?" Maya asked directly.

"I don't have a problem with Diep or the reports he has been giving us—I just sense that we are sitting on something here that is going to grow and we don't seem to have a handle on what it is."

Maya silently concurred.

At that moment, Jimmy Buttero thrust his large frame into the office. He had been running the CIA with great skill for six years. A former diplomat with credentials in anti-terrorism, he was highly regarded and had experience inside three government agencies. Sometimes he was blunt and impatient, but Jeff and Maya knew him as an able partner. He was followed in by the recently appointed head of the FBI, Eileen Johnson.

"Let's get started." Jeff pulled up extra chairs to his large conference table. "I had a call from Homeland Security earlier this morning. Harold Harper is out of town and Paul Blake is tied up on a crisis related to the Gulf of Mexico, so Homeland isn't sending anyone to this meeting. I'll get back to them with whatever we discuss. Also, I'll make a report to NIA, as they didn't feel it essential for them to attend when I told them all the agencies would be represented. Eileen, could you to review what we know to date about this case?"

Eileen was in her 40's, smart, intense and had been a popular choice to replace the former FBI Director. She had started as a street cop and was the first black woman to be promoted to the number two spot in the Bureau before becoming Director. She scrolled to a page on her notebook computer and looked up. "We know that there is at least one factory either in western Canada or in the western US—or maybe factories in both places—working on acquiring or harvesting some types of poison. We're not sure what they are. We had a low-level source, courtesy of the Agency, who found this out. And then our source disappeared. We think she was murdered."

She looked up at the group. "More recently, we have had reports that there is increased 'chatter' about spreading poisons, presumably in the US. We don't know where the attacks are planned or when this will happen. We've also found out, via Secretary Tchernov's office, that there may be an initiative in Vancouver to rent a fleet of fishing boats or other small craft, to be used sometime in the next eight weeks. We think there may be a connection with the poisons case, but we cannot be sure at this point."

Jimmy Buttero moved his chair slightly, leaning forward. "When you say you don't know if there is more than one plant, our information has been that the place we had under surveillance in the Denver area is now completely discounted, so doesn't that leave just the Canadian location?"

"The combined report doesn't mention Denver," Eileen replied smoothly, "but it suggests that there may be another US plant because NSA is reporting numerous cell phone and text messages about moving something. The messages are originating in Colorado, California, Oregon and Washington—as well as in Vancouver. We know two of the suspect Yemenis whom we have been tracking for the last two years are in Vancouver; one of them has chemical expertise."

"Tell us what is known about the boat leasing," Jeff said to Maya.

She glanced down at the written report she was holding. "At least five fishing boats of relatively modest size—nothing over 50 feet—have been rented by a man who calls himself 'Gerard'. He is one of two brothers who are naturalized Canadian citizens of Algerian background. We know he has one brother, who calls himself 'Luc', and who works for a trash company but is suspected of having been part of a gang responsible for selective murders of both moderate Muslims and others. Neither one of them has an actual criminal record. The date Gerard has given for needing the boats is June 2nd, and he pretends to be affiliated with Vancouver Technical College."

Maya again consulted her notes. "He has said he needs the boats for a research expedition. He has asked for no special supplies other than for a reliable captain and one or two crewmembers on each boat."

"And the chatter suggests that some kind of lethal attacks are likely to happen at about this same time?" Jimmy asked.

Jeff intervened. "As Eileen said, we don't know anything specific, but right now I'd bet on poison gases—Sarin, maybe. But that's just a guess. It may be that there are two operations that are going to take place at the same time to confuse or scare us. Jim, I'd like you to talk a little about what could be a related matter."

Jimmy Buttero stretched his long legs and adjusted his glasses. "Yesterday, we linked up some of the chatter and communications Eileen mentioned with a man we thought had dropped out of the bad guys' world. He's Syrian by birth but with French parents. He has lived in Canada a long time and used to do some importing and exporting in the US, but never anything we could catch him at. He goes by several names, although his given one is Georges Labadie. We know he got as far as Kansas City last week before we lost track of him, and he resurfaced in San Francisco. There is nothing to connect him to any of the people Eileen and Mike have been talking about except this report from the NSA."

Buttero held up a single piece of paper. "This is the report that I sent to you late last night, Jeff. We'll work with Eileen's people to get the name he's operating under now and what he may be doing. And we'll see if we can find anything to connect him to Al-Kodari. Is there anything else in all this to connect Kansas City?"

No one volunteered a connection.

Jeff looked around at the group. "Let's go around the room and get best guesses of what we have here. Eileen, let's begin with you and the Bureau."

"It may be that this Georges is responsible for collecting the toxins and getting them to the boats. Possibly the boats are going to be met by some mother ship, bringing in the bad stuff from off shore. The boats must be going to move them into ports where the surveillance could be considered inadequate. After that, there must be some way to move them into the population, so we should be looking at trucking companies, even car rental companies and small aircraft. That's an assignment I'll make as soon as this meeting is over."

"What about you, Jim?"

"I'm not sure I agree that the boats are related to all this. They may be set up for another mission. I think we should put all available resources on the possible US lab—wherever it is—and try to find any other processing plants. We'll focus more assets in Vancouver. See if we can find out where al-Kodari is these days. If there is really a threat of a poison attack, can't we get cooperation from the Canadians to round up some or all of these people and restrict their movements for the time being?"

This was a suggestion Jeff Sanchez already discussed with the President and with Maya. Their consensus was that it would be more useful to let the known activities proceed. Stopping these people at any point was easy but finding out who was involved, and why, was critical. But Jeff did not want to cut off this discussion. "Maya?"

Maya weighed her words, recognizing that Jeff shared nothing with the group about the conversation they had with the President. "I think the boats are key to a scheme we don't fully understand yet," she began. "It may be that they are going to pick up illegals, or they could be a decoy. I'd like to find out more about Gerard and Luc as well as this Mr. Labadie. I also wonder who is behind all this. We can trace an Algerian connection, probably also Iraqi, Yemeni and Syrian, maybe Egyptian or Jordanian, and Mr. Buttero's 'Georges' is interesting—but we don't see any big name in this yet, unless it's al-Kodari, and that speculation is coming from one informant. If we knew who was sponsoring the poison developments, we might find motives and that would reveal more about the means."

Maya looked at Jeff, who nodded at her to continue. "Maybe we're seeing a trial run being put together. Maybe whatever they plan to do with the boats is just the beginning of a bigger plot, or an experiment to see if they can do something first on a small scale. If we found the other place, or places, where they are assembling the poisons that would help, too. And I think Ms. Johnson's idea about looking at other transportation systems is good. Do we have the resources to do that?"

"After I brief the President, I'm sure we'll have what we need," Jeff responded, taking in all the participants as he spoke. "Even if this plot is small potatoes, we need to find out and stop it. Thank you all for coming. I'll get back to you—and to Harold and to the NIA—with a formal memo on next steps. Oh, and just in case we should need it, let's give this investigation and our group a code name. Any suggestions?"

"How about Trial Run?" Eileen suggested, and everyone nodded. Then they stood up.

The meeting lasted 15 minutes and there would be clear assignments, thanks to Jeff. That was all they could expect at this point.

CHAPTER ELEVEN

Maya's driver left her in front of Ruth's Chris Steak House in Bethesda at precisely 6:30 p.m. An early hour, but then she did not expect that the eating part of dinner with her Russian counterpart, Colonel Pyotr Olenshinsky, would begin immediately.

Pyotr arrived in an unmarked embassy limousine. After maneuvering his broad shoulders out of the car, he looked up to see Maya waiting for him just outside the door. Surprise and pleasure spread into a broad smile. "My dear, you need not have waited outside—I'm sure they would have shown you to our table!" He enfolded her in a bear hug. Exactly the same height but more powerful of build, he always thought of Maya as his "little friend." Pyotr was a few years younger than Maya, educated in Russia and France, decorated for his army service, and highly intelligent.

"Pyotr—so good to see you. *Kak pozhivaete?*" While they seldom spoke to each other in their native language, a few words now and then cemented their friendship. "I was hoping Elena would be with you!" Maya meant this sincerely as she always enjoyed Elena's sense of humor and stories of her upbringing in Ukraine. But, of course, this trip was all business.

Relations with Russia these days were cordial, despite some on-going ideological differences. Cooperation on such fronts as the Middle East cemented mutual admiration between the two Secretaries of Defense, and Maya planned to use this occasion to probe for information on several subjects.

After they were shown their red velvet curtained booth and Pyotr ordered Chivas on the rocks for himself and a bottle of Dom Perignon for the table, he took her hand. "Elena sends her love and says she is unhappy not to be with us. I spoke with her just before leaving the Embassy."

"How is she, Pyotr, and how is that book of hers coming?"

"Oh, I think she enjoys complaining about the writing, but she loves her teaching at the university, and she's been asked to guest lecture at the Sorbonne next semester, so we're both excited about that. She goes back to Ukraine often to continue her research for the book, so she gets away from me—she's there now, visiting her sisters."

"And the boys?" Pyotr and Elena had two sons.

"The older one is pursuing an advanced degree in physics and he still has the good job with Senemca. Someday, I think, he and his wife would like to move to France or the US. The sailor, the one like me, is getting another promotion. But I think he wants to go into politics in a couple of years. I tell him he needs to marry a rich girl to do that!" Pyotr laughed heartily. He often complained that despite his own distinguished career, first in the Russian navy and then in the Defense Dept., he and Elena lived on only modest means. Maya suspected otherwise.

There was a pause while their waiter deferentially described the specials. They listened politely, while Maya rehearsed Pyotr's likely next lines in her head, while a slight smile played over her face.

"I'll have the porterhouse, rare, with the broccoli, and a large baked potato with butter and sour cream—extra sour cream!" Pyotr ordered decisively. Maya was startled; no mention of extra bread. "And, another basket of this wonderful bread!" Pyotr added. Maya suppressed the rest of her smile.

Pyotr tactfully did not ask about Maya's personal life. With both her parents dead and only one sister, who lived in LA, there was not much family to ask about. He knew her early history. Shortly after joining the US military, she had married a young captain who had died three years later of acute leukemia. There had been no children. Why she had never remarried, Pyotr did not know.

During their drinks, they talked about mutual friends, news of other governments' current defense activities and other safe subjects. Then, Maya asked, "Pyotr, how are the GLONASS replacements coming—is the money still there?"

Pyotr leaned back with a slight grimace. "Yes, we are holding on to the money, but it's not easy. We are about six months behind schedule on the new construction. Our President keeps grumbling about the European Union's Galileo project—he thinks that it will interfere with our frequencies. I don't think the Europeans know what they are doing. They are still facing delays even though they have six satellites up."

Pyotr was feeling expansive after the drinks. "Let me tell you about our new heavy-lift air transport plane!" he said, smiling. "The Anatov is going to have a big brother!" With this, he launched into a description of the new plane that Maya had seen in classified briefings but was perfectly willing to hear Pyotr talk about.

After enjoying the superlative steaks, they had coffee, refused dessert, and Pyotr indulged in a Calvados. "My friend," said Maya, when it reached 11 p.m., "you and I have a formal meeting in the morning—and I must prepare for that. You never know what the Russian Secretary of Defense will bring up." She was only half joking, since Pyotr was perfectly capable of being a wonderful dinner companion only to become hard-nosed in a formal meeting hours later.

They embraced outside the restaurant and got into their chauffeured vehicles. As the cars separated on Massachusetts Avenue, Maya thought, "I wonder if we will be able to keep this spirit of cooperation going. I wonder how much they would do for us in a crisis and when we are going to need it." The presidents of the two countries currently were on cordial if guarded terms, but Maya had started her career when the Soviet Union was in full sway and she remembered strained relations. "Could I rely on Pyotr if it came to a crisis?" she thought to herself, and then hoped—as she always did—that such a crisis would never come.

CHAPTER TWELVE
May 16

Raul remembered his promise to Carmen to help with unearthing background information about Vancouver Office Supply and Service Company. After returning from another highly classified trip, he checked his home email account just before getting ready for what he hoped would be a very pleasant dinner in Palo Alto. His initial search uncovered little. The company started as a family-owned concern fifteen years ago but was sold three years ago to an investment group with a few other holdings in the Northwest, most in service businesses. The principals in the group were easily checked out and looked legitimate, but since it was a private corporation it was possible that others not listed on standard records were involved in the financing or management of the company.

Therefore, before leaving on his trip, Raul had passed on an inquiry to a researcher he often worked with at the Agency. Finally he got a reply. It simply read, "No special history on Vancouver Office and Supply. One of the principals in the initial investment, Philip Miller, was a former journalist who was kidnapped and held for a short time in 2005 in Iraq. Quit the journalism business. Let me know if I can help further." Raul took time to compose a short message to Carmen, noting his findings and concluding, "They seem legitimate."

He glanced at this watch: it was time for him to leave. Raul offered to pick up Judith at her apartment, but she said she would likely join him for dinner straight from work so he drove directly to Nola's in Palo Alto. As he had arrived a few minutes early, he asked to be shown to a table and immediately ordered a Campari and soda. Five minutes later he enjoyed watching the lovely young lady in the form fitting gray suit and black silk shirt walk towards the table. As he rose to greet her, he noticed that she had braided her long black hair and twisted the braid at the back of her head. Her only jewelry was exquisite gold double loop earrings in her delicate ears. She wore no rings. From what little he knew about her, she was never married.

"Judith, you look lovely as always—and straight from the office, too!"

He took her hand and held it briefly, then pulled out her chair, waving the solicitous maître d' away.

"I cheated!" she said with a laugh, giving his hand a squeeze. "I brought the suit in with me this morning and changed in the ladies' room. The light's not so good there for make-up, so I hope my lipstick is more or less on my lips."

Raul refrained from commenting about her lips which, he thought, were one of her best features—full and slightly bowed. He was not surprised about the lack of facilities in her office. She worked for a consulting firm that helped people in poor communities find land and money to construct homes and businesses. Their offices were in an old building in downtown San Francisco. Judith told him she worked with them for eighteen months, following a more lucrative career in banking. "But I couldn't stand not helping more—at the bank, we said 'no' so often. Now I can help people find the 'yes.'"

They met when she called his architectural consulting number, and he accepted the brief work assignment offered because he liked the sound of her voice. He always served a client or two for his business to maintain his cover. When he finally met her, in her dingy offices, he liked everything about her. Even if working with Judith Abrams and The Community Building Foundation started as a way to maintain his work cover, it rapidly became a personal pleasure.

"May I order a drink for you?" Raul asked as their waiter approached.

"Dry sherry," Judith said promptly, and it arrived within moments.

"And, how was your day?" Raul asked with real curiosity.

"Frustrating," Judith answered. "We have so many good projects waiting to be funded and the money is still hard to find, but we are gaining friends. Thank you, by the way, for your first report. We thought that particular building had possibilities, and the county just wanted to tear it down without an appraisal."

Raul smiled. He was charging less than 50% of his normal fee and was thinking about volunteering his services to the Foundation for future work. He preferred not to analyze his motives too closely.

Judith's sherry came in a cut crystal glass. Raul liked Nola's for all their elegant touches. "And how was *your* day?" Judith asked, smiling at him.

"I did some research for a friend, designed a new island for my kitchen, and I worked on your project, but I didn't bring any of the drawings. Can we schedule a meeting in your office later this week?"

"Of course," Judith replied, laughing, "even if my project ranks behind your friend and your kitchen island."

He had casually mentioned before that he had an interest in gourmet cooking, which made Judith curious as he spoke very little about himself otherwise, although he once mentioned having a sister in California.

"Give me a couple of days and I'll call you about getting together at the office. We have a new woman starting Monday, Andrea Miller, and I will be responsible for training her, so I'm not quite sure of my schedule at the beginning of the week." Judith took a sip of her sherry, not seeing Raul's eyebrows rise slightly.

"Common name, Miller," he noted. "I ran across a story about a former journalist by that name today, some old magazine I unearthed. I hadn't heard of him but he was apparently held captive in Iraq at one time."

"And he's writing again now? For whom?" Judith said, eyeing the menus that had been discreetly placed before them.

"The story I read said he isn't. Maybe that experience soured him on journalism. Apparently, he invests in businesses and buildings now. Philip Miller. Not exactly a memorable name, but I'm surprised I don't remember anything he wrote if he covered the war."

Judith opened her menu and remained silent. There was a pause in the conversation, which Raul attributed to her not being very interested and wanting to order. "If you like stream-caught trout, it's excellent here," he offered.

She put down the menu, smiling, but there was something serious in her eyes. "Actually, I think I'll have the lamb," she replied, "and I'm fine with white or red wine, depending on what you are having."

Raul admitted to himself that he knew little of her dietary habits and had wondered if as a Jew she observed any restrictions, which was one reason he had suggested the fish. "I'm going with the filet mignon, so red will work— do you want to choose?"

"No, I'm very limited in my knowledge so you please do that!" Judith smiled again, this time seeming to focus more on him. He picked up the wine list and found one of his favorites—the Shotfire Ridge Shiraz.

The food and wine came promptly, with the wine smoothly decanted and allowed to breathe. Raul felt that the evening had become subdued, so he decided to ask her more about her family. He had, of course, checked her out via his own sources before ever asking her out, including with the Agency, which had no unusual information about Judith Abrams.

"My mother was quite liberated for her background—growing up in a traditional Jewish family with my grandparents emigrating from Russia—and she was the one who insisted I get a good education, learn a profession, plan to make my own living if a nice man did not come along." This time, Judith's smile was broad and genuine. "My father adhered more to older traditions, but he, too, supported me. We had bankers in the family, so he was not too disappointed when I went into the profession instead of getting engaged right out of college."

"And was there someone to get engaged to?" Raul asked with another raised eyebrow. "Or am I being too personal?"

"Oh, no, that's all right. There was someone, but he went to the east coast for a job and we drifted apart. I wanted to stay in California, primarily to be near my parents."

"No brothers or sisters?"

"None, just some cousins I seldom see and don't really keep up with." Raul sensed that little bit of sadness or seriousness he glimpsed in her earlier. A small family, no one her own age that she was close to. He thought of Carmen and their relatively large, extended family and found Judith's hard to imagine.

For dessert, they each ordered the Pears Helene and espresso. "My rack of lamb was delicious—thank you for introducing me to this place!" Judith said enthusiastically.

Raul smiled. There were many more good restaurants he wanted to introduce her to, but he sensed that this relationship needed a bit of time to develop. They chatted about some of the architectural features of grand old buildings in the San Francisco area as they enjoyed their coffee.

Then Judith said, "You mentioned that this Philip Miller now invests in buildings and businesses. Is that here in the San Francisco area? Is he someone my company should perhaps get to know?"

Raul hesitated. It perhaps was imprudent to mention anything about his research project, and he certainly was not about to compound the error by revealing anything substantive to her. "I didn't get the impression he's in California, although maybe somewhere else on the west coast."

She nodded. Another lead for the company going nowhere, Raul thought. It must be so difficult to raise money for the work they were doing. He would have to try to help her more.

"Let me walk you to your car," Raul offered as they left the restaurant. The night was mild.

"I'm at the end of the second row," Judith said, pointing out her Volvo. When they reached her car, she turned to him. "I've really enjoyed this evening— thank you. I don't think I've felt this relaxed in weeks, and dinner was superb."

Raul took her face in his hands lightly. "And for me, it has been a special pleasure. May I call you next week, and not just about the office appointment?"

"Yes, I would like that," she said, patting his right hand and turned to open the driver's door with her remote. He held the door open for her.

"Watch for fog," he ordered as she smiled up at him and started the car. He watched her drive away, and his most vivid memory of the evening was her beautiful eyes smiling at him. At least he hoped it was a smile.

CHAPTER THIRTEEN
May 25

In Goodland, Kansas, Farley McDonald was closing up his office. The entire shipment of balloons was sent that morning by a convoy of special trucks to the two FBI drop points—one in Seattle and one in Los Angeles. Each of the balloons was packaged in a PVC piece that looked like a fishing rod tube with a screw top. Part of the requirement that the FBI gave Farley was that each balloon was to be fitted with an automatic fill valve—like a tire inflation valve—with a plastic hose barb fitting located about six and a half feet down from the top of the balloon. A pressure relief valve was located near the bottom of the balloon. Load spreading tapes and payload attach rings were also attached.

The most difficult part of the work had been to design a balloon that could be taken out of its shipping container and launched in two minutes in a 10-mile per hour wind. In the end, they had beaten the requirement: the ingenious packing solution involved the use of ordinary sewer pipe with built-in helium tanks. It turned out that the balloons could be launched in a 15-mile per hour wind in less than one and three quarter minutes.

Farley had beaten the delivery schedule by 24 hours, even though the quality control process took longer than expected, primarily because of the government man stationed at their plant who insisted on testing at least two balloons from every batch. Mr. Ricotti put this requirement into the contract; it was not unheard of when working with certain US government agencies, as Farley knew, and certainly the FBI had the right to request this extra step—they were paying for it, and price had not been an issue, either.

His secretary stood just inside Farley's weathered oak office door. "Do you think we'll ever see any of our balloons flying over Kansas?" she asked, with a twinkle in her eye.

"How's your distance vision?" Farley shot back. "When they're up there, they should be way above even where an airplane could find them."

After Farley was alone in the building, he picked up the phone and called the special number Mr. Ricotti had given him if they ever needed to communicate directly. Farley had called it before, and it was always answered with a simple masculine, "Hello?" Today, he let the phone ring five times before a voice came on and said, "No incoming calls are being accepted at this number." The person on the other end hung up. When Farley redialed, the line was busy. "Odd," he thought to himself. All he wanted to say was that the last shipment had gone out, and they had sent a fax to this effect two hours earlier. "Probably won't hear from Mr. Ricotti again—if that even was his name," Farley thought to himself.

He decided to go home. Doris wanted to talk about going to Switzerland and Italy. Farley was getting into the swing of European travel and fine dining. He was even building a wine cellar in his basement.

CHAPTER FOURTEEN
May 26-28

On Saturday by 10 a.m. at Kamal's lab the last truck was being loaded. He composed a text message on his cell phone: "The children have all left now and will be with you soon." The message was sent to his contact in Los Angeles. This was the signal that all had gone well. His next message would be to Ahmed with slightly more detailed information.

Vancouver Office Supply and Service Company rented two factory buildings in the US, one on the outskirts of Seattle and one in Long Beach, south of Los Angeles. When the trucks arrived on Monday at each location with the balloons from Kansas, a small group of men began their work. It was simple enough. Every balloon tube was mated to a helium filled tank. The moderate pressure tanks, approximately three inches in diameter and nine inches long, were loaded with ninety-nine percent pure helium to a pressure of 450 psi at sea level standard conditions.

Each tank contained a pressure gauge, a shut-off valve, and a two-meter length of surgical tubing, which was securely mounted into a second, twelve -inch long tube with an end cap and short coupling. Two meters of surgical tubing connected the helium shut-off valve and the barb fitting on the balloon fill valve. The men assembling the units then slipped the short tube coupling over the long (balloon) tube to complete assembly of the transportation and launch tube. The whole package, when assembled, weighed less than twenty-two pounds and was less than ten feet in length. It looked like a piece of sewer pipe or the pipes sometimes used to carry fishing rods.

The balloons assembled at the Seattle factory were loaded into trucks and driven to Port Moody, outside of Vancouver, BC. The boxes were labeled to indicate joint US-Canadian scientific weather balloons.

In the same modest building north of the Sea-Tac Airport in Seattle, where the balloons and helium tanks were being mated, a ground-floor section of the building was set aside for another task. At midday, the moving vans were arriving, carrying the packages originally shipped from Kamal's lab in Colorado. The previous day, the moving vans from a metal parts fabrication plant near

Calgary, run by Kamal's cousin, also arrived with special packages concealed under crates filled with metal parts intended for US factories. That shipment successfully passed US Customs as it entered from Canada; the supplying company shipped fabricated parts to the US for several years now and there was no special reason for the overworked US Customs agents to examine more than a few of the top layer boxes.

Kamal also arranged for a shipment of pallets loaded with what appeared to be Styrofoam cooler boxes. At the warehouse, Ahmed appointed a chief deputy, an American, one of his most trusted men in the movement. The deputy ordered that twelve work tables be set up in the special section and he selected fourteen men to perform the final assembly process. Twelve of them were to do the actual assembly and repackaging for final shipment, while the other two were quality control inspectors. They worked twelve-hour shifts for two and one half days.

Ahmed's chief deputy at the Seattle warehouse opened one of the Styrofoam payload containers to inspect it, exposing the electronic circuit cards, batteries, wires and electromechanical parts that were wired together and glued to various facets pre-casted inside the box. The boards included the circuit cards of the GPS units that Rafik so carefully selected. The deputy turned the box on its side and saw nine cylindrical cavities on the bottom. He noted the small switch lever and light emitting diode located in a depression near the outside of one corner of the bottom of the box.

He turned to the men. "Do not touch any of the electronics inside the box and especially this switch on the outside. It turns the electronics on and will run down the batteries if it is activated too soon. You will also notice that the inside of each of the cylindrical cavities is lined with a polypropylene sleeve and that there is a latching mechanism at the top of each hole. You will be attaching one of our scientific instruments to each of these mechanisms."

"Why are four of the holds outlined in red?" One of the workers asked.

"You will see in a moment, please." The deputy then opened one of the containers from the Calgary shipment and very carefully withdrew a cylinder that looked like it would just fit inside the holes in the bottom of the cooler. "The scientific instruments in these cylinders are extremely fragile and you must handle them with great care."

He motioned the men to step closer to the worktable. "You will notice the outside of this cylinder is encased in a hard plastic sleeve and that there are three fins attached to this sleeve at the top end. These fins can be bent over so that the package can be inserted in these holes. I will demonstrate that in a moment. You will also notice that there is a small plastic rod with a ball machined on the end fixed to the centerline of the top of the package. This is the ball that you will insert into the latching mechanism inside the cooler box. I will also demonstrate the technique for you in a moment. First, I want you to look at the bottom of the cylinder. It is also rimmed with red paint. Later, you will see blue cylinders. Red cylinders go into red holes. Blue cylinders go into blue holes."

There were a couple of snickers among the workers.

"Be serious. Look at the bottom. You see in this indentation in the Styrofoam, another very small toggle switch handle with an off marking on one side. Next to it is a small red glass LED lens. This switch must always be left in the off position. Turning it on, even for a moment, ruins the expensive instruments inside." The deputy knew that if the switch was turned on before it was placed inside the cooler box it would immediately explode and shower everyone in the room with whatever was in the container.

"Finally, if you look carefully on the side of the cylinder near the bottom, you will see a round, black protrusion. This is a spring-loaded switch that must be pressed in during the mating sequence. I will be demonstrating this step." Once the cylinders were inserted into their matching cavities, the switch could be turned on because the spring-loaded switch kept the circuitry in a safe mode.

"You will also see two additional glass lenses on the bottom. Those only need to be kept fingerprint free. At the very center of the bottom of the cylinder you will also see a small plastic pull ring. This is for testing. Again, these instruments are extremely fragile. Do not touch the instruments or the switches. If you should accidentally drop one of the packages, even a short distance you must stop everything and call me for advice. You will not be punished. Do not hide anything."

At this point, the deputy walked the cylinder back to the pallet and carefully placed it back in its shipping box.

"I will now walk you through the assembly steps. We will work slowly and carefully. One of our inspectors will monitor your progress and offer suggestions. General rules are only one person at a table and only one action at a time. Never leave a cylinder on the table. It should always be in your hands until mating is complete."

"First, I retrieve a cooler box and open the cover. Since I already have this box here I will not repeat this step in this demonstration. Check the switch on the bottom to be in the off position. If it is not, call me. Examine the insides to be sure everything is secure and in order. Then go to the open red pallet and retrieve an instrument cylinder.

"Second, I carefully unwrap a cylinder and immediately check the switch position to be off. I then carry the cylinder to my worktable and fold the fins tightly against the sides so that the package will just slip into one of the holes. Red into red. I carefully push the cylinder into the hole, fins first, and place one finger on the black spring loaded switch and slip it under the edge of the liner while continuing to insert the cylinder. Being careful not to touch the lenses or the switch on the bottom of the cylinder, I continue to push until I feel contact with the latching mechanism inside the box. I can see this contact and I continue to push until the pawls open and I hear and feel a distinct click. The mating is complete.

"Now, I test the mate by applying a two-pound load to the test ring using this simple fish scale test puller. One final look at the switch and lenses and one is loaded. Only now do I go to the pallet and extract a second cylinder. When I have inserted 4 red cylinders, I then go to the second set, the blue set, of cylinders and continue the process 5 more times. At this time the quality control inspector will pick up the whole package and place it on its corresponding shipping pallet. You will be expected to take a 10 minute break before continuing on to the second package."

The twelve men were expected to complete approximately 200 balloon packages in each twelve-hour shift. It would take them three shifts to completely load all 600 packages with 5400 payloads. Each man worked one shift, then had twelve hours off, then began the next shift, each working three shifts.

If everything went well, they could be finished with their assembly by midnight Wednesday. There was a bonus for completing the work sooner. When they were close to finishing their work, the deputy called a special number. Trucks arrived, and the packages loaded into them. Then, on top of the crates with the newly assembled boxes, they would stack crates of medical instruments, quite clearly marked. One third of the trucks went south to Long Beach, California, while the rest crossed the border and drove to Vancouver, BC.

CHAPTER FIFTEEN
May 30-31

Ahmed cleared US and Canadian border formalities at 2 p.m. Wednesday afternoon. His papers were in order. He had several letters of appointment, plus his fake British passport, to substantiate his identity. On the passport, he was listed as Kas Pradep. If anyone bothered to look up Dr. Pradep, he was listed as a faculty member in London, with a distinguished accumulation of publications and frequent appointments abroad.

He wanted to spend a few days checking locations in Vancouver, BC. On Thursday he expected that two convoys of trucks from Seattle would come to the border, declare their cargos of medical instruments and scientific weather balloons, and cross without incident into Canada. The actual medical instruments, which were purely for decoy purposes, would be carefully unpacked and saved at a Port Moody location where there was a former high-bay boat storage facility, now leased to a company listed as Marine Supply and registered in Seattle. The real cargo would also be unpacked, placed on insulated pallets, and locked up until the trucks from Vancouver Office Supply and Service Company arrived to off-load the balloons.

As they had planned, at the same time on Thursday, Georges Labadie would be overseeing the delivery of the payloads and the balloons in Long Beach. The people working in the Long Beach storage facility were also part of their movement, so Ahmed had few worries about security.

§ § §

On Thursday, at noon, as Ahmed drove up to the Port Moody depot, the first group of trucks from the US pulled into the parking area outside the former boat storage facility. Ahmed parked his rental car quickly and joined the team of men he had hired, who were already unloading the packages. The truck drivers had no idea about their cargo. When they loaded the boxes, all they saw was that each box was labeled "Medical Supplies," and the bills of lading simply identified the boxes the same way. The drivers were pleased not to have to assist with the off-loading, and they were able to get signatures on their documents and leave within the hour.

Ahmed knew that the building was well equipped in case of an accident, and he instructed Raymond, the team leader, to take the team through several safety drills. "We want everything ready Friday night. May Allah be with you." Ahmed shook hands with Raymond and watched as all fourteen men went immediately to their stations and began to unpack the cargo that had arrived. The balloon boxes would be arriving shortly, and they, too, needed to be checked out and stored. The next hours would be among the most critical in the program. Ahmed felt a degree of concern but also heightened anticipation and a rush of adrenalin. He hoped everything was on schedule in Long Beach. They came so far—soon, the world would know what they could do.

CHAPTER SIXTEEN
May 31

On Thursday, Gerard made morning phone calls to two of the boat captains. His message to the first was that the boats would be needed to put out to sea on Saturday, weather permitting, and that they would be going out about thirty miles from shore, then returning. Since he had negotiated the original contracts the plans changed, and now he called the second captain to let him know his vessels were needed the following Tuesday but to deploy only as far south as Newport on the coast of Oregon. Both fleets were to operate in international waters during the critical part of the day. He left no message for the reserve fleet since he was not sure it would be needed at all.

Someone in the hierarchy—Gerard did not know who—made the decision that two northern fleet deployments were better than one, although there would be only one fleet in California. Everything depended on the weather forecasts. They needed the right prevailing winds at the right velocities, both at the surface and at altitude. Gerard checked the predictions on the NOAA weather site, which he was doing daily. Things were picking up. He felt good about that since he liked action.

One of the other things that made him feel good was that he had gotten his friend, Rahmid, a moonlighting job as crew on one of the boats in the first fleet and planned to talk with Rahmid about the second sailing, too. He vouched for Rahmid by telling a senior member of the team that Rahmid was a friend "from way back."

"They'll pay you cash, no complications with forms and things," he advised Rahmid over coffee.

"I can use the money—my cousin needs help providing for his new son," Rahmid told him.

Gerard nodded. "My brother, Luc, said he was serious about offering you a job at his trash hauling company, too. He had to go away, though, and we don't know when he's coming back."

Rahmid smiled at Gerard. "You are a good friend. Where did Luc go—or is it a private matter?"

For a moment, Gerard stared at his coffee and frowned. "He didn't tell me. He left a note. Luc does not always tell me what he does, but he'll be back. His note said in a week to ten days."

CHAPTER SEVENTEEN
June 2

Morning in Vancouver, BC, dawned clear, cool and with moderate winds, eight to ten knots, from the west—perfect for the mission. Gerard arrived at the dock at 5:30 a.m. While an early departure was not really necessary, it was decided by those planning it that the fleet deployment should look as much like a normal fishing fleet departure as possible—and fishing boats went out early.

There were signs of crew movement on all five boats. The parking lot leading to the dock walkways had plenty of room open for the trucks that would be arriving shortly. Gerard made sure no one parked in front of the walk to the docks since the unloading had to take place there. He wished he could accompany at least one of the boats, but his instructions were to stay on land and continue to coordinate.

He was with the captain of the *Filly* when the first truck pulled up. At the same time, he saw a black Dodge Neon park next to the truck. Gerard excused himself to the captain and walked back to the parking lot.

"You must be Gerard!" said the slender man who got out of the Neon. He held out his hand. "I'm Kas. I'm in charge of the trucks and assigning the crewmembers their duties."

Gerard shook hands, noting that this slender, dark-skinned good-looking man had a very firm grip. He was dressed in Dockers, a plaid shirt, a lightweight jacket and boat shoes.

"All the boats are here and should be ready to load in a few minutes," Gerard told Kas.

"How many crew members does each boat have?" Kas peered over Gerard's shoulder toward the docks.

"The captain, one or two mates and three of our people," Gerard answered. "I interviewed all the captains personally, and they are all experienced." Gerard did not say that he had been given strict orders not to employ any boats that required more than three crewmembers. In two cases, the captains said they could do the job with just one other man, provided that the scientists on board were able-bodied, and Gerard guaranteed this.

As they talked, the second and third trucks pulled into the parking lot. "There will be one more truck today," Kas noted, and as he spoke, the fourth truck rounded the corner and came toward them. "I will supervise the unloading. Please make sure your captains and crews are ready, and then we will start."

Gerard hurried down the dock to let the captains know that the cargo would be ready for loading in a few minutes.

Kas spoke briefly with each truck driver and then watched as they opened their trucks' rear doors to access the cargo. In the first two trucks, the balloons, integrated with their helium tanks inside the PVC sewer pipes, were in wooden boxes, ten balloons to a box. From the last two trucks, large crates were carefully removed and placed on the dock. Gerard knew only that the payloads for the balloons were in these crates, but he was not sure what was inside the Styrofoam boxes nested in the crates. Each truck driver brought one extra man to help with the unloading. The drivers and their helpers were not, however, going out for the voyage. Their job was strictly to move the boxes into position.

While the unloading proceeded, two white vans pulled into the parking lot next to the Dodge Neon and fifteen men climbed out. They were dressed more or less alike—in work pants, warm jackets, baseball hats, deck shoes. Gerard recognized Rahmid immediately and called out pleasantly to him. Kas stood nearby but did not ask for any introductions, though he noted Gerard singled out the man "Rahmid." All the crew milled about with Gerard, and there was some brief conversation.

Kas beckoned to Gerard, who came back down the dock from the boats. "Gerard, please have our crewmembers introduce themselves to the captains. They can also help with loading the boxes on the boats and securing them." Gerard nodded, smiling briefly at Rahmid, and then led the fifteen men down the dock. They were pre-assigned to the five boats and so separated into teams to help with the loading.

The movement of the boxes to the boats was swift. By 6:25 a.m., all the trucks were empty, the truck drivers and their helpers prepared to leave, and the men from the van stowed the boxes on board each boat, under the supervision of the boats' own crewmembers. Gerard watched with some curiosity as Kas spoke occasionally with the men doing the work, always appearing to give advice and encouragement. He noticed that Kas shook Rahmid's hand, apparently having realized he was a friend of Gerard. Gerard knew very little about Kas other than that he had made some of the crew assignments and supervised the trucks and the loading.

"Would you like to go out on a boat?" Gerard suddenly asked Kas.

"No, I will remain here to stay in radio contact," Kas answered, producing his VHF radio and an Iridium Satellite handheld unit. Gerard planned to see that the boats got off the dock safely. Then he would return around the time the boats should be back. He offered to pay each captain upon his return, and all of them accepted that arrangement.

At 6:30 a.m., Gerard checked the weather reports on his Blackberry and saw that they were going to have ideal conditions. Winds were still at eight to ten knots, from the west, with no storms predicted. At 6:40 a.m., the captain of the *Filly* signaled that he was ready to leave the dock. Gerard quickly checked on the other boats. Only the crew of the *Little Miss* signaled that they needed a few more minutes. At 6:45 a.m., *Little Miss* indicated they were ready, and the fleet loosened lines and began pulling away from the dock, one by one. The waters were calm, and the temperature was 65 degrees Fahrenheit.

Gerard stood at the end of the dock with Kas as they watched the boats move into open waters. Gerard was curious about several things—who was actually in charge of the cargo deployment once the boats reached their designated spots, what the men from the van told the boat crew about what was happening, whether he would have any trouble with the captains or their crews being too curious after the trip was over.

As if reading Gerard's thoughts, Kas said, "We have a senior man on each boat and even he does not know all the details of the mission today— just that it is something scientific that will help us. He will make the final decision on whether the balloons should be sent up, based on the weather when the boats reach their assigned position. Just as you have told the captains, our men will say only that they are from the university and this is a scientific mission. It will be enough."

This final statement, said with quiet authority, intrigued Gerard. He suspected initially Kas was not merely a middleman, assigned to supervising the crew and the trucks. Now he was sure of it, although he could only guess at what role Kas really played.

"I will be back in eight hours—or earlier, if I get word that the boats are returning before schedule," Gerard told Kas.

Kas nodded and reached out his hand. "Thank you for all your work."

Gerard returned to his truck and drove off.

Kas placed a short call on his VHF radio to Nassir, the most senior of the men on the boats. All was going well. Next, he activated the Iridium handheld unit and walked around the docks and the parking area for a while before settling down in his car. Later, he took a very short lunch break. He never wandered too far from the dock, although his communications systems permitted him some freedom. There was a minor problem to deal with, once he learned that Luc was missing, but he would find time for that later. If anything went wrong with the boats, he needed to be the first to know and to make decisions.

CHAPTER EIGHTEEN

Rahmid was assigned to the *Filly* with Nassir and one younger man. "How long will we wait before we start opening the boxes?" Nassir, who appeared to be about 50 with shaggy graying hair and a weathered face, looked at his watch. "We got an assigned position, based on latitude and longitude. It's off the coast a few miles, in international waters. The weather radio report and the wind indicator make it look like we got about two and a half, three hours to run before we reach the right spot."

Rahmid nodded. He decided that this was not the time to ask more about the cargo. He already knew it was balloons with a scientific payload attached, but he planned to be very cautious about interrogating Nassir. He already learned by talking with the boat's crew that they knew nothing of the mission, other than that it was connected with a university.

The winds stayed calm as the boats moved southwest further into the Pacific Ocean.

Rahmid looked over the side of the boat, watching the color of the water darken as they reached deeper waters when, just a few minutes before ten, he heard Nassir speak into his satellite unit. "We are nearly there. All the fleet in sight. You got a winds aloft reading?" There was a short reply that Rahmid could not hear. Then, "You want me to give the signal to the others?" Rahmid did not hear Nassir address anyone specifically, but he was sure the person being called was Kas.

Apparently the answer was affirmative. Nassir went into the cabin and said a few words with the captain, after which the boat slowed considerably. Nassir returned to the open deck and activated his VHF radio, choosing channel 72. "To fishing fleet from Ober Dock, Vancouver: please ask your captains to turn the boats and run with the wind. I repeat: all boats must run with the wind at the same speed as the wind. We make wind speed at eight knots. We deploy mission now. Repeat, we deploy mission now. Please acknowledge." Rahmid heard the crackle of the radio as each of the other boats acknowledged the message. Then Nassir turned to him and the other helper. "Come on, we move the boxes out here and get started."

The men had to work with two sets of boxes. One set contained the balloons packaged in their pipes with the helium tube caps. These boxes were already stowed on the aft deck. The second set contained the payloads, which were mounted in the Styrofoam carrier containers. It would be the first man's job to open the payload carrier crates that had been stowed in the cabin just ahead of the aft deck and to bring out each container individually to Rahmid and Nassir.

Several days ago, the fifteen men were trained on how to attach the payload carrier containers to the balloon lift rings. Since the actual payloads were already mated to the carrier containers at the factory in Vancouver, they unpacked them carefully and got them to the person assigned the task of hooking them on. Rahmid was the "hooker" on the *Filly*.

On the aft deck was a twelve by twelve foot square area in which to work. In that space, a small worktable, fitted with a pipe cradle, was placed in the middle of the launch area. A helper assisted with each balloon launch after he brought the hooker a payload container.

When they began the actual launch sequence, Nassir and Rahmid placed a balloon launch tube in the cradle on the table so that the tube lined up with the prevailing wind directions. Nassir was the designated "gas man." He removed the end cap and stretched the inflation tube out to expose the shell material of the balloon. Their helper became the "bag man," carefully pulling both ends of the balloon shell out of the container so that about six feet of material was exposed before he held up the top section of the balloon shell, so that a gas bubble formed when helium was released. Nassir then opened the helium shut-off valve to inflate balloon. Meanwhile, Rahmid hooked the payload carrier to the balloon ring.

As soon as the helium filling was complete, Nassir pulled the surgical tubing free from the balloon. "If we don't do this just right, there's not enough helium to let the balloon to get to its altitude. It will come down before it should—before we get our scientific readings," Nassir explained patiently.

Now, the other man walked the bubble away from Nassir in such a direction that the inflated balloon was horizontal to and off the deck. Nassir then extracted the remaining balloon material from the pipe and held all the slack material off the deck until it was taut. He held the balloon ready for release, and as soon as the balloon material straightened out and the balloon bubble rose above any obstacles, he let go. Afterward, the used pipe pieces were rejoined and moved to a storage area at the front of the boat while a new pipe assembly took its place in the cradle.

By the second launch, Nassir, Rahmid and the other man completed the entire process in two minutes per balloon. The goal for each boat was to have all launches completed within three hours. As each boat only launched forty balloons, the schedule gave them ample time. Rahmid remarked to himself after the first several launches, "These balloons go up fast!"

During their work on *Filly*, they could see that the other four boats were having the same success they were. Only one balloon, from *Dock Side*, appeared not to have inflated properly and fell back into the water. No one attempted to retrieve it.

They worked steadily for an hour, and then Nassir said, "Time for a break. I brought coffee." He went forward to the captain's station to report that all was going well and then he returned to sit down. The break was short, and then they went back to work. The pattern continued: swift, efficient launches while Nassir checked wind speeds with the captain every fifteen minutes. They were averaging nine knots. Rahmid also noted that there were no other vessels near them during the launching.

At 12:15 p.m., Nassir called the other boats. Within a few minutes, each boat reported that they, too, completed launching. After the last reply, Nassir again spoke into his satellite unit. "All payloads launched." There was an answer, and then he said, "Only one. Weather still good. We return unless there is something further." There was another short answer, and then Nassir walked forward to speak with the captain of *Filly*. He also spoke again into his VHF radio. "All clear. We return now."

The slow running engines of all the boats shot to life and the fleet turned toward a direction Rahmid assumed led back to Vancouver. He decided that this was the moment. "Should they have tried to get that balloon that fell into the water from *Dock Side?*" he asked Nassir softly, out of hearing range of anyone else.

"No, no importance," Nassir responded, still looking out over the water toward the rest of the fleet who were behind them but catching up.

"We won't get any less data?" Rahmid persisted, careful to keep his tone deferential; he was not even sure what Nassir knew.

Nassir barked a short laugh. "We get enough data on everything in and around the Pacific ocean with all these balloons!"

The answer confused Rahmid and made him wonder what was actually in the payloads. He decided to risk one more question. "Are those payloads fragile—what if a balloon went down on land?"

Nassir laughed again, but this time he looked directly into Rahmid's eyes. "Might be a lot of broken glass!"

The boats returned to their dock without incident. Several hundred miles south of Vancouver, BC, the Los Angeles fleet was also returning to its base in Long Beach. They, too, completed their mission, although on one boat there had been some difficulty with two of the balloons that resulted in their being under-inflated.

CHAPTER NINETEEN

When Rahmid got home Saturday night, his cousins were visiting. He excused himself after dinner and typed a text message to Col. Diep, detailing his day, including his final conversation with Nassir. Then he pressed "send." He pocketed his Blackberry and rejoined his cousins and aunt, spent some time chatting with them and then said that he wanted to walk to the store to buy cigarettes. On his way down the two flights of stairs from the apartment, he remembered one detail of the day he forgot to put in his earlier text message. He stopped in the foyer, made sure no one was around, and typed two lines. Then, he hid the Blackberry by dropping it in a vase filled with silk flowers that sat on a high shelf near the entry. He used this safe place many times; Col. Diep warned him about taking the special phone anywhere that it could be stolen or lost. He would pick it up when he returned from the store.

Rahmid did, in fact, want some cigarettes and strolled two blocks to the small grocery store that was always open. After he purchased his Camels, he started back to his apartment.

"Rahmid! I didn't know you lived in this neighborhood!" Rahmid turned at the touch of a hand on his back and saw Kas. Rahmid smiled and extended his hand.

"Yes, I live very near here—are you visiting someone?" They walked toward an intersection. The building beyond the crossing to their right was under construction.

"Yes, my sister's cousin. I hope you had a good day on the boat?"

They crossed the street; there was no traffic. Rahmid started to reply when he felt a dull pain somewhere near his waist. He staggered, and Ahmed caught him, half dragging him toward the unfinished building.

"Here I will help you," Ahmed said, and the pain in Rahmid's back intensified. During his last conscious moments, he was aware of blood on the ground and realized it must be his. When Ahmed heaved Rahmid's body into the construction hole, Rahmid was already near death.

Ahmed waited a moment and then climbed into the hole, buried the knife as best he could in the soft dirt and rapidly searched Rahmid's pockets and shoes. In the top pocket of Rahmid's shirt, he found a crumpled piece of paper with a single number on it. He took this, pocketed it, and climbed out of the hole. He threw a tarp that he previously left lying near the hole over Rahmid's body.

He wanted to leave Vancouver then, but he needed to be "Kas" for three more days to see off the second fleet of boats. Luc was stupid and inept and probably got killed for it. They still received no word on him. Ahmed sighed; this was not what he enjoyed doing. Further, he was unsure how much Rahmid compromised their operation. He decided to find out where the number connected as quickly as he could. It might lead to another traitor who needed to be eliminated.

§ § §

Judith also made a decision late on Saturday. She had agonized for a few days since her date with Raul about sending a message that might embroil her in something she was not sure she wanted. But it needed to be done. Using her home email account, she addressed it to "Pparker" at the FBI. The message simply said, "Are you interested in meeting Mr. Miller? Call me any time today or tomorrow night at home." She signed it simply "Judith," the name she always used now.

In Alexandria, Andy Shannon checked email just after midnight on his "Pparker" account and found Judith's message. He decided to risk a phone call. When he heard her voice, a mixture of feelings hit him. Regret, for one, since he once hoped to be more than a friend to her but never was able. Anxiety, for another, since he knew the tightrope on which she walked and, as he cared about her, wanted her to be safe. Guilt, too, as he was responsible in a major way for how she lived now, but he knew as surely as he knew anything that she was better off than when he first knew her in graduate school.

"Judith—I got your message. Good to hear from you. Have you really seen Mr. Miller?"

"No, but a friend mentioned his name and that he may be investing in properties on the west coast. At least the name is right."

Andy paused. The conversation was one that should be held on a secure line. If the information was good, he was not going to take any chances. "Judith, can you be available at 6 in the morning your time and can you use your special phone?"

"I'll be awake and with the phone on," she answered quickly. And then, "I hope you are doing well—it's been a long time."

He felt gratified that she asked. "Yes, quite well, thank you. Work keeps me busy. I wish we could persuade you to come out here." He did not add "without your new friend," whom he suspected was male.

"Until tomorrow then," she said and rang off. "Well, Saleeth," she told herself, "you are involved now."

CHAPTER TWENTY
June 2-5

The first victims were a Guernsey cow and her calf. On Saturday night, a balloon drifted ashore in southern Oregon. While the look-up table in the computer attached to that particular balloon's payload container should have provided the drop command to the payloads when the balloon was over one of the several hundred population centers programmed into it, the computer was faulty. It misread the GPS signals, so the payload was instructed to drop into a pasture, several hundred miles west of the area where the coordinates would have signaled that it was the right place to drop. The first glass bulb payload was released and shattered on command at 100 hundred feet above the ground. The powder it had contained blew around as it descended. Late in the evening, the large Guernsey, still nursing her young calf, looked up and inhaled some of the spores as did her calf.

Nothing happened to them until Tuesday morning, when blood began running out of their ears and they convulsed and fell. By the time the rancher found them, they were dead. The rancher arranged to have them hauled back to the barn and then he called the vet about an autopsy. He was suspicious about the cause of their deaths and used gloves, which he later discarded, as he removed the salt lick as a precaution, since he noticed the white powder around it. Then, he herded the remaining cattle to an adjacent pasture and locked the gate behind them. The vet, overworked at this time of year, promised to do an autopsy within two days.

A significant break-through came when the computer on a balloon deployed by the Long Beach fleet behaved correctly. Having read that it was near San Francisco, it began releasing its payloads, and one of the shattered light bulbs sprayed powder above the schoolyard of Emerson Elementary in San Mateo. It was Sunday, but the parent-teacher organization had organized a weekend work party to fix up the children's outdoor play equipment.

A retired lawyer, the grandfather of one of the fourth-graders, saw what looked like a thin white cloud float into the far northeast corner of the yard. He immediately walked over to the school principal. "There's something odd over there. I saw a little cloud of something white that just seemed to drop out of the sky. It could be dangerous, and it could be someone wants to hurt the children. I think we should call the police."

The principal was a take-charge person and she sensed the danger immediately. Rather than taking the time to walk into the building, she pulled out her cell phone and dialed "911." The police arrived within three minutes since a cruiser was in the vicinity.

By this time, unnoticed, a second bulb from the same balloon successfully exploded and sprayed its powder near the trash bins of the schoolyard, obscured by some shrubs. The first policeman on the scene scraped up some of the powder and put it in a plastic bag. "We'll take a sample of this into headquarters," he said politely to the principal and the group of parents and teachers who now gathered around them as he scraped a tiny sample of the powder into a plastic bag.

Just then, another policeman yelled, "something over here!" and they all converged near the bushes where the second light bulb had exploded. The socket end of the bulb lay on the ground, with some shards of glass and powder near it. The police bagged all the fragments and started back toward their van. The senior officer said to the principal, "We'll let you know what we find. Has anyone threatened the school or the children that you know of?"

Worried glances were exchanged, but she said firmly, "No, nothing like that, and I'd know about it!"

"We will have to cordon off this area of the school yard," the officer directed, "and I would advise that you keep everyone away. We will let you know what our analysis turns up." With that, the police roped off the area with yellow tape. All the volunteers stood around in stunned silence. The principal decided to excuse the PTA members. "Let's try this again next weekend," she said, "when we're sure people aren't trying to play pranks on us." Privately, she felt great concern—was someone targeting Emerson and, if so, why? She knew of no disgruntled former students or teachers or staff. She was principal for five years and the school was doing well. She felt both alarmed and frightened.

The most deadly incident began unfolding in the Ojai Valley near Santa Paula. A rancher had just acquired four new Arabian horses to add to his already impressive stables. The value of his ranch was in the millions of dollars. Balloon No. 226 dropped its first payload in the valley where a bulb exploded near the ranch, resulting in the spores floating down over the west corner of the rancher's property.

Some of his horses were out milling around in the paddock. The new Arabians were all in the field nearest the barns. The horses shied as the unexpected white stuff landed in their pasture, but a few of them were close enough to inhale it. Other horses grazing farther away joined them. At the end of fifteen minutes, eight horses were contaminated. Some of the spores from the bulb descended on the exercise paddock, and a young groom who exercised the horses also inhaled some of the powder.

The carnage began Monday afternoon when the groom was the first to collapse, unconscious and bleeding. When the rancher walked out to check on the exercising, he uttered an exclamation and then shouted to his other helpers, who came running from the barns and from other work areas. Eight horses were in various stages of dying, and his young groom was bleeding. The men corralled the healthy horses and got them back into the barns. Then the rancher ran into the house and called the police.

But it was the senior on-duty detective at the San Mateo police department who, late on Sunday night, called a special number, known only to law enforcement agencies, at Homeland Security and reported, "We have confirmed anthrax in a school yard," that set the Federal ball rolling. Harold Harper at Homeland Security was alerted immediately by the supervisor of the young man who had taken the call from San Mateo. Harper was unable to take the call, so the supervisor left a message on his secure phone. She then contacted the FBI, CIA and NIA.

At the FBI, the message went straight to Eileen Johnson, who sent orders to dispatch two agents to San Mateo. Then she picked up her secure phone and called the White House, where the operator relayed her call to Jeff Sanchez. She explained briefly what she had been told. "Jeff, I don't know what we have here, but it could relate to our meeting the other day," Eileen said.

Jeff thought she was right. "I'll get word to the President and to Maya. Are you personally coordinating with Jimmy?" he asked.

"I haven't called anyone at the Agency yet—you came first—but I will. Consider us coordinated, and I'll put in place a liaison with Harper's office. I got the call from a supervisor at Homeland—I guess Harold is too busy." It was unlike Eileen to be sarcastic, but none of them thought much of Harold Harper's dedication to his job.

"Eileen, I'll call Maya and ask her to check any reports coming in from their people. And, if you could do me a favor, please let me know the minute your agents report in—or, if you get a report of anything else suspicious."

When Jeff put down the phone, he made a decision—call Maya first, then the President. He rationalized that if, by any chance, Maya's people uncovered something, he could give more information to the President. "Maya," he said with some relief after she picked up on the first ring, "I hope I'm not disturbing you too much but Eileen just called and Homeland Security has been notified by the San Mateo police that they've found anthrax in a school yard."

There was a brief silence on the other end, then, "So, they've started."

"Have your sources reported anything more?"

"I'll find out. Normally, nothing would come to me unless it's top level, but our Colonel might have sent something that I have not yet seen. Let me get back to you."

Jeff was forced to leave a message for the President with the operator at Camp David.

He had one more call to make and this was to the Centers for Disease Control in Atlanta. When he reached the on-duty director, he explained the situation. "It's possible there may be other locations that are being targeted," he added, not going into any detail. "I need to have you put our special depots with the supplies of ciprofloxacin, tetracycline and penicillin on high alert so that they can get these drugs to people who have been or may have been contaminated. We have reason to believe there could be additional attacks—probably on the West Coast."

Since 9/11, the CDC had built up massive supplies of the three drugs most effective in treating people who inhaled anthrax, and, fortunately, there had been no occasion to tap into those large supplies. "But," thought Jeff to himself, "this may be the time they are needed—if we can find people who are contaminated quickly enough." The problem, he knew, was that while treatment of a contaminated person over a 60-day period was usually successful, if you waited until symptoms appeared, it was probably too late. And decontamination of exposed land and buildings was extremely difficult. He hoped Elliott called back soon.

CHAPTER TWENTY-ONE
Evening, June 2

After dinner, Johnny Diep was enjoying a late-night Clint Eastwood "spaghetti western" with his wife when the call came from the Pentagon. He moved into the bedroom to take it. "This is Roy," the caller said. "Someone called the special number a few minutes ago. We traced the call to a cell phone registered to a company in Vancouver. Did one of your people give out the number or did you?"

Col. Diep sat down heavily on the bed. "No one that I know of, but let me check. The only likely way that number would have been obtained was if one of my people lost it or if it was taken from them."

"We've traced the incoming call to a cell phone and it's registered to the Vancouver Office Supply and Service Company. I've sent the number on to Operations."

"I'll check with my operatives and get back to you," Johnny told Roy.

Without moving from the bed, he tried all three numbers he had for Rahmid. Nothing. He received Rahmid's text message earlier and prepared a report for the Pentagon. He saw no reason tonight to worry about Rahmid, who was with relatives. He tried his two other operatives; both answered and both were positive that they never lost the special number. Col. Diep programmed his alarm clock to ring every two hours; he would continue trying to reach Rahmid tonight and visit his apartment discreetly in the morning, but he was not optimistic. The question was, if anything had happened to Rahmid, how much information had he parted with to the person or persons who may have harmed him?

§ § §

Meanwhile, on Sunday, Jay Sheldon enjoyed a short flight in his Mooney over the Santa Barbara Channel Islands. He liked to keep current, and this Sunday was a perfect day for flying. He took the plane to 10,000 feet when he saw two objects floating ahead of him and at a slightly lower altitude.

They appeared to be about 300 feet apart and drifted east. He pulled out a pair of powerful binoculars he kept in his flight bag and looked more closely.

The objects looked to him like balloons with small boxes attached below them. He had seen weather balloons before and assumed that's what these were. He checked for traffic, corrected his course, and headed for the balloons. When the first one was only a few hundred feet to his left, he descended so that he was almost level with it, at 8500 feet. He could see no writing or other identifying marks on the balloon itself or the payload, which now appeared to be a rectangular box. Jay was puzzled but not alarmed. Lots of things went on at the military bases and with NOAA on the coast of California. As he turned to resume his course back to the fixed based airport, he convinced himself that this was some NOAA weather or Air Force maneuver. As soon as he landed, he made a Pilot's Report to the FAA, indicating what he had seen and reporting the altitude, latitude and longitude. He also made a note in his log and added a mental note to write on his blog about his sightings.

CHAPTER TWENTY-TWO
June 3

Col. Ty Green got off duty at 7:00 a.m. at Peterson Air Force Base in Colorado and checked his laptop for personal emails. As a major, he was originally assigned to the Cheyenne Mountain Air Force Station before it was all but disbanded and put on "warm standby" in 2006. When he made Colonel, he was placed in charge of surveillance equipment at Peterson. The job entailed supervising the staff that monitored the few big land radars still in use in the US. The radars were now superseded by satellite tracking, but the radar ground stations were kept active in case a massive attack on— or failure of—the satellites occurred.

As a private pilot himself, he enjoyed reading the blogs of other pilots, and he routinely checked Jay Sheldon's blog, as he did this afternoon. "Wonder what those balloons were that he saw," Ty thought to himself. "Satellites probably couldn't pick up anything at those altitudes. Maybe we should try to look for them with the radars," he mused and then put the thought aside. None of this was important.

§ § §

On Sunday at 6:00 a.m., Pacific Coast Time, Saleeth sat by her living room window and waited for her cell phone to ring. When it did, Andy began the conversation where they had left off, saying, "Do you really think this is our Philip Miller?"

There was a pause. Then she said, "I haven't heard from him or about him for a long time, but I did not expect to. I didn't know he was still using that name, but he may be. I don't know why he would be investing in or owning companies."

Andy thought to himself, "More questions than answers," and gave a silent salute to the real Philip Miller, who never survived his kidnapping in Iraq and whose identity was boldly stolen. He left no direct survivors; only a handful of people in the US government knew he was dead and that someone else stole his name. All those who knew were under orders to keep quiet. But with Saleeth it was more than that; the person who had presumably stolen Philip Miller's identity was her brother.

"Judith, I know you can't contact him directly, but do you think you can verify this? Or at least give me the name of the friend who told you about him?"

She hesitated; she saw no reason to bring Raul into this—he was a new friend and valuable for her current business, perhaps even for her personal life, if she ever hoped to have one. Then she realized that she must, as always, think about duty to her government first. "His name is Raul Cabellero. He's an architect."

"I'll run him through our computers and see if at least he is someone you— we—can trust. You don't think he dropped this name on purpose, do you?"

Again she hesitated. "I don't know, but I don't think so. I did ask him a few more questions but he did not seem to know anything more about 'Mr. Miller.'"

"Well, if you see your friend Raul, try to bring this up again. Meanwhile, I'll check him out. Thanks for getting up early," Andy said. His voice softened a bit and they said their goodbyes.

Saleeth was not expecting any other calls, and left the phone on the coffee table as she went into her kitchen to fix oatmeal. But before she could even heat the water, the phone rang again. She answered immediately and heard Andy's voice.

This time he was laughing. "He's with the CIA!"

"Who?" she asked, feeling confused and for a dizzying minute wondering if he meant her brother.

"Raul! He's primarily assigned to Latin American projects, and the architect work is a cover. How did you meet him and what do you think he knows about you?"

Saleeth sat down abruptly in a kitchen chair. "We met through work! Wouldn't he have checked me out if he thought I was anything other than what I appear?"

"He probably did, but we've built you a pretty good legend, so he probably thinks you're a nice, single Jewish working girl. And maybe he didn't try to in-vestigate you too much—I'll bet he's just plain interested in you!" As painful as it was for Andy to say this, he thought now of the intelligence situation and of what could be done to locate "Mr. Miller," not of his personal feelings.

Saleeth heard this with decidedly mixed feelings. She hoped Raul was in-terested—but, again, she found herself in a situation where her personal life was compromised by her brother and her past.

§ § §

In Seattle, Rafik was finishing supper and was thinking about going outside for a cigarette. Just as he stood up, his cell phone beeped and he saw he had a text message. It read, "Call the Paris Travel Agency tonight." Rafik was surprised. The "Paris Travel Agency" meant a message or a command from the highest level of the organization—even higher than Ahmed. Technically, Rafik and Ahmed ranked equally. Their initial assignments meant that Georges was in charge of the balloon procurement, Rafik was the electronics expert, and Ahmed was the project director, overseeing Kamal, the two labs and all the packaging of the poisons plus most of the other logistics. But with Ahmed in the country—or perhaps still in Canada—Rafik expected any orders would come directly from him. He pulled out a disposable cell phone from the drawer in his kitchen where he kept such supplies and dialed the international number. After two rings, the call was answered, in French, with a simple "Paris Bureau— Artur ici."

"It's me," Rafik said softly, "I got your text message."

"One moment, please," the voice said, now in English.

Rafik waited; his desire for the cigarette was now acute.

"Our friend, Kas, may be compromised," said a new voice, deeper in tone and heavily accented. "After the next fleet departure, we need to have you and Mr. Ricotti complete the mission. One of you will deliver the first message. But do not do so without an express command from here. We will get back to you about that. We also need to have you make sure Kas is put on a plane. If you need extra resources, we will make them available. You can text to the Paris Travel Agency and we will get back to you with a number to call, if necessary." The connection went dead.

Rafik sat down slowly on one of his two kitchen chairs. He forgot momentarily about his desire to smoke. The next "fleet departure" was to be in twenty-four hours. "Put on a plane" meant only one thing. Rafik hoped he had a working number for Georges Labadie. They previously expected to contact each other infrequently since Ahmed was the go-between for the three of them. Rafik wondered how Ahmed was compromised, but he supposed that it did not matter. Had Ahmed, by any chance, switched sides? This possibility was beyond Rafik's comprehension. They came from different cultural backgrounds, but they knew who the enemy was and the current campaign felt their whole-hearted support. Ahmed worked so long and so hard to make it happen;

Rafik had supported him, and so had Georges, every step of the way. For their leaders across the ocean to command this change in plans, meant something irretrievable happened. And Rafik might never know what. Now, however, he knew he must act.

CHAPTER TWENTY-THREE
June 4

The internal mechanisms at the FBI, Homeland Security and the CDC were gearing up to focus on the apparent threat detected in California. So far, the press knew nothing about the anthrax story. The agencies involved were only aware that anthrax was deployed by some unidentified means.

But they were also unaware of what was about to happen at the Riverview Golf Resort, just outside of Las Vegas, where the Western States Republican Governors convention convened the day before. The date was well publicized in the press and security was tight, as fourteen governors attended, but Monday dawned bright and sunny and no one was particularly concerned about a threat in so serene a setting.

Gov. Fritz Nachtman was thinking about his handicap and whether he could get lucky with his wedge on the front nine. He was in a foursome with the governors of Utah, Nevada and Oklahoma, the last of whom, Gayle O'Connor, could out-drive all of them on a good day.

"Let's toss for driving order." suggested Utah's governor.

"Fine—here's a quarter" and Louis Dalberto, Nevada, produced a Nevada quarter. Emery and Fritz each called heads and each won. Then they tossed again and Fritz won to be first on the tee.

After all four of them drove just over 200 yards on the generous, slightly sloping fairway, they drove their two electric carts smartly toward their balls. Two threesomes waited to start behind them. The plan was to play nine holes before lunch, have a working lunch, and then play nine more holes. The real business of the convention was to strategize about how to elect a Republican to the White House in the next election, and that conversation could take place on the golf course as well as off.

The Nachtman foursome holed out and was ready to drive on the par three, second hole, when Gayle O'Connor saw what looked like a small patch of fog ahead of them, half way up the third fairway. She pointed it out to Louis, her cart partner, who took a pair of binoculars out of his bag to get a better look. "That's funny looking stuff but I don't think it's fog, not out here,"

Louis said. "We'll get a better look, I guess, when we get up to the third tee." They continued on the second hole, with the next threesome close behind them.

Emery drove first from the third tee. The cloud of whatever it was dissipated, but they saw traces of a fine, white, powdery substance on the fairway, and also some small pieces of glass. Emery reached the spot where the white powder lay on the ground. It covered an area of several yards. Without thinking too much about it, he stooped down and ran his finger over the powder, then raised his hand to smell it. Fritz reached his ball, which was near the outlying area the powder had reached, and did the same.

Louis and Gayle, who were further back, saw what was happening and rushed up. "Don't touch them—don't touch that! It may be poisonous" Gayle yelled. Early in her life, she trained as an emergency technician before going into the security business, and her instincts told her something very wrong happened here. She bent closer to the white substance but could not identify it.

By the time Gayle called the clubhouse on her cell phone and she and Louis jumped in the nearest golf cart and sped back, five of the governors who had come to Riverview were contaminated. Fortunately, the last threesome finished playing the first fairway and was warned by Gayle and Louis to turn back. When they got to the clubhouse, Louis, whose normally tanned skin looked pasty, said, "I've called the local police. If we really think it might be poison, I should call Homeland Security," and he left for the clubhouse office.

His security detail, who were not on the course, joined him—two tough, fit-looking men who played college football in Nevada years ago. Louis knew a particular friend in Homeland Security, Inez Esperanzo, and he placed the call to her. "Inez," he began, trying to keep his voice steady, "we have a situation here." He went on to describe what was happening.

"Louis, we know there is anthrax in at least one location in California," Inez told him immediately. "Do all you can to quarantine the golf course. Alert the local officials. We'll be sending someone there as soon as we can."

Louis hung up. He was the governor; he had the power to act. If he acted now it would secure his state, his people. But out on the fairways, five of his friends were potentially poisoned. Who could have planned such an attack? Who would want to?

Inez immediately called Harold Harper. Upon reaching his secretary, she explained that her call was top priority.

"Mr. Harper is not available right now, but I have a contact number for him if you want me to relay your message," said Simone, ever efficient. "Also,

Paul is here if you want to speak with him." Paul Blake was the second in command at Homeland Security and as aggressive and quick as Harold Harper was slow to make decisions.

"Yes, I'll talk to Paul. Thank you."

After Inez explained the call from Louis, she heard Paul sigh. "Inez, something's happening out there—as you know, we have a report of anthrax in California. We're sending someone to each site where there has been an incident. The CDC is gearing up to release antidotes. The FBI and the President's office have been informed. Thanks for calling me. I haven't reached Harold yet but I'll continue to call the shots."

"Paul, if I can help, please let me know," Inez replied. This was a little out of her area, as she specialized in natural disasters like floods.

"I will, and thanks again, Inez. We may need lots of help from everybody before this one is over."

§ § §

On Monday evening, two hours after a lab report from Las Vegas had confirmed the presence of anthrax on the Riverview Golf Resort's golf course, Jeff fired off a memo to the Trial Run team. It read:

"We have anthrax in two states—California and Nevada. We don't how it's being deployed but a fragment of a light bulb was found in the schoolyard in San Mateo. We have no known motive or suspects. I'll be contacting the FAA to see if they have a trace of any aircraft flying unusual patterns in the West but if planes were using Visual Flight rules, they'd be hard to track. The intelligence about an attack mounted from Western Canada is vague. I need the following: FBI to check on the glass fragments; Homeland to coordinate with the CDC so we stay ahead of any possible widespread contamination. I'll convene our next meeting as needed."

CHAPTER TWENTY-FOUR
June 5

Ahmed rose early on Tuesday, prepared to be Kas for one final day. His original plan was to leave Vancouver and travel east in Canada, eventually reentering the US under a completely different identity for what he hoped would be the ultimate act of this mission. But at a few minutes before midnight, he received a text message on his secure phone. It read: "Lovely day for a boat ride—avoid planes." It appeared to come from "Travel Agent." Ahmed stared at the message for a few seconds. There was no direct communications with Paris for a few days nor was he expected to contact them unless something went wrong on his end, and it had not. He was also not talking directly to Rafik or to Georges, but he kept them aware of the status of the operation through his reports.

Now, someone who knew him—and knew the codes—was warning him. He took a guess as to who it might be. A young, gay operative at headquarters more than once let Ahmed know he was interested, which Ahmed treated politely but coolly. But the identity of the sender mattered less to him now than what he should do. If the message was deliberately erroneous, it meant someone was directing him into a trap.

Ahmed showered, dressed, and placed all the necessary items into a black travel bag before he pulled out a map of the coastline and made his decision.

§ § §

Gerard also woke early. The first fleet deployment, last Saturday, went so well that he was promised a bonus. Today, Gerard was mildly annoyed and again had much to do before the boats left port. He planned to confirm with Rahmid that he could work again, but when he tried him Sunday and again on Monday he got no answer and Rahmid never returned Gerard's message. By late Monday, it was too late to find a substitute. Gerard expected to see Kas again and thought Kas would not be pleased that they were one crew-member short. He wished Luc were around to consult.

At 5:45 a.m., Gerard pulled up to the docks. All the captains worked with their crews to prepare room for the cargo. Like before, at 6:00 a.m., the trucks pulled in, although Gerard saw no sign of Kas yet until his black Dodge Neon swerved to a stop next to Gerard's car minutes later. Gerard went over to meet him.

"Good morning. I hope your weekend was good," Gerard said politely, and in English, although he was secretly tempted to speak French Canadian just to see if this somewhat mysterious dark-complexioned man, whom he took to be Indian or Paki, would understand that.

Kas held out his hand and shook Gerard's firmly. "It was busy," he replied.

"The boats are being loaded but we've got a minor problem," Gerard continued. "One of the men, Rahmid, didn't call me, so now I don't expect him to work today."

To his great relief, Kas actually smiled. "It's all right! I have been thinking that I should help more than I did on Saturday. If you can stay here or close by and handle our communications, I'd like to be crew for the day."

Gerard was amazed and pleased. Perhaps Kas was not so high up in the organization after all. "Will you go out with Nassir, then? That's the crew where we are short."

"Of course!" Ahmed answered quickly.

"Come, then, and I will introduce you. You will go out on *Sea Lady*." He waved Nassir off the boat and introduced the two men. After a handshake, Nassir went back to *Sea Lady*, and Kas began supervising the off-loading of the trucks, all of which were now in the parking lot.

The process was completed within forty-five minutes. Kas paid the drivers and sent them off. The boxes—identical in size and shape to those that had been off-loaded at the dock the previous week—were securely stowed on all the boats. Kas unlocked his car and took out his bag, a thermos of coffee and a small metal box from the glove compartment. He looked around. Everyone was temporarily occupied; Gerard was on a cell phone call and walking away from the cars, while the boat crews were all at work making ready. Kas locked the car and placed the car keys in the small metal box, bending down and attaching it just under the front passenger side door.

He waited until Gerard completed his call and then walked over to him. Extending his hand, he said, "I will see you here when we return, yes?"

"I'll be here," Gerard answered enthusiastically. "If I need to relay anything to you, I'll call *Sea Lady*. If you need me, you have my cell phone number."

The two men shook hands and Kas headed down the dock toward *Sea Lady,* her engines already running. He never looked back.

CHAPTER TWENTY-FIVE

On Tuesday morning in Los Angeles, Georges Labadie, whose own oversight of the Long Beach boat deployment the previous Saturday went well, prepared to enjoy a rare day when he didn't have to be anyone but himself. Specifically, he planned to go to the health club and then arrange a trip to Tahoe, which would be for business, of course, but not until next week. He was at his home computer, about to log off and leave for the club, when a message came up on his mailbox from "Chauffer." It read:

> "Need to speak with you about a request for a Paris trip. Please advise number to call or ring me."

This, he knew, meant some difficulty. Rafik had not communicated with him by uncoded email since the beginning of the plan, when they all agreed on a long list of names and email addresses they would use on a one-time basis for urgent correspondence. They all changed their cell phone numbers regularly, but he thought of one that he knew would work for Rafik, since Ahmed confirmed it to him recently. He picked up his desk phone with the scrambler and dialed the number. Rafik picked up after three rings.

"Yes?"

"Is this my chauffer and can you talk?" Georges asked quickly.

"Yeah," Rafik said, and Georges thought he heard the sound of a car engine being shut off. "I had a call from the Paris Travel Agency. They want us to put our friend on a plane to Paris. They said there will be further instructions about the mission later." It was clear to Georges that Rafik was being careful about what he said.

There was a long pause on Georges' end of the line. "What is the status of the boats he was overseeing?" Georges asked, also weighing his words.

"All underway, I believe, as of this morning, but I need to check—and yours?"

"Saturday went well. Have you talked with our 'passenger' in the last twenty-four hours?"

"No. I was waiting for him to call me, but now I'll have to call him. He should have been with the boats this morning."

"Can you do the chauffeuring yourself if you can reach him?"

"Yes, unless you want to join me." Rafik gave a short, harsh laugh.

"I don't think that's a good idea, unless you want me to. Think about it. And how is the Travel Agency going to get in touch with us for the next steps? Our friend was supposed to do something important soon!" Georges became increasingly angry at what might be a massive screw-up on the other side of the ocean—and after all their careful planning!

"They just said that they would. Do you have a number I can keep in touch with you on?"

There was another pause. Then Georges said, "I'm going to email you some weights for packages I am shipping. Use them in order and only once. I can be with you in less than twenty-four hours if necessary. Notify me when you have taken him to the plane as well as when you hear from the Travel Agency."

The health club could wait. He picked up his scrambler again and dialed a landline number. It rang four times and then reverted to voice mail. "Hello. I'm not here to take your call right now but please leave your name and number and a short message. Thanks."

Georges waited for the beeps to end. "Good morning! Or, at least it's morning here! About our trip to Tahoe—I can get away two days earlier, so I can be there Thursday. How does that sound to you? The course may be less crowded before the weekend. Give me a call." He rang off, irritated. No telling when he would get a call back, and now the trip to Tahoe was more urgent than ever. Not that he particularly enjoyed gambling, although the golfing was pleasant. He was careful, more so, obviously than Ahmed had been, although Georges struggled to believe that Ahmed had done anything to jeopardize their mission. It was Ahmed who was so passionate; Georges cared about the cause but he was in it for the money and, yes, the excitement. Plus he held a certain distaste for Americans.

§ § §

Seven hundred miles away at Peterson Air Force Base in Colorado, Ty Green was studying the large radar screen, having just come on duty. His deputy, who was preparing to leave for the day, reported when Ty arrived. "We're seeing what look like a lot of sparkles or blips on the radar screen over the western states. They seem pretty random, but they're in clusters and they appear to be moving east. Should I check the Pentagon's secure notices to see if there is some kind of an exercise? We haven't been alerted to anything."

Ty saw them immediately. Moving steadily west to east in an unorganized way were occasional small bursts of faint returns on the screen. It was impossible to identify whether they were objects or some type of reflection, as it was not unusual to see reflected signals that amounted to noise from the radars. The pattern, however, triggered something in his mind, and he suddenly recalled reading Jay Sheldon's flying blog. These might be balloons, since they would have little to no metal for the radars to see, causing them to look like small blips on the radar screen.

"This could be a NOAA event," he said to the Major. "Have we gotten anything from them about a special launch?" The Major consulted his computer screen and scrolled through several pages. "Nothing, sir."

"Let's do the usual FAA notification. I'll do our internal report, and I'll assign someone to investigate with the other agencies. I'm sure it's routine."

The Major left and Ty rang another office to have them report the sightings to the Chief of the Air Force and to the FAA's regional offices in Denver and Los Angeles. He was annoyed that a US government agency would send up any type of balloons without notifying the proper authorities, including the Air Force, but it wouldn't be the first time.

CHAPTER TWENTY-SIX

ea Lady handled the gentle waves well in the Strait of Georgia, and Ahmed saw it was a perfect day for the deployment. Before they started, the surface winds reading showed ten knots, and the forecast was for a calm, clear day.

He and Nassir exchanged few words, although Nassir looked at him with open curiosity as they got underway. Based on the distance they needed to travel in the two straits and then in open water before beginning to unpack the crates and begin filling the balloons, they had about an hour to go before working with the payloads.

"I have never been on these pleasant waters before!" he announced to Nassir. "Perhaps it would be polite for me to ask the captain if I can stand with him for a while and use his binoculars—there is so much to see!" And without waiting for Nassir to reply, he climbed the short flight of stairs up to the captain's station on the top deck.

"Good morning, sir!" Ahmed said heartily to the bearded, burly man at the wheel, who was dressed in jeans and an oversized sweater. "My name is Kas Pradep. I am new on this university project and am glad to be with you and your crew. I was wondering if you could point out some things we should look for."

Ahmed was fully prepared to play "Kas" down to the literal naming of some of his publications and explaining how he became connected with the supposed university project, but the captain's first words were simply, "Morning. Name's Sig Olsen. Glad to have you aboard. Not much to see, but I'll answer any questions if you have 'em."

Ahmed moved to the captain's side. "What land are we seeing there to our left?" as he pointed to what was evidently a city.

"That's Bellingham. In Washington." Sig seemed a man of few words.

"May I borrow your binoculars"? Kas asked politely.

"Sure. Just leave 'em up here." Sig steered around a sailboat that proceeded at a safe distance to their right.

Ahmed picked up the binoculars and focused them. He saw a large harbor with a commercial port and what looked like at least one private marina. The port was moderately busy, with boats maneuvering out to the channel and trucks coming and going on land. "Do you have competition from the fishing boats in Bellingham?"

"Some. But it's a big ocean." Sig was clearly not going to share his inner thoughts.

After almost two hours underway, the teams on each of the boats began unpacking the boxes, attaching the payloads, filling the balloons and sending them up. Ahmed asked Nassir for instructions and was given an efficient lesson in the plan he, himself, designed—but, of course, Nassir would never know that. Nassir assigned Ahmed the role of "hooker."

As he began to fill the balloons from the helium canisters, Nassir became talkative. "Saturday we had light winds—today almost the same, and it's warmer, too!" He turned his face up to the sun and smiled. "If I could afford to make my living as a fisherman I would be out here every day." Ahmed continued to work, refraining from any questions about what Nassir really did. "And you, you a university professor, yes? And you a member of our cause?" Nassir asked, looking directly at Ahmed.

Ahmed cursed himself for not having found out more about Nassir; it was always possible that someone in the group was a spy or a traitor. "Oh, yes, I teach—and do research and write. And, yes, I strongly believe we in our organization must show what we can do." Ahmed hoped this reply would be sufficient enough to allay any concerns Nassir might have.

"When our balloons can deliver spying technology they will never see and never catch, that is wonderful thing," Nassir responded and smiled again up at the sun. Then he went back to work.

The first balloon from *Missfit* lifted rapidly out of sight above them even as Ahmed and Nassir prepared to release their first one. When all the boats released their balloons, Ahmed wished briefly that he could use his digital camera to take a picture. It was an impressive sight—the more so if one knew the contents dangling under each balloon, ready to drop their poisons in hours or days, depending on their individual destinations as directed by their preprogrammed satellite units.

The total deployment took just over two hours. After Nassir communicated with the lead crewmember on each of the other boats, he informed Ahmed they were ready to begin their return to Vancouver. "It will take less time to go back—I can see from the current," he informed Ahmed. Ahmed looked up at the still brilliant sky.

"I'd like to give the men a break for lunch as we go back," Nassir informed Ahmed, who nodded.

"I have some coffee in my thermos—I would be pleased to share that with you," he offered Nassir.

"Yes, that would be good—I have some bread and cheese, and I will share that with you, too."

Ahmed excused himself to use the boat's one head and to get his thermos. It was stowed with his black bag under the bunk in the aft cabin. He retrieved them. No one was around. He carefully unscrewed the top on the thermos and unzipped the black bag. In a minute, the maneuver was completed. He washed his hands and then went back on deck. Nassir found two dented metal coffee cups in the galley and was sitting on a deck box, unwrapping the bread and cheese, which he cut in half with a pocketknife. "For you!" he said, pushing some of the food toward Ahmed.

Ahmed opened the thermos and poured two cups of coffee. "Thank you," he said and took a bite of the cheese on the bread. "Your wife must have made this bread—one cannot buy anything like this in Canadian stores!"

Nassir beamed. "I baked it. It is my hobby!" And with that, he took a long swig of coffee.

Ahmed watched while Nassir finished his bread and cheese and the first cup of coffee. Ahmed ate more slowly. "Here," he said, pushing the thermos toward Nassir, "you finish it. I had two cups before we started out."

Nassir smiled. "You were maybe nervous about a sea voyage, but see—today has been very calm. We are lucky," and he began his second cup of coffee.

Ahmed got up for a stroll. He took his coffee cup with him. When he was half way around the deck and no one was looking, he emptied it over the side. There was not much to see until they reentered the channel, and if his timing was right, nothing much else would occupy anyone's attention for about fifteen minutes. Then, he confidently expected, all hell would break loose.

At 2:30 p.m., *Sea Lady* was running next to last in the fleet. They would easily reach port in a couple of hours and no one was hurrying. The boats were making about 15 knots. Ahmed again visited Sig Olsen and again borrowed the binoculars, hoping to see some sea life, perhaps a whale, but he was unsuccessful. Then he heard a shout from the aft deck. He rushed out of the wheelhouse and down the short flight of steps. Nassir was lying on the deck, writhing in pain, and the youngest helper was bending over him.

"He says he has a great pain in his stomach," the man said, turning to Ahmed and looking very worried.

Ahmed knelt down next to Nassir. "Is this where it hurts?" he said gently, touching Nassir's abdomen. What he got in response was a moan; Nassir was nearly doubled over. Ahmed straightened up. "I think it is his appendix—it must have burst. We must get him to port as quickly as possible."

The first mate, who had joined them, went pale. "But we are another hour or more from Vancouver!" he said, his voice trembling.

Ahmed spoke calmly. "Go and tell Captain Olsen that we must get to the nearest port. I will take responsibility for any problems this causes and will see that any inconvenience is paid for. This man could die if we don't get him to a medical facility very soon." The first mate ran up to the wheelhouse. Somewhat to Ahmed's annoyance, Sig Olsen emerged a few seconds later and ran down to where Nassir was still writhing on the deck. His hands and face were clammy, and he continued to moan.

"Do you have any medical training?" the captain asked Ahmed without preamble.

"No, but I saw my brother die from acute appendicitis," Ahmed replied, "and if it isn't that, it must be something else quite terrible. I am senior in this mission and I will take full responsibility for anything to do with your boat. The university will reimburse you, but we must get him to port."

Sig straightened up. "I'll radio Bellingham. They'll have an ambulance when we get there." He ran back up to the wheelhouse to use his VHF phone. The first mate brought a blanket and a glass of water, covered Nassir and went up to the wheelhouse. Ahmed looked down dispassionately. He knew nothing about Nassir and did not wish to. Nassir would likely die, although the dose of poison he gave Nassir was the smallest amount that still induced these symptoms.

He looked up. *Sea Lady* was now passing all the other boats in the fleet and breaking off from them. Bellingham, off to their right, was approaching rapidly. Ahmed waited until they were docking and the confusion of getting Nassir off the boat was at its height. He would, of course, help with that, but he would not be getting back on *Sea Lady*. He went below to get his black bag. He was about to become an American.

CHAPTER TWENTY-SEVEN

June 5, in Washington, DC

Paul Blake sat with his eyes focused on the far wall at 8 a.m. on Tuesday. He was minutes away from his meeting with Harold Harper and he had to think. Harold disliked long briefings; it was questionable whether he even read the briefing paper Paul emailed him last night. The subject of the apparent anthrax attack was complex. Harold would want facts and would be annoyed if Paul were not able to outline a clear plan of action. Finally, he got up, picked up his slim folder and began the long walk from his modest office to Harold's considerably larger one.

"Is he ready for me yet?" he asked Simone, Harold's long-time secretary, who sat primly at her walnut desk. Simone, he thought, covered for Harold in many ways and on many occasions.

"I'll buzz him." She smiled while reaching over for the intercom.

When Paul entered Harold's office, Harold got up and came over to sit in one of the easy chairs around the oval meeting table. "Thanks for coming in and for the briefing memo. I read it. What more do we know about the anthrax, and have they found any more of it? How are we keeping it out of the press?" Harold seemed to be in a good mood and focused.

"We don't have anything new since late yesterday. We haven't gotten any more reports of the stuff being found anywhere else, and there doesn't seem to be any connection between the incidents so far, so it may be an elaborate prank or a clumsily planned attack that isn't going to do much. The White House has asked the local law enforcement agencies to keep the wraps on this for the time being."

"What does the FBI say about this? Don't they have any good informants, or the Agency for that matter?"

Paul went over the highlights of what had been discussed in Jeff's office the preceding day. He concluded by saying, "We may have to be ready to send out additional teams on short notice if this stuff appears anywhere else. I need to know if you want to personally approve additional personnel or if you want me to authorize people if you are not reachable." He did not add, "As you seem not to be on many occasions."

"Phone me after your next meeting with Jeff and the team. I want a briefing, of course, but if we have to move quickly, I'll authorize you to deploy our people." With that, Harold got up and strode back to his desk.

His tone was dismissive, and Paul walked out with a curt "will do."

CHAPTER TWENTY-EIGHT

At noon on Tuesday, Jeff convened his meeting with the Trial Run team. This time, he had an electronic white board where he could jot down notes that could be printed later.

"Let's begin with any updated information. Anyone?" Jeff looked around the room. Eileen, Jimmy, Maya and Paul were present. NIA offered to staff the meeting as well, but Jeff had declined and agreed to continue his liaison role with them.

Maya began. "Our agent who sent in the report about the boats launching research balloons is now convinced his informant is dead. No one has seen or heard from him in four days. All his contact numbers have been deactivated. Col. Diep is doing some more investigating but is not optimistic." They sat soberly for a few moments.

Maya continued. "We don't, of course, know exactly what the boats that were leased—or the balloons, if they are related to this—are supposed to be doing. Or how—if at all—this episode is in any way related to the anthrax attacks. But, we have been tasking our military surveillance satellites to look for balloons over the Pacific and the West Coast—so far, without results. It's possible that they are flying at altitudes where the satellites cannot see them."

Eileen half-raised her hand. "We now have a report that aerial surveillance working off shore from Long Beach, California on Saturday spotted some boats—fishing boats, they looked like—that may have been launching balloons. We're trying to get more information, and we are working with Jimmy's people to interview all captains out of Seattle and Vancouver, BC."

"Can the balloons be seen by radar?" Paul asked. Jeff was pacing.

"Depends on whether they have any reflective surfaces," Maya answered. "Unfortunately, we've deactivated some of our conventional ground radars now that we're depending almost entirely on satellite surveillance and guidance. And unless there are really large reflective surfaces on the balloons, the satellites would not be able to see them. But, we still have staff at Peterson Air Force Base watching the images we do get via the active radar ground stations. They might be able to see something."

"The President has asked for special tracking," Jeff informed them, "so, Maya, I'd like to have you make sure the Air Force gives us the best they've got at Peterson." He sat down again.

"Has anyone from the Governors' conference gotten really sick?" Maya asked.

"Not yet, and we're getting them the best medical attention available," Paul answered. "But we aren't absolutely sure who might have been contaminated, although we think five of them were exposed to the anthrax, so everyone who was anywhere near the golf course is quarantined and being decontaminated."

"There is something else from our agency," Jimmy offered. "We've had some evidence that the person who stole the identity of a US journalist and who may be a terrorist or linked to terrorists is participating in a Vancouver-based company. The company looks to be legitimate, but a building they were renting in Seattle burned to the ground last Saturday night. We don't have anything to link this to the anthrax attack, but since the rumor about the boats leaving Vancouver was raised at our first meeting, I thought I should report this. Also, we may have an informant who knows how to get in touch with this person, Philip Miller, but no contact has been made—or at least verified—yet. I'm going to direct that we use this informant to make contact as soon as possible."

"We're putting out alerts to all our western regional offices that there may be an anthrax attack that could be widespread in the West," Paul reported. "We've asked them not to talk with the press, but we don't know if the San Mateo incident is going to get any press attention—someone who was at the school might report it. And I am, personally, coordinating with the CDC. They have their stores of antidotes ready to administer on a wide-scale basis in the west if needed."

Just as Jeff was about to summarize their reports, Paul Blake's mobile phone rang. He listened grimly and then reported to the group. "About an hour ago our office got a report that very small clouds of a white substance had been seen by pedestrians near the Mormon Temple in Salt Lake City. A similar report had come in to our office from Boulder, only this time the locations of the drifting powder were the main campus of the University of Colorado and a children's playground nearby. The city is essentially shut down, pending more information. We're testing for anthrax."

As the team was trying to digest this information, Jeff's assistant rang him. "Turn on your TV to CNN," she said.

Jeff activated the large screen while the reporter was saying,

"Again, we repeat that we've just learned that in Klamath Falls, Oregon, the mayor, whose brother-in-law heads the Homeland Security office in Portland, told him about an anthrax alert, so he decided to do some investigating before anything happened in that peaceful city. He ordered that the city's water supply, which comes from Upper Klamath Lake, be tested for any dangerous substances. A lab technician at Oregon State University checked for anthrax spores, but after he and his team took water samples, he ordered that tests be run for other toxins as well. They've found unmistakable evidence of the toxin Cryptosporidium. We understand that the mayor has alerted the local police, the state police and the governor and is appealing for National Guard troops to bring in and supervise distribution of bottled water supplies to the city.

"To let our viewers know, this is the first time we've learned of any nation-wide anthrax alert. Anthrax can be deadly, but if exposed people are treated quickly they may not die. The microorganism Cryptosporidium, commonly known as 'Crypto,' works to cause Cryptosporidiosis, a diarrheal disease. While this isn't usually fatal to healthy people, it can lead to serious infections and prolonged weakness in people with weakened immune systems—such as young children, the elderly or those with other diseases. Crypto often infects people who drink contaminated water, but it can be found in other substances such as soil and food or on surfaces that are touched. People and animals become infected after accidentally swallowing the parasite. The organism is resistant to chlorine, although Nitazoxanide is an FDA-approved treatment for diarrhea caused by Cryptosporidium. No one in Klamath Falls had been exposed, as far as we have been able to learn." CNN paused for a commercial break.

Jeff immediately called his assistant. "Tell the President we're going to Skype with him if he's available." In thirty seconds, they saw President at his desk. Jeff informed him of the CNN report.

"Contact the Prime Ministers' offices in Ottawa and London and the President's office in Mexico City. Tell them we think we have a situation where poisons are being spread. Ask them to stand by for any help we may need—and to be alert in their own countries. Tell them we have antidotes that the CDC has stored for the anthrax decontamination and that we can make plenty of Nitazoxanide available for anyone who might get diarrhea from the Crypto poisoning. Until we know who is doing this, we don't know the scope of it.

"I'll have my press secretary issue a brief statement to the White House press within the hour. He'll report that we have five confirmed locations where anthrax has been found, in addition to the Cryptosporidium in Oregon, and that the FBI, Homeland Security and the CDC are working on this—and that we have no evidence of any widespread attacks. I'll have him schedule a press conference for tomorrow morning, and I'll address the nation tomorrow night on television—even if we don't know much more. We have to be able to tell people that we are on top of this."

Just as their call ended, Jeff was again buzzed by his assistant. "FAA Administrator Glovere on the line for you. She says it's urgent."

"Switch her in," Jeff said, putting the call on speaker phone. They all heard the deep voice of the current head of the FAA, herself a former naval and civilian pilot with excellent administrative credentials.

"Jeff, I'm calling you directly because I've seen the CNN story about the Cryptosporidium in Oregon, and there is something you should know. We've just seen a report from the Secretary of the Air Force's office—quite confidential, you understand—that at Peterson they spotted groups of drifting blips on their screen, apparently moving west to east. They could not find any agency report on any activity that would explain this, including anything classified. The Air Force Colonel who heads the radar operation there believes what they saw could have been balloons. I know it may be a long shot, but could the poison have been dropped from a balloon?"

"Ada," Jeff said, "I'm meeting with a special emergency team now, and there is something else going on that we've kept quiet. We have evidence of an anthrax attack—we don't know how wide-spread—that has at least affected sites in California and Nevada. All that has been found at the sites is what looks like fragments of what could be light bulbs, plus some evidence of the spores. We have deaths, so this means the anthrax has been out for at least three or four days. If this stuff is being dropped from aircraft, is there any way your people can check on flight plans in the areas where we have contamination, or even do a trace on VFR flights that might not have registered flight plans?"

There was a short pause on the other end of the line. "We can check all records of filed flight plans. We keep records for twenty-four hours of 'flight following' requests from VFR flights, but if this is being done by bad guys, I would assume they did not ask for flight following."

"Ada, get me anything you can," Jeff said, "and if we get any evidence aircraft were involved, I'll call you. Oh, and tell your people to keep this quiet. The press is already going to whip up people into mass panic with what they've got!"

CHAPTER TWENTY-NINE
June 5, in Vancouver

By 3:00 p.m. Tuesday, Johnny Diep knew he could not wait any longer to go to Rahmid's family. With a sinking feeling, he went to the apartment building where Rahmid lived with his aunt and one of his cousins. He decided to pose as a prospective employer. As he entered the foyer of the four-level building, he looked around. It was a modest entrance, clean but plain with one rug, a small table with a lamp on it and a shelf on the opposite wall, decorated by a large vase with artificial flowers. No elevator. Johnny walked up the two flights to the aunt's unit.

As soon as he knocked on the door, a small woman wearing a headscarf opened it. "Yes?" she said, staring at Johnny.

"Good afternoon," Johnny began. "My name is Ming Lew. I've come to talk with Rahmid Shalif. He has applied for a financial position with my company— I am in the restaurant business, and he was supposed to meet me today for an interview, but there must have been some misunderstanding as he did not come and I could not reach him on the phone number he gave me. I hope I have not come at an inconvenient time."

"Mr. Lew, he is not here. I am Raisa Shalif, his aunt. We have not seen him since Saturday. We think he is on a trip." The woman lowered her eyes and made a gesture that seemed to beckon Johnny further into the apartment. "Sit down, please, Mr. Lew," she said, and he took the nearest straight-backed chair. "We have not seen my nephew in several days. We had a small party here Saturday evening, and he said he was going out for cigarettes. He never returned and he has not called. He has been working part-time and sometimes he is called away suddenly, but he always calls me. I am very worried."

Johnny thought quickly. If there was any information that Rahmid had left in the apartment that could be of value, he wanted very much to get his hands on it. "Rahmid struck me as a very sincere and very honest young man," he said warmly to Raisa. "I must tell you that I gave him some valuable and confidential information about our company last week and asked him to study it and bring it to the interview. There were copies of our financial information.

I am very sorry that he has not been in touch with you—or with me, but if it would be possible for me to retrieve the information I gave him that would be very helpful. I will, of course, hold open the job until we hear from him. I'm sure there has just been some emergency that he had to attend to."

Raisa rose. "He has a small room in the back. If he had information from your company, I'm sure he meant to return it. You may look on his desk. He did not have so many personal things." Johnny let her lead the way to Rahmid's room, which was, indeed, spare.

One book, the Koran, lay on his small desk. No sign of a PC, tablet or cell phone. Johnny was wondering how he could decently ask to open the two desk drawers when Raisa said, "He may have put the papers in a drawer— you may look in them." She moved slightly to let him get to the desk but did not leave the room. Johnny opened the drawers and made a show of looking. There was a small book of phone numbers, and he debated whether to try to take that but decided against it. After looking carefully at the contents of the two drawers, he turned to Raisa. "I don't see the papers here. Perhaps he mailed them back to us. When he returns, please tell him I still want to meet with him—and to return the papers."

After thanking Raisa, he left the apartment and walked back down the two flights of stairs. He thought again about how modest the building was. "Can't even afford fresh flowers!" he remarked out loud as he again eyed the tall vase with artificial flowers near the door. Then he stopped. He taught Rahmid to be very cautious and not to carry with him anything that could incriminate him in the event he was ever waylaid. So far, there was no evidence that anyone took Rahmid's mobile phone. If that was the case, where was it likely to be? He had not seen it in Rahmid's room. Of course, it could still be with him and inoperative for a variety of reasons. The time of the text message had been Saturday night, so Rahmid had the phone with him, but could he have hidden it somewhere before he went out?

On a whim, Johnny reached up and took the vase from the shelf. He later wondered what he would have done had someone entered the foyer just then, but no one did. He carefully removed the flowers and turned over the vase. A Blackberry Curve fell to the rug. He stooped down, picked it up, pocketed it, and returned the flowers and vase.

When he was safely inside his own apartment half an hour later, he examined it. It was clearly Rahmid's Blackberry as it displayed the number on which he had contacted Rahmid several times. He even found the text message Rahmid had sent him about the excursion on the boat. Following that message, however, he also found a short message, also meant for him, that, for some reason had not been sent. It was also about Rahmid's day on the boat. The first sentence began, "Before we went out on the boats today, I met the man who seemed to be in charge, but all I got was his first name—Kas."

91

CHAPTER THIRTY
Late afternoon, June 5

Don't swim in the lake, don't drink the water!" Internet news sites and newspapers screamed on their headline banners. The major broadcasting networks, local radio and TV stations and cable news stations all provided details about anthrax and Crypto and how the poisons seemed to be spreading—and what to do about it. Frightened parents kept their children away from community pools and boiled their drinking water. Many communities created safe water stations where people could pick up bottled water. Animals were provided with sheltered water for drinking, and any that displayed signs of Crypto were immediately tested.

"Local hospitals have their hands full," the TV announcer reported. The CDC sent out a nation-wide bulletin, which was carried by all the press and major web sites, urging that anyone who was possibly exposed to anthrax be treated immediately, since recovery could be complete if the treatment began immediately after exposure. But if people waited until symptoms appeared, it would generally be too late to save them. When this news got out, people in all the communities where confirmed spores were identified began frantically calling their doctors and checking themselves in to clinics and hospitals. Medical staffs were nearly overwhelmed; Internet and press reporters fed the panic.

All day, reports flooded the CDC, the FBI and local police about outbreaks of severe diarrhea in communities in southern California, Arizona, Utah, Colorado, New Mexico, Wyoming and Montana. Many school systems decided to close. The head of the national boy scouts organization consulted with his counterpart at the national girl scouts and with heads of the national YMCA and YWCA. At 2 p.m., Eastern Time, they issued a statement to the press: "We believe it is in the best interests of the members of all our organizations that we immediately cancel all outdoor camping and athletic events until our government can assure us that this threat is over."

What no one outside of the terrorists yet knew was that of the nine payloads on each of the 600 balloons, four were filled with weaponized anthrax spores; the other five contained the microorganism Cryptosporidium. The computers in the payload boxes calculated their positions based on dead reckoning that, in turn, was based on reading the position information from GPS/GLONASS receivers. Each computer was programmed to command its payloads to drop anytime the balloon was within a prescribed circumference— a few miles—of any one of a certain number of specific latitude-longitude intersections that were programmed in as "look up" tables.

The majority of the look up tables specified drop sites that concentrated on Midwestern and Eastern cities, since those cities accounted for the highest population concentrations. Some balloons had tables that also included Western population centers, which was why payloads had dropped near San Francisco and Los Angeles, as well as in Las Vegas, Oregon, Utah and Colorado. Wind currents and other meteorological factors meant that no drop could be guaranteed to hit any particular target. The on-board GPS/GLONASS receiver continually provided the current payload position. A pressure sensor provided information on low altitude abort situations, which meant the payloads would be ejected and would subsequently explode at 100 feet above the ground if the balloon descended below 10,000 feet, regardless of whether or not it was near a programmed target.

In New Orleans, where no poisons of any kind had been reported, an ambitious politician called a press conference. "I have every reason to believe the United States is under an unprecedented attack by dictators from South America," he said, providing no evidence whatsoever but gaining headlines not only locally but on the evening news broadcasts and on all the Internet news sites.

A prominent Atlanta evangelical minister went on Fox News to say that every American should pray for the country, leaving the clear impression that he had little faith that the government could—or would—do what was needed.

By 3:00 p.m., the three major US stock markets had all lost more than eight percent and were continuing to dive. "I may have to order the markets closed tomorrow," President Bradley said and immediately asked his secretary to convene by teleconference the Working Group on Financial Matters that included the Secretary of the Treasury, and the three chairmen of the Fed, the SEC and the commodity Futures Trading Commission.

At the conclusion of their conference call, President Bradley said, "I'd like to see how the markets open tomorrow before we take any drastic action." They all knew, according to the SEC's rules, revised in 1987, that if there was a ten percent decline in the Dow-Jones Industrial Average, trading must be halted for at least an hour if the drop occurred before 2 p.m.

"What if we see a steady decline from early morning on?" the Treasury Secretary, a former banker, asked.

"Then we'll convene an emergency teleconference," Elliott responded. "We may have to close the markets earlier but let's not decide that now."

They all agreed, although several of the group's members had deep misgivings about how widespread the poison attacks were going to be and how the public might react.

As Abu watched the international news from his compound near Paris, he remarked to his trusted aide, "It's working. The Americans don't know what is happening!"

CHAPTER THIRTY-ONE
June 5, in Seattle

After he left the fishing boat, Ahmed moved easily from Bellingham to Seattle. He found a willing cab driver to whom he had paid cash for a one-way trip.

Now in Seattle and in a room at the YMCA, Ahmed saw the CNN report about the discovery of Cryptosporidium in Oregon and knew he must do three things. First, he must activate a new identity. Although he registered as Philip Miller, he doubted it would be safe to be Philip for very long—or ever again. Secondly, now that his own life was in jeopardy, he needed to stay alive and undiscovered long enough to deliver the message to the US Government—the message that was at the heart of all their work and effort.

He was not sure what orders about him came from Paris, but now he trusted almost no one. Yet, the plan mattered more to him than his life. Third, he needed to get out of Seattle and find a way out of the country after the next phase of the plan. This last seemed the hardest to him, for he never gave up the thought that he could find Saleeth, but he failed to do that even when he could move about easily. Still, some part of him hoped a miracle would happen. "If Allah wishes," he said to himself.

He doubted that he could continue to access his money safely for very much longer, so he decided to withdraw several thousand dollars before leaving Seattle, though not so much as to cause the bank to make a report on the transaction to any agency. Two people apparently knew that there was a price on his head—Rafik and Georges Labadie, but they might need to enlist others. He counted on the fact, however, that they would do as the organization desired, eliminate all enemies swiftly and quietly. He also trusted Kamal not to betray him.

It even occurred to him that if he could eliminate Rafik and Georges, he could be in sole charge of the operation and see it through to completion. The people in Paris valued success above all else. Yet something went wrong; someone in Paris thought he betrayed the cause. "Never," he said out loud, pounding his fist on the bedside table. But he had to be cautious now. "Deliver the message and get out of the country," he said to himself.

First, he would check bus and train schedules for any points south or east of Seattle. Then, he would go to the bank and leave the next morning, using another alias as he made his way either to the Los Angeles area or to Denver. He was undecided as to which place was safer, but first he would try to find out how much the US Government knew and how much damage had been done. He turned up the television volume.

CHAPTER THIRTY-TWO
June 6

At 10:00 a.m., the Trial Run team reconvened in Jeff's office. The notes from the previous meeting were emailed to everyone in the group, plus a short agenda that Jeff proposed. Jeff also summarized all the information that came in to the CDC regarding the anthrax and Crypto contaminations.

Maya reported first. "We're in touch about the Air Force's sightings on the radars at Peterson Air Force Base. We don't know of any connection to the anthrax and Crypto attacks at this point, but it seems possible that the radars are seeing balloons, which are, in fact, being used to drop the poisons. If that's the case, we assume there must be some kind of guidance system for the drops—unless they are simply random. The Japanese sent balloons over the Pacific to the US for a few months in World War Two, intending to drop fire bombs—the Japanese term was *fugo*. Our government hushed it up, and it wasn't very successful, so the Japanese called it off. But those balloons had no way of hitting specific targets, and the ones we're dealing with would probably have some form of guidance."

Jeff leaned forward. "The FAA is still checking flight plans in the LA and Las Vegas areas for the last few days to see if there has been anything unusual, especially with small aircraft."

"If they're using aircraft, they have to be renting or borrowing them, and we should be able to trace that," Eileen offered. "I'm having our agents check all the airports in the Northwest and Nevada to see if there have been any suspicious rentals or planes stolen. If they're using balloons, they must be deploying them from a number of places, or as Maya said, how could they guarantee where the poisons would be dropped?"

Paul was frowning. "Maybe they don't especially care where the poisons land. Maybe the idea is to create significant panic and death?"

Others were thinking the same thing, but no one wanted to acknowledge this possibility. Then Eileen asked, "If they are using balloons how long could a balloon stay up, and wouldn't they eventually drift higher and higher?"

"A day or two unless they are pressure regulated," Maya replied. "NASA and NOAA keep some of their balloons up for a week or longer. Jeff, we need to ask the NSA to monitor all frequencies—do frequency sweeps—to see if they can detect that there is some kind of radio control of objects aloft going on."

Jeff made a note.

Just as they were all taking a minute to make notes and think, Paul's phone rang. "Yes?" There was a pause. "I'm with the emergency team now. Please email Jeff with all the information as soon as possible."

He rang off. "Anthrax has been discovered in Wrigley Field in Chicago. There is a game tonight but one of the groundskeepers saw some kind of small explosion and then something drifting down on the stadium and felt it was suspicious. The police came. They investigated and finally found a trace of what looked like flecks of white powder on two rows of the bleachers. The police lab has identified it as anthrax. At this point, it doesn't look like anyone but the groundskeeper had direct contact with it. He's being treated. They're postponing the game but not telling the press why, which is probably a break for us."

They all looked at him.

"It's moving farther east," Eileen said softly.

Jimmy rummaged around in his briefcase and pulled out a note. He put on his glasses, looked at it, then looked up. "This may not be important, but a few weeks ago, one of our operatives asked for a check on a company that is based in Vancouver—Vancouver Office Supply and Service. Seems that his sister, who is also an operative and who works for Bay Electronics, had an order from the Vancouver company for 200 Navigon GPS units. The company checked out—not much history on them."

Paul turned to Eileen. "Can we check with all other GPS suppliers in the world to see if they have had any orders from this Vancouver company?"

"We can, of course, but it won't prove anything," Eileen answered.

"Yes, but can we find out immediately if this company is still in business and if it is reselling the units and to whom," Paul continued.

"Suppose that they could somehow use GPS units to program the drops from the balloons!" Jeff jumped up and looked intently at the map on the table. "Maybe they are using planes and balloons and even trucks and cars to get the poisons spread—but we could trace the balloons and maybe intercept them if we knew they were part of this and where they are heading."

Maya looked thoughtful. "We can deploy all the satellite assets we have at the Pentagon, but if there are balloons flying at altitudes around fifty or sixty thousand feet, our surveillance satellites wouldn't be able to see them. We do, of course, have the radars."

Paul was also looking at the map. "Maya, could you issue an order that the radars in Hawaii and Alaska and Colorado must begin trying to track these balloon-like objects 24/7?"

"Of course," she replied, "but we can also send up F-18's. Their radars are good enough to see anything that has even a small radar cross-section, although we don't know if whoever made these balloons has employed stealth technology which would make them almost impossible to see. They may have been very cleverly designed. If we spot any of them and can get their altitude, we can ask NOAA to give us an estimate of how fast they are likely to be moving and what their ground-tracks and distributions are likely to look like." She could see the questions in several people's eyes. "What I mean is, we need to know how spread out they may be."

Jeff made another note. "I'm also going to issue an order via Commerce to get the name of every company in the world that manufactures balloons. Of course, we have no guarantee that we are even going to find balloons involved in this or that they would have been manufactured here, but it's worth a try." They nodded in agreement.

Jeff was about to end the meeting, when his buzzer rang. He took the call and reported to the group with a grim look.

"The futures on the stock exchanges were way down at 8:30, so the President reconvened the Working Group and ordered the stock exchanges to close down immediately. They'll review the situation again tomorrow morning."

§ § §

In Seattle, Ahmed had decided to travel to Los Angeles, which he thought would be an easy place to conceal himself—and to escape from later.

He took a taxi to an office building on the outskirts of Seattle that was two blocks from a used car lot that had seen better days. He walked to the lot and after he had been there about ten minutes, a middle-aged, overweight man with thinning red hair strolled up to him as he was looking at a twelve-year old green Altima.

"Good car for the money," the salesman said heartily, shifting his bulk from one foot to the other.

"If I pay cash, can I drive it today?" Ahmed asked, configuring his accent to sound as neutral as possible. They negotiated and settled on a price of $3,100, though Ahmed carried about $12,000 total. He insisted on a test drive, which was uneventful. The Altima had some dents, "but it will get me to LA," Ahmed thought.

He paid cash, and the salesman executed the title exchange while a young black man washed the car in the one-stall washing apparatus behind the lot. Ahmed watched as the young man put temporary dealer's plates on the car. He drove back to the YMCA and collected his bag. He checked out, paying cash. He was on his way to Los Angeles.

CHAPTER THIRTY-THREE
June 6, in Texas

Two of the balloons, No. 84 and 91, drifting toward Texas, made it to Austin, the state's capital. Balloon No. 84 released two payloads over the state fairgrounds during the height of the fair and just as the evening's activities were getting underway.

"Look, Mom, snow!" said a little boy, watching a very faint-looking powdery substance descending around a bench.

"Don't get near that!" his mother yelled, sharply pulling up on his arm, but it was too late. Several other people inadvertently inhaled the curious substance.

Another light bulb from balloon No. 84 exploded above the open stadium where the tractor pull was about to start. The weaponized spores drifted over the crowd. Several dozen more people inhaled. A few of those exposed were suspicious because they saw what looked almost like tiny specks in the air immediately around them and sought medical treatment within hours, but in the end, twenty people were contaminated, remained untreated, and died from the anthrax spores dropped on the state fair that night.

The other payloads released by Balloon No. 84 near Austin caused only minor damage to some domestic animals that ingested the Crypto microorganisms from their water dishes. But in Dallas, Balloon No. 91 dropped a payload of anthrax over the Dallas-Fort Worth Airport. Some 50 people, most of them baggage handlers, cab drivers and parking lot attendants were exposed.

"Man, what's that weird stuff?" one cabby asked another as they were sharing a cigarette break near the north parking lot. He was squinting into the sun and saw what he thought were very large dust particles.

"You think it could be that stuff they were talking about on TV?" the second one asked.

"Don't know, but we're too near it for my liking. I'm gonna call my doctor tonight!" the first one replied. His friend decided to do the same thing, and the quick action saved both their lives. But in the coming days, 46 people, including two foreign travelers from Argentina, died. The diagnosis in every case was anthrax poisoning.

CHAPTER THIRTY-FOUR

June 6, in San Francisco

On an impulse, Raul had called Saleeth in the afternoon on Wednesday, and he found her in her office. "Judith, this is your consulting architect, reporting in!"

"Raul!" she said quickly, and he heard the lilt in her voice, which made him happy. "How are you?" she asked.

"How are *you?*" he replied, "and can I tempt you away from your training of new employees to have dinner with me tonight? I know it's short notice but I just returned from a trip a day early."

There was a pause, and then Saleeth said, "I'd love to, but tomorrow night would be much easier of me—if you have it free." She wondered if she had sounded too dismissive; she did want to see him again even if it was getting complicated.

"That's fine," Raul replied, hiding his disappointment. "I'd like to try that good fish restaurant, Scott's Seafood Bar and Grill, if you're up for that."

"Fine!" Saleeth answered. "Do you want me to meet you there?"

"No, I'll come to your place and pick you up—say around seven?"

"I should have accepted for tonight," she thought to herself. She would have greatly enjoyed Raul's company, but she had made up her mind to do something else tonight, and whether it would be successful or not she had to try. She was going to try to find "Philip Miller."

When she got home to her apartment she went to a small safe in her bedroom closet, entered the combination and opened the door. She pulled out an ancient, leather covered address book. It held the names and addresses of many family members and friends whom she had not seen or talked to for years. After all, she was Judith Abrams now—and had been for some time. But in the back, concealed under the leather binding and accessible through a small slit, was a piece of paper with several phone numbers, email addresses, and mailing addresses. She did not think any of them would reach him anymore, but two of them should enable her to reach a female relative at home who might know something—and who could be trusted. It was too late to make a phone call there so she tried a text message. Using special software to conceal its origins, she simply wrote, "An old friend misses you. She misses her brother also and would like to know where he is. Could you reply if you are still there?" It was signed "S."

CHAPTER THIRTY-FIVE
Late on June 6

At 9:02 p.m. on Tuesday night, the network pool feed camera zoomed slowly in on President Bradley as he sat at his desk in the oval office, with the seal of the United States behind him. All the major networks had suspended their regular programming to carry his speech. He looked composed but serious as he began.

"My friends and fellow citizens, some events have occurred in our country in the past three days that may mean we have a terrorist or terrorists trying to attack some of our vital resources." The camera drew closer. The President reached for his notes and read, calmly and slowly, the sites where anthrax spores and Crypto microorganisms were known to have invaded.

"All the necessary Federal government agencies, including the FBI, Homeland Security, the National Guard, and state and local police and forensic specialists have been mobilized to stop these attacks, find out who is behind them and help those who are affected. The Centers for Disease Control are playing a major part in getting antidotes to everyone possibly affected. Their efforts are already successful in every city where anthrax and Cryptosporidium have been discovered. Unfortunately, some people have been sickened, and there has been loss of life, but our highest priority is to end these attacks and help all of you who may be suffering at this moment. My job is to protect our country, and I will do everything in my power to continue to do that. I want to deliver a message to the people behind this: you will not succeed, and you will be found and punished.

"We do not yet know the motive of the people behind these attacks, but we are gathering valuable evidence. We will post all new information on the White House web site as soon as we know anything more. I will also hold a press conference tomorrow afternoon and report to you on any new information and progress we have made. Until then, if you have any questions or concerns—or if you have any information that might help us, please contact one of the agencies you will see on the screen at the end of this broadcast. I am deeply sorry to have to report these events to you, but I want you to know I am doing everything in my power to bring them to an end. Thank you, good night, and God bless America."

§ § §

At a large dacha many miles from Moscow it was early Wednesday morning. Daylight found its way through the windows of Vassilly's bedroom as he got up, dressed, and activated the scrambler on his satellite phone. He reached the Paris number after three rings. "I see we are having some success across the ocean. You should be pleased."

He heard a short laugh in return. "I'd be more pleased if they didn't keep asking for more money—you'll have to write some checks soon and so will I," Abu remarked dryly.

Vassilly smiled to himself. "Ah, yes, but then we should have a new source of income very soon if we are truly successful. And, after all, it's still your family's money you are contributing."

His correspondent did not reply directly to that but said, "There has been a slight complication. We think our Mr. Miller talked to some people he shouldn't have. I've issued orders for him to be returned here, permanently silent, but I have not had any report in the last 12 hours about this assignment."

"Can you trust the other two?" Vassilly asked with some misgiving.

"Yes, no doubt, unless they are stupid enough to get themselves killed— or arrested, but we've taken great precautions against that."

"And you don't know that Mr. Miller has actually done anything to hurt us?"

"No, and our source for that information is also unreachable."

Vassilly sighed; it was so difficult working across time zones, with half a dozen different countries and cultures involved. Still, they agreed on the principals of what they were doing, and they all stood to benefit if everything went even reasonably close as planned.

"Well, keep me informed. I will be here in the country for two more days, then in Moscow. But don't call me at my office. It's bugged." At that, they both laughed. His correspondent had no doubt every conversation he had with Vassilly was recorded, but he didn't care. Vassilly was proving enormously useful, even though he didn't trust him.

§ § §

In a luxurious villa in Riyadh, Amal was awakened in the predawn because her iPhone chirped at her. With her husband away and the children still asleep at the other end of the hallway, she got up and put on the light to read the message that came through. It was signed "S," and she knew what that meant. Many months passed by since they contacted each other, and she knew she must not initiate communication unless it was a matter of life and death. But now here was a message—and a request. She quickly tapped out an answer: "I am here, my cousin. I will try to find out about your brother. Shall I send to this number again?" She did not sign the message.

Where to find him and how? So far as she knew, no one in the family heard from him anymore, not for a year. He apparently left Iraq some time ago and was rumored to be in Syria. While he occasionally called her husband and others in the family, he never revealed his location or exactly what he was doing. "I could wait for Abdul to return from London and talk with him, but I would have to be careful in my inquiry," she thought. Then she remembered the stories about a young man who had worked with Ahmed in Iraq and who had moved on to Paris. He showed so much loyalty and devotion that her husband and others had joked about the young man being "in love" with Ahmed. "If I could find him, would he know where to find Ahmed?" she asked herself.

She decided it was worth trying; gossip was a favorite pastime among her and her husband's friends. No one would take any special note of her question if she slipped it into the right conversation. With this decided, Amal got up to bathe and dress. She instructed the household staff that she wanted to host a dinner party at the villa the following Friday.

CHAPTER THIRTY-SIX
June 7

At 6:55 a.m. on Thursday, Harold Harper boarded a commercial flight at Dulles for Las Vegas, where he would board a smaller plane for Tahoe. When he went on these short vacations, Harold always flew commercial and paid for the flights himself. "Wouldn't do to create a scandal with the Government Accountability Office," Harold thought wryly. This trip would be relaxing and, with a little luck, lucrative. Over the past eighteen months, he built up his bank account—or accounts, as he was careful to put his "consulting money" into several different banks. Still, if he wanted to retire early, buy a place in the Bahamas, maybe remarry—although after 20 years with Lydia he was not sure he wanted to repeat the experience—he needed some reserves.

"And it's not as if I'm doing anything to hurt the country," he again reminded himself. "Helping the Israeli intelligence service is always in our interests." He convinced himself of this almost two years ago after his second interview with Svi Levi, his new friend and official contact. In order to secure the contract, Harold gave Svi confidential information that the Israelis could verify, such things as locations where terrorists were held and interrogated and names of undercover agents employed by the US Government. After Svi contracted with Harold, they rarely met, but once in a while they had an outing. And they both liked golf.

Harold was famous in his office for not taking long vacations, but everyone knew he enjoyed shorts breaks, usually to play golf or go fishing. Just before boarding the plane, Harold phoned Paul Blake, but he did not answer his office phone or his cell phone. Harold left messages on both and also sent a text message that said, "Please provide me with an update on any new developments as soon as possible. Will contact you later today." Whatever developments there were, Harold wanted to be able to give Svi an update that evening and a more complete report the next day. That, after all, was why they paid him.

§ § §

Jeff arrived at his office in the Executive Office Building at 7:00 a.m. on Thursday. Earlier, at 5:00 a.m., he received a call from Eileen Johnson. "Jeff, we've found three companies on the west coast here in the US that sold GPS units to Vancouver Office Supply and Service," she began. "We have the name of the purchasing agent, Silvio Franchetti, and his name is on the electronic directory at Vancouver Office Supply and Service Company, but so far we have not been able to contact him—or anyone directly at the company. Is it all right if I call you again as soon as we learn anything?"

"Yes, please, Eileen. This may be the break we need."

"Oh, and one more thing," Eileen added hastily. "So far, it looks like all the units he purchased were dual GPS/GLONASS receivers. That may be significant."

Jeff was well aware that the US and Russia cooperated well for years, as both countries had their own constellations of satellites that served their militaries and their civilians with satellite-based positioning information. Both militaries used some aspects of each other's systems. They coordinated frequencies and exchanged information. In the mid-1990's, several European nations decided to develop a European version of the GPS/GLONASS system, naming it Galileo. Some non-European nations joined in, but constant squabbles about funding and control delayed the completion of the system. Then the first satellites launched experienced problems. Also, Galileo was almost entirely dependent for income on civilian, non-military uses. The GPS and GLONASS systems were under-written by their government users, and so offered nearly free services to private civilian users.

Not getting back to sleep, Jeff decided to drive in to work. When, by 8:00 a.m. he heard nothing more from Eileen, he picked up his office phone and called Maya's secure cell phone. "Maya, it's Jeff. Eileen Johnson called me at home early this morning." He explained the conversation. "This might mean both our GPS system and the Russian's GLONASS are being used in this attack. If they are using them to program how the balloons are managing their payloads, I need to know what we would have to do to alter the GPS signals and how fast it can be done. Also, I need to know what the Air Force people at Peterson are seeing, if anything, on the radar with regard to balloons. And, Maya, you need to tell me what you think about scrambling fighter jets to shoot them down—if we can identify them and find them."

"I was planning on attending your 9:00 a.m. meeting. I can come straight to your office now. See me at 8:30 a.m. if you can, so you and I can talk."

"You have it," said Jeff.

CHAPTER THIRTY-SEVEN

CNN and NPR teamed up to provide hourly updates about the spreading anthrax and Cryptosporidium scares. On Thursday, at 7:30 a.m. Eastern Time, beginning a half hour segment of CNN's morning broadcast and at the same time on "Morning Edition," both networks switched to Ben Shongren reporting from Chicago. "I'm standing here at Wrigley Field with Omar Havaz, who saw an explosion and then a cloud drifting down over the stadium yesterday," Ben began. "Omar, can you tell us exactly what you saw?"

Ben moved his hand mike gently toward Omar, who looked as if he had not slept much in the past 24 hours. "I was working near the dugout and I was looking up, I guess, and saw what looked like a firecracker, like, you know, the kind you shoot off on July 4. It sort of exploded over the bleachers."

Ben moved the mike closer to Omar. "And what else did you see, Omar?"

Omar looked right at Ben and said, "Then I saw a little puff, you know, like of smoke. It sort of came down over the stands. And some glass. That came down, too, but just little pieces. And some foam stuff, but little pieces."

"Thank you, Mr. Havaz, I'm sure this will be very helpful to the police." Holding the mike now and facing the camera, Ben concluded, "This is Ben Shongren reporting from Wrigley Field in Chicago for 'Morning Edition' and CNN. We will have further reports for you as we learn more about this situation."

At home in Kansas, Farley McDonald watched television from the kitchen. He half heard Shongren's report, but now he turned toward the TV and froze. "But how did whatever it was that exploded get there?" he asked himself. A cold feeling crept into Farley's stomach. Laying down a carton of eggs, he moved to the kitchen phone.

He dialed the number for AeroProducts' headquarters in Dallas. When the operator answered, he asked for George Steelman's office and got George's secretary, on the first ring. "This is Farley. I need to talk to George immediately if he's there." He hoped Steelman would be at work this early.

"Good morning, Mr. McDonald. Mr. Steelman is with Mr. Goldberg in the conference room, but I can transfer you if that's all right."

"Please do," Farley answered, somewhat relieved that he could speak with both owners.

"Farley, how are you!" he heard George Steelman's hearty Texas voice, followed by a softer greeting from Mark Goldberg.

"George," Farley began, "several months ago you sent me a job that we did for the FBI. We fabricated 600 balloons for them. Do you remember the FBI official who first met with you there?" He could hear George and Mark exchanging a few words.

Mark's voice came on the speakerphone. "It was a Mr. Ricotti, from their field office in Denver. He showed us identification and gave us a number to call to check him out. He told us he had checked on AeroProducts and on you, since you are the one with the clearances. Why? Did something go wrong with the order? I thought we saw payment several weeks ago?"

Farley felt foolish, but he persisted. "When you say you checked on him, how did you do that?"

Again, he heard exchanged words before Mark answered, "We called the number he gave us and also had Accounting check out all the information he supplied. Farley, what is this about?"

"It may be nothing, and if that's the case, I apologize for disturbing you, but I've been following all the news on the attacks—this anthrax and Cryptosporidium that's been coming down in some places—and I think it's possible that this stuff is being carried by balloons."

He heard an exclamation at the other end of the line. This time it was George. "And you seriously think our balloons may be involved? Why?"

"What we built was supposed to be able to carry research equipment. Some of the news reports say the authorities have found very small glass fragments near where they've also found anthrax spores. Our balloons were designed to carry a six pound payload. They could have carried payloads with small containers in them. And there's something else. I had only one phone number for Mr. Ricotti, and he asked that we conduct our business by fax. I've done classified work off and on, but this seemed unusual. I think we ought to check again, now, and see if he is who he says he is. If not, I am recommending to you that we call the FBI in Washington."

There was a slight pause on the other end of the phone, and then Mark said, "Farley, this sounds a bit farfetched, but we trust your judgment. If there is even a remote chance that this Mr. Ricotti is bogus and our balloons are involved in something this terrible, we need to do all we can. We'll get back to you. Will you be in your office today?"

"Either there or home," Farley replied.

"Very good. You'll hear from us. And if there is anything to this, the FBI may get in touch with you before we do." Mark and George rang off.

Farley sat quietly for a few seconds then went back to fixing breakfast for Doris. He decided not to tell her about his suspicions or this phone call. But he certainly did not feel like eating.

§ § §

Outside the White House, a picket line of more than one hundred people waved signs that read "Mr. President, save our children—stop the poisons." Jeff saw the pickets before the President did. A crowd was gathering around the picketers and the crowd seemed sympathetic. A man yelled, "What are you doing for us?" and other voices could be heard cheering him on. Jeff knew the police would soon disperse the crowd, "but not before all the television cameras get a picture of this," he thought grimly, and he was right. By noon, video was on all the networks and Internet sites. The story lead on one site read "President implored to stop the carnage—what is he doing?"

In the Midwest, one young governor who had political ambitions of his own called an emergency press conference. "I am asking our neighbors in Canada to send troops across the border into our state to help us, if necessary," he proclaimed with great self-importance, ignoring the fact that what he was proposing was legally impossible. "We cannot have every family in America staying behind locked doors without food and water," he continued. And, of course, the networks all carried his words, too.

CHAPTER THIRTY-EIGHT

At 8:30 a.m. on Thursday, Maya walked into Jeff Sanchez's office and closed the door. Jeff rose to meet her. "Maya," he began, knowing they had only thirty minutes, "we have to assume they are using balloons. The FAA has found no evidence of airplanes involved in this."

Maya nodded, "We're having the F-18's scrambled shortly. And I know we have additional reports from Peterson that they are continuing to see faint radar returns, although there are all kinds of government and privately commissioned balloons flying around so their radar sightings don't tell us anything definitive."

"What is the status of our own GPS constellation now, and what do you think our options are?"

"All of our 28 operating fifth generation satellites provide signals for both military and civilian users. The accuracy of the civilian signals can be degraded and errors introduced to increase position uncertainty—you know we call this practice 'Selective Availability'. With SA, we could decrease accuracy by as much as 100 meters or more. However, there are compensating programs that give users information on the accuracy of the GPS signals, and these programs could resolve positions to a few meters."

"So, using SA probably wouldn't help us to confuse their guidance systems?"

"Right. But another alternative is to shut down the civilian signals to deny all but military users access to position readings. Other than for very brief tests, we haven't done this for more than a few days since 9/11. To shut down the civilian signals again means involving the FAA because all but the smallest private planes use GPS for guidance in flight and even for landing. It would also affect ships and boats and even private citizens who used GPS to locate themselves."

"Is there any other alternative?"

"Maybe. The GPS signals could be 'frozen' to provide incorrect longitude and latitude readings to civilian users, and this freezing could be limited to the times when the satellites were over a specific area, such as North America."

Jeff tried to picture how this would work. "If I were flying a plane and planning to land at a longitude of 38 degrees, and my GPS kept telling me I was at 50 degrees, I would keep flying east until the GPS told me I was at 38 degrees. The same would be true of latitude. So, I would just keep flying until I saw the correct latitude and longitude readings."

"Exactly! And while doing this would also mean that the GPS system could not be relied on by civilian users in the geographic area where the signals were frozen, it has the advantage that *if* the terrorists' balloons were relying on GPS signals, they could be fooled into thinking that they were not yet over their targets. So, they would presumably keep moving east until they read position data telling them they were either over the correct target or past it."

"If that's how they've set it up," Jeff mused, "then once we turn the system back on and unfreeze the lat-lon information, the balloons will probably drop their payloads immediately, thinking they have overshot their targets— but by then we could have them out over the Atlantic."

"And the freezing option also has the added advantage that the payload computer would not automatically switch to the GLONASS system for its commands. If the computers think they are getting active signals from GPS, presumably they will keep relying on GPS."

"And we don't know of anyone purchasing just GLONASS receivers for this Vancouver company," Jeff reminded them both.

It was 8:45 a.m. Jeff picked up the phone and dialed the direct line for Ada Glovere.

"Ada," Jeff said. He took a deep breath, for what he was about to ask would not be easy. "It's Jeff. We now think the anthrax and Cryptosporidium are being deployed from balloons guided by GPS. I've been speaking with Maya about our options." He went on to explain what they were, adding, "So if we freeze the GPS, aircraft couldn't use the system. How much time would you need to alert your air traffic controllers and get the whole system back to using pre-GPS technology?"

There was a long pause on the other end of the line. Then, Jeff heard the words he was hoping for: "If this is a national emergency, we will do whatever it takes. I would prefer a few days lead time, but if we can have at least 6 hours, I think we can avoid total disruption of the air traffic system. Would it be possible for you to call me after your meeting today?"

"Call me anytime—I'll interrupt the meeting, if necessary."

His buzzer sounded, and he picked up his intercom phone. "Yes?"

"Eileen Johnson is here, sir, and she says it's urgent. Do you want to talk with her?"

"Have her come in."

Eileen's normally brisk stride accelerated as she entered. "We may have a break on the balloons. We got a call fifteen minutes ago from our people in Denver. A company in Dallas, AeroProducts, was calling to check on someone who represented himself to them as being with the Bureau and who ordered 600 balloons from them three months ago. The name he gave them, 'Nicholas Ricotti' doesn't exist, at least not with anyone in the Bureau! And, none of the contact numbers they had for him work now. The actual fabrication was done by their factory in Goodland, Kansas, which is run by Farley McDonald. The owners are on standby to talk with us if we need them, and so is Mr. McDonald."

Eileen sat down next to Maya. Jeff continued to stand. "Eileen, let's proceed with our meeting at 9 a.m. If your people learn anything more from Mr. McDonald or the owners in Dallas, have someone report it to you during the meeting. We're going to have to make some decisions."

"Let me use the next five minutes to make a call," Maya said, standing, and Jeff nodded.

When Maya had closed the door to the anteroom, she thought about the best way to approach this request. Finally, she did two things: she called her office in the Pentagon and asked that they send a coded cable to Secretary of Defense for Russia, Col. Pyotr Olenshinsky, saying simply, "Please call me. Highest importance. Try special number first, then my office." She carried a phone for which only a few people in the world had the number, and Pyotr was one of them. Then she took that phone out of her briefcase and composed a similar message, directing it to a number that she knew was Pyotr's personal phone. It would be late at night in Russia, even if he was there, but she knew he would answer as soon as he could.

CHAPTER THIRTY-NINE

The entire Trial Run team convened at 9 a.m. in Jeff's office. As usual, Paul was a few minutes late, but this time he had a good excuse.

"We have a new death count," he said, looking around gravely. "Boulder is the worst—the anthrax blew around more than we expected, and there may have been more than two drops. We're up to twenty-nine people contaminated there for whom it was too late to start decontamination. And Texas is bad, too, because of the State Fair and the contamination at the DFW Airport. Three deaths so far. Adding them to those we know are also contaminated, we have 276 possible deaths to face. And this isn't counting animals. FEMA has issued a 'Code Red' for all major cities and ports. We are working with the CDC and the National Guard. We're trying to get clean water to people. The CDC's phone lines are swamped. People are panicked, and those who can't get to their doctors or hospitals are calling the 800 numbers. We need to have something to tell the country today, as soon as we can."

"Thank God Congress is in recess," Jeff thought to himself. "That's one less group of people in Washington who might be a target."

He faced the team. "Let me start by summarizing what we have learned—and what we think we may know." He reviewed his discussion with Maya about the GPS and GLONASS constellations, the options they had discussed, the information about the GPS units, the radar sightings from Peterson Air Base, the newly acquired information about AeroProducts' balloons, and his request to Ada Glovere.

He was about to ask Maya to speak when Eileen suddenly waived a hand in the air. "Wait! I've just gotten a text. Our people interviewed the head of the AeroProducts division that manufactured the balloons for the supposed Government agent, and I'm getting a transcript of the interview right now."

"Forward it to me and I'll put it on the screen," Jeff said, stepping over to Eileen and noting that the download was in progress.

Within two minutes, they were all looking at the following transcript of the FBI's interview with Farley McDonald:

Agent: *Mr. McDonald, can you tell us exactly what the balloons look like, how they work, and what they are made of?*

Farley: *They are helium filled balloons with a total lift capability of 13.2 pounds at 56,000 feet. They look somewhat pumpkin shaped with a nominal diameter of 15 feet. The material is optically transparent but it is covered with a fine silk net that allows the payload to be attached. They would be hard to see.*

The balloon envelope is what is called a super pressure balloon. I designed these with an over pressure of 1 pound per square inch. They should stay above 45,000 feet on a cold night.

The shell material is a 7-micrometer per layer, 3-layer polyethylene co-extruded film using the Stratofilm-420 resin film with a density of 0.913 gm/cubic cm and high strength and ductility at normal surface temperatures. The total weight of the balloon shell including reinforcing caps at the poles, payload netting, ring, and fill and vent valves came in at only a little over 5 pounds. Because of the short time allowed me to design and build these balloons, I actually subcontracted to a Japanese company named Ube Chemical Industries for the high technology gores. All I did was bond them together.

Agent: *How long will they last Mr. McDonald?*

Farley: *Unless they are torn up in storms, they could last for several months, but the design called for the ability to stay up at least seven days.*

The transcript ended and Jeff projected a new document on his screen. "Look at this computer report I got late last night from NOAA. They have predicted the possible flight path and dispersion pattern of the balloons *if* they were launched somewhere out over the Pacific, not too far from shore, and designed to reach an altitude of 50,000 to 60,000 feet. I'm also thinking of the leased boats that could have been the launch platforms."

They all looked closely at the report. Jeff continued, "They would all be moving east, and could cover the entire continental US in six or seven days, depending on weather patterns." The notes from NOAA clearly indicated that things such as severe down-drafts, occurring in thunderstorms or elsewhere, could perturb a balloon's flight path and even cause it to move around in a vortex over one area for several hours or days. "We could have some downed balloons if something goes wrong with any of them."

Maya stood up. "All right, let's assume balloons are the main culprit. We still don't know how their commands are programmed in. If the payloads are relying on GPS signals to be released, then, yes, if we freeze the GPS signals, they would probably not make the drop until they received the right signals. But they may have some 'drop anyway' command that would eventually be activated. They may rely on dead reckoning to account for temporary or permanent loss of either the GPS or GLONASS signals."

Maya moved over to a map on Jeff's wall. "If we are lucky, they would drift out over the Atlantic Ocean. If we can see them on radar or locate them with the F-18's to know they are doing this, we can reactivate the correct civilian signals when they've cleared land. At that point the programs on board should recognize that the balloons have overshot their targets and the payloads will be dropped. We could have them all floating over the ocean, and perhaps only some sea life and, God forbid, some ships at sea will be affected. As a last resort, we could also shoot them down out there."

Jeff interrupted her. "I've thought of most of this, too. I understand about the use of dead reckoning, but if we really can fool their on-board computers so that they continue to rely on GPS and not switch over to GLONASS, maybe we can make this work. What are we doing about the Russians?"

Maya sat back down. "I've asked Col. Olenshinsky to get in touch with me as soon as possible. If we do freeze signals on our GPS system when the satellites are over North America, we need to ask the Russians to do the same with their GLONASS. They have been very cooperative with us on this program, but I don't know if Col. Olenshinsky will be willing—or able— to help us. If not, we have to hope that when we freeze our GPS signals the terrorists have not figured out some way of commanding the computers to use the GLONASS system as an alternative to our GPS. And we have to hope that *all* the balloons have dual receivers so we can fool all of them with our GPS commands."

Jimmy Buttero reached for his coffee cup. "We're still trying to get a line on the whereabouts of this Georges Labadie. We don't have anything to tie him to any of this right now, but he's been on the periphery of other plots we know about. And, of course, we're working with Eileen's people to see if anyone can locate al-Kodari, but we don't think he's in North America at this time. I am having my operative, Andy Shannon, call in someone who may be able to identify Mr. Miller, who we think is al-Kodari. Also, I've directed more research into this Vancouver company that ordered the GPS's. They seem to have vanished into thin air—no one at their leased location answers. The company may be a red herring anyway, but we think we have an additional name to check on."

Maya knew she needed to talk about another alternative. "I'm getting increasing pressure from the Air Force to allow them to take fighter jets up to intercept and shoot down the balloons. I've decided that this is too risky, since we would not be able to control what happens to the payloads in a shoot-down. So at 7 a.m. I directed the Air Force to send up three F-18's since their radars should be able to see anything like balloons as long as there is some reflective surface on them. That way, we may able to get some kind count on the balloons still aloft and see how fast they are moving. If this factory in Kansas manufactured them, we know there were 600 ordered—but we cannot even be sure if all of them were launched."

Paul turned to Jeff. "Do we have any more information from the FAA on the possible use of small planes in dropping the poisons?"

Jeff shook his head. "Nothing for now. But the FAA has inquiries out to all the commercial and fixed base airports to check on recent rentals of small aircraft or even thefts and any suspicious flights. If Ada tells me that the FAA can go back to using old-fashioned technology instead of GPS, we'll do our trick with freezing the GPS signals, hopefully no later than 6 p.m. today. We've scheduled a press conference at 4 p.m. today. I'd like for us to have a conference call at 2:00 or 2:30, so please hold the hour between 2:00 and 3:00 and I'll get back to you."

CHAPTER FORTY

June 7, in Moscow

Col. Pyotr Olenshinsky worked late on Thursday and saw Maya's text message a few minutes after she sent it. He guessed what she might want. It would be the middle of the morning her time. He would take a chance and call her special number.

Maya was walking to the garage of the Executive Office Building when her special phone rang. "Yes?" she said, hoping the signal would not get blocked out as she proceeded underground.

"Maya, I got your message," Pyotr began.

"Pyotr, I'll be back in my office in 20 minutes—please tell me where I can call you."

"I, too, am in my office, working late. Call me on the special line."

Once at her desk, Maya activated her scrambler and called Pyotr back. "Pyotr, you know about what is happening here with the anthrax and the Cryptosporidium." She went on to summarize their thinking about the balloons and how they were guided.

"We've made a decision to freeze our civilian signal information on latitude and longitude when our satellites are covering North America. We'll probably start this at midnight tonight, after the FAA, NOAA and our Coast Guard has time to alert users. This should cause the balloons' computers to be fooled and they'll drift out over the Atlantic. Then we can shoot them down without worrying about the anthrax and Crypto hurting anyone. I am calling you to ask if you would be willing to alter the GLONASS civilian signals to conform to our plan. We're also tracking where the balloons may be now."

She did not mention the ground radars or the F-18's, but Pyotr assumed they would rely on both. He considered offering the use of one or more of the Russian spy satellites and then realized the balloons' reflective surfaces were too small for them to be of use.

"This does not come as a surprise," he answered slowly. "We are worried here, too, about this poison attack. Do you have any evidence yet of where it is coming from?"

Maya knew he expected her not to tell him the truth, even unofficially, but she said honestly, "No, nothing. We are following leads and there may be a Middle East connection, but we have nothing concrete."

"Then I will take this request to my superiors immediately. Am I to consider this an official request, Maya?"

"No. It's unofficial. If for any reason you must refuse, we do not want to cause you a problem. If you can help us, we will make it official but not release any information about it. We do need your answer as soon as possible though, Pyotr. Call me any time today or send me a message. I will be available to talk at any time. And Pyotr, thank you."

"I will let you know what we can do. I hope it will be the right answer." Pyotr sat at his desk for a few more minutes, looking again at the world clock and a world map. Having the balloons drift out over the Atlantic before dropping their payloads when they could be shot down was logical and would not imperil any Russian interests. He wondered if they knew whether balloons were the only delivery method. Of course, Maya would not share with him anything more than she needed to at this point. And he would do the same in her position.

He now faced two choices: he could authorize the freezing of the civilian users' GLONASS signals and explain later to his superiors why, or he could get permission. "Always safer to get permission," Pyotr said to himself. He was two years away from an early retirement, which he expected to enjoy and did not want to jeopardize. Most people high up in the Russian government and even in the military got good civilian jobs now when they retired early. He saw no reason that this request, if properly presented, would cause any problems. After all, it meant the Americans owed him—and his government— a favor in the future.

Pyotr picked up his private line and dialed a government number. No need to contact the President directly on this one; the Chief Deputy for Security would do and was, indeed, nearly as powerful as the President himself. In the days of Putin, that would not have been the case—no deputy would have had any power, but Putin was long dead, killed in his own car on an icy road years ago. Today, the President was the real leader and he had several powerful deputies. When Pyotr reached the office of the Chief Deputy for Security, he got voice mail. Mildly annoyed, Pyotr left a message. "Call me. It's urgent. We've had a request from the Americans." He felt reasonably sure he would get a call back soon and was not mistaken. Within thirty minutes, his secure line lit up. "Da?" he answered.

"Tell me about the request," Chief Deputy for Security Vassilly Rementrov said.

Vassilly listened carefully to Pyotr Olenshinsky. He took no notes and did not record the call. He was not surprised by the request—he thought it would come but perhaps not so soon, depending on when the Americans realized how the poisons were being spread. The balloons needed at least a few more hours if not another day. And they still needed to deliver their main message while the threat was real.

"Pyotr," he began, "this is a grave matter. Some of our aircraft may be affected as well as some belonging to our friends in other countries. What evidence do we have that what the Pentagon is saying is happening is really happening?"

Pyotr sat back in his chair. This was not going to be as easy as he thought. Still, the threat of terrorism anywhere in the world had—at least in recent years—been one where the US and Russia saw nearly eye to eye. But he knew Vassilly was a cautious man. "Vassilly, even CNN is carrying the news of the balloons! And we know there is Cryptosporidium in some of their water supplies and people have been contaminated with anthrax. We can do this without much disruption—and none to our military. Our civilian aircraft and ships can use the Galileo system for a few days. If the President will authorize it, I can make sure all our transportation people know what we will be doing with GLONASS, and I can authorize contacts with our friends in China and India and elsewhere."

"I must check with the President. He may be difficult to reach, but I can contact him. Are you in your office, Pyotr?"

"Yes, and I'll be here until I hear from you."

"You will hear from me soon," Vassilly reassured him.

<h1 style="text-align:center">CHAPTER FORTY-ONE</h1>

June 7, in Tahoe

Just after noon on Thursday, the room phone of George Labadie, alias Svi Levi, rang. "Mr. Levi, Mr. Harper has arrived and we have given him your message to call you," the polite desk clerk said.

"Svi! Good to hear your voice!" Harold said when Georges answered. "I'm here, not too much the worse for wear from the airlines and ready for some lunch or a game of golf—or both!" Georges smiled to himself. A couple of beers should be productive before the golf game, and certainly a good wine with dinner even more so.

"I'll meet you in the Grill Room, Harold," he said and slipped on his alligator loafers as he started to hang up the phone.

"Give me about ten minutes," Harold asked hastily. "Have to check on messages and I may have to make a call or two. See you down there at 12:30."

Harold already knew he had messages, but the only one he intended to check on now was from Paul Blake. He dialed Paul's private line and Paul immediately picked up, with a quick "Hello?"

"Paul, I got your message. I assume you have a briefing on 'Trial Run.'"

There was a short pause while Paul activated his scrambler, knowing that Harold would have done the same at his end before placing the call. "I do. Would you like a coded text message or a fax or just a brief verbal report now?"

"Just give me a rundown on the phone now. I'll be busy this afternoon but we'll talk again later today. Of course, I'll keep my phone on so you can reach me if it's an emergency."

Paul relayed all the information from the morning meeting in Jeff Sanchez's office and concluded by saying, "the President will decide about whether we freeze the GPS signals. And he has a press conference at 4 p.m. today."

Harold was secretly delighted. Not, of course, to learn that more anthrax and Cryptosporidium were being spread, but that there was so much that he could report to Svi. "Thank you, Paul," he said gravely while making some notes on the pad near his phone. "Call me when you have any new information— or if we need to talk." He hung up, pulled on his white wool golf sweater and turned out the lights. Svi would be pleased, especially with the part about the likely Russian cooperation. Israeli-Russian relations were not always the best, and the fact that the Russians would help the US at such a sensitive time should reassure Svi and his government, Harold thought.

CHAPTER FORTY-TWO
Afternoon, June 7, in Washington, DC

After talking to Jeff Sanchez, Ada Glovere personally called the chief operating officers of the major US, Canadian and Mexican airlines and had her deputy call the other carriers. She also spoke with her counterparts in Canada, Gander, and the UK who controlled air space where the frozen GPS signals would fool the GPS receivers. Her staff notified the International Maritime Organization and all counterpart aviation agencies in the rest of the world, since many ships and aircraft used the GPS system once they came into the North American coverage area. Finally, she talked with the President of the National Business Aviation Association and ascertained that the NBAA could help get out the word that, beginning at 6 p.m. Eastern Time and for at least the next forty-eight hours, the GPS system would be degraded and that all aircraft should rely on pre-GPS guidance VOR's and inertial navigation systems. That meant many of the newest aircraft, which did not have the older systems, were grounded. There would be significant disruptions and costs to the American people, "But this must be done if it can help," Ada told her executive team. The FAA itself sent out the official "Notice to Airmen" or NOTAMS, with the new information, and Ada picked up her desk phone to call Jeff Sanchez at 2:08 p.m. and told him what was going on.

"Jeff, please just promise me that you will keep us in the loop on this one. If I'm not available, I will have people in the office here who can handle anything you need and who can reach me. Jeff, how bad is it?"

"Bad, Ada, but what you've done will help us a lot. And we're getting great cooperation from Homeland Security, NOAA and the Coast Guard who are notifying their constituencies. I'll stay in touch. We've released a bulletin to all the news media and the President is still going to hold his press conference at 4 p.m. today."

Jeff hung up and looked down at a text message that had just come in from Eileen. It read: "MacDonald, AeroProducts, told agents Ricotti had accent, maybe French Canadian. Gave full physical description."

"Well, at least maybe now the FBI can get a bulletin out," Jeff thought, messaging his temples. He decided to convene the emergency team by conference call at 3:00 p.m. and asked his secretary make the arrangements.

CHAPTER FORTY-THREE

Night, June 7, in Moscow

Pyotr glanced up from his computer when his secure line rang an hour after he had called Vassilly. "Yes?" he said, expecting to hear Vassilly's clipped tones.

"Pyotr, aren't you coming home tonight?" It was his wife, Elena—always a welcome interruption, but now he was disappointed not to hear from Vassilly.

"Darling, I'm working on something important. Don't wait up for me. I'll come home when I can, but I must wait for some calls."

Elena knew enough about how much of Pyotr's work was classified not to ask any questions. "I'll leave some dinner for you in the refrigerator, top shelf. But wake me when you come in. I worry about you."

Pyotr waited fifteen more minutes and decided to try Vassilly again. Time could make a difference to Maya and the Americans, and if GLONASS was going to be reprogrammed he wanted to give the order as soon as possible since the reprogramming could take up to two hours. But when he called both Vassilly's office number and his confidential cell phone, he got voice mail on both. He also left urgent messages. He decided to wait another hour and then give the order to reprogram. "Surely, they will not say no to this," he said. "Or they may want to attach some conditions or ask some favor in return, but we can deal with that later. At the very least, I must tell Maya something."

Sixty minutes later there was no word from Vassilly. Pyotr called both numbers again, but this time his only message was, "Please call me back." He then dialed the number at the home of the Air Force Colonel in charge of the entire GLONASS program. The call transferred several times before a sleepy Sergeyev answered. He came immediately awake when he heard Pyotr's voice.

"Serge, we may need to freeze the civilian signals on GLONASS just for those satellites moving over North America. If I get permission to do this, we need to freeze the latitude and longitude readings in that zone so that anything moving east will think it is still west and north of its real location." Pyotr referred to his charts and gave Serge the exact latitude and longitude readings at which the signals were to be set. "We are doing this on a temporary basis to help the Americans. You must have people ready to contact our airlines and all the other related agencies and users. Also, you must be ready to give the order to your people to reprogram the system immediately when I tell you that we can, which I hope will be in the next hour."

Serge was pulling on clothes even while he held the receiver. "Have we authorization from the President?" he asked, struggling with his shoes.

"He is being made aware of this plan," Pyotr answered confidently and hoped this was true. "I expect his authorization and then I will call you, but you must be prepared to have our people act quickly."

"Very good, Pyotr, I am now at work!"

Pyotr sat back in his chair. He would wait a few more minutes in his office for a call from Vassilly and then leave another message for Vassilly to call him at home if necessary. Pyotr knew the decision making process could be slow but he was already beginning to feel some disappointment that his government might not realize how grave a situation the Americans faced.

Pyotr made one more call. He dialed Maya's private line at the Pentagon and was put through to her. "I have made the request, and I am awaiting authorization. I expect to receive it soon. We should able to reprogram within two hours of notifying all the affected agencies. There may be some conditions but I will get back to you if there are."

"Pyotr, we owe you for this one, so if there are conditions we will try to meet them. I hope this did not cost you much personally."

"Not at all," Pyotr said smoothly, "but let us keep closely in touch so I can report to our President on the success of this cooperation and we can go back to normal operations as soon as possible. I will let you know as soon as we begin the reprogramming. And, Maya, I'd like to keep this out of the press over there as long as possible. Can you do that?"

"You have my word," Maya answered, looking at the time and realizing that the conference call with Jeff and the emergency team would be in ten minutes.

Pyotr decided to go home. Vassilly could find him at home as well as at the office. He was reaching for his briefcase at the side of his desk when all the lights in his office went out and he heard the air-conditioning sigh to a stop. "Damned power outages!" he said aloud. At least the emergency lights would be on in the hallways, and he could walk down the four flights of stairs. Getting his car out of the garage without the automatic garage doors opening would be another matter, but he could walk home if absolutely necessary.

But he saw no emergency light coming in under his door. Instinct made him pause for a moment. Bent over to the side of his desk with his left hand on the handle of his briefcase, he heard the door to his outer office softly open. Col. Olenshinsky had not survived active service in the Russian military for thirty-five years for nothing. He kept a flashlight in a lower left-hand drawer of his desk as well as a gun. He opened the drawer. Very deliberately, he straightened up in his chair. Two shots rang out. Then a third.

CHAPTER FORTY-FOUR

Vassilly stayed in a crouched position in front of Pyotr's desk for another few seconds. He knew Pyotr had shot him in his left arm, which felt hot, and in the dim light he saw blood on his sleeve. No movement came from the other side of the desk, so he slowly got down on his knees and crawled around it. He carefully picked up Pyotr's right wrist. The pulse was uneven. This was the moment to put a final bullet in Pyotr. But, was that necessary? He was sure Pyotr could not identify him. As a precaution, he had entered the building in full view of the guards and shown his identification. After that, out of sight of the guards, he put on a head mask. Then he doubled back and shot both of them. He then disabled the electrical system in the building and was wearing the mask when he entered Pyotr's office. No, better to let him live. A dead Pyotr meant a full-scale investigation, and that was not desirable. Vassilly spent a long minute frisking Pyotr to find his cell phone, which he finally spotted on the floor, next to the desk drawer.

After pocketing Pyotr's cell phone, Vassilly stood. He still had his gun in his waistband. Now, he put it in the inside pocket of his coat. Moving around the desk, he found the phone and dialed a high-level security number. "This is Vassilly Rementrov. I am in the office of Col. Pyotr Olenshinsky. We were going to meet here and were startled by intruders and we have both been shot. I am not seriously wounded but I cannot rouse Col. Olenshinsky. I do not know where the intruders are; they may still be in the building. I cannot reach the guards at the front of the building. Please send help."

Vassilly knew he had less than ten minutes to make the scene look as if an intruder surprised the two of them. First, he wadded up a large white handkerchief and applied it as best he could under his shirt to the wound in his left arm, which was bleeding somewhat less but still felt hot. He considered planting his gun in some piece of furniture in the office, but then reconsidered, since he shot two men with it—the two guards at the front desk, both of whom might be dead—and now Pyotr, who might not live. He already concealed the black mask in his trouser pocket.

Next, he overturned the chair in front of the desk as if he had fallen out of it. He scattered the papers that were on Pyotr's desk and knocked several of them to the floor. Finally, he went back to the door handle and wiped it with his handkerchief to erase any prints. A second later, two armed soldiers appeared at the door. "Mr. Chief Deputy—are you all right? We came as soon as we could! The two security guards at the front of the building were also attacked."

Now came the hardest part. "I am bleeding in my arm and must get to a hospital. But please see to Col. Olenshinsky. They must have shot him in the chest. I was more fortunate. They only hit me in the arm. They did not rob me, so perhaps they were after something in this office."

The two soldiers, already joined by two medics, were bent over Pyotr. One medic gently probed the wounds in his chest and arm. At the door a man and a woman entered with a stretcher. "Can we take you to the hospital, too?" asked the most senior officer who had arrived from Central Security.

"No, no—I have called my driver, and we will go immediately to the hospital where my own doctor is waiting," Vassilly replied.

"Sir, we will need to debrief you in the morning to get a full report on this incident. Can you give me any information now on the intruders? Was it one man or two or more?"

"I really am not sure," Vassilly replied. "I was a few steps from the door of Col. Olenshinsky's office when all the lights went out. I managed to get to the door and pull it open. Two men ran past me out of this office and shot at me, but I think I also heard other footsteps further down the hall. Col. Olenshinsky must have heard the men and got a gun out of his desk to face whoever was there, and he got a shot, too."

"Was anything taken?"

"I don't know. We were going to discuss a highly sensitive matter, and I remember him saying there was only one copy of the documents he wanted to show me. That may have been what they were after. I will stay and help you search if you like." And, with that, Vassilly made a good show of getting down on his knees to look under the desk and around Pyotr's body.

"No, no, sir—we will secure the office!" the young officer said, appalled that he was delaying Vassilly from getting to the hospital.

"Then I'm leaving." And, with that, Vassilly walked slowly from the office.

Vassilly never called his driver. He drove his own car and parked it two blocks away from Pyotr's building. His arm throbbed but he had two more tasks to accomplish quickly. One was to get rid of the gun, which he intended to toss into the Oka Canal on his way back to his office. The second was to find out what orders, if any, Pyotr gave with regard to GLONASS. Vassilly thought Pyotr would not have dared to command any interference in the system without official sanction, but he had to be sure. He drove by the river, waited at the far end of the bridge until there was no traffic, quickly got out of the car and, under the guise of lighting a cigarette, took out the gun with his handkerchief around it and dropped it into the water. Back in his car, he sped to his office.

Once he was at his desk, he activated his computer to find the number for Col. Sergeyev Yvetshenko, who would surely have been the person Pyotr would have contacted if any orders had been given about GLONASS. He reached Serge at home on the second ring. "This is Chief Deputy for Security, Vassilly Rementrov," he said sternly. "I regret to report to you that late this evening, Col. Olenshinsky was attacked in his office. I was on my way to meet him, and he was apparently startled by intruders who also shot at me. We were both wounded, and Col. Olenshinsky is now being taken to the hospital, where I will go shortly. Col. Olenshinsky and I have been talking about a very important and sensitive matter this evening. It has to do with GLONASS. I need to know if Col. Olenshinsky has given you any special orders concerning GLONASS in the last twenty-four hours."

Serge was at first startled and then horrified to get the call, but he rallied quickly. "Yes. Col. Olenshinsky had told me he was trying to get the President's permission to reprogram the civilian signals on GLONASS to help the Americans."

Vassilly cursed silently and said calmly, "Col. Yvetshenko, I can assure you that the President and I are very much aware of this situation, but there are factors Col. Olenshinsky did not know about. You are not, under any circumstances, to order a reprogramming at this time. I will personally notify you if this order changes, but it comes from President Lebrovny himself. If Col. Olenshinsky does contact you, please refer him to me. I plan to stay closely in touch with the doctors and monitor his condition."

Serge could only agree, so he hung up. He remained at his kitchen table with a full cup of coffee. "What could the circumstances be?" he wondered, but he knew he had to follow the orders of Chief Deputy Rementrov. "Still, perhaps I can visit Pyotr in the hospital tomorrow," he thought, worried for Pyotr's survival and for his wife. "First thing in the morning, I will try to see him."

He tried to think what might happen next. Maybe it would take a while to hear back from Vassilly? "So perhaps I should begin talking with the Air Force Command and the civilian agencies in the morning to prepare them for what we might have to do?" The more he thought about this, the better the idea seemed. Finally, he took off his clothes and slipped back into bed. He set his alarm for 5 a.m.

CHAPTER FORTY-FIVE
Afternoon, June 7, Oregon

At an air base near Portland, Oregon, Lt. Col. Dan DeCarlo was getting a full flight briefing from his Colonel, who received the urgent and unusual request from the Secretary of the Air Force. Major Doug Velander had just joined them in the hangar, where the F-18 was being pre-flighted by another airman. "So you and Doug will take up the F-18 immediately for surveillance."

The Colonel moved them a few yards away from the plane. "Gentlemen, this is classified, but Washington thinks these poison attacks might be coming, in part, from balloons carrying and releasing the toxic materials. They want surveillance in the Western sector, especially from Oregon down to Arizona and as far east as eastern Colorado. Based on radar sightings, they may be somewhere between 40,000 and 70,000 feet. Based on what NOAA has apparently calculated about drift and what the radars have seen, there may not be any balloons still flying in this sector, but they want to be sure. If you see anything, send a text report immediately."

He gave them a text address. "I'll also be here for you to debrief me when you land. The ground controller will be giving you your coordinates as soon as you are in the air. I'm authorizing you to stay up and continue with the flight as long as necessary. You may need to refuel. That will depend on what orders the ground controllers give you."

Dan and Doug confirmed that the young captain had finished with the pre-flighting and climbed aboard the F-18. They rolled out quickly. After they reached their first checkpoint, they received further orders. "Looks like they want us to head north over Washington, then east to Montana," Dan said, consulting his charts. In the end, they covered this route, plus a portion of Wyoming, Colorado, Utah and Nevada, before they returned to California. They did, in fact, have to land for one refueling stop.

CHAPTER FORTY-SIX
Afternoon, June 7, Washington, DC

Even the best-designed products malfunction. Out of 600 balloons, two of the computers partially failed, causing drops over a horse farm in Ojai and a Kansas feedlot. Twenty balloons experienced anomalies— six because of inadequate filling from their helium tanks, four because of shell punctures, nine because of downdrafts from upper air disturbances and thunderstorms, and one because of a battery problem.

At noon Eastern Time on Thursday, June 7, Balloon No. 101 was punctured by some unknown object in flight. Helium leaked out slowly, and the balloon began to sink. When it descended just outside Nashville, all nine payloads ejected and fell, exploding their light bulbs into tiny fragments and distributed the poisonous spores over the sprawling estate of a state senator.

Eileen Johnson got the alert call from a Nashville agent at 2:56 p.m., four minutes before the start of the emergency team's conference call. Before joining the Trial Run conference call, she sent back a message directing everything that was found be turned over to the CIA for backward engineering, and she copied Jimmy Buttero and Paul Blake on her note. Then she dialed into the conference call.

At 3:00 p.m. on Thursday, Jeff Sanchez's secretary logged Jeff on to the Trial Run team's call. Within two minutes, all the other members of the team were on the secure line.

Jeff started. "Now, who has new information?"

"I do," Eileen Johnson replied. "A few minutes ago, I had a report from Nashville that a large balloon landed on the grounds of an estate there. They found some kind of Styrofoam box nearby, with batteries, wires and circuit cards. One of the cards was identified as a GPS. We have a team of agents investigating, and I've sent a note directing that everything found be turned over to our lab for backward engineering. If we can get some information from at least one of the balloons about how the GPS is programmed, we may have a break. Also, we're checking the description of Mr. Ricotti from AeroProducts against our known terrorist database."

Jeff was about to ask Jimmy Buttero about their further work on uncovering Mr. Miller when his secretary slipped a note in front of him. It read, "President Bradley wants you to call him immediately." "I have to call the President," Jeff told the others. "Please continue without me and I'll rejoin." He hung up and dialed the four-digit extension he knew so well. This time, Elliott Bradley answered it directly.

"Jeff, we've had word from CNN that they got a call from a man saying his group is behind these poison attacks. He wants to speak to Wolf Blitzer at 4:50 p.m. Eastern Time today, but only on a confidential line CNN must provide and not for broadcast. I'm going to postpone my press conference. CNN offered to let us listen in on the call. I'd like you in my office a few minutes before five."

Jeff sat back in his chair. "Mr. President, may I tell the other members of the emergency team?"

"Of course," Elliott replied, "and they are welcome to be here while we listen if they want to come."

"We're having a conference call right now, Mr. President. I will tell them."

Jeff switched back to the conference call. Maya was saying they needed to keep Russian cooperation—if, in fact, they received it—highly confidential for the time being. When she finished, he told them the news. "The President invited all of us to be with him. That's not an order," he added, recognizing that some of the team members were juggling many assignments at the moment.

Murmurs of surprise filled the line, and then everyone but Maya agreed to be in the President's office. "Jeff, please call me immediately afterwards," Maya requested. "I have a conflict because of my meeting with the Secretary of the Air Force."

CHAPTER FORTY-SEVEN
Afternoon, June 7, Oregon and Washington, DC

At 1:45 p.m., Pacific Daylight Time on Thursday, Ahmed sat in his parked car in a supermarket parking lot in Southern Oregon. He was uncertain whether or not CNN would really patch through his call to Wolf Blitzer's producer, which was what he asked for in his call two hours ago. "I had to give up valuable information to convince them this is authentic," he said, feeling some uneasiness at having revealed the details of the building fire in Seattle. But he knew they would have made that connection later anyway. CNN would have had enough time now to check with the Seattle authorities and know that he had given them details not yet released to the press. He was given the name of Blitzer's producer, Jean-Beth Reque, and a direct line to call. By now, he assumed that every phone line at CNN in Washington was being tapped. And that the White House was notified.

"They will hear our message now, no matter what happens to me later," he said.

He called two minutes later. Two phones at CNN were connected to the special line CNN's Washington bureau chief gave Ahmed. From 4:00 p.m. on, the line was monitored. By 4:15 p.m., Homeland Security and the CIA staff joined the FBI in the CNN control room. Andy Shannon led the CIA's detail. All members of the news staff were sworn to secrecy so that, no matter what the caller said, they could not reveal the information without explicit permission from the president. No one at CNN balked at this; they were professionals but they were also Americans.

At precisely 4:50 p.m., the two phones rang. Ahmed heard a voice on the other end and quickly placed the muffler over his cell phone's microphone.

"Am I speaking to Miss Jean-Beth Reque?"

"Yes, and I was expecting your call. May I ask who you are, please?"

Ahmed did not bother to respond directly. "You will please connect me with Mr. Blitzer."

There was a short pause and Wolf, not yet on the air, picked up the second phone. "This is Wolf Blitzer. Go ahead, sir."

"You will please listen. This is a message for President Bradley and his people. I will not repeat it, and you cannot reach me again. Many people are being killed in your country today, and there will be more tomorrow and still more in the days to come. Some people we did not intend to die will do so, and that is unfortunate, but your government caused many, many of us to die, including our beloved leader."

Wolf interrupted Ahmed immediately. "Excuse me, but I need to know if you are authentic—how are people dying or going to die?"

There was a pause, as if the interruption was unexpected. Then he began again. "They are being poisoned—we released several deadly substances. We can control who becomes sickened. We can attack every city in the United States. And this is just our first attack. We can also target allies of the United States and will do so unless our conditions are met. They are:

"First, all who were moved to other prisons in the US and Great Britain when Guantanamo was shut down and are now standing trial or about to stand trial must be released and repatriated within one week. Secondly, the US must remove all economic sanctions against all Arab and predominantly Muslim countries around the world and persuade the UN to do this as well. Third, the US must contribute two hundred million dollars within five days of this call to the Children for a Righteous World Fund. The payment must be made with small, cut diamonds. There will be instructions sent to your President about this very soon. Finally, two wrongfully imprisoned men must be sent back to their native countries within seven days: Mohammed Haru from Egypt and Pavez Riari from Pakistan."

When the voice stopped, Wolf glanced at two more notes he was handed. "If all these demands are met, will you be able to end the deaths in the US from your poisons?"

"No, but we would not send out more of a new kind," Ahmed replied calmly. "If our demands are not met, we will mount a further attack and begin to kill off candidates for your political offices. We will also strike one US ally within two weeks."

"Who can we say is behind this? What is your movement? What is your cause?"

"We represent the will of the greatest number of the people in the world. We are against the evil in Western governments and will work for thousands of years, if necessary, to conquer it by whatever means necessary."

All three of the agency representatives in the control room gave Jean-Beth signs to get Wolf to extend the conversation, but she knew it was coming to an end. "May we say who you personally represent? Is it one country, one cause?"

The reply came back in one word: "Justice," and the line went dead.

CHAPTER FORTY-EIGHT

Even before anyone could react, the FBI official, who used his smart phone to text headquarters, reported "he used a cell phone—not trace-able."

Jean-Beth looked at her boss. "What do we do next? Air something about this during the next half hour?"

The senior FBI agent answered her question. "No, we need to check with the White House. You can broadcast whatever the President says is OK."

"And I want a copy of the recording with the call on it as soon as possible," Andy Shannon added. "We need to start a voice trace." Privately, he thought about a way of tracing the voice that would not involve the Agency's computers.

The FBI called the President. President Bradley listened to the question about what CNN should do and said politely, "I have my National Security Adviser here. Please give me ten minutes to discuss this and get back to you."

"Well?" the President said, turning to the small, assembled group.

Jeff spoke up promptly. "I think we let CNN go with most of it. We don't know enough about the anthrax and Cryptosporidium attacks to know what these people can or cannot do now and we need to alert the public. Maybe they could let Wolf talk generally about what we do know—and that we are working on stopping the attacks. Then let him talk about this message in general terms, saying something like 'terrorist contacted the President' but not specifically what was said."

Paul added, "Maybe we could let CNN say that demands have been made and say this has just happened—and the President is working with his highest level security people."

Eileen waited to speak and now said, "There were too many people in that control room listening."

They all turned to her, puzzled, but President Bradley understood. "So, no matter what I tell CNN to let Wolf say—or not say—what the terrorist said is going to get out."

"It might," Eileen replied. "We should be able to trust CNN and who ever was there, but this is unprecedented and they are a news organization. Mr. President, I recommend that we let the whole story go on the air tonight."

"Then I will speak to the nation tonight at nine, but I will not state the demands in detail. Jeff tells me that everyone at CNN has been sworn to secrecy, and I hope we can be sure of that. We can hold a press conference when we know more, hopefully some time tomorrow. Jeff, you may call CNN back and tell them they can talk about the fact the terrorists called but not give details."

The President turned to his desk and rang his assistant's line. "Let the staff know I'm going to go on the air again tonight from the Oval office and that the networks need to be informed. We are looking at scheduling a press conference late tomorrow but that's not firm."

"Mr. President, what can we do in the meantime to help you?" Jeff asked.

"We need information about the two men they want released, about this fund—I suspect it's on the list of terrorist-sponsored organizations—but I need to know who runs it, where it is headquartered—everything. Tonight, I'll just say we are working on all this. We don't know who made the call or who he represents, but we won't yield to demands of terrorists."

The President got up from his desk. "Thanks for all the work you're all doing. I understand we're very close to being able to reroute the balloons. However, if we can't divert all of them, we may need to scramble the fighter jets and shoot down the ones they can find. We'll try to do this over relatively unpopulated areas. Paul, I'm expecting Homeland Security to coordinate with every local resource center in all major cities to be on alert not only for further attacks but to provide emergency shelter for people if necessary."

After the Trial Run team moved out of the Oval Office, the President turned to Jeff. "I'm going to call the Secretary of State to tell him to get our ambassadors to talk with all our allies over the next several hours. I don't want them to hear of these threats first from me on international television. Give me a few minutes for that call, and then we'll get to work." He sat back down at his desk. Jeff left to get some hot coffee. It was going to be a long day.

CHAPTER FORTY-NINE
Late Afternoon, June 7, Western States

In Tahoe, Georges and Harold Harper finished a good nine holes of golf and were drinking at the bar. CNN was on the in the background when Wolf Blitzer reported on Ahmed's call. Both of them—for quite different reasons—immediately stopped talking and listened to the news as Wolf ended his report by saying, "CNN will follow this breaking story and will have more to report in the next half hour. We have been informed that President Bradley will address the nation again at 9 Eastern Time tonight. CNN will carry his speech live."

"I've got to call my office," Harold said immediately. "Might be a while. Can I meet you back here?"

"Sure," said Georges, "but if I'm not here I might be taking a shower, so wait for me. We can have dinner any time, I checked, and they'll seat us when we want to eat." Georges tipped the restaurant's maître d' handsomely for that privilege. "I suppose we ought to watch your President at 9 so let's plan to be through with dinner by then."

Harold almost ran to his room and locked the door. He checked his phone and saw a text message from Paul, asking him to call.

Paul picked up after the second ring. "Harold, thank you for calling. Have you seen the CNN report?"

"Yes," Harold replied without going into any detail about his locale. "What do we know about who is behind this, and what's happened with the poison attacks since last night?"

"We don't seem to know anything about the people doing this, but the message sounded like they have al-Qaida connections. We keep thinking we have contained the movement's actions in this country, but maybe we haven't." Paul related their specific demands.

"This fund that he mentioned went on our prohibited list more than five years ago. We're looking into all the areas he spoke about. The CIA will have more information about the prisoners they want released. But I have some good news—we have confirmation that the balloons carrying the toxins are being guided by GPS, and beginning at 6 p.m. today, the Air Force will freeze the civilian signals on the satellites to fool GPS receivers as to their lat-lon positions. We hope this will send them out over the Atlantic and that they will drop their payloads into the ocean. We are not yet sure the Russians will cooperate with us by reprogramming GLONASS, but we are hoping to hear soon."

Then he went on. "The President wants our office to coordinate all the local emergency efforts in the major cities, and I have given orders to proceed with that. We'll be using 'Plan Cobra' and I should be able to give you a further report in about two hours, before the President speaks, if necessary."

"Text me if we need to talk," Harold replied quickly. "I'll be tied up in a meeting tonight but I can get back to you immediately. I'll check in with you after the President's talk if we haven't spoken by then." He hung up. Now, he wanted to make some notes so he wouldn't forget to tell Svi everything.

§ § §

Dan DeCarlo and Doug Velander had swept the first part of their route without seeing anything out of the ordinary. The big radar on the "Growler," as the F-18 was called, had not picked up evidence of any balloons at 50,000 feet or above—or below. They were near the Canadian border in eastern Montana when Doug spoke into his microphone. "May be something up ahead."

"Altitude?" Dan asked—they were holding steady at 60,000 feet.

"I make it about 5,000 feet below us, twenty miles ahead. It's a very weak signal."

Dan steered the aircraft toward the blip they were seeing and started reducing the F-18's altitude and speed. Within minutes, going 250 knots, Dan spoke into his mic, "Looks like it could be a weather balloon. I'm going to go around it and come back. Look for markings and anything you can see about the payload." As the plane sped past the object, it did, indeed look like a weather balloon. Dan had seen many of them before. This one appeared to have no markings. They were above it, so Dan decided to turn the plane and come back under it. "Going to 55,100 feet," he announced.

On the second pass, with both of them looking left and up at the balloon, they saw the rectangular Styrofoam box. Still no markings. "Make a note of the location and start the gun camera," Dan said to Doug. "Our gun video camera should reveal plenty of details when the shots are analyzed. I'm going to go straight south on this heading—we may see more of them." He communicated with the ground controller, got permission for his desired direction and altitude, and took the jet back up to 60,100 feet.

They proceeded south over the western side of the Dakotas and just as they came to the border of northern Nebraska, Doug spoke again. "Picking up two more bogeys fifty miles out, moving east, somewhere between flight levels 56 and 60."

Doug maneuvered the aircraft toward the objects, again slowing the speed and reducing his own altitude. This time, they found two balloons about five miles apart. The appearance was the same and again the high-resolution video camera recoded images of the balloons and their payloads. Doug sent a text message, reporting the sightings to the number they had been given.

In the next two hours, they were able to verify sightings of fifty-two more balloons, all moving east over the states of Nebraska, Kansas and the Dakotas. Nothing further south or west. Dan made a quick fuel stop in Nebraska. He then got permission from the ground controllers to alter slightly the originally planned route and crisscrossed all the northwestern states several times. After a final pass above the midsections of Oregon and Washington, they turned home. "Coming in," Dan radioed the airfield, and they landed at 1:00 p.m.

As soon as they landed, Dan reported to the Colonel, "I think we saw a pattern. They're moving east at about the same altitude and longitude but at several different latitudes and they're carrying boxes that look like Styrofoam. We did not spot anything west of the Dakotas."

Doug added, "They barely showed up on our radar. Whatever is in the payload must have a very small radar cross section. It's hard to see these balloons when we go by them at 250 knots. I guess the photo intelligence lab has started detailed analysis of the video footage."

The Colonel shook their hands. "Excellent job, gentlemen." He subsequently made a full report to the number at the Pentagon that he had been given. Within minutes, that report went straight to the President's National Security Advisor and to the President himself, along with copies of the video camera file.

CHAPTER FIFTY

Evening, June 7, in San Francisco

I've been looking forward to this!" Saleeth said enthusiastically, reaching for Raul's hand after they had been seated at Scott's Seafood Bar and Grill. Raul squeezed her hand in return. "Me, too."

Instead of meeting at 7 o'clock, they had agreed Raul would pick her up for a very early dinner so they could watch the President's speech later. Saleeth talked for a few minutes about her work and the architectural project on which Raul was consulting for her. "She is really beautiful," Raul thought, watching the light come into her eyes when she talked about the foundation's clients. She was wearing a mauve cashmere sweater, black sateen pants and sling-back black heels. Her hair was loose, and she had only a pair of gold earrings and a watch as adornments.

When their drink orders came Raul said, "I highly recommend the gray sole. Imported from Scotland, of course, but worth it." They both ordered the sole with lobster bisque to precede it and a bottle of Chablis to accompany the fish. Raul leaned back and again observed Saleeth, who was still looking with interest at the extensive wine list in its leather binding. "I've always wanted a wine cellar," he said impulsively, "but it's so hard to fit one in when living in an apartment."

"Don't you ever want a house?" she asked, finally looking up and closing the wine list.

"Well, someday, but as a bachelor and with all my travels I haven't thought much about that yet," Raul answered. Instantly, he began thinking about how much fun it might be to go house hunting with Judith, and wondered what her tastes were like. Other than seeing her apartment, he did not know. Equally impulsively, he reached across the table, took her hand and held it for a few seconds. "I want this evening to be fun, to be about good food and good wine and even wine cellars, if you like. I think we both work too hard!"

She laughed and relaxed into the back of the banquette, gently removing her hand from his as she did so. "I would like that, too!" she answered just as their drinks arrived.

Dinner moved at a leisurely pace with easy conversation between them. Raul talked about safe things such as his sister and his early life in Colombia. Saleeth said less but laughed in her low, attractive voice, and shared her own reminiscences from time to time.

Finally, after enjoying ripe peaches and cream, Judith said, "We need to get back to my place to watch the President's speech. We can have coffee there. I have an excellent Turkish blend. And I do have brandy—and some other things."

Raul was delighted with this offer and paid the check as promptly as he could without seeming rude to the waiter. They retrieved their car from the valet and drove to Judith's apartment.

Raul found the apartment simple but tasteful. Prints from several contemporary artists, primarily oriental, brightened the beige walls. "Comfortable furniture," Raul remarked to himself, noting the prevalence of leather and wood. Far too many of his female friends had considered bamboo or metal as the choice for sitting and eating on. Raul preferred more traditional—and sturdy—pieces.

After she had turned on the lamp in the living room, she excused herself to make the coffee. "I hope you like it strong!" She returned in three minutes with two cups.

Raul had just turned on CNN. Wolf Blitzer announced the President and the shot of President Bradley at his desk with the seal of the US behind him faded in. He wasted no time on pleasantries.

"Fellow Americans, today we heard from one of the terrorists behind the failing plot to intimidate our country by dropping poisons. Before I tell you about the conditions he mentioned, I want to reassure you that we now know that the poisons—anthrax and Cryptosporidium—are being delivered from balloons that are guided by geopositioning satellites, and we have taken measures to reprogram our satellites so that the GPS receivers on the balloons will respond to false readings and carry the balloons and their payloads out into the Atlantic Ocean where we are designating a 'no fly, no shipping' zone. Here is a photograph of one of the balloons, taken by some of our assets earlier today." The camera zoomed in on a blown up image of the balloon.

"We will make every effort to collect the payloads when they land in the ocean and destroy them. I can't guarantee to you that there will be no loss of ocean life in this procedure, but all branches of the Armed Forces and the NIA are cooperating to ensure the least harm possible to human and animal life. Also, if you are a user of GPS, please be advised that the system will continue to give false information for a period of time. The relevant government agencies, including the FAA, the Coast Guard and NOAA will further advise users and all the media as to the status of the GPS system.

"It is also possible that the terrorists are also using other means of distributing the poisons, so I have asked Homeland Security to declare a red alert at all airports, sea ports and railroad terminals. That status will continue until we know we have stopped all forms of delivery. If you believe you have come in contact with anthrax, you must seek decontamination assistance. The Centers for Disease Control are releasing their ample stores of Ciprofloxacin, tetracycline and penicillin in order to provide enough treatment for all affected people. If you do not have professional medical help readily available, please call the Centers for Disease Control directly at the number now shown on the screen below me. The CDC can also prescribe treatment for Cryptosporidiosis if you have contracted it or feel you are in danger of doing so."

The camera moved in for a tighter shot of the President's face. "We do not yet know precisely what group is behind this vicious attack. However, we are receiving information hour by hour that will help us identify them. Tonight, one of their people called CNN with some demands, which were intended for me to hear about, and I did. The threat made by the anonymous caller was that if these demands were not met, further attacks would be mounted on the US and possibly on one or more of our allies.

"I have asked Secretary of State Goldovsky to call the presidents and prime ministers of all countries we consider our friends and allies around the world. We will share with them all the information we uncover about this terrorist group and their methods. We will not, I repeat will not, allow these threats to further disrupt our way of life or the way of life of our friends and allies. We will carefully evaluate the demands made and will act in the best interests of our country and those of our friends.

"I have asked that the stock markets reopen tomorrow as we believe we have contained the worst of this attack. It should be safe for you to move about in your work and school and other pursuits. As soon as we have additional information, I will again report it to you. In the meantime, if you see, hear or otherwise learn of anyone or anything suspicious, please contact your local law enforcement agencies or call the Homeland Security toll-free number you will now see on the screen. Good night, and God bless America."

An 800 number for the CDC and another one for general reporting of suspicious activity appeared for a full sixty seconds on the screen, which faded to black after the President finished speaking.

Saleeth and Raul sat quietly for a few moments. Raul thought, "I wonder what someone like Judith, with her Jewish background, thinks of all this?"

Saleeth thought, "I wonder if he is involved in any of the Agency's work on this—and what he would think if I told him that I may be?" Instead of talking, she went to get more coffee and her brandy snifters since Raul expressed a preference for Cognac.

Raul poured a generous portion of Remy Martin into each. "All we need is a fire in the fireplace—except that this is June, and we're in California!" he joked. They were both sitting on her low sofa, and Raul moved a few inches closer to her after his first sip of the very strong, black Turkish coffee, which he had sweetened.

His right hand hesitated a moment, and then he began gently to stroke the back of her head. Saleeth turned slightly toward him and smiled but did not pull away. After a few seconds, she took his face in her hands and kissed him. The kiss lasted a long time, and at the end of it, he stood up and took her hand. "Is this all right?" he said softly, and she nodded. She led the way to her bedroom, where only a small night-light illuminated the thick off-white carpet and scarlet patterned bedspread.

Saleeth slid off her heels and reached over to begin unbuttoning Raul's shirt. When she finished, she shrugged off her sweater and swiftly unbuttoned her pants. Raul kept pace and when they had no more clothes on, he took her in his arms and held her very close. "You are so beautiful," he said softly into her hair. He could feel her hard, upturned nipples, and his own erection was pressing against her. She moved to the bed and pushed him down on the sheets. Then she knelt before him.

He knew that she was doing everything she could to please him, but he wanted to please her, too, and after some minutes, he stood, picked her up and laid her on the soft sheets. Then, holding back for as long as he could, he slid inside her. He could not know it, but she was thinking in that instant, "This is the only man I will ever again want inside me."

CHAPTER FIFTY-ONE
Evening, June 7 and Morning, June 8

Ahmed had driven south into California and sat in his darkened motel room, watching yet another CNN report of his own threats and what the President had said. With his own life in danger, he had to make two decisions rapidly. First, should he remain in the United States long enough to oversee the next stage of the plan if their demands were not met? And, secondly, should he try to contact Paris to find out who had betrayed him and reassure Paris that their fears about him were groundless? To answer the first question, he decided to contact Kamal.

To be on the safe side, since he knew cell phone calls could easily be picked by NSA, Ahmed decided to go to the lobby and use one of the two pay phones in enclosures that he had seen near the small coffee shop. "At least, if they are listening to all the cell phone calls, they won't hear us!" he said to himself.

On the second try, he reached Kamal at home. "Yes?" he heard at the other end. Ahmed took a deep breath. "Kamal, it is I. I want to thank you for all your work—you see we are making progress."

There was a slight pause at the other end of the phone, then, "I am with my family. May I call you back?"

"No!" Ahmed said forcefully. "I have had some problems with my phone but I must talk with you. Can I call you back at this number in one hour?"

"I will arrange it," Kamal answered.

"Good. If anything happens, I will try you every ten minutes beginning in an hour until I reach you. It is important or I would not ask this."

"I will be here," Kamal replied.

He left the hotel and walked rapidly toward an all-night chain drugstore, where he found some pay-as-you-go phones. To be safe, he bought three. The incurious night clerk, who was reading a paperback, rang up the sale, gave Ahmed the phone card inserts entitling him to fifty dollars' worth of calling time on each one and went back his reading.

Ahmed found a coffee shop across the street from the drugstore and bought himself a cup of espresso. "They don't make it properly in the US," he observed, not for the first time.

At 11 p.m., Ahmed went back to the hotel and dialed Kamal's phone number again.

"Yes?" Kamal again answered.

"I can give you two numbers at which you can reach me at least for the next two days. Please write these down." Ahmed recited the numbers for two of the three new phones. "Wait for me to contact you again before you ship the special package. We may not need it, but if we do, I will be in Washington, DC, to oversee its arrival. Is everything all right at the factory?"

"Yes, we are continuing to manufacture and ship the paint products for our regular business. No one has come to see us who should not have. But I have the special truck ready if we have any visitors. Is the shipping address for Washington still all right?"

Ahmed paused. He did not know how much of their operation had been compromised, but he had no choice at this point. "Yes, and I'm sure the fish market people will be very pleased to receive it," he answered. Then he added, "Kamal, I may need some money. You can take it out of the special account. I will let you know where to wire it if I need it. Can you do that?"

Kamal was puzzled but as always compliant. "Of course, Ahmed. Please let me know anything you need!" Kamal paused, and then he said, "Today, I was proud to be a part of the cause."

"Thank you, Kamal, we must pray that they listen and do the right things." Ahmed disconnected his phone. He felt certain he could count on Kamal, but now he had to answer his second question and decide if it was safe—or even wise—to make contact with Paris.

Ahmed turned back to the television. To his great satisfaction, he heard a Fox reporter say, "We have just learned that the Cleveland water system, which gets its water from Lake Erie, has been tested positive for Cryptosporidium. The mayor of Cleveland has shut down the water processing plant and ordered emergency water supplies to be made available at fire stations and all other city facilities. All cities taking their water from Lake Erie are being warned to shut off municipal water. This is a disaster!"

All that night, Ahmed wrestled with the thought that he should go to Washington, DC, regardless of what he learned by talking with the "travel agency" in Paris. "And perhaps I had better make my way to Washington *before* I contact them," he thought, not sure now whom he could trust. "We had a plan, and I am executing it—with the help of Kamal and a few others.

If I can get across the country and continue to follow our plan, then our goals will be met!"

He checked out of his hotel early to begin the long drive to Los Angeles. He took stock of what he had to work with. He still had three cell phones, his notebook computer, his gun, two credit cards that should still work, enough money to get himself across the country and a couple of passports that should be safe. He had decided to become Kas Pradep for this trip, but he knew it would be a risk to fly. And, for now, with the GPS system not working, many commercial flights were grounded. Yet driving would be exhausting and take so long.

His research a few months ago had suggested an alternative: getting a ride on a jet with seats to rent if he could find one. The Orange County John Wayne Airport, south of Los Angeles, was home to many business aircraft. He would gamble that by the weekend, the GPS would be restored and planes could fly. If not, he had the Altima, and so far it was proving reliable transportation.

During a lunch stop at a café with Internet access, Ahmed found what he was looking for. Two businesses that owned jets based at John Wayne Airport advertised they would welcome passengers if they had space available. One company was affiliated with a laboratory at Cal State Long Beach. Ahmed was unsure how much luck he would have contacting them, but he sent a short note to their email address, introducing himself as a visiting professor from England, in need of transportation to the east coast, preferably Baltimore or Washington, DC, since he was scheduled to lecture at Johns Hopkins. He provided one cell phone number.

Ahmed continued to work at the computer, checking what news agencies were now saying about what the US government was doing. He also reviewed alternatives if the charter flight did not work out. But within ten minutes, he had an answer to his email: "Provided that all flights are not grounded, we have a flight leaving Saturday, June 9, at noon for Washington, Dulles Airport. If you want a seat, please be at the airport no later than 11a.m. The price is $950 and we accept cash or a credit card. There will be a security check. How many bags do you have? We would prefer a phone call from you to confirm." A name, phone number and directions to the hangar were provided.

Ahmed left the café and dialed the number on one of his cell phones. After introducing himself, he said, "Please book me a seat. I will pay you in cash and will be there no later than 8 a.m. I have only carry-on bag." He would keep the Altima until the last minute. If the flight left, he would abandon the car at the Orange County Airport. Otherwise, he would drive to Washington, DC.

CHAPTER FIFTY-TWO
June 8

Maya was wide awake at 2 a.m. on Friday and thought of trying to reach Pyotr again since she had heard nothing. "But surely he will call me or send me a message."

Then, at 4 a.m., her phone rang. She picked it up immediately and heard Jeff Sanchez's voice. "Maya, go to 'scramble-secure'. I'm very sorry to be calling you in the middle of the night, but I just received the CIA's preliminary analysis of what was found at the garden party in Nashville—the balloon payload. I think you should read it. I'm forwarding it to the President and to the FBI also, and the Director General has promised that his engineering people will get a full report to us no later than midday Thursday."

"Can you give me an idea of what it says?" Maya asked, now fully awake.

"The whole system uses off-the-shelf hardware, and when you see the report, you'll note that they are using GPS/GLONASS receivers—or at least they did on this balloon. The on-board computer makes the drop decisions based on calculating the payload's radio distance to pre-programmed target locations. The Agency engineers found over 6000 targets loaded into this particular target table. Essentially, they're loading light bulbs with the toxins, and they are using explosive charges so that the bulbs spray the contents when they break open. One of the payloads didn't get released from its housing, which is a Styrofoam box, and so they were able to see how it worked. Also, the Agency engineers were smart enough to get the CDC involved—they 'safed' the light bulb and sent it down to the CDC, and they're working on analyzing the contents.

I'll start sending you the preliminary report as soon as we're off this call. Let me know if you have any questions after you get it. We should have the full report in time for our Trial Run team meeting this afternoon. You'll see that the decision to freeze the GPS and GLONASS signals is exactly the right way to deal with the balloons—assuming the Russians cooperate. If not, we may still have a problem on our hands."

Maya thanked Jeff, hung up, and went to her computer. The report was loading. She did not expect to sleep at all for the rest of the night.

(See Appendix One for the full report that the CIA's Directorate of Engineering sent to the Director General of the Agency, and which he then made available to Jeff and the President.)

CHAPTER FIFTY-THREE

Harold Harper awoke early Friday in Tahoe to find Paul's message. Harold called him immediately. Paul detailed the reports from Cleveland. "The President has authorized use of the National Guard to help get clean water to people in Cleveland and Erie and other cities taking water from the lake. Meanwhile, the CDC is recommending that the cities heavily chlorinate their water supplies, but we don't know how much good this will do. We do, however, think the Russians will be cooperating to reprogram GLONASS. As of midnight, about two-thirds of our commercial airlines were grounded. The news media are having a field day with this."

Harold waited for a break in Paul's report. "Are any additional steps being taken to identify and find the terrorists? And what are we doing about meeting their demands?"

"Yes, we are taking steps. I'm not privy to all of them, but I do know we are trying to track down at least a couple of people who have raised suspicions in the past. One seems to be a French-Canadian and one from Iraq or Syria, but there's some confusion even about their identities. I've been more involved in the efforts to control the poisons. Harold, I think it would be good if you could be on the scene here. When will you be back in Washington?"

Harold had already thought about cutting short his trip, but not before he could give an update to Svi. "I'll try to leave after my meeting today and try to hitch a ride with the Air Force if I can. I'll send you a message later about my schedule and we can meet Saturday when I get in—if that won't disrupt any of your plans."

Paul laughed briefly. "Most of my plans have been pretty well disrupted."

Harold next brought up a number for his Air Force contact on his laptop. After making the call and learning that a National Guard plane would be leaving at 11 p.m. out of Los Angeles, he arranged for a limo service to get him from Lake Tahoe to LA. "This will put me back in Washington, DC, by Saturday morning," he thought with some relief. Then, he went down to have breakfast with Svi, who was uncharacteristically late. Harold ordered black coffee and opened the *LA Times,* which the waiter had thoughtfully provided.

When Georges joined Harold in the dining room and they had both ordered, Harold leaned across the table, which was in the far corner of the dining room, and said, "I have some more information for you on our current crisis."

"Let's take a walk after breakfast and you can tell me," Georges replied. He did not trust waiters, other patrons or possible bugs under tables.

They discussed the fine points of putters over breakfast and then went outside. "Let's walk over to the Pro Shop. I need more balls," Georges suggested.

As they walked, Harold recited most of his conversation with Paul. "And you still think the Russians are cooperating?" Georges asked with some surprise. "If it's true, something has gone wrong there," he thought to himself.

"That's what I was told," Harold said, thinking he understood his Israeli friend's skepticism. "And we seem to have a handle on who two of the bad guys may be—I'll let you know names when I have them, but the intelligence is that one may be French Canadian and the other an Iraqi or Syrian." Harold thought of his upcoming meeting on the weekend, which should give him more information to send back to Svi.

Georges did not respond to this. He rightly guessed that intelligence was pointing to him and to Ahmed, although it sounded like they had not picked up on Rafik. He must be very careful from this point on about how to have Harold contact him. But he certainly wanted to continue the contact. After Harold told him about taking an earlier departure flight that day, Georges realized that he might have to leave the Gulfstream in Tahoe and take a limo back to LA himself until the GPS system was restored. A minor irritation but one he had not anticipated. He turned to Harold. "After our golf game this morning, I'll have an envelope for you—with a bonus. You are helping Israeli-American relations greatly."

Georges went back to his room and made a call to a number in Paris. "I have a report to make," he said when Abu answered, and he summarized what he had learned from Harold. At the end of the report, he added, "It looks like the Russians are cooperating with the Americans by reprogramming GLONASS. I thought you had a way to stop that?"

"We do have a way, and I think we've done that. GLONASS should not be a problem. Have you heard from Rafik?"

"I reached him very late last night. He has found no trace of our friend but he has ideas of where to look. And I'm curious—who was it that alerted you that our friend may not be trusted now?"

Abu paused. He did not want to admit to Georges that he was not absolutely sure of the source—or why he believed the information. Finally, he said, "Let's just say my source found out something about our friend's family connections that makes us think he could be ready to betray us—if he has not done so already."

Georges had to accept this at face value. "What's the best number to reach you at from now on?"

"I'll be at this number or try my other cell phone," Abu replied patiently. He knew the strain on the team in America had to be great right now.

CHAPTER FIFTY-FOUR

On Friday at 7 a.m., Jeff Sanchez had a call from Eileen Johnson. After he had called Maya, he had sent Eileen the CIA's preliminary engineering report on the Nashville balloon's payload.

"Jeff, we've had another break. I got word late last night that a fisherman working out of Long Beach called in to the Coast Guard that he had discovered a deflated balloon with some kind of package attached to it in the ocean. We asked the Coast Guard to send it directly to the CIA—to their Directorate of Engineering—and here is what they've found.

The Styrofoam box and internal electronics appear to be identical to the Nashville balloon box they were also back engineering. Saltwater getting into it made the electronics inoperable but the package had all nine drop payloads attached. They opened the drop payloads and shipped the light bulbs off to the CDC. The CDC in turn has confirmed that each of four of the light bulbs contained 25 grams of anthrax. Each of five of the remaining light bulbs contained 25 grams of Cryptosporidium. We are up against a system that uses at least 600 balloons with 3600 drop payloads to carry almost 200 pounds of deadly toxins targeted for some very large number of identified population centers, and we are not sure we have stopped it."

Jeff felt his adrenaline pumping. "Meet me in my office at 8 a.m. if you can make it," he said.

At 8:05 a.m., they were both seated in Jeff's office. "I've sent messages to all the other team members," Eileen began, "and can I assume you have notified the President?"

"I called him at 4 a.m. and again after you and I talked an hour ago. He's already read the CIA's preliminary report on the Nashville balloon," Jeff answered, pouring himself his third cup of coffee for the morning.

Jeff's secretary had quietly slipped in with some orange juice and rolls for them. Jeff ignored the food. He had another issue on his mind. "Eileen, go over for me again how you have gotten the diamonds and how you can trace them."

"It's easy to get 3-carat stones. Our friends in Israel are helping us by locating some here in the US and shipping more over," Eileen said, with a slight smile. "Not all of them will be clear color—some will be yellow. A few of the yellow diamonds will be fake, and very good fakes. Inside of them we're putting miniature radio transmitters. We want to trace where the diamonds are taken to, and hopefully get the key people before they realize we are tracking them. Also, we have researched the Children for a Righteous World Fund. After we froze their assets in 2002, they closed up shop in the US and moved to Algeria. They operate out of an office in Algiers. That may be where the diamonds will be sent. We're relying on Jimmy's people for information, and the Agency tells us that the Fund has not been linked to any known terrorist activities since they re-opened, but we cannot be sure of that."

"It's risky," Jeff replied. "If they find out about the radio transmitters or get suspicious, they could take more harmful actions. I will brief the President and see what he thinks. I have a meeting with him at 12:30." He walked over to a window to look out. The weather was warm and all the trees were fully leaved. He wished the day could be as benign as it looked from his window.

"We did have some good news from the Air Force yesterday afternoon," he continued, noting the report from the F-18 Doug Velander piloted over the western states. "The F-18 working the Midwest saw balloons in Ohio, Kentucky and Tennessee, and the one working the East reported another thirty, all north of Georgia but all the way up to Maine. They saw some already out over the Atlantic. They got a count of 410 in all, which obviously isn't all 600 if, in fact, that many were launched."

He moved back from the window and sat down. "What have you learned about our ability to track down this Mr. Miller or Georges Labadie?"

"I've got two people on this fulltime, and they're liaising with the Agency. The Agency people are due to report to us this morning. We can call them in a few minutes. Do you want to participate?"

"Yes, but let's conference in our whole team." He stood up, rubbing his eyes and stretching.

"I wonder how much sleep he has had in the last few days," Eileen thought to herself. He had circles under his eyes and his voice cracked with fatigue. "Jeff, if we can do anything more—anything more than we are doing, you let me know. We all want to help—we want this to be over."

Jeff turned to her and gave her a weak smile. "I know, Eileen. And thanks. We have a couple of days, maybe, before we have to meet all their ultimatums."

"Has the Pentagon confirmed that the Russians actually froze the signals from GLONASS?" Eileen asked as they stood.

"Not yet, but Maya believes we will have good news on that shortly."

Jeff rang his secretary to set up the conference call. Joining Jeff and Eileen were one of Eileen's aides, the rest of the Trial Run team, and Andy Shannon from the CIA. Jeff began the call.

"You've all gotten the complete reports from the CIA's Engineering Directorate with regard to what they found in the Nashville payload, plus the CDC's analysis, so we now have complete information on the system and how it works. The President agrees that what we now know validates the decision not to shoot down the balloons over the US but to try to reprogram their routes. First, let's talk about our attempts to trace Georges Labadie and Mr. Miller who may or may not be Ahmed al-Kodari. Will the FBI begin? Eileen?"

"We're getting excellent cooperation from the company, AeroProducts, where it was probably Labadie who ordered the balloons. We know some of the aliases he has used in the past and are tracking all of those, and his physical description matches our records. We've been less successful tracking Mr. Miller. On the assumption he is al-Kodari, we have bulletins in the hands of all TSA people, all Amtrak stations, all bus companies and all rental car companies. We don't have a good track on his last whereabouts or what other names he may be using, and he could easily be out of the country by now. We are also getting good cooperation from our Canadian friends. Andy do you want to add anything?"

Andy Shannon spoke slowly and deliberately. "Mr. Buttero asked me to call in our operative who may be able to identify al-Kodari. She will be coming to Washington, DC, and then we will create a plan for her to identify him. I will have more on this possibly by late today."

"Anything else on this aspect?" Jeff asked.

"Just one thing," Andy answered. "The informant Col. Diep was using went out on a boat that was releasing the balloons on June 2. That night, he disappeared. Col. Diep found the informant's cell phone four days after he disappeared and on it was an unsent text message that referred to someone who was around the boats who had introduced himself as 'Kas'. There was no other information of interest that Col. Diep could find on the phone, which he has sent to us. We're examining it. We're running checks on the name 'Kas', but it's a common name in India and Pakistan so it may be awhile before we get a lead. It seems most or all of the people closely connected with the deployment used aliases. We've asked the Bureau to add this name to their TSA bulletins, but without any last name or physical description, we don't expect much right now."

Eileen reported next. "I've briefed Jeff this morning on the status of the payment, and he will brief the President today. But we are still waiting for instructions on where and how to deliver the diamonds."

"As for the repatriation of Haru and Riari, neither of them is being held in the US," Andy Shannon told the group, "but we have access to them. The plan at the moment is to have both of them sent to the UK, to a military base there—we already have assurance that MI5 will handle this. They will remain there until the terrorists have allegedly made good on their promises. In reality, MI5 will not send them back either to their own countries or to our bases but will work with us on a suitable place to transport them. However, they will be led to believe—as will the outside world, and, of course, the terrorists—that they are about to go home. I must add that we're not sure either of them will be very welcome in Egypt and Pakistan, so they may be quite content to be removed to London and stay there!"

"Only if they like rainy weather," Jeff muttered. "Paul, I know Homeland Security and State are dealing with the prisoners who were at Guantanamo and are now in the US, but can you bring us up to date on that aspect?"

"We will have all of them at military bases within the lower 48 in five days, making it look like they've been moved to their homelands.

Jeff took a quick sip of coffee. "The death count this morning stood at 305, and we are afraid it will climb this weekend, especially in the cities bordering Lake Erie. We're super-chlorinating all water supplies we think have been affected. The Army, the National Guard, CDC and Homeland are all working overtime to contain the damage."

Maya waited for Jeff to finish and then added, "We are monitoring the entire GLONASS constellation and have seen no changes yet."

"And we're working with Eileen's people to interview the boat captains in Vancouver who might know anything about what happened there. This may even help us with finding 'Kas'," Andy reported.

Jeff decided to wrap up the call. "I'll be briefing the President in less than an hour. If there are any developments I need to know about between now and then please call me. The President will probably want his press secretary to issue a statement soon about any progress he feels we can announce. We should text each other with any new developments today, and I'll call another meeting or conference call as needed. But let's plan on a call Friday morning if we don't convene before that. And, thanks, everyone. We may be through the worst of this."

As they rang off, Eileen said to herself, "Not likely. We don't even know when, where and how we are supposed to deliver the diamonds."

CHAPTER FIFTY-FIVE

Providing instructions for the drop of the diamonds meant one more challenge for Ahmed before he left California. Originally, the plan had been for him to call CNN again, but he now felt it likely that all CNN's lines were tapped. He had the number for the *Washington Post's* "Readers' Hot Line" and decided to call that number on Friday. He found a pay phone inside a hospital about a block from his hotel in Los Angeles. He took out the folded script that he had written for himself two days ago. He did not trust himself to remember all the details without reading it. When he reached voice mail for the "hot line," he lifted the piece of paper and read:

"This is the organization that is seeking justice from the United States by distributing poisons until our demands are met. The diamonds for the Children for a Righteous World Fund must be placed in two sealed, watertight containers. There must be no tracking devices in the packages. On Tuesday, June 12, between 4 and 5 p.m., these containers must be placed in the back of a small motorboat that will be tied up at the Alexandria Sailing Club. The boat is painted blue and orange and will have a French flag on the stern. There must be no powerboats or sailboats moving in the area. It must be reported in the *Washington Post* on Saturday that the White House knows how to pay the money to the Children for a Righteous World Fund but that details cannot be released. If these instructions are not carried out or if your Government tries to follow the boat, further attacks will take place in the US and in other countries. I am the person who contacted Miss Reque at CNN. I tell you this so that you know this is not a prank."

Ahmed felt more relaxed than he had in days after making the call. He would be flying out on Saturday, assuming, of course, that the aircraft he was booked on was allowed to fly. "We have so many of them grounded," he thought with amusement.

§ § §

In Riyadh on Friday night, Amal's dinner party progressed well. The main course of lamb met with great enthusiasm. As they all ate, she casually brought up names of many mutual friends who were living outside the Kingdom, some in Europe, some in North America. Into this conversation, she dropped Ahmed al-Kodari's name. All of them knew him or knew of him, but no one seemed to have seen or heard from him lately.

Later, as she and her guests were strolling in the family garden under the stars and enjoying the strong, black coffee, Amal caught up with her friend, Nour, whose husband, Ali, was Amal's husband's second cousin. While they lived in Paris much of the year, where Nour taught philosophy at the Sorbonne while Ali worked as a lawyer for one of the large Saudi conglomerates, they often returned to Riyadh for Ali's business interests and to visit family and friends.

Taking Nour's arm, Amal said, "Nour, I heard from one of my mother's sisters, my Aunt Fatima, in Jordan a few days ago. She is very sad not to hear anything from her nephew, Ahmed al-Kodari. We spoke of him tonight at dinner, and it seemed none of us know how to get in touch with him, but it is her wish to speak with him, perhaps to see him, before she dies, which could be soon. Do you think you or Ali could find any way to get in touch with him?"

Nour continued walking a few steps without speaking. She remembered Ahmed as a handsome and intelligent man with a beautiful sister. She recalled that they were also cousins of Amal. They often traveled in Middle East diplomatic and business circles with their parents. Her private reaction was that Ahmed had become a radical and joined up with shady forces in Iraq, but she knew that there was only vague evidence to support this. The story as she knew it was that the sister, Saleeth, had apparently committed suicide in America— a sad thing, but then they did not know the whole story. If Amal's elderly relative now wanted to get in touch with Ahmed, and she could help, why not? "I'll see what I can do after we get back to Paris. Ali knows the company where Ahmed used to work. I will let you know."

"Thank you so much. I think there was a young man there—perhaps his name was Kareem?—who worked for Ahmed and liked him very much. At least that's what we used to hear! If you find him, he may be able to help. Perhaps you can say an elderly relative would like to be in touch and that this is her dying wish. I remember Ahmed as a polite person—and he was at one time close to his family."

"All right, Amal, I will do everything I can. But if I succeed, you must promise to come to Paris and visit us!" They both smiled—a bargain easily kept.

164

CHAPTER FIFTY-SIX

On Friday, Rafik finally tracked down Kamal at his home. After apologizing for bothering him, Rafik said, "I have lost track of Ahmed, and I urgently need to speak with him. I have money for him and several messages. He may be in danger, and I need to warn him."

"Oh, he called me just a day ago. He will be glad about the money because he said he might need some and I was to send it," Kamal began, genuinely pleased to know that Rafik was seeking to help Ahmed. Then several thoughts came to him at once: why hadn't Ahmed just called Rafik if he knew Rafik would have money for him? And, weren't Rafik and Ahmed supposed to be communicating anyway? What was the danger Rafik spoke of? Was it possible the danger could be from Rafik himself? Kamal met Rafik once and instinctively had not completely trusted him. Kamal had the deepest regard for Ahmed and knew Ahmed was heading the operations in the US. If Ahmed was in danger then he, Kamal, should try to protect him. He took a deep breath.

"But, I am not sure how to reach Ahmed just now. He said he was in Mexico and perhaps would be leaving there soon. He was going to phone me. He said his mobile phones had been compromised and he left no numbers where I could reach him."

Rafik suppressed an oath. "Did he say where he was staying in Mexico? And did he say anything about traveling to Washington?"

"No, he did not say exactly where he was. I had the impression that he might have been calling from some public place. There was noise in the background. He did not say where he was going next. All he said was that he would call me back in a few days." The lies came easily to Kamal, now that he felt he might be helping Ahmed.

Patiently, Rafik said, "Kamal, this is extremely important. If Ahmed calls you back, find out exactly where he is and get a contact number. Then call me immediately—you have my numbers."

"Yes, Rafik, I will do that," Kamal answered. "I will do everything I can to help."

Rafik rang off. Maybe Ahmed was in Mexico. He would activate his contacts there. But it was also possible Ahmed had deliberately misled Kamal. He might be on his way to Washington, DC. After all, if they needed to carry out the next part of the plan, it would originate there, although none of them needed to be "on the ground" when it did.

CHAPTER FIFTY-SEVEN

On Friday morning in Vancouver, Johnny Diep's luck came back. He had not been satisfied with the investigations of the FBI and CIA agents. They had not found a captain who sailed with Kas, but there was one captain whose boat had been used and whom they had not interviewed since he had been out of town for a week. The Captain's name was Sig Olsen. Johnny began making inquiries.

He was having breakfast in a small restaurant in Johnson Fishing Village when a young man came up to him. "Excuse me for interrupting. I'm Pete Greeves. I understand you've been asking about fishing boats that might have been chartered for a scientific mission on June 5. One of the boats I own was chartered, and I asked one of my best captains to take the run. He's over at that next table, the tall guy, if you want to talk with him. His name is Sig Olsen."

Johnny got up slowly. He pulled his windbreaker off the back of his chair and walked over to the table where Sig and two other men were eating. "Excuse me, sir," he said to Sig. "My name is Col. Po Diep. I work for the US Government, and I'm involved in an international investigation of a scientific excursion that took place earlier this month. I'm especially interested in talking with the captains of the boats that were deployed on this excursion on June 2nd and 5th. Do I understand correctly that you may have captained a boat on June 5th for this mission?"

Sig Olsen looked up at this slight but well-spoken Asian man who was standing next to the table. Sig liked the honest look he saw in the man's eyes. "Pull up a chair," he said to Johnny, and when he did, Sig continued. "I did run a charter that day. Had a lot of trouble, too. On the way back, one of the men who was working on the mission got sick. We had to stop on the way back in Bellingham, WA, to get him to a hospital. Poor guy died later, I heard. Is that what you're investigating?" This was all news to Johnny, who tried to stay calm.

"I was not aware of such an incident, but we are trying to find a man who may have been on one of the boats and probably introduced himself as Kas. Was he on your boat and was he the one who became ill?"

"No, the man who was ill was Nassir. Never got a last name, but one of the other two men introduced himself as being from the university and I think that he said Kas, or something close, was his first name."

"Did he give you a last name?"

"Let's see—something Indian or Paki, I think. Pra-something. Maybe Pradep. I think that was it: Kas Pradep."

"And do you know where Mr. Pradep might have gone after you returned to Vancouver?"

"Oh, he didn't come back with us. He went with the ambulance people in Bellingham. I just assumed this Nassir fellow was his responsibility."

"And had you ever seen or met either of them before?"

"Nope, never, wish we hadn't had the bad luck, but I guess they got all of their research balloons launched anyway." Sig Olsen finished his coffee and looked inquiringly at Johnny.

"Mr. Olsen, I very much appreciate this information. Some colleagues of mine who are helping with this investigation may also be in contact with you. We'll try not to take up too much of your time."

Sig looked keenly at Johnny, who had started to get up. "This is about the poison attacks in the US, isn't it? Those balloons were carrying poisons."

He was not the first captain they had interviewed who suspected what had happened, and Johnny felt sorry for him. "Yes, but I cannot tell you anything more at this time, and please be assured we are not blaming any captains for anything. Some very bad people are behind this. We just want to find them."

They shook hands, and Sig watched him leave. June fifth had not been a good day for him, although he had gotten paid. Now he learned that, inadvertently, he might be part of a terrorist plot. "By damn," he said to his two friends as he sat back down, "if I could find any of those people, I'd give them a one-way trip out to sea. No charge!"

When Johnny Diep was alone, he sent a short message to his contact at the Pentagon with the information he had just received. It felt like a good morning's work.

CHAPTER FIFTY-EIGHT
Midday, June 8, Washington, DC

Just before noon at the Pentagon, Maya reviewed Jeff's note to the Trial Run team, informing them that the instructions for the diamond drop had been called in to the *Washington Post* and that the call was believed to be authentic. She was about to call Jeff when her secure cell phone rang, and she answered it immediately, hoping it was Pyotr finally.

Instead, she heard a female voice say, "Maya? It's Elena Olenshinsky. I need to talk with you. Is this all right?"

Maya tensed at the sound of urgency in Elena's voice. "Of course, Elena, is anything wrong?"

"Pyotr has been shot. It happened in his office last night. I would have called you sooner but he has been unconscious and we were not sure he would live. There were two bullets and one is near his heart."

"My god, Elena, that's terrible," Maya exclaimed with real emotion and also a sinking feeling. "How did it happen?"

"We are not sure but he was waiting to have a meeting in his office and some people apparently broke in. They took some files. We don't know any more than that. I have been with him at the hospital ever since they called me. Maya, it's the middle of the night here now and Pyotr regained consciousness for a few minutes an hour ago. They have guards posted outside his door, but he whispered to me that he wanted me to leave the room and call you from home, so I came home. Maya, he said to tell you, 'they have not reprogrammed.' Does that make any sense to you? He seemed quite agitated."

Maya let out a deep breath. Two catastrophes! "Yes, Elena, it does make sense. Are you going back to the hospital now?"

"As soon as I can. I want to gather some clothes and other things Pyotr might need. Then I'm going back. Oh yes, he lost his mobile phone—or they took it—so he can't make any calls. But I'll let him know I talked with you and I'll let you know how he is in a few hours."

"Elena, I'm so very sorry about all this. Please tell Pyotr I will be thinking of him—and of you—every minute."

Maya was about to hang up but then asked, "Elena, you said he was going to have a meeting. Do you know who he was going to be meeting with?"

"They didn't tell me but whoever it was reported the shooting. I think he was injured, too. Is that important, Maya?"

"It may be. Elena, if you can find out who it was without causing yourself or Pyotr any harm, I would very much like to know. And Elena, he's tough and he loves you. He'll pull through." Maya tried to make her voice sound as warm and reassuring as possible.

Maya hung up and immediately dialed Jeff Sanchez's office number, asking to be put through. "Jeff, we have a problem," she began and related her conversation with Elena.

"I'll notify Homeland Security and the rest of the team," Jeff said wearily. "We're already on high alert at major public places. If there are balloons out there with payloads programmed to track only the GLONASS signals, we may not be able to divert them in time to prevent another attack. We can account for 540 dual GPS/GLONASS units having been sold to the Vancouver Office Supply and Service Company, and we know there were 600 balloons—if not more. So, we don't know what the other 60 receivers are or where they were purchased. They could be dual units or GLONASS only. If you could have your people get a report from Peterson about what their radar is seeing now, that could help. And, Maya, if we have to scramble F-15's or F-18's—or even F-22's or F-35's—to find them and shoot them down, President Bradley may authorize that now. I'll brief him. If you find out anything, call me on my mobile phone if you can't get through on this line."

As soon as they ended the call, Jeff called Paul's office. "Bad news," he said and then explained. Paul thought for a few seconds. "So far, they've hit a political gathering, several water supplies, the spaces in front of official buildings, a ballpark, a fair, and some neighborhoods. Not all these sites were on the list of targets loaded into the Nashville computer, so we can't be sure that all of the computers were programmed with the same list. In fact, we can be pretty sure they weren't. But we can bet that they'll have the big cities in the East targeted and maybe specifically with the GLONASS only balloons."

Jeff had to agree. "I'll get back to you with whatever information Maya gets from Peterson and maybe that will help us decide what to do. Hopefully, it's only a few balloons relying on GLONASS—or maybe none now if some of them have been lost or already dropped their payloads—we just don't know."

Jeff was about to place another call when his secretary put Maya back on the line. "We have the information from Peterson, and I've asked them to send you a full report electronically. It's good and bad. Good that they can still see occasional blips on the radar screen that are probably the balloons. Bad in that we don't know if they are seeing all of them and bad in terms of the apparent direction. There seem to be two waves of balloons now, all of them pretty widely dispersed. They are seeing some still in the mid-west, spread out between about Illinois and Pennsylvania, and they can identify some more clusters between Atlanta and the south end of Maine. That covers a pretty big territory."

"Maya, what are you thinking now about the option of just shooting down the remaining balloons?" Jeff asked.

"If we shoot and just hit the balloons, the payloads will fall and then explode. That way, they'll spray the poisons like they've been doing. We could gamble and assume most of them are still going to drift over the Atlantic but if any are using GLONASS only receivers, they may drop their payloads before that. Maybe you had better ask the President about that."

In a few more minutes, Jeff had the read-out from Peterson. In fifteen more minutes, he was in President Bradley's office, looking at the President's computer wall screen. "I agree with Maya," the President said, pacing now behind his desk. "We know they bought dual GPS/GLONASS receivers based on the data the FBI gathered on sales, but we don't whether they bought other GLONASS-only receivers. If I were running this as a bad guy, I would have done that."

He continued, "Let's keep getting updates from Peterson and scramble a couple more F-18's in the Midwest and on the East Coast. If we have to shoot down some that are moving toward populated areas, we can probably do that over relatively open land and limit the damage. Of course, it may be that they present too small a target for us to be successful, and if we are lucky, maybe they'll all move out to sea without dropping their payloads."

Jeff returned to his office, called Maya, and relayed the conversation. "We'll get 30 minute updates from Peterson and I can have two F-18's in the air for you within minutes," she promised and phoned the Secretary of the Air Force to pass on the orders.

CHAPTER FIFTY-NINE
Late evening, June 8, in Moscow

On Friday evening Col. Sergeyev Yvetshenko reached the door of Pyotr's hospital room before he was stopped. "Sorry, sir," one of the two guards posted at Pyotr's door said to him. He looked embarrassed. "We are not allowed to let anyone in to see Col. Olenshinsky except his wife and the President himself or his deputy. We will, however, tell Col. Olenshinsky that you were here."

Serge was incensed. He was a full colonel in the Air Force with an unblemished, indeed a distinguished record. "I have business with Col. Olenshinsky!" he replied indignantly.

The second guard moved closer. "Sir, we are under orders."

"Whose orders might those be?" Serge challenged, his blond head a full six inches higher than that of the second guard.

"The Chief Deputy for Security," the guard answered, eyeing Serge. The guards devoutly hoped they would not have to use weapons to usher Serge away from the door. He outranked them and was a well-known military man in the country. They did not like this duty but they had their orders.

Serge made a quick decision, turned on his heel and said, "I will be speaking to the Chief Deputy directly!" So Vassilly Rementrov was restricting access to Pyotr. He wondered if this had something to do with the GLONASS business or if they were worried that the attack on Pyotr might mean his life was in danger and so no one was going to be allowed to see him except his wife. Probably the latter. Serge had difficulty believing that Pyotr's shooting could in any way be related to orders about what to do with GLONASS. And, it had been clear in the phone call from Sec. Rementrov that Pyotr had not known all the factors affecting the GLONASS decision. "Perhaps I should just obey orders and stay away, for now," Serge thought. Just as he was opening the door to leave the hospital, he almost ran into Elena, whom he had met socially on occasion.

"Mrs. Olenshinsky," he said, reaching to take her right hand in his, "it's Col. Yvetshenko. I just tried to visit your husband, but the guards at his door said no one may see him except for you—and the President himself. Please tell me, how is he?"

Elena stopped, distracted, and looked up at this imposing blond man in his blue uniform. She remembered meeting him and that Pyotr had spoken well of him.

"I'm sorry they would not let you in! There must be some misunderstanding. I did not know that no one would be allowed to see him. He has been unconscious but he came out of it for a little time this morning. I went home to bring him some clothes and other things. He seems to be stable but they say a bullet is lodged near his heart and another one near his left lung. They may have to operate, but they're waiting to see because it could be dangerous."

"I am glad to hear that he is holding his own. He is a strong man. Please tell him I was here and that I am thinking of him. If he wishes to contact me, I will, of course, take his call." Privately, Serge thought, "and I hope he is well enough that he can call me."

"He won't be able to do that as there is no phone in the room and they say he can't be given one until he is better. He was robbed of his cell phone, too, but I will tell him you were here. Perhaps you can come back, I mean, when they will let him have visitors?"

She held his hand for a second more and then dropped it. "Thank you for coming," she said and moved past him, through the door.

"Mrs. Olenshinsky, Elena!" Serge called out as she was now several steps past him. "Here is my card. It has my mobile number on it as well as my office number. If Pyotr has any messages for me, you can call me. But please tell him the main thing is for him to rest and get well." She came back, took the card, glanced at it and put it in her coat pocket. Serge watched her walk quickly back through the hospital's lobby. "I wish I could help them more," he thought, "but maybe there will be something I can do soon."

§ § §

Elena had watched Pyotr drift in and out of consciousness, and he often spoke a few words in both conditions. But for the last few hours, he had been conscious most of the time and had begun inquiring about where he was and what happened. She told him what she could, leaving out the part about Maya's wanting to know who Pyotr was meeting with when the attack happened. That question could wait until he was stronger. But hoping to make him feel better, she did include her encounter with Sergeyev Yvetshenko and that the

173

guards outside his door were not allowing any visitors. Surprisingly, at this news, Pyotr tried to sit up, which alarmed Elena.

"You must stay quiet—you are wounded!" she said firmly but softly, pushing him back down into the bed. "I did not mean to alarm you. Col. Yvetshenko was very nice, very concerned about you. That's all."

Pyotr's eyes were fixed on hers now, and his gaze was clear—even angry. He had been trying to focus in his mind during the times he was awake on a smell that kept coming back to him. It was important, he knew, but he did not know why. Now he knew. He pulled Elena's hand close to his chest, and then as she leaned toward him, he gently pulled her head down to within inches of his own.

"Elena, please listen to me carefully. I am not hallucinating. I think I know what happened to me now, and we can talk about that later, but I need for you to get a message to Serge. It's very important but don't tell anyone else. You must do this right away. Do you understand?"

Elena looked into his eyes, alarmed. He did seem lucid. "What is the message, Pyotr?"

"Call Col. Yvetshenko. Try his mobile phone. Tell him I told you to give him a message, and that I know who attacked me. The message is simple. 'Proceed with reprogramming immediately. It is a matter of life and death. Our enemy is on the inside.' Can you repeat that?"

After Elena had repeated the message twice, looking puzzled, Pyotr released her. "Go now. If anyone asks, tell them you are bringing me some more of my clothes or my reading glasses. Come back as soon as you can. I love you."

He lay back on the pillows, exhausted with this effort. Perhaps he was putting Elena in some danger, but he hoped not. He also hoped that Serge would understand the message and reprogram the GLONASS. He relaxed a bit as he watched Elena leave his room. And then he thought, "Vassilly should not smoke those expensive Cuban cigars that he has made especially for him. I could recognize that aroma anywhere."

§ § §

Sergeyev Yvetshenko was at home when he received the call from Elena at 8 p.m., Moscow time, on Friday. For a few minutes, Serge sat in silence, weighing his options. He had never heard back from Vassilly Rementrov, and he had never doubted the authority of Pyotr Olenshinsky until this moment. Still, many things could be going on about which Serge knew nothing. Was Pyotr a traitor? Had the wounding affected his brain? Were there other players here about whom Serge knew nothing? Yet, in the end, it was a simple matter for him. He knew, of course, what was happening in America. He could surmise how the attacks were being carried out. He could not imagine why Russia would not do what they could to help.

"I am forty-six. If they fire me—and do not put me in jail—I can find work." He had a brother-in-law in Germany, a cousin in Australia. "My wife will go with me, no questions asked." More than this, though, he trusted Pyotr and his own instincts. He turned on another light in the room so he could be sure to read all the telephone numbers correctly and booted up his computer. He made two phone calls to the central operations number for GLONASS and followed up with a coded message. Essentially, he was having his people notify the civilian air control operations center and the central military air control operations center that there would be a "temporary reprogramming" of the "non-military" signals on GLONASS, beginning in 6 hours and "not to exceed 48 hours."

He noted in his messages that he would keep two telephone lines open, one a landline and one his mobile. Serge switched off his desk light and went to the small kitchen to find something to eat before driving to the GLONASS operations center. Then he remembered to call Elena. She answered her mobile phone on the second ring. Serge had no way of knowing if she was at home, in the car, or back with Pyotr, so all he said was, "It is done." He was quite sure she recognized his voice.

At the Russian Civil Air Operations Center, Valentin Chermenov was surprised to receive Serge's message. But he did not doubt that the GLONASS reprogramming was being done for legitimate reasons. Under the protocol he was supposed to follow, he should have relayed a copy of the message to the Chief Deputy for Security, Vassilly Rementrov, for verification and additional authorization.

Valentin did not do this, however. He had never liked Vassilly, not since the Putin days when Vassilly had clearly been one of Putin's handpicked stars. Vassilly had several times snubbed Valentin at Moscow events, not considering the hard-working, less prestigiously educated Valentin to be his equal. Plus which, Valentin's current mistress was an American businesswoman whom he eventually hoped to marry. "I know what is happening in America. Maybe GPS and GLONASS are being used to guide the balloons!" Valentin surmised to himself. "If we are doing something to help the Americans, then I'll cooperate." He spent the next several hours coordinating with air traffic control and the airlines.

CHAPTER SIXTY

Afternoon, June 8, in Washington, DC

President Bradley was increasingly preoccupied all morning Friday with the fact that they could not know if there would be more deadly poison attacks. At 2 p.m., he went to his computer and opened up the Google Earth page that showed the entire District of Colombia area and its nearest suburbs. He had a bad premonition.

At 2:10 p.m., Jeff's phone rang and he heard Elliott's Bradley's voice. "Jeff, I think the terrorists have to have looked at programming in coordinates that would make it likely to have at least one payload drop over the DC area—and probably New York as well—and maybe over all of our east coast ports. We're going to have to scramble the jets and try to shoot down whatever is still up there if we can find the balloons and not put too many people at risk."

"Mr. President, I know the Pentagon scrambled F-18's early this morning—let me get a status report and get back to you." He put in a call to Maya.

Maya's return call to Jeff came exactly two minutes later. "The F-18's in the eastern sector were directed to look at everything from Maine down to Atlanta, and they've spotted four balloons that look like the others. Two are drifting in the direction of Potomac, Maryland, and could turn south, depending on the winds. The other two are heading east just about two miles south of DC. From what the radar is telling us, there appear to be a couple of blips further south and west, but they are faint and the F-18's haven't reported anything in that area yet. If they have the dual receivers, they would still be taking their readings from GPS, so they should drift on out to the Atlantic. If not, they could make their drops. From the positions the F-18's reported, there could be hits near population centers if we shoot down the four balloons they saw, but we'll prepare to do that on the President's order."

"Thanks, Maya. Please keep your mobile open for me; we may need updates more frequently now."

Jeff dialed the President. "Sir, at least one balloon is heading toward Potomac, Maryland and could be overhead in Maryland or Northern Virginia in the next hour or half hour. Another one is behind it, but about a mile further south. Two others are also moving into the mid-Atlantic region. Radar reports suggest a few more drifting further south of here but no F-18 sightings yet."

"Jeff, have Maya order the F-22's and F-35's on high alert for scrambling and ready to shoot down the balloons we can still see over land if they are not right over cities. And please come over to my office. We have to make this decision very soon."

The President went back to his computer screen. Coordinates for the Capitol, the Pentagon, the White House and the Reservoir just off MacArthur Boulevard in McLean, Virginia—which provided all the water for much of Northern Virginia and the District of Colombia—had all been programmed in as targets in the Nashville payload. The Reservoir had a cover, of course, but the cover was designed so that rainwater could leak in. And so would any poisons that were released over it—like Cryptosporidium. "I'll bet anything that they hope to release the Crypto over us and try to poison our water supply." he thought. "And still no help from the Russians!"

What none of them could see at the moment that the President called Jeff was four balloons, all launched on June 5 and all with GLONASS-only receivers, moving toward their targets—Norfolk, which houses that Navy Ship Yard and the Port of Virginia, and northern Virginia, home to the CIA and—as the President had identified—the Reservoir.

§ § §

At the GLONASS command center on the outskirts of Moscow, at 10 p.m. on Friday, Valentin Chermenov, was putting in place all the necessary software commands to reprogram GLONASS, having notified the requisite authorities to alert all aircraft, ships and other users. He had completed most of the sequence when one of his computers simply quit. It had happened before, and Valentin cursed. "Oh, well, five minutes one way or another won't make any difference!" he thought, recognizing that two of the satellites had yet to have their frequencies frozen.

Just at that moment, his boss, Col. Yvetshenko, came through the door. He found Valentin leaning over the farthest right computer screen and grumbling. "Major Chermenov, what is the matter? Have you carried out my orders of last night?"

Valentin straightened up. "Yes, Colonel, but we have had a computer failure. All but two of the satellites are reprogrammed."

Serge sat down at the middle terminal. Without a word, he hit several keys and waited for new lines to appear on the screen. He had helped set up the software programs to control GLONASS; he could by-pass the current failure. In five minutes, at 10:20 p.m. Moscow time, he leaned back and motioned Valentin over to the screen. "Look, I've by-passed your sick computer!" he said, not unkindly. "That should take care of the last two satellites. I'm sure it would not have made too much difference if we had not done this, but it shows, Valentin, that we must maintain our equipment and have more redundancy. I would like to see a plan for more redundancy from you by Monday." From what Serge could see on the active screens, all the satellites were now reprogrammed. It would take a few minutes for the freezing of the signals to take effect.

§ § §

At 2:30 p.m., Jeff was with the President; Maya and the other members of the Trial Run team, along with Harold Harper, were conferenced in.

"I very much regret that I'll have to give the order in the next ten minutes to begin shooting down the balloons we can find that are approaching populated areas, including Washington, DC," the President began. They could all hear the stress in his voice. "We have put out an alert for all states from Maine south to Georgia that toxins may be released. The CDC is on stand-by, as is the National Guard and Homeland Security."

There was a momentary pause.

"Sir, the F-22's and F-35's are scrambled. They are acquiring targets," reported an anonymous voice from the Pentagon at 2:35 p.m.

And then, to everyone's considerable surprise, they heard Maya's aide actually shouting on his line, "They've reprogrammed GLONASS! They've frozen the signals! They *did it!*"

Maya recovered first. Her aide was not in her office but in the Air Force's nerve center in the Pentagon. "Details please!" she said in her most authoritative voice.

The others on the conference call heard faint exclamations from the people in the room with the aide. "We saw the signals on some of the satellites change about fifteen minutes ago—and just now, the last two shifted to what are clearly frozen signals. We have confirmed this, and we are continuing to monitor their constellation."

The President stood and clapped Jeff on the back. "Great work—many thanks to all of you," he said into the speakerphone.

"I'm going to ask, Maya, that you scramble F-18's in all sectors again this afternoon to observe how many more balloons may be up there and that your people keep Jeff fully up to date, and he will keep the rest of you alerted. I am ordering the F-22's and F-35's to stay up for another hour as a precaution, and then they can stand down. After that, I'll have my press secretary make a short report in the press room. He can say that we have received assistance from the Russians so that all the guidance systems of the suspected balloons have been effectively disabled and the balloons will be moving on toward the Atlantic. I do not expect to have to give any orders to shoot them down. And, if we can confirm that these are the last of the balloons, we should be able to restore the GPS signals by midnight tonight."

CHAPTER SIXTY-ONE
June 9

When Saleeth saw Amal's message, it was 2:15 p.m. on Saturday. She was working in her apartment, simultaneously drinking coffee while checking news bulletins on CNN. There had been news earlier, saying that the Pentagon now thought the threat of the poison attacks was substantially over and that the GPS system was restored to normal operations.

She debated whether to call Andy Shannon before calling Amal, but what good would that do? Better to find out what Amal had learned, if anything, and then talk with Andy.

Saleeth went to her kitchen, sat at the table with a pad of paper and pencil, and dialed Amal's number in Riyadh.

On the second ring, Amal picked up, with merely a "Yes?"

Saleeth drew a deep breath. For all her successful cover, for all of her new life, hearing the voice of her second cousin after so long sparked many deep emotions. "Amal, it's me," she said, hoping Amal would recognize her voice. "No names, please."

Amal had been prepared for the call but not for the emotion that engulfed her as well in hearing Saleeth's voice. "I miss you," she said simply. Then, willing herself to steady her voice, she went on. "The person about whom you asked may be in the North America but my source could not say where, except that perhaps Canada, or California, perhaps Washington, DC. It sounded like Washington was more likely. And that he may be hiding or in some kind of trouble."

"Did you talk with this source directly?" Saleeth asked.

"No, but Nour did. You will remember her. Nour is in Paris and so is the source. He implied that some people may be looking for the person we are discussing."

"Amal, this is important. Is the source someone that others could talk to, if it became necessary? Is it likely he knows more than he would tell Nour?"

"I don't know. I think he, himself, felt in danger, but I could give you a name and contact for him if you wish. Should I do that in an email?"

"Yes, please," Saleeth replied swiftly. "We cannot talk long now, but this is very, very important—and you have been a great help."

There was another pause, and then Amal said softly, "Will I ever see you again?"

"When the time is right, yes. Until then, you have my gratitude and my love. I must go now."

After they hung up, Saleeth waited until she had the email from Amal, with Kareem's name, working address and telephone number, just as Nour had provided them to Amal. "Please, let this be of some help," Saleeth thought as she prepared to send a message to Andy Shannon. "And, if Ahmed is here somewhere, please let them find him—for everyone's sake."

When Andy Shannon received Saleeth's message, he immediately relayed it to Eileen Johnson and to Jimmy Buttero, reiterating that the Agency would be bringing her to Washington, DC, very soon. Then he sat quietly at his desk for a few minutes. He knew his emotions were barely in control where Saleeth (or Judith, as he now always thought of her) was concerned. He so very much wanted to protect her, "and I can't, not really," he thought, discouraged. Although he had tried. Andy followed the rules, most of the time, but he had gone off the reservation a few times in the past when he thought the situation required it. He had done it again recently, and now he wondered why his actions had not produced the desired results. "Maybe they still will," he thought and realized he had done all he could, for the time being.

CHAPTER SIXTY-TWO
June 11

On Monday at 8 p.m., President Bradley again addressed the nation from the Oval Office. The Trial Run team gathered with Jeff to watch the broadcast on closed circuit. The President's principal message would be to reinforce the fact that the Government believed that the spread of the toxins was being contained because the balloons were no longer dropping payloads and because the CDC was getting anti-toxins distributed broadly. The satellite guidance system was restored and flights were returning to normal, but he also needed to convey a message—that he knew the terrorists would see and hear—that their demands were being met, without saying that in so many words.

"My fellow citizens," he said near the end of his talk, "while it is never the policy of the United States to yield to demands of people who wish to do us harm, we do need to take steps that are in our best interests. So, today, we have moved two people who have been under our supervision for some time back to their home countries. You may have seen news coverage of these events earlier tonight on the networks. The two men in question are no longer a threat to the United States, and that is why they have been sent home. We will be dealing with other issues raised by the perpetrators of this attack, but we will not take any steps that would further endanger the health and safety of this nation. I will be back to speak with you over the next few days as events warrant. I want to thank the many people in our government and in the private sector who have given us their cooperation. We have, together, averted a larger disaster. I pledge to you to do all that I can to bring an end to this episode and guard against its repeat in the future. Thank you, God bless America, and good night."

The team members sat quietly for a minute, and then Paul spoke up. "I think we have to assume that if the terrorists' demands are not met, or don't seem to be met, there will be more attacks. We are taking every precaution against this, but we still do not know where the original poisons were fabricated, so we cannot guarantee that more will not be released."

Eileen intervened. "We have good evidence now that the man called Kas Pradep, who is probably Ahmed al-Kodari, is here in the Washington area. We got a tip, through one of our agents, who found out from the pilot who is a friend of his about a charter plane coming to Dulles Airport that carried someone calling himself Kas Pradep. We also got a pretty good recording of his voice from the call where he booked the ride on the charter. Andy Shannon at the Agency played it for their operative who can identify al-Kodari's voice, and she was sure it was him. Andy's bringing her in to DC now. Al-Kodari may be here to supervise the pick-up of the diamonds—or for some other reason. We don't know. We still don't have a good trace on Georges Labadie and we're trying to get more information about a possible third collaborator, who goes by the name of Rafik Muhaimin. He is a known associate of Labadie, and there is some evidence that he may know al-Kodari."

"What's the plan to contact al-Kodari, or any of these people, when we have supposedly met their demands?" Paul asked.

"You heard the President tonight," Jimmy began. "That was an indirect message to them that we have moved Mohammed Haru and Pavez Riari, although, of course, we didn't move them back to Egypt or Pakistan. And, tomorrow we make the drop of the diamonds. Assuming we have any direct communications with the terrorists in the next day or two, we'll tell them we are making arrangements to repatriate or otherwise free the former Guantanamo prisoners. By the time they learn this isn't necessarily true, we should have been able to trace where the diamonds go and detain at least the ringleaders."

Jeff took up the narrative. "Our ambassador to the UN will bring up the topic of sanctions tomorrow. We don't, off course, intend to ask that they all be removed but everyone knows that decisions at the UN usually move slowly, so we think we can stall on this one. If it becomes an issue, we can always target one of the smaller countries where we have sanctions imposed and ask that those be eased. But we are hoping to have all the bad guys in custody long before we have to do that."

"We'll have people watching the drop tomorrow, of course, but from remote locations, using binoculars, and we're also going to use one helicopter, marked as if it's a DC police chopper." Eileen reported. "Our plan is to let the bad guys get the diamonds and then trace the transmissions. Or, if we are lucky, we may see who takes the boat and where. We have no tracking equipment in the bags themselves—too easy for them to find. But we did make some fake yellow diamonds, and they have radio transmitters. We'll begin tracking the packages as soon as they are dropped, and we'll have to keep our fingers crossed that somebody high enough up in this conspiracy gets involved so we can arrest him—or them."

"We still have the CDC on high alert and all state and municipal agencies cooperating to be on the lookout for additional poisons. Some may be spreading from different sources that we don't know about. I'll also have a new report for all of you tomorrow," Paul added, looking as tired as he felt.

"Let's adjourn for tonight—unless anyone else has anything?" Jeff suggested. "Let's have a conference call tomorrow at 8 p.m."

CHAPTER SIXTY-THREE
June 12

Early in the morning after taking a red-eye, Rafik checked himself into the JW Marriott on 14th Street, NW, in the heart of Washington, DC. He had decided to travel to Washington since that was where he felt Ahmed would most likely come. Before he had booked his trip, he had made a quick visit to Fed Ex to send an important package, addressed to himself at the Marriott. He hoped it arrived on time.

The only way Rafik thought he could get an early clue as to Ahmed's whereabouts—if, in fact, Ahmed was in the area—would be through Luis Jimenez. Rather than risk a phone call, Rafik took a taxi to the waterfront just below L'Enfant Plaza and found the Freshest Fish Market, which Luis owned. He found Luis busily supervising the morning's shipment of fish. They had never met in person, but as soon as Rafik identified himself Luis turned over his duties to one of his workers and led Rafik into a small office. Luis closed the door and offered Rafik a chair.

"I am here to help with the plan," Rafik began, wondering how much he could trust this man who had supposedly been a member of the movement for some years. "Unfortunately, I have lost touch with Ahmed because we had our codes intercepted and had to get new phones. When I last spoke with him, he had indicated he, too, might come here for the next phase. Have you heard from him?"

Luis studied the man across the desk from him. He was older than Luis himself by several years—maybe in his late forties—swarthy, with an accent that sounded French to Luis. But most important, Ahmed had said nothing about wanting to contact Rafik—or about Rafik's coming to Washington. Rafik had no official assignment here as far as Luis knew. Luis had known Ahmed for many years and had been recruited by him. In some respects, he owed his life to Ahmed. Luis made a quick decision.

"No, I haven't spoken to Ahmed for at least two weeks. He sent me a note about a package to be delivered here, but that is the last I heard from him. Is there something wrong with him that you know of? Has he been compromised? You said the codes had been intercepted?"

Rafik looked at Luis carefully. Was it likely he had not heard from Ahmed? "I had a message from Paris not to use the current codes and not to contact Ahmed until we received more instructions, and when I tried to reach him via an unsecured number, it was out of service."

"OK, but our message was delivered by television, wasn't it? So, didn't Ahmed make that happen? I thought you would know where he was!" Luis returned Rafik's level gaze.

"I think Ahmed may be in Mexico or even be out of North America. He felt he had some enemies in the movement. He may be in hiding. We can never be too careful. But, he has been the head of all our operations here for most of the past year, so I feel it is my duty to find him and to be in touch with him. I want to be sure he knows he can trust me. We don't want anyone acting on his own now—not when we are so close to accomplishing our goals." Rafik made his voice sound warm, his tone urgent. "So, since I am here, I am willing to take any assignment. If you were expecting Ahmed, perhaps I can fill in for him."

Luis played with a pencil near his telephone. "Ahmed was never supposed to be doing anything official here, although we would have welcomed him. The drop today is being well covered; my people have their instructions. However, if you would like to wait here and see me after it is over, that is fine."

Rafik hesitated. His real motive in seeing Luis was to get some clue as to Ahmed's whereabouts. On the one hand, if Ahmed himself was in the area, he might be expected to get near the scene of the action. On the other hand, if Rafik exposed himself too much and something went wrong with the 'drop' or anything else, he would have further compromised their mission.

"I will stay at my hotel. You can call me when it's over. I think that is best, but if you feel you need an extra hand, I am here. I am especially good at driving!" Rafik meant this humorously, but Luis did not smile.

"Give me your contacts, your cell phone or whatever, and you will hear from me tonight. We are scheduled to pick up the package between 4 and 5 p.m. I should have it in the proper hands no later than 7."

Rafik gave Luis a card from the hotel with the main number and his room number scribbled above it, plus the number of the cell phone he was currently using. "I am registered as Silvio Franchetti. Again, if you need me urgently, try the cell phone first. I will be waiting to hear from you."

They stood, shook hands, and Luis asked if Rafik wanted a taxi. "No, I think a walk back would be fine," he answered courteously. As they left the small office and he moved out onto the pavement, he wondered how Luis could keep this business going and still do his work for the movement. Plus, the smell of fish was overwhelming.

§ § §

At the same time Rafik was returning to the Marriott, Andy Shannon was on an early morning, pre-arranged phone call with Saleeth. "And so," he was concluding, "we need you here because we believe your brother is coming here or is here already. We need you to help us get to him. We'll have all the travel arrangements made for you within the next two hours, and I'll send you a message. Call me back if you have any questions when you get them. I'll pick you up at Dulles Airport."

Saleeth sat quietly at her desk for a few minutes. The first thing she focused on was that she wanted to see Raul or at least talk to him to tell him she was going away for a few days. She called him on his cell phone and got his voice mail. Hearing his voice, even that way, sent a small tremor through her, and she thought, "I should not be getting involved. I never let myself get involved before, even with Andy, and I know how much he liked me. Maybe I will always have to be a fugitive. Maybe I should not bring anyone else into this." And yet, she had deliberately changed her life two years ago; she had deliberately pledged her cooperation to and gone to work for her new country. Why, now, should she have to give all that up, as well as any chance at personal happiness, just because her brother might or might not have made bad decisions? But she had committed to going to Washington. She left a detailed message for Raul and hoped she could see him before she left.

CHAPTER SIXTY-FOUR

The problem," Eileen was saying to Jeff over the phone at 1 p.m., "is that we really don't know where al-Kodari is—or what identity he is using. The Agency's photographs of him are old and not very good. Andy said his operative was not absolutely able to identify the voice, either, but she thinks it's him. And he may not even be in DC any longer. We're going to gamble that he will have something to do with the drop and have extra people looking for him this afternoon."

"Review for me again what assets you and the Agency have in place for this afternoon."

"We'll have agents in two of the sailboats at the dock of the Sailing Club. The instructions were that no boats were to be moving in the area. But we'll also have agents in the club and at Reagan National Airport, which has a good view of the dock. We'll have a helicopter with DC Police markings moving up and down the Potomac in the vicinity. We might get lucky and be able to follow their boat, but we don't want to spook them since we want to trace the diamonds to their destination. Do you want to come over to the airport or the Sailing Club and watch?"

Jeff thought about it—it would be exciting to be on the scene, but he had work to do. "No, I'd better stay here. Thanks, anyway. I would like to be on the phone with you or someone you designate while it's all going on, though, so I'll keep a line open."

"It'll probably be me," Eileen said. "I'll call you when we get in place—that should be around 3 p.m. Call me if you need me in the meantime."

§ § §

Four blocks south of the Freshest Fish Market on Water Street, SW, the Captain's View restaurant was preparing for the lunch crowd. Most of the customers would come from nearby hotels or businesses, but a few would come by boat. The two docks outside the restaurant could accommodate a number of powerboats and dinghies. At the end of the outer dock, a 25-foot fishing boat, tied securely to a cleat, bobbed gently. It sported a blue and orange paint scheme and had a small French flag flying off the stern, just behind a large, covered bait box. This much patrons in the restaurant could see.

If they had looked closer, they would also have seen bubbles coming up from the water near the boat, then moving away from the boat. What they could not see were Luis' two cousins, Marcos and Raphael, in full scuba gear, practicing their approach and retreat from the boat. After a few minutes, the bubbles moved along the Potomac River, paralleling Water Street. At the dock used by the Freshest Fish Market, the two scuba divers emerged into a small, covered tent, where they shed their gear before walking up to the Market. Luis then collapsed and retrieved the tent, which he stored near the dock.

"Timing?" Luis asked when the three of them were in his office behind a locked door. "It should take no more than ten minutes to swim back, although maybe more with the packages," Marcos said, looking at his large, illuminated waterproof watch.

"Perfect," Luis replied. "Be ready to go at 4 p.m. I will give you the signal."

CHAPTER SIXTY-FIVE

Early on Tuesday morning, Ahmed visited the branch of a national bank near his hotel to pick up the wire-transferred money that he had asked Kamal to send. The $4,000 was given to him in 100's and 50's, which he zipped into an inner pocket of his black bag that also contained his Glock. He returned to his hotel and put $2,000 in his room safe, along with the rest of the money he had brought from Seattle. Then he left the hotel and walked a few blocks to the Metro and rode to DuPont Circle. While he was at the bank, he received a voice mail message at his hotel from Luis. Ahmed decided to call Luis back from a pay phone after riding into the District. He felt certain that Luis would tell him Rafik was looking for him, maybe Georges, too. He knew that Georges must be in town to take the diamonds.

Ahmed did not trust the Americans to meet their part of the bargain and actually deliver negotiable diamonds, although the news about the transfers of Mohammed Haru and Pavez Riari, if the President's message could be trusted, was good—and surprising. He had seen on television just this morning, too, that the US ambassador to the UN had introduced the topic of lifting sanctions on several small predominantly Muslim countries. Maybe spreading poisons— and the threat of more to come—had had its effect. But the next phase of the plan would have to be carried out if there were any slips. In one way, Ahmed hoped the US government would slip up—the next step was one he had planned personally.

Ahmed got off the Metro red line and walked to the DuPont Plaza hotel. Two pay phone booths near the men's room afforded him his opportunity. It was one o'clock. When he dialed the Freshest Fish Market, he was put through to Luis. "Can you talk?" He asked, adding, "No names—this is not secure."

"Yes," Luis answered. "A friend was here looking for you this morning. I believe he is sometimes called 'the Chauffer'. It was not clear why he wanted to find you but he said he had lost touch and all codes had been compromised."

"What did you tell him?"

"Only that I had not heard from you recently—not since two weeks ago, and I did not know where you are."

"And where is he?"

"At the JW Marriott—some of our friends must be doing well!" Luis gave Ahmed the room number. "He said he is registered as Silvio Franchetti."

"Did he say what he plans to do in Washington?"

"He said he might try to watch events this afternoon or just stay in his room—and that he was here to help. I got the feeling that he was here to look for you; I did not give him an assignment or tell him much, but I am sure he will be back. How do you want me to handle him?"

"Just keep with the plan. Do you know if our courier has arrived in town?"

"Yes, earlier today. He telephoned. Are you going to make the call this afternoon or should I?"

"I'll do it, but call me when you get underway or if there is any change in your plans. If, for any reason, you cannot reach me, then you must make it." Ahmed gave him one of his two remaining temporary cell phone numbers.

"And is there anything else I can do to help you?" Luis asked.

"No, thank you. You have arranged everything well. I will call you after it is over tonight, or you can call me. If, for any reason, you have not heard from me by tomorrow morning, it means things are not going well. But I hope that does not happen."

Ahmed left the hotel. He was undecided about his next move. He found a small, inexpensive café on New Hampshire Avenue and seated himself at a window table. For the day, he had donned a driving cap and tinted glasses. As he waited for his lunch, he thought out his plan to trap Rafik. With the information Luis had given him, the plan primarily hinged on timing—and luck. "And I will be the hunter, not the hunted," he vowed silently.

Ahmed left the café, got in a taxi and had the driver take him to Macy's, which was near the JW Marriott. In the basement, he found a pay phone. He dialed the number of the hotel. When the operator answered, he said, "I would like to leave a voice mail message for Mr. Silvio Franchetti, who is in room 1216."

"Sir, I can try to connect you," the operator offered.

"No, I just tried the room and no one answered. Please put me into your voice mail system." Within seconds, he heard the automated voice say, "Please leave your message for room 1216 after the tone."

Ahmed, not trying to disguise his voice, said, "I have missed you. I will be calling you at 2:30 in your room. Please do not leave without talking with me." He hung up. Less than two hours to kill. Ahmed decided to walk around the area. There were a few things he needed to know.

CHAPTER SIXTY-SIX

Rafik had left his room at noon to pick up his FedEx package and to have lunch in the lobby. He was waiting to call Georges, who should recently have arrived. Not having a real assignment for the rest of the day, Rafik had decided to stay closely in touch with the action. He reasoned that if all went well, he could at least report this to Paris, despite the embarrassment of not having any "good news" about Ahmed. It was also quite possible that if Ahmed were really in Washington, he, too, might show up at or near the drop site in the late afternoon. "I will be prepared for that," Rafik said to himself.

After finishing his lunch, Rafik returned to his room and using his cell phone, called the number for one of Georges' safe cell phones.

Georges answered on the third ring. He did not tell Rafik where he was staying, nor did Rafik ask. "And you, you are here in town?" Georges asked with some surprise.

"Yes, tracking our friend. I am quite sure he is here as well. I will not interfere with today's activities unless you need me to help." Georges suppressed a sigh; all this was complicated enough without a manhunt—and he still could not believe Ahmed had somehow betrayed them or was trying to.

"My assignment is later today, as you know," he told Rafik. "If something goes wrong, I may call you. Will you be reachable at this number?"

"Yes, or another one; let me give it to you." Rafik repeated the number of a second phone. "If all else fails, you may leave a coded message for me here at the hotel," and he repeated that number, too.

"Well, let us hope that I can give you a good report," Georges replied, "and I should add—good hunting."

Rafik put away his cell phone and for the first time noticed a blinking light on the landline phone next to his bed. He picked up the receiver and dialed in for his message. After he heard it, he immediately called the hotel operator. "I had a message earlier. Is it possible for you to tell me the phone number of the person who called? I want to return the call."

"Sorry, sir," the operator said. "We don't have that information. Would you like to place a call now?"

Without answering, Rafik hung up. He felt his pulse racing. Clearly Ahmed had been in touch with Luis, which meant Luis had been lying earlier, but that did not matter now. In less than two hours, he might be able to accomplish his main assignment. He walked over to his suitcase into which he had zipped the FedEx package with the bullets and his Browning 9mm. He unwrapped the package and loaded his gun. Now he had to think about how he would get a dead body out of the hotel—or wherever he and Ahmed finally met.

CHAPTER SIXTY-SEVEN

Saleeth's flight was scheduled to leave at noon. After she went through security at LAX, she turned her cell phone back on and found a message from Raul, asking her to call him and to tell him the precise details of her trip. Her first instinct was to call him back immediately, but then she thought, "What am I going to tell him? What am I going to say? I can say I am on my way to Washington, DC, for part of my job, which is true even if he doesn't know what job I'm really talking about. Or, I can wait until I know more about when—and whether—I'll be back. Or maybe I should just send him a text message, telling him I will call when I can." She rested her head against the wall next to her seat. The white wall felt cool, and it relaxed her. She had been up most of the night, first to pack, then unable to sleep. She had left detailed messages for her staff at work, saying she would be back in a few days and that her trip had to do with a family matter. That, at least, was true.

She could picture Raul. Tall, with his slightly off-center smile and deep set eyes. She thought of their night together after the President's speech. She thought about her feelings for him. She took her cell phone out of her purse and dialed his number.

As soon as he answered, she heard background noise. "I'm in a taxi!" he said, almost shouting. "But I'm so glad you called. Where are you?"

"I'm about to fly to Washington, DC—it's work related. We've got a good possibility of some funding and I don't know how long I'm going to be gone. Where are you?"

"Also traveling, but I'll be back in three days. If you're not going to be home by then, maybe I'll fly to DC and join you!"

Saleeth thought quickly. "No, don't do that—at least until we have talked. My trip might be short. Let's just stay in touch. I'll let you know when it looks like I can come back."

Raul bit back the next question he so badly wanted to ask: "Are you alone?" He simply said, "All right—and Judith, when we do see each other, there is something important I want to ask you."

She closed her eyes. Was this a personal question? Could it be *the* question? No, they certainly were not at a point in their relationship where he would consider proposing to her. "I'll look forward to seeing you and talking with you," she replied, trying to make her voice sound as warm as possible. "Have a good trip—wherever you are." The line went dead. "I wonder if I'll ever be able to tell him who I really am," she wondered and sighed. The next few hours and days might mean a turning point in her life—or nothing. She did not know, except that she had to do this.

She needed to make one other call, this one to Andy Shannon. No need for security on the line. When he picked up, all she said was "I'm at the airport. Flight should be on time," and hung up.

Andy pushed back from his desk and went to the staff break room. He felt like celebrating, even though he knew her arrival could mean complications. "But perhaps she will also be tremendously helpful," he thought as he poured himself eight ounces of strong Colombian coffee. He didn't need the caffeine to give him a jolt but it tasted good anyway. "Philip Miller, I think we're going to get you," he said to himself, "if your friends don't get you first!" Andy's exposing Ahmed to his own people had not gotten Ahmed eliminated—yet— but the people who wanted him captured or dead were multiplying on both sides.

CHAPTER SIXTY-EIGHT

At 2:15 p.m., Ahmed walked back to Macy's and looked for a cab. He let the first one go by as the driver was a young woman. One minute later, a Yellow Cab pulled up to let two women out. The driver, an African-American with short graying hair, leaned over to the passenger side and called to Ahmed, "You lookin' for a ride?"

Ahmed smiled and got in. "Please drive around the block while I check the address." The driver shrugged and pulled back into traffic. He was used to the eccentricities of foreigners, and now that DC cabs were metered, he would make money even if they stood still. As they turned up 14th Street, Ahmed leaned through the Plexiglas window that the driver had left half-open, as he did not take Ahmed for a criminal. In Ahmed's hand were four fifty-dollar bills, which the driver could see quite clearly.

"I would like to ask you a question," Ahmed began, holding onto the bills. "Does this cab have the kind of locking system where you can lock all the doors from your side and no one else can unlock them?"

"Sure thing," the driver said.

"Then I would like to ask you a favor," Ahmed continued. "We are going to pick up a friend of mine who is staying at the JW Marriott. After we do that, I will give you an address near the waterfront. I want you to begin driving there but take us by way of some streets where there will not be much traffic. When we are on one of those streets, I want you to say there is something wrong with your engine and pull over. Then I want you to leave your key in the ignition and then get out of your cab and run—I don't care where. I will not hurt your cab and it will be waiting for you somewhere near where you left it when you look for it later. You can tell the police or your cab company that you were threatened, even mugged."

"You gonna do anything bad to my cab?" the driver said, without looking at Ahmed as they slowed down for a red light.

"Nothing that some cleaning won't be able to fix," Ahmed replied pleasantly.

"Cleaning's gonna cost you another two hundred," the cabbie said, now accelerating.

Ahmed reached for his wallet and extracted four more fifty-dollar bills. "I have to make a call now. We will need to be in front of the JW Marriott at 2:35 p.m."

The cabbie took the money and pocketed it. "What has this guy done to you?" he asked with a touch of sarcasm but also curiosity.

"He's been seeing my wife," Ahmed answered quietly.

The cabbie half turned around. "Dudes like that, bad things gonna happen to them." He continued east on G Street.

"Yes," Ahmed said soberly, pulling out his cell phone.

The hotel operator put him through to Rafik. It was exactly 2:30 p.m.

"It's me," Ahmed began, "and I am sorry to have been out of touch. There have been some problems, and I have been in some danger, but everything should be all right now."

"Where are you? You must have found out I was here from Luis! We need to talk. Can you come up to my room?" Rafik actually hoped Ahmed would not agree to do that as he did not want to kill Ahmed anywhere inside the Marriott.

"No, there is no time to do that. We must both go to the market. There has been a change in plans. I have a cab and we will pick you up across the street from your hotel in five minutes. It is a Yellow Cab, and I will be in the back seat." He did not give Rafik time to argue. "Be there!" He disconnected. "We need to go across the street from the Marriott," he instructed the driver.

Rafik pocketed his gun and room key and took the elevator to the lobby. "If I cannot do anything to him on the way to Luis', I'll find a way to do it after the drop," he told himself. One way or the other, he now had Ahmed in his sights. "But I have to be careful." It was possible Ahmed knew he was walking into a trap—and Ahmed was too clever to let that happen easily.

Outside the hotel, Rafik saw the Yellow Cab parked across the street, with a man in the back seat. He waited for traffic to clear then crossed the street. When he entered the cab, Ahmed held out his hand and smiled. Rafik took it. "This is very good fortune to meet up with you here!" he said heartily. "We were afraid something had happened to you."

Without acknowledging this, Ahmed leaned forward and said to the driver, "Water Street Southwest, please, the Freshest Fish Market." They started down 14th Street but then turned left on E Street.

"Is this the way?" Rafik said, immediately alert. "I went there earlier and this wasn't how we went."

"Big tie up on 14th Street," the cabbie said loudly, without turning around. "Gonna take a better route." Already the traffic was lighter and he sped up.

"When did you get to Washington?" Rafik said, hoping he could get some idea of what Ahmed had been up to.

"Two days ago. I had to come by way of Mexico. It is a long story. There are some untrustworthy people in our movement, and I found this out, so I had to take precautions."

Rafik nodded and turned to look out the window. He was still puzzled by the route they were taking. Just then, the driver turned south on 10th Street and suddenly slowed down, easing into a parking zone that was vacant.

"What's the matter? What are you doing?" Ahmed asked, preempting the same question from Rafik.

"Damn engine light's coming on again. I gotta check under the hood." He left the key in the ignition, reached for his leather case, opened the door slowly, activating the locking mechanism as he got out—and then began running with long, powerful strides north on 10th Street.

"What?" Rafik began as he felt the blunt end of a gun connect with his skull. He moaned and slumped in the seat.

Ahmed looked out the window of the cab. The street was deserted. "Why were you instructed to kill me?" he asked, hoping Rafik could still hear him.

Rafik looked up at him, puzzled. He had his hand in his jacket pocket to pull out his own gun when Ahmed brought the Glock down on Rafik's hand. "Tell me or I'll kill you!" Ahmed said, louder now.

"Paris said you have betrayed us. Georges and I have been trying to find you but to help you." Rafik moaned again, trying to use his left hand now to get the Browning.

Ahmed did not waste any more time. He steadied the Glock and shot Rafik through the forehead twice. Then, reaching into Rafik's pocket, he took out Rafik's wallet, room key and the Browning 9mm, all of which he slipped into his pants. He reached through the Plexiglas and unlocked the doors. Still no one on the street. He got out, opened the door on Rafik's side, and pulled his body into the gutter. Then Ahmed got into the driver's seat, started the cab, made a U-turn and drove it three blocks further east, leaving it outside a fast food store. He hoped the cleaning bill for the cab would not be too much. He looked at his watch. It was time to make the call.

CHAPTER SIXTY-NINE

Ahmed walked to a vacant store on F Street that had a large, recessed entrance where now only dirty scraps of paper and other small garbage resided. He moved to the back of the entrance and pulled out one of his disposable cell phones, dialing a number he had memorized.

A voice answered, "This is Jean-Beth Reque." Ahmed recognized her voice. He had been prepared to speak with an assistant or even ask for Wolf Blitzer, but this made it easier.

"You know who I am," he began, enunciating clearly and speaking slowly. "You must call the government and tell them that the place of the ransom drop has been changed. They must be at the Captain's View docks on Water Street, SW, in DC no later than 4:15 p.m. The blue and orange fishing boat with the French flag will be tied up at the dock. They must put the two packages into the bait well of the boat, untie the boat and push it out into the Potomac River. If they are more than ten minutes late, we will begin Plan B immediately. There must be no following or attack on our people. If there is any interference, we will conclude that your government has not met its part of the bargain. If you question who this is, I will repeat some details of my earlier call to Mr. Blitzer." Without waiting for her to respond, he repeated things he had said earlier that had never been released to the press. Then he asked, "Have you heard me?"

"Yes!" Her voice was shaking. "Yes, and I will report this. Can you tell me where you are?"

Ahmed disconnected the phone. So far, so good, although he was willing to bet any amount of American dollars that CNN would rush cameras to the scene. "Let them," he thought. "They won't see much."

§ § §

Eileen heard Ahmed's message within minutes of CNN's call to the FBI. "Oh my God," she said to herself but calmly dialed her contacts at the CIA and Homeland Security, plus the DC police. "They've switched the drop point—the boat is at a dock on Water Street." She gave them the exact location. "We'll have our two agents who were going to place the packages do it there, but we need everyone to stay as far away from the dock as possible while still keeping surveillance.

"Best place may be from the commercial boat sheds next door," the Chief of Police offered.

Two large boats that gave pleasure cruises on the Potomac were housed at covered docks half a block from the restaurant. Eileen's deputy, who was also listening in, said, "I'll call all agents right now to reassign positions."

Eileen next dialed Jeff Sanchez and explained the situation. "Do you want to try to get near the dock area?" she asked him.

"No, but call me when everything is in place, Eileen, and if you can give me a live run-down while everything is happening."

Just then, Elliott Bradley walked into Jeff's office. Grasping the situation, he said, "I think I'll join you on the line with Eileen when the drop starts." They both moved to Jeff's conference table where a speakerphone was set up. It was 3:55 p.m.

The two FBI agents originally assigned to deliver the diamonds in their water tight bags now sped north on the GW Parkway from Alexandria, Virginia to the 14th Street Bridge where they could cross back into Washington, DC and get to Water Street. The other agents assigned to surveillance moved as quickly as they could. The helicopter pilot got his new coordinates and was told to fly back and forth from Georgetown, north of Water Street, to the Wilson Bridge, well to the south until he saw the boat. His primary mission was to follow the boat once it was released from the dock.

At 4:14 p.m., the two lead agents roared into the Captain's View parking lot, which at this time of day had plenty of spaces available, and left the car in a "loading zone only" space. Each one carried a bag. Without speaking, they walked to the end of the outside dock, having easily identified the blue and orange boat. No one else was on the dock, and there were only two other small boats tied up. Both agents had miniature cameras on their belts that were automatically filming everything.

When they reached the boat, they saw that it had eight small cement blocks between the seats but nothing else unusual. They found the cover to the bait well unsecured, so the first agent put down his bag and lifted the heavy cover of the box, in which there was some rope but nothing else. The first agent deposited both bags into the well and shut the cover. They looked around. Still no one visible other than some waiters, two of whom were agents, in the restaurant preparing for the dinner crowd. The second agent knelt to untie the boat's painter. When the rope hung free in the water, both agents moved alongside the boat and gave it a good shove forward so that it cleared the dock and headed straight out into the Potomac River. The light chop made ripples on the river. Without waiting to see where the boat was heading, the agents returned to their car and pulled out of the parking lot. They noticed that DC police had cordoned off the area and were turning away a CNN camera truck.

"The boat is adrift," Eileen reported on the conference call line. "We should have a good reading from the helicopter about where it's going and who approaches it."

From what all the agents and the helicopter could see, the boat seemed to be moving slowly north with the current. What they did not see in the next few minutes was the stream of bubbles coming from under the boat—the movement of the small waves obscured them.

Raphael used the saw to cut open the bottom of the bait box, and then Marcos grabbed both packages, while Raphael secured one to each of their diving belts, using rope they had brought and also the extra rope in the bait well. The cement blocks had served to keep the boat from wiggling when Raphael cut through the fiberglass. They turned and began swimming toward the Freshest Fish Market. The boat continued to drift north.

When they reached the dock, Luis was waiting for them in the small tent. He took the bags as they handed them up, then helped them shed their gear. Luis transferred the bags to a dock cart that had often been used to transport fish from boats to the market. He threw a tarp over the cart, which he wheeled up to the parking lot next to the market. His two cousins disassembled and stored the tent, then reentered the market and went back to work at their usual tasks. In the parking lot, a run-down gray garbage truck was waiting, with its engine idling. The driver, dressed in dirty overalls, boots, a baseball cap and dark glasses, got out of the cab to help Luis load the bags into the back of the truck, already filled with discarded boxes and other garbage. Then the truck pulled away.

Luis looked at his watch. 5 p.m. Right on schedule.

CHAPTER SEVENTY

The boat's still drifting!" the helicopter pilot reported fifteen minutes later. "They'll have to send someone out to get it sooner or later, so we'll stay on this route," he reported, moving north toward Georgetown. The FBI had high-speed power boats tied up at the Washington Marina, ready to move on command. Scuba divers were also available if the fishing boat was seen to be sinking. So far, no one had seen any markings on the boat that would indicate its ownership. Jeff Sanchez and the President had given up on the play-by-play conference call, with Jeff asking Eileen to call him if there were new developments.

At 8:30 p.m., the blue and orange fishing boat drifted ashore and beached itself at the north end of Georgetown. The helicopter identified the location and scores of police, FBI agents and CIA personnel descended on the boat, no longer fearing reprisals of the terrorists. What they found was a very waterlogged bait well, and then they knew. "Interview every business along the waterfront in DC!" came the command from Eileen's office. More agents immediately scrambled to begin. But the diamonds were far away.

§ § §

Georges drove the garbage truck he had leased at a high price for a few hours from a very willing driver back to the parking lot next to his hotel in a seedy section of Northeast Washington where he had stayed the first night. Before leaving the Freshest Fish Market, he had promised to call Luis later to verify that the diamonds were real. There would also be a call to Rafik, a message sent to Paris, "and there should also have been a call to Ahmed," Georges thought with some regret. The plan had been so well organized—and well carried out, so far. It was a pity that Ahmed had somehow removed himself from the action. But if there was good news and all their demands had been met, there was no need for Ahmed any more. If they had been double-crossed by the US Government, several things would happen next.

Now, back in the parking lot, George carefully removed the two bags from the back of the garbage truck and placed them in a lead-lined box in the trunk of his rental car, which was parked a few feet away. He had brought a second box, but the bags both fit into the larger box. He had already checked out of the hotel. He drove the rental car a few blocks away, pulling into a parking garage near Union Station.

As soon as he was in the parking garage, he took the box with the diamonds out of the trunk and put it in the back seat of the car. He got in the back seat himself and closed the door. Opening the box, he took out the bags, unzipped them, and dumped all the diamonds into the box. He then took the two empty bags, which he strongly suspected of having some type of homing devices in them, and walked to a truck parked further down the aisle. The doors of the pick-up were locked but he was able to open the gate in the back. He tossed the bags into the truck's covered bed, closed its gate, and walked back to his car. He waited a few minutes to see if anyone came, then he drove out of the garage and headed for the hotel near Georgetown where he had a new reservation.

At the hotel, he self-parked in the underground garage. After checking in at the front desk, he returned to the garage. He went around to the trunk of the car and removed the box with the diamonds, which he placed on the passenger seat in the front of the car. He took out a flashlight and his jeweler's eyepiece. He sifted through the diamonds quickly with his hands, briefly testing their weight—it would be easy to spot fakes if some or most were synthetic, but he did not detect anything wrong.

Next, he took one out at random and looked at it with the eyepiece. A beautiful, clear, 3-carat diamond. He looked at another, and another. He saw that a few were yellow diamonds, more were white. He was almost satisfied most of these diamonds were genuine when he picked up one of the yellow ones with the tiny radio transmitter embedded. In the light of the flashlight, Georges was quite sure of what he was seeing. He closed the box. When he returned it to the trunk, he zipped the box into a large suitcase with wheels.

"Bastards!" he thought, not without some sense of triumph since they had all suspected the government would try to trick them somehow. Now he had some choices to make. Abandon all the diamonds here? No, too risky, and he was staying at this hotel, and maybe someone would see him take the boxes out of the car. "No point in giving them back all their money!" Take them up to the room and remove those with the radio transmitters? How many were there like that and could they find him even while he was examining them? Georges thought and came up with a plan.

He retrieved the box of diamonds and the empty box. While he avoided removing the diamonds all the way from the protective lead cover of the box this time, he began a manual sort for all the yellow diamonds—whether real or synthetic, hoping that he was right and that the white or clear diamonds had nothing wrong with them. Within ten minutes, he had a pile of yellow diamonds in the left box and a much larger pile of white diamonds in the right box. Now came the most dangerous part. He left the box with the yellow diamonds in the front seat and locked the other box back in the trunk, inside his large, wheeled suitcase. He started his engine and drove out of the garage; fortunately, his room key let him in and out without paying the attendant.

He then drove along Pennsylvania Avenue to Key Bridge, crossing the bridge into Virginia. He drove north on the George Washington Parkway, and as he drove, he lowered his window. It was dark now. He opened the box next to him with his right hand. Very carefully, he began transferring diamonds to his left hand, taking it off the wheel and steering with his knees. As he drove, he tossed a dozen yellow diamonds out onto the road. He then drove to the first overlook where he could turn off. He made the right-hand turn, got out of the car, and tossed the whole box with the remaining yellow diamonds and the synthetics, over the side of the wall into the upper Potomac River. "Let them dive for them!" he said to himself, knowing that the radio transmitters would not send signals under water. He got back in his car. He continued north to McLean and then took a circuitous route back to Georgetown. No point in getting into a police action on the GW Parkway, because by now it was likely the little radio transmitters were telling people where the diamonds were. And Georges was right. Within 10 minutes of his disposing of the first radio-equipped fake diamond on the road, a helicopter was hovering over the northbound Parkway.

Georges made his way back to Reagan Washington National Airport and parked in the Signature lot. This part of the airport was reserved for business jets. Luis's cousin Raphael was sitting in the passenger lounge, holding but not reading the most recent issue of Newsweek. Georges wheeled in his suitcase, sat down next to the man, and said, "I believe you need this for your flight."

Raphael looked up from the magazine, smiled, offered his hand to Georges, and said, "Why yes." No names were exchanged. The younger man went up to the service desk and said to the red-haired agent, "Please let my pilot know that I can be ready any time now."

"Certainly, sir, your flight plan calls for a departure in 30 minutes. I will let him know." Without any further exchanges, Georges got up and left, returning to his car and heading back to his hotel. He had not been followed. He had some calls to make. It would be interesting to see if Paris wanted to activate Plan B.

CHAPTER SEVENTY-ONE
Evening, June 12, in Northern Virginia

Saleeth allowed Andy Shannon to seat her at one of the tables toward the back of Magianno's Little Italy at Tyson's Corner. He ordered a Heineken; she ordered a glass of Merlot, and they settled back. Andy decided to start without preamble. "We think your brother may be in the DC area, and we believe he is linked to the spread of the poisons, although clearly there is some larger group behind this. We don't know exactly what his role is. We also have reason to believe that his own people think he has betrayed them—or at least is acting as a double-agent, so they may be after him, too." He did not add that Ahmed might already be dead.

"This makes it tricky, because to get any kind of message to him, even from you, we have to know who can reliably deliver it—and how. We know he—they—are using the media. His first message was on CNN, and he later called in to the *Washington Post*. So, we could try that route." Andy and his colleagues had discussed the pros and cons of such a plan in detail, but he wanted to see how Saleeth would react to this suggestion.

"He would know it is a trap if you do something like that. Is there no one who can reach him, even indirectly, to tell him they know where his sister is?"

Andy paused, as if thinking about her suggestion. He could not tell her, just as he could not tell anyone in the Agency, that *he* had sent the message to the terrorist organization through a CIA sympathizer. Andy hoped the message would reach the top ranks of that organization. What he had told the low-level man was that Ahmed had betrayed al-Qaida by confiding in a relative who, as Andy had reported, "now works for the US Government." What had been done with the information was less clear, especially since it appeared that Ahmed had been alive as recently as today. Andy's intent had been to have Ahmed taken out by his own organization. That appeared not to have happened. Was Ahmed now acting on his own? Not likely, so he must still be in touch with members of the organization who trusted him—but who were they?

"We could try a different kind of media approach—something subtle. Several of the remaining big newspapers are willing to sell small personal ads on the bottom of the front page these days and they also run them near the lead stories on their web sites. We could run one that says something like, "Philip Miller—your sister is in town. Please call her at the Mayflower in Washington, DC" and run it in the *Washington Post*, the *New York Times* and the *LA Times*. People would probably think it's some kind of promotion for the Mayflower. Of course, it might not work, but we could give it two days and then try another strategy."

"And you think he is still in the US?"

"Well, today, there was an event—we complied, more or less, with the terrorists' demands. It happened in DC. We think Ahmed made a call to CNN, and he may have been near the action, although he could have moved on by now. We could try the ad, at least."

"And am I really staying at the Mayflower?"

"Yes, you are, but as Judith Abrams. However, we'll have another room adjacent registered to 'Saleeth' with a special female agent in it. The rooms are connected."

"And if he calls?"

"Our female agent who sounds like you will answer. She'll tell him she is not alone and to call back. We'll come and get you, or if he leaves a number, ask you to call. We will not leave you alone at any time. If he asks for a meeting, we will confer. Please don't worry—it is you we are thinking about first."

Saleeth sat back and looked at Andy. "It is *you* who are thinking of me first," she thought, with mixed emotions. She always liked him. He had been persuasive when she had first met him; they had had a close but never intimate relationship. After she had "come over," largely due to his persuasion, he had always treated her professionally but she knew he was interested in her. Perhaps without Raul in the picture—if he was in the picture—she could consider another level of relationship with Andy. "But this will have to wait," she thought, just as she had postponed any specific plans to see Raul. "I will sort this out later."

"If you think the ad will work, please try it. Perhaps we can think about other strategies, too," Saleeth said, draining her glass. She had finished her lasagna, and Andy was cleaning his plate after his veal special. Tiredness washed over her, but she knew he would want coffee—and more conversation.

"There is one other option. I have a cousin in Saudi. She has a contact who we think is or could be in touch with Ahmed. I can get word through her, to him, to get in touch with me, but we'd have to think of phone numbers or email addresses that would be safe for him to use."

This came as no surprise to Andy, since he assumed she had some remaining contacts from her old life, however infrequently she used them. "Let's try the newspaper and their web sites first," he replied. "That's quick, and if he's reading any of them and even if he's not in the Washington area, it might work. We'll wait for the two days, and if he hasn't made contact, we'll consider your foreign sources."

During the drive back to DC, they spoke little. When she checked in to the Mayflower, the female agent, Nania, who would be in the next room accompanied her on the elevator. Saleeth said good-by to Andy in the lobby; they shook hands. "See you tomorrow," he said, after she had thanked him for dinner. He did not say when or where or under what circumstances, but she knew she would be seeing a lot of Andy in the next few days.

CHAPTER SEVENTY-TWO
Evening, June 12, in Washington, DC

The first call Georges made after getting back to his room was to Luis. "We have mixed news," he began. "Most of the diamonds were real, but some were fake and they put radio transmitters in those. I got rid of them. They are all over the George Washington Parkway and in the Potomac! The good ones are on their way to the delivery point."

Luis was quiet for a moment and then said, "I see."

Georges continued. "I will notify Paris and, of course, Rafik. As I have not been able to speak with Ahmed recently, I will leave that up to Rafik. One of us will be back in touch with you. Thank you for all you have done."

After the call, Luis sat in his darkened apartment and thought. His loyalties were split between the cause and Ahmed who, while part of the cause, clearly was in trouble. "I must contact him," Luis thought. "Surely there can be nothing wrong with that." He had only one phone number that Ahmed had given him. He dialed it promptly.

After two rings, he heard Ahmed's voice, "yes?"

"No names," Luis said hastily, hoping Ahmed would recognize his voice. "Do you know who this is?"

"Yes!"

"We got the items. Some were fake and had radio transmitters. They are gone. The rest are on their way to their new home. I do not yet know what I am supposed to do. One of your friends is going to contact Paris to get instructions. Am I supposed to let them know, now, that you and I have talked?"

Ahmed had anticipated this question. With Rafik out of the way, he knew he should not trust Georges either, but now that the US Government had broken at least part of their promise, the next step in the plan would have to be activated. "If I am going to die, at least I can perhaps see that this gets done," Ahmed had thought, and he knew they needed Georges to help. "Call the person who called you tonight," he instructed Luis. "Tell him you are in touch with me but you do not know where I am. Tell him I will be involved if Paris orders that we take the next step, as I am sure they will. I will call you back in four hours with a new phone number where you can reach me. Do not call this phone again."

While Luis and Ahmed were having this conversation, Georges tried repeatedly to reach Rafik but without success. "He should have called me before now," Georges reasoned. In any event, Georges felt it was now up to him to make the call to Paris and get instructions.

He dialed the first contact number he had, knowing it was very early morning in Europe. The phone was picked up on the third ring. "Travel agency," said a male voice.

"I am calling to report on a trip," Georges said, hoping that whomever he was speaking to would recognize the code.

Abu responded, "Go ahead, please."

"A package is on its way to you. It is not complete but it is of value. They tried to place transmitters in some of the items, which I have gotten rid of. I have not been able tonight to reach either of my principal colleagues. The one whom you wanted returned has been missing for several days, but it is he who has been delivering the messages to the press. The other one is not answering his phone. I need instructions about our next steps."

Abu had not slept that night. In fact, he had been watching CNN International and various other channels. Nothing had been reported about the diamonds, but it had been reported that two suspected international terrorists whom the US had apparently been holding in undisclosed locations were being returned to their home countries. Egypt verified that Mohammed Haru had landed on Egyptian soil. There was no official confirmation from Pakistan about Pavez Riari, but a BBC stringer reported that Riari had been secretly returned to a military base near Karachi. Earlier, Abu had seen a CNN report that one of the former Guantanamo prisoners, a middle-aged man called Ali, had already been repatriated to Saudi Arabia. The report went on to say that the US was speeding up efforts to repatriate an undisclosed number of other such prisoners, all currently being held in the US in local prisons.

"So, they are doing most of it," Abu blurted out to Georges. "But now, they have shown bad faith with the diamonds." Secretly he hoped they would have to activate the next step in their plan, for he felt it was in its own way far more ominous in terms of a threat that would tell the corrupt US Government that the movement could penetrate to their very heart. "Killing people with poisons should scare them but we need to show them we can strike at their heart any time—we are many, and our cause is just, and they do not have a way to stop us, so they must cooperate.

"We will activate Plan B. You will have to contact your friend who runs the fish market and tell him it is time. The package he needs must be sent from the factory. If you cannot reach the 'chauffer', you must call the lab to have the package shipped. Time is of the essence. If there is any opportunity, the actions should take place in the next five days. Some of that will depend on circumstances and what your fish market friend is able to arrange. Be sure he is paid well this week—he has earned it. Call back here in twenty-four hours and give us a progress report. I may not be here but someone will answer."

Georges tried again to contact Rafik but failed. He decided to make one more call to Luis to tell him that his services would be needed. He dialed the now familiar number.

But before he could even mention his conversation with the "travel agency," Luis said in a low voice, "there is something I must tell you. I am in contact with Ahmed. He wants to talk with you."

Georges' adrenalin started pumping. "So he's alive!" he said to himself. To Luis he said, "Arrange it and let me know how the contact can be made."

CHAPTER SEVENTY-THREE
June 13

Jeff's conference call got underway at 11 a.m. "What is the CDC reporting about the outbreaks?" Eileen asked.

Jeff gave the report. "Cleveland still has about 250 people hospitalized, but they have not admitted anyone new in the last 24 hours. Two of the people in Boulder whom we thought were decontaminated have also died—both were elderly. CDC is still getting reports of contaminated water sources but most are in the West and Midwest. The death toll nationwide appears to be under five hundred, but that could be revised upwards if some of the people being treated cannot be saved or we find more anthrax contamination where it's too late to help." He paused. None of them mentioned the few dissident politicians and rabble rousing talk show hosts calling for an investigation of all their agencies and for the President's resignation.

"Are we any closer to identifying who arranged for the boat that collected the diamonds, and are any of the transmitters working?" Paul asked.

Eileen answered. "Apparently they got rid of all the stones with the transmitters—we found some on the GW Parkway near one of the pullovers, and we've dredged some out of the Potomac. So, we have temporarily lost track of the shipment. As for the boat, there were no markings, it was old, and we are trying to trace where it might have been bought. We've interviewed everyone who owns or rents establishments along the waterfront in southwest DC and so far nothing has turned up. We assume there was a transfer of the bags after they cut them out of the bait well but we don't know where they went from there. All of the merchants on Water Street are going to be interviewed again."

Jeff continued, "The President thinks the terrorists will likely move to another kind of attack now within the US, as al-Kodari—or whoever it was—threatened to CNN. Does the Bureau or Homeland have any evidence of anything else underway? Are we still keeping close watch on all the borders?"

Paul decided to let Eileen go first. "We have all possible surveillance going on. And thanks to Maya, we have total cooperation from the military, but we're not seeing anything, at least nothing we can identify as unduly suspicious."

"I've asked to meet with Harold Harper this afternoon to brief him and also to ask him to give us more resources," Paul added, "but we don't know of anything new right now. The CDC and National Guard are standing by. They've cancelled all leave and are on high alert."

"Let's just think for a few minutes about what would be their most likely next step—that is, if they are going to do anything right away." Jeff tried to sound patient.

"Maybe it won't be something massive, like the poisons," Paul offered. "They may want to make a statement, something that would be frightening but not necessarily large. They have to know we are exercising peak surveillance. Or would they try something like a kidnapping or a killing of someone prominent, and if so, who would it be?"

Eileen and Jimmy both spoke at once, with Jimmy prevailing. "They could do that, but all our senior government people are getting extra protection now."

Jeff broke in. "If there is no more new intelligence, I'm going to tell the President what we have discussed, and I assume he will still want to address the nation at 9 p.m. If anyone learns anything before his talk, please call me and hold open a slot between 7 and 7:15 p.m. in case we need an emergency call to discuss any new developments."

Jeff sat in silence, staring out the window for a few minutes. He was worried about many things, not the least of which was the President himself. "At least he's safe as long as we can keep him in the White House and the Executive Office Building," Jeff thought, knowing how difficult that would be and wondering how long they would have to wait for the terrorists to play their next hand.

CHAPTER SEVENTY-FOUR

While the Trial Run conference call was going on, Georges Labadie, dressed as a Texan, complete with boots and hat, sat on a park bench in DuPont Circle, holding a Starbucks cup and the *Washington Post* in his lap. He had been sitting on the bench for ten minutes when an orderly, apparently from some nearby hospital, sauntered up to the same bench and sat down. He, too, had a Starbucks and the *Post*. After a few seconds of silence, he spoke. "Rafik is dead. He had an unfortunate accident. You will read on page B-4 of the *Post* about an unidentified body found yesterday on E Street. He was given some bad information. I take it you have talked with Paris. What is the order?"

Georges' eyebrows raised a fraction but he controlled his curiosity. "We are to proceed with Plan B. As our friend was to have obtained the package, I take it you have it or know how to get it?"

"I've arranged it. Is Luis ready?"

"I gave him the instructions from Paris and he is. It's only a question of which day, and we will have to wait for him to tell us that, but there should be plenty of opportunities."

"This coming Saturday would be the best, I think, but I will stay in touch with Luis."

"Where can I reach you?"

"Give me your contacts, and I will reach you," Ahmed answered. "I cannot afford to let anyone know my whereabouts—even you may have the same bad information that Rafik had."

Georges did not let himself show any expression. "I never believe bad information. Besides, I have a well-placed source, as you know, and I do not want to jeopardize my ability to work with them just now. You are safe from me." Georges handed Ahmed a slip of paper with two cell phone numbers written on it, plus the name of his hotel.

Ahmed pocketed the paper. "I will arrange to get the package to Luis today. I will give him a contact number where you can reach me in an emergency or if you get more information from your source. Will you be in touch with your source soon?"

Georges shrugged.

Ahmed stood. "Thank you for your part; it has been well played." Then he walked away.

Georges watched him go and sat for several more seconds before getting up. It was time to see if Harold was up for some fun and games.

CHAPTER SEVENTY-FIVE

The package was in Kamal's safe, waiting to be sent, following instructions from either Rafik or Ahmed. Since Rafik was permanently unable to issue those instructions, Ahmed used one of his disposable cell phones to call Kamal in the early afternoon.

"It's me," Ahmed said, "safe and well and proceeding. Thank you for wiring the money. Now, I need you to send our special box. It must go to the Fish Market." He gave Kamal the address and reminded him to put it to Luis' attention. "Please have it sent out today."

Kamal was excited to hear from Ahmed and wanted to ask several questions, but he refrained. "It will be done. Will you be there long?"

"A few more days, perhaps. I will be in touch. All is well." Ahmed rang off. He needed to see Luis and called him next. "Meet me on the Mall near the hot dog vendor in an hour, if you can."

"I'll be there!" Luis said, trying not to let his excitement show.

Ahmed took the subway and then walked the last block. It was a warm day, and he was still dressed as an orderly. He had bought the clothes at a Pennsylvania Avenue shop specializing in uniforms. The green outfit helped keep him cool. When Luis arrived, they began walking slowly toward the reflecting pool.

"You will need to offer your services for your special work this week," Ahmed began.

Luis had expected this. "I have already called my friend, Dimitri, and he is looking at the schedule. It looks like a dinner on Saturday might be the first chance, but there could be something sooner."

"Saturday would be good. It's the Norwegian ambassador, isn't it?" Ahmed asked.

Luis nodded. "And two nights later, the Arts Awards, and I think another head of state later in the week."

"You will be receiving a package from Colorado tomorrow. It will contain everything you need, but we will talk. I will call you tomorrow evening. I hope by then that you may know your assignment schedule." Luis nodded. Ahmed clapped him on the back, "and don't worry about your own safety—we will get you out of there so that you will be in no danger."

"Thank you, but my safety is not as important as the cause. I am proud to help."

"You did well with the diamonds—thank you. They will help us greatly, even if the Americans tried to harm us. But we expected that. They are not to be trusted. But perhaps after our next message they will be more willing to cooperate."

§ § §

Georges Labadie, sitting in his expensive hotel room in Georgetown, overlooking the Potomac, was also leaving a message—this time, for Harold Harper. To be on the safe side, he called Harold's personal cell phone, and left a short message on the voice mail. "I'm in town. Send me a message and let me know if you are available for lunch or dinner." He had no doubt Harold would recognize the voice of his friend, Svi.

But when Harold called him back about fifteen minutes later, he sensed some hesitation in Harold's voice. "This is a difficult time for me," Harold began after they exchanged greetings and Georges repeated his invitation to get to-gether. "And I don't really think I should see you in the city."

"Can you get away to meet me somewhere else, then, say in the next day or so? I have some time I can spend here on the East Coast," Georges asked as pleasantly as possible. He never wanted to seem too eager.

"I have a friend in Annapolis who lets me use his house for the month while he is on an assignment in Japan. He comes home Saturday. We can meet there tonight if you want. He has a housekeeper, but I can give her the evening off."

"Perfect—just give me the address and I'll Google the directions." Harold told him the address and Georges began firing up his laptop while they were still on the telephone. "I hope you will have many things to tell me?"

"Oh, yes, and even more by tonight," Harold answered, now with a bit more enthusiasm. They agreed to meet at 6 p.m.

Georges checked his watch. Should he call Paris and tell them that Rafik was probably dead? "But if I do that, I have to reveal how I know—and I may get an order I don't want to hear," he thought. "Besides, I only have Ahmed's word on this. It's really none of my affair." Georges had worked for more than one organization in his long and elusive life. He did not intend to feel trapped into continuing to work for this one, even though he generally supported the cause. "Let's get through this week first," he thought. After that, he could re-assess his personal situation.

§ § §

Saleeth saw Raul's text message just after 1 p.m. It read: "I'm back home. Can I come to visit you in DC?" She and Nania had strolled out to a small French restaurant on Connecticut Avenue. She showed Nania the message. "He's a personal friend—but he's also Agency. I need to answer so he will not think anything is wrong."

"Does he know who *you* are?" Nania asked. She had only been briefed on this part of Saleeth's evidently complicated life two days before.

"No, he doesn't. It's purely a relationship that developed because of my non-profit foundation job." Saleeth paused. Right now, she did not feel her life was her own, but she felt a need to confide in someone. "But I like him—he is someone with whom I would not like to lose touch."

"OK, but don't encourage him to come here. Maybe you'd better call him today? He might be more persuaded if he hears from you."

"I'll do that," Saleeth answered and quickly typed a text message. It read: "I'll call you at your apartment tonight at 7 p.m. your time. If you cannot be there then, give me a number where I can reach you." She sat back, feeling that while she had little control over events, she was at least going to be able to talk with Raul.

CHAPTER SEVENTY-SIX

In Europe, during the middle of the afternoon on Wednesday, Abu made a phone call to Russia. Vassilly answered and sounded as if he was in a very good mood. After listening to Abu's news, he said, "So, they tried to trace the diamonds, did they? Typical—and stupid. But that is what we are dealing with. I trust you have commanded that the next step be taken?"

Abu paused. He was growing to dislike Vassilly's tone of superiority. After all, Russia was not calling the shots in this. "Yes, we are going to take the next step but we need to deliver a very clear message after we do that so they know we have the upper hand. We'll also ask, of course, for another payment—this time with a wire transfer. But I must tell you that, given the lack of success of our poisons on the east coast in America, we suspect that *your* part in helping us to use your satellites was not successful."

Vassilly caught the irritation in Abu's voice. "Of course your people will take care of the next step—and they will be successful. Remember, our attack killed hundreds of people and our demands are being met. And I am doing what I can here to ensure that our leadership is fully in line with your objectives. We have had one bad actor, I think, but I do not expect him to cause any more problems. Is there anything more you need from me at the moment?"

"No, but I will be in touch when we do. It may be soon." Abu hung up. It was becoming difficult to know whom to trust these days. Even in his own family he knew there were dissenters. "But I am carrying on *his* cause," he thought, as he had many times, and that thought strengthened him.

CHAPTER SEVENTY-SEVEN

J ust before 2:00 p.m. on Wednesday, Jeff's secretary rang through to let him know Jimmy Buttero was on the line.

"Jeff, I want to talk to you about the President's address tonight. We learned from Eileen that there was a dead body discovered down on E Street yesterday. Normal police records did not turn up anything on his identity, but the DC Chief of Police had the presence of mind to call the Bureau because he'd heard something about the events in the Potomac. I guess he thought it suspicious that a man who looked to be a well-dressed foreigner was found dead without any papers. We've combined forces and come up with something interesting on the victim after we checked the fingerprints with Interpol.

"He is an Algerian national, Rafik Muhaimin, and he's used a number of aliases. He's also been connected with al-Qaida. The police found a matchbook from the JW Marriott in one of his pockets. We checked the hotel and found that they had a guest who registered as Silvio Franchetti, which was close to one of his known aliases. Their guest has gone missing, so he's probably the victim. This may be nothing, but if Muhaimin's one of the people involved in the poison attacks, it would be a good thing, don't you think, if the President could say we've taken him out? No need to say he is dead."

Jeff sat back in his chair. Giving the President some good news to report would improve everyone's outlook, but they had to be careful not to appear to be further reneging on the deal they had agreed to with the terrorists. "Jimmy, let me talk with him about it. He may not want to say anything or be very specific yet. If he wants more information, should I call you or Eileen?"

"Call Eileen—she told me she'd be completely available to talk with you about this or anything else."

Elliott Bradley listened intently to Jeff's information on the phone and invited Jeff to come to the Oval Office. By the time Jeff stepped through the door, Elliott had all but made up his mind. "Jeff, if we talk about one of the terrorists being dead, they might think we are not moving ahead with the supposed repatriation of the Guantanamo prisoners or with pushing to remove the sanctions. Hopefully, they believe we have moved Haru and Riari. What are our friends in the news media doing to help us?"

"All major media are reporting consistently that the Guantanamo prisoners are being readied for transport back to their home countries or to Turkey or Australia, where, as you know, their officials have agreed to play along. We don't think there have been any leaks about what is really going on. Also, our U.N. Ambassador is speaking again this afternoon about removing sanctions on Arab countries. Of course, we know that Israel and England will help us by blocking any vote. We have to assume the terrorists know that we had fake diamonds in the package since we found so many of them on the GW Highway and in the Potomac, but they would still have gotten about one hundred million dollars worth of real stones. So, we don't know if all of this points to their working on another attack—or not. Would you even want to consider postponing the speech?"

"I think the people want to hear from me, even if it's not with a complete story," the President said, easing himself into a straight-backed chair. Lately, his back bothered him.

"There is one more reason you might want to wait," Jeff began. "We have a reasonable hope of contacting the man al-Kodari, who may be the ring-leader, and if we can contact him, we should be able to capture him. Would you rather wait and see if that happens in the next couple of days?"

"Are you that close?" the President asked.

"We hope so—either the procedure we have set up will work quickly or not at all."

"I'll still make the address, but I'll keep it brief and hint that we may have more to say later this week. But I'm prepared to cancel tonight at the last minute—and I'm relying on you and your team to let me know if I should do so."

Jeff felt he must make a formal statement. "Mr. President, your key agency people are doing everything possible to get to the bottom of all this and give you reason to reassure the American people, but we are all very concerned for your safety."

The President looked up from his chair at Jeff, who looked back at the President gravely. "Oh, Jeff, I know you are all doing everything you can—and we'll beat them. I'd like it to be without any more deaths, but we have to be realistic and recognize this may not be the end." Elliott stood and moved over to Jeff, putting his arm around Jeff's shoulder. "We'll have a break through soon, and I'll be careful. Hang in there."

CHAPTER SEVENTY-EIGHT

Afternoon, June 13, in Moscow and Washington, DC

Pyotr remained in the Moscow hospital. They had decided to leave the bullet near his heart and not perform a second operation; he was gaining strength by the day. He had no illusions that he was not under some kind of house arrest, and he was concerned for his life but much more so for Elena. He thought about escaping but could not figure out how to do it. He also thought about trying to contact President Lebrovny directly—but perhaps the Russian President was involved with the terrorists' plot? And then, one sunny morning, as he lay in bed, watching the birds out his window, he knew what he could do. It might not be successful, but he had to try. He reached for the pad of paper and pencil that he was allowed to keep near the bed. Elena would visit within the hour. He began to write, in English.

When Elena arrived later, she bent over and kissed him on both cheeks and while she did so, he whispered, "I'm going to give you a letter. It's for Maya—you must find a way to send it securely. It's under the sheet below my right hand." She prolonged her embrace and then pretended to fluff up his pillows while reaching under the sheet. She slid the paper out and put it into her large handbag without looking at it. It felt like just one sheet of note-paper. Elena had many friends in Moscow, and she knew that getting a letter to one of them to be mailed, faxed or even hand-carried out of the country should not be difficult.

Later that afternoon, she invited herself for tea with a British friend who graciously agreed to hand-carry the letter the next day upon her return to London and to fax it from there. In the scheme of things, it would help that Elena's friend was actually with MI-5 and did, in fact, read the document she was carrying. She dutifully took it with her on her long airplane ride, faxed it to a special number in Washington, DC, and made a copy of it, giving the original to her superior.

He raised his eyebrows when he read it. "Are you sure this is authentic?" he asked her.

"Almost certainly—his wife handed it to me, and she did not appear to be under duress."

"Our Prime Minister will be interested in this, I think," said the head of MI-5 and rang a number that he knew well.

§ § §

When Maya's special assistant received a "top secret" fax late in the afternoon, she immediately delivered it to Maya, who read the letter twice. Then she picked up the phone to call Jeff. When she learned he was with the President, she asked to be transferred in to their meeting. "Mr. President, if it's possible, I'd like to come across the river to meet with both of you," she said. "It's important." They agreed immediately.

Maya arrived at the Oval Office and handed the President and Jeff copies of the fax. The original was in a safe in her office. President Bradley's first question was, "Is this authentic?"

"I've personally talked with the British agent who faxed it, and she received it from Elena, Pyotr's wife, yesterday. I also recognize this as Pyotr's handwriting, so yes, I have no reason to believe it is anything but authentic."

"But he is accusing one of the highest officials in the Russian Government of being part of a terrorist plot against the US—and he wants me to contact President Lebrovny to have this man, this Vassilly, taken out of commission!"

"Mr. President, we have to think about the down-side if you don't contact Lebrovny. If this Vassilly is part of the plot, he has already tried to kill Pyotr and stop the GLONASS reprogramming—and we don't know what else he may be doing even now. If he's not a part of anything, it could be embarrassing for you and even for President Lebrovny but that would not be as bad as letting him continue."

"There's another alternative," Elliott offered, starting to pace. "I can talk with President Lebrovny, tell him what we know although not necessarily how we know it, and ask him to put Vassilly Rementrov under surveillance with very tight security. They may need to do that anyway to find out what else he is up to."

"Mr. President, if I may," Maya began. "I think you may have to tell President Lebrovny how we got this information, or he may not act. Of course, if Lebrovny is himself involved, then there is no hope. In any event, I think it would be good if Pyotr and Elena could somehow be removed immediately from Russia and from the influence of Rementrov but done in such a way as not to arouse Rementrov's suspicions."

"And how, exactly, should I suggest that President Lebrovny spirit the Olenshinskys out of the country?"

"There is an international conference on advanced missiles and surveillance satellites starting in two days in Hamburg, Germany. We have six people going. Surely, the President of Russia could order Col. Olenshinsky to attend? I gather he is more or less under house arrest in the hospital, but he says he is well enough to get out, so he could be flown to Germany. We can work with the Germans on providing security for him once he is there."

"And perhaps we could even have one or two of our people go to the hospital to escort him in light of his injuries? I like it—so that's the tack I'll take!" President Bradley said, with a small smile. "Though I don't think I'll mention tonight in my talk to the nation that we now think a renegade Russian or Russians may be behind all this!"

As Jeff and Maya left the President, he was already on his phone, asking his assistant to set up an urgent call to President Lebrovny in Russia.

CHAPTER SEVENTY-NINE
Early evening, June 13, in Annapolis, MD

Georges arrived at the house in Annapolis just ahead of Harold Harper, so he waited in his rental car in the driveway. "I need to know where their government has increased security," he thought to himself. He could guess that the borders were heavily guarded.

When Harold pulled up in his own car, an aging BMW, he greeted Georges and immediately invited him in. "Do you like the view?" The two men settled into white leather chairs overlooking a veranda that led down to a dock where a 25-foot Grady White rested on a lift overlooking the Chesapeake Bay.

"Americans live well," Georges thought, not for the first time. "So," he began, after Harold had thanked and dismissed the housekeeper and their first round of drinks had been poured, "How is your government dealing with these terrorists now? I haven't seen anything about more cities being attacked."

"We hope that is over," Harold answered, frowning slightly, "and the President is going on the air tonight to say so. But we are worried that there might be another attack planned. The terrorists made demands, and we haven't met all of them exactly as specified. The one who called CNN last week said that if we didn't meet their demands, they would launch a second attack in the US and in two weeks on one of our allies. We are, of course, concerned about Israel, and I'm sure you know that our people are working with your people at the highest levels."

Georges, of course, neither knew nor cared anything about what was being done with or for Israel, but as "Svi" he had to pretend interest. "Yes, the cooperation between our two countries is excellent, and the Brits are helping, too. Maybe even the Russians, although we don't trust them very much. But this must be taking up all of your time!"

"It's taking up the time of lots of people. We have increased security along the Canadian and Mexican borders and along the Atlantic and Pacific coasts. Of course, we can't watch every movement. The President's concerned that we have so much unguarded coast line and that the terrorists might try to bring in weapons or poisons by boat or small plane—or even try a kidnapping and get someone out via the water or by air."

This was useful information for the future, but so far nothing indicated that the Americans knew what might actually happen next. "You say that your government has not met all the terrorists' demands. What haven't you done?"

"Well, we planted radio devices in fake diamonds that were mixed in with the real diamonds that they demanded. They found most of the fakes, we think, and took the real ones. And, we're pretending to move some Guantanamo prisoners but we won't move them all. If we have to move some, they are going to Turkey and Australia." Harold decided not to say anything about Haru and Riari as he did not know how much had been shared between US intelligence and Israeli intelligence.

"And what about President Bradley? Is he canceling all engagements and going in to hiding?"

"Not at all. He is insisting that it's business as usual at the White House."

Georges continued to interrogate Harold about various security measures being taken. As he usually did after he had met with Harold, he would go back to his hotel and record their conversations on his iPod. Georges had an excellent memory. Tonight, he did not expect to learn much more of interest, but he wanted to watch President Bradley's address on TV with Harold. Eventually, he turned the conversation to golf and their next possible outing. After more than an hour of enjoying drinks and the view of the Bay, they moved into the spacious kitchen to enjoy a supper of crab soup, cold roast beef, baked potatoes, and blueberry pie that the housekeeper had left for them.

They were having coffee when Harold said, "I forgot to tell you—we think there might be a Russian or Russians connected with these terrorists. I know that will interest your government since, as you said, you don't trust the Russians very much!"

Georges concealed his surprise and asked, "Is there someone or some group specifically that you suspect?"

"I don't know a name yet, but I'll find out. Maya Tchernov has a source that has apparently told her someone high up in the Russian government may be helping the terrorists. If it's true, we don't know the extent of the help— or how many other people could be involved." Harold knew Svi would like a name, and he made a mental note to ask Paul for all possible information on this subject.

CHAPTER EIGHTY

Evening, June 13

Two hours before the President's address to the nation, Jeff Sanchez sent a short text message to the Trial Run team to let them know there would not be a conference call but that he was still available if anyone had late-breaking information that he should deliver to the President. The only person who did have information for him was President Bradley himself, who called Jeff at 7:15 p.m. to report on his phone call with President Lebrovny.

"Jeff, I honestly don't think he knew anything about how Rementrov may have tried to stop the GLONASS reprogramming. He trusts and admires Pyotr Olenshinsky and was quite amenable to our having him invited to the conference in Germany and also to providing him with an escort to get there. Lebrovny is notifying the hospital himself that Col. Olenshinsky is to be discharged tomorrow and that one or two from our embassy will be assisting him in his departure. We have to get him the name of our people, so please arrange that within the hour."

Jeff thanked the President and immediately put in a call to Maya. "Let's use two of your people who work at the embassy," Jeff suggested. They reviewed names and came up with two experienced agents who worked directly for Defense but with the cover of low-ranking diplomats.

When they hung up, Jeff went through the approved route to get a message to President Lebrovny as to who the US would be assigning from their embassy to escort Col. Olenshinsky. He wondered briefly if Pyotr would be suspicious and perhaps not want to leave with the Americans, but Maya had assured him that she would inform Elena of the plan.

Jeff then contacted a high level official in MI-5 to tell him about the plan to get Pyotr out of Russia—a plan about which his contact in MI-5 heartily approved.

"We'll have to work together to keep him safe after the conference— maybe move him from Germany to London or to the US," the MI-5 official suggested.

At 9 p.m., when the pool feed camera zoomed in on President Bradley, he looked rested and composed. "My fellow citizens, I wanted to speak with you again tonight to report on our progress in containing the vicious poison attack on our country that has concerned and affected all of us." As he spoke, detailing the status of those cities that had been hardest hit and noting the number of people still hospitalized, his voice was firm but gentle.

When he reached the middle of his speech, however, his voice dropped a note and his eyes narrowed. "We have good information now about who the key people are behind this attack. I will have more to report to you about this in the very near future. We also know that this is not the work of any government, although the people involved may in some cases work for foreign governments." He then detailed many of the security measures being taken by Homeland Security. As he reached the end of the talk, the camera came in for a last tight shot.

"We will take any and all steps necessary to ensure that the American people will be safe in their homes, in their schools, in their workplaces, in their places of worship. I value the cooperation of every citizen in this endeavor. I will be back with you as soon as we have meaningful information. Good night and God bless America."

CHAPTER EIGHTY-ONE

Raul watched the end of President Bradley's speech while frequently checking his watch. He knew Judith was supposed to call promptly at 7 p.m. West Coast time—if she could—and he knew what he wanted to say. His phone, however, rang at 6:25 p.m., and he picked it up on the first ring.

"Hi. Can we go secure?" he heard and immediately recognized the voice of one of his closest friends, Cornel Pollock, at the Agency. After he had taken the necessary precautions, Cornel said, "You remember a couple of months ago when you asked me to check out the new lady you were dating, Judith Abrams?"

Raul's hand froze on the phone. "Yes?"

"And I said we had no records on her. Well, I'm on a new assignment as of this week which lets me into some compartments I didn't have access to before, and as part of what I've learned, Judith Abrams doesn't exist. 'Judith Abrams' is a legend we've invented."

Raul sat back heavily into the soft red sofa cushions. "Are you telling me she's *Agency*? Or something else?"

"She works with us, yes, and she's also under deep cover. Her real last name is al-Kodari. Her first name is Saleeth. Her brother is Ahmed al-Kodari. He's a known bad guy, and right now we think he may be one of the leaders in the recent poison attacks. She 'came over' two years ago after being recruited by one of our agents. She's solid, but I thought you should know in case you're still seeing her."

Raul needed time to absorb this. "Thanks for the call. I have seen her a couple of times. Don't know if she was ever going to tell me! I'll be careful."

In the intervening minutes before his next call, Raul tried to readjust his thinking. She had played the part so perfectly that he had never suspected she was anything other than what she had led him to believe. But did that change his feelings for her? She had to maintain her cover—perhaps she even felt herself to be in some danger now if her brother might be one of the terrorists involved in the attacks. Would she ever have confided in him? Could they have any future together? His quandary continued right up until the moment the phone rang.

He picked it up immediately and heard her voice. "Judith, I'm so glad we can finally talk. How are you? How is your visit going?" He tried to keep his voice as normal as possible.

"We have some difficulties here, but I hope to be back in California before too long. And how was your trip?"

"Successful, tiring, a bit boring with all the time on the airplanes." He paused. "Judith, I have some free time, and I'd really like to see you. What if I fly there tomorrow? Can you spare a little time for us to be together? I'm perfectly happy to do some sightseeing while you're in meetings, but maybe we could at least have a quiet dinner somewhere."

She had known he would want to come. And she wanted to see him. What if her assignment proved futile? She would then, of course, simply go back to California. But if Ahmed found her and agreed to see her—then what would happen? Raul might come, and she might not be able to be with him at all. Still, he was Agency, too, and perhaps she could get permission to confide in him. But would that really be wise? "Raul, I do miss you, but right now is not a good time. I must try to get this grant, and then I'll be back in California as soon as I can. And we can talk each day!"

He heard the slight note of uncertainty in her voice. "I don't want to interfere with your work," he said, truthfully, "but I hope we can be together soon. We have important things to talk about."

"If this is a good time to talk, I'll call you again tomorrow. If I can't call at this time, I'll send you a text message."

He knew he had to be satisfied with that, for now. "I'll be here, waiting for your call!" he said, trying to hide his disappointment. After they hung up, he went to his computer to check out flights to Washington. "Just in case," he said to himself.

§ § §

Another phone call took place later that night, between Georges and Abu, after Georges had returned to his hotel room. "Sorry to wake you," he said politely when Abu answered his phone, "but I have two pieces of information that cannot wait. First, it's business as usual with the leader, so that should mean a normal schedule. Secondly, they think a highly placed Russian might be involved. You don't have to confirm or deny that to me, but I thought you should know. And they seem to know who it is. I'll get a name as soon as possible from my source."

"You did the right thing to call me," the sleepy voice said. "I will await your full report." There was no more conversation. Abu did not go back to sleep that night. Georges composed and sent to Abu a coded text message, detailing all the information learned from Harold. Then, he watched a late movie and slept peacefully.

CHAPTER EIGHTY-TWO
June 14

On Thursday morning, Ahmed followed what had become his temporary routine. He left the lobby of his hotel, bought a *Washington Post* from a street vendor, and slipped into a small coffee shop for a light breakfast. He always scanned the first few pages of the *Post* to see if it said anything about the attacks and what the US Government knew. He finished a front-page story about the President's address from the previous evening and was about to turn the page when his eye stopped at the small personal ad at the left-hand bottom of the page.

It read: "My brother, I am staying at the Mayflower Hotel in Washington, DC, under our family name. I need your help. Please call me. Saleeth." A telephone number that he assumed to be that of the Mayflower's switchboard followed. Ahmed carefully put down his coffee cup. His hand was shaking. "There could be more than one Saleeth," he thought to himself, "but this could be her! Or, this could be a trap." But what kind of trap? And what if this ad really was placed by his sister—how would she know what city he was in?

Ahmed hastily paid for his breakfast and rushed out to the same street vendor's stall. "Do you have the *New York Times*, the *Chicago Tribune, The Dallas Morning News*, and *The Los Angeles Times*?" he asked. "Coming up," the young black man said, and laid all four newspapers in front of Ahmed. "That'll be six dollars and sixty-five cents," he said, and the money was in his hand almost before he had finished speaking.

Ahmed sat down on a park bench to check the four papers. There, in the same position in the *New York Times* and *The Los Angeles Times* was the identical ad. "So she doesn't know where I am—but she thinks I might see this!" he thought, somewhat relieved since he felt that if the ad ran only in Washington, someone must know he was here and it might not be Saleeth. "But where has she been?" he asked himself. "And if she is dead, then who is placing these ads?"

Instead of going back to his hotel, Ahmed strolled in the small park and then for several blocks on the city streets in this pleasant Washington suburb, almost losing track of where he was. He reviewed carefully the options he had and the probable consequences. Always he came back to one essential thought: if she really had placed the ad, and if she was alive and in trouble, he had to contact her. "Even the next step of our crusade can go on without me," he admitted to himself. "If this is a trap and I am caught, our cause will proceed." With that in mind, he started back to his hotel. There was a pay phone in a booth in the lobby. He dialed the number from the newspaper ad.

As it happened, Nania and Saleeth were together in Nania's room. The switchboard knew to route any calls to "Saleeth al-Kodari" to the room registered under that name, which was Nania's room. When the phone rang at 8:48 a.m., Nania answered. "Yes?"

There was a pause at the other end, and then she heard a voice say, "May I please speak to Saleeth?" Nania mouthed to Saleeth "it's him," and handed over the receiver.

"This is Saleeth. Who is this, please?" she said, trying to keep her voice steady.

Another pause, then, "Tell me the names of our four cousins on our mother's side."

Saleeth repeated the names of the two girls and two boys.

"And which one hit you with a tennis ball, and how old were you when it happened?"

"It was Yasir—he was ten and I was seven. You told him you would tell his father, and he begged you not to and then he gave me a sweet." A sound like a long, drawn out sigh came over the line. But she had her own game to play. "And now I must know who this is. What did I give you for your fifteenth birthday and what did our mother say?"

"It was a book—a book of pictures about Paris, and our mother said she would take us both when you were older. I said I would rather go to New York!"

"Ahmed? Are you somewhere we can talk? I am with my friend, but I can talk in front of her. I am so glad you found my message. I don't know what city you are in—or even what country!"

"I can talk, but I want to see you first. I am in Washington, DC, on business. Are you in any danger? Where have you been? I have been trying to find you for two years!"

She heard the agitation in his voice and the rising anger. "Ahmed, I made a very unwise marriage. But I am gone from him now. It is possible he may try to find me, even harm me, so I must be careful. My friend, Nania, is helping me. Her family lives in this area. I will meet you but only in a public place and with Nania nearby. Do you know the Washington Monument? We could meet near the street vendors' stands. Please understand that I want to trust you, but I have to be sure you have not been put up to finding me by *him*," she paused slightly, reviewing her script in her mind. "He is of our faith, so he is, perhaps, someone you know." She, Andy and the other agents had discussed whether she should say this to Ahmed, but concluded that she had to show some reason to be cautious about meeting him, so this was the story.

Ahmed had to think quickly. If this was a trap, he should not accept her invitation under any circumstances. If they were going to meet at all, it would be better if he selected the place of meeting and made sure it was secluded and that they were completely alone. On the other hand, how could he ensure this? She could have agents prepared to follow her anywhere. If they met inside a building, it could be surrounded. Meeting her in public might be best anyway, as he could slip away if there were other people around. She sounded frightened, and he had never known Saleeth to pretend to emotions she did not feel—or to lie to him. Furthermore, if her need was legitimate, he could not allow her to think that he was in any kind of danger or needed concealment.

He made his decision. "I have meetings until 3:30 today. Go near the Monument at 4:00. I will look for a vendor who sells coffee. But, really, I can come to your hotel room then, too. Wouldn't that be better?"

They had anticipated that he might counter her proposal and suggest a different place. "Ahmed, I am sorry, but I need to know that you will not be bringing anyone with you. I know this sounds silly, and I am very sorry for what I have put you through. Please—let's just meet today and I can tell you things. I would so very much like to go home when this is all over!"

His heart melted. She could be nothing but sincere, he knew now. "I will be there. If you cannot come, I will call you again this evening at your hotel room. Stay with your friend at all times." He was about to tell her he loved her and forgave her for all she had put him through, but he knew he could tell her this in person later. "Saleeth, my dear sister, I will take care of you!" he said and gently replaced the phone in its cradle. At least she had not asked him for his cell phone number. "I must be very careful this afternoon to seem normal," he thought, rising to stare out into the hotel lobby. So many months of waiting and now just a few hours. "Allah be praised!" he said out loud and smiled.

The FBI had put a trace on the call as soon as Nania had texted that he was on the line, but the call as too short for them to find the pay phone. No one was particularly worried, however: the plan had worked and he had agreed to a meeting.

CHAPTER EIGHTY-THREE

On Thursday at 1:00 p.m., a box from Colorado was delivered to Luis Jimenez at the Freshest Fish Market. Ahmed called Luis. When Luis heard Ahmed's voice, he said simply, "Our box has arrived."

"Good, and what have you heard about your assignment?"

"It will be for Saturday night. They have ordered from us, as usual, and I will report four hours before the event.

Ahmed was encouraged. "I will call if there is any change in the orders, but as of now, we want you to proceed. As I have told you, we won't abandon you."

Luis appreciated the reassurance, but since he had joined the movement, he had been prepared to die for the cause, if necessary. "I am not afraid. I am glad to help," he said simply, and Ahmed smiled for the second time that day but felt he needed to add something. "If anything happens to me that I cannot contact you further, you will hear from our other friend—and you can trust him." Ahmed certainly hoped Luis could trust Georges, who would be the only one left giving orders if he, Ahmed, met with some "accident." Even now, he was having second thoughts about the meeting with Saleeth, but he knew he would go.

§ § §

By 10 a.m. West Coast time, Raul had completed his trip report and was doing some reading on line. As usual, he scanned the major newspapers. He scrolled down to the bottom of the *Washington Post's* first page and stopped at the small personal ad. Was this his Saleeth?

"They are using her to lay a trap," he said out loud and banged his fist on his computer table. "They are putting her in danger!" Quickly, he pulled up flights from San Francisco to DC and found one that left at 2 p.m. He could just make it. He booked a first class seat, using his personal credit card. He would report to the Agency that he was taking two days' vacation—that should be enough. He knew he would have to check in when he got to DC, even though this was private business. "I can't let her do this on her own—at least, I should tell her that I know who she is," he vowed to himself.

After booking his flight, he packed and prepared to leave for the airport. "Judith or Saleeth—whatever I will call you in the future, I am coming," he said as he went back on line to book himself a room at the Mayflower. Raul seldom operated impetuously. "Maybe it is a good thing that I am doing this," he thought. "Maybe it tells me that I have finally found someone whom I care about enough to motivate me." He sent a short email to Carmen to let her know he was traveling again and where he would be staying. Then, he drove considerably above the speed limit all the way to the airport.

§ § §

In Paris, Abu had finished a modest dinner with one of his trusted aides. He had confided about the message from Georges, including that Washington might know about the Russian connection. "But we had to use them to get the poisons," Abu repeated.

"Yes, but if the Americans don't really know who is involved, what great harm is there in their suspicions?" His slightly older companion took a long drink of coffee. "We have other matters of greater importance just now! And, we will likely need the Russians again to supply weapons."

Abu had made a decision. "Georges has told me that he can get the name the Americans think is this bad Russian. If they know it is Vassilly, then we have to do something. We cannot afford to jeopardize the movement because of him. And, besides, he has promised eventual support from his government, but we have seen no evidence of that. How do we know he is not just working for himself?"

His aide stood up to pour more coffee for them both. "Do you think you can get the Council to agree to do something if the Americans do know?"

"Yes, but we need to have a plan first. If I go to the Council with this, they will want to know what we are proposing. They are not likely to want to cut off our Russian ties."

Abu leaned forward. "If it is Vassilly that the Americans know about, suppose I invite him to a little meeting as we did with our friend, the Turkish businessman, a few years ago? I mean the one who sold us the weapons that misfired?"

The aide smiled, and they both helped themselves to more coffee.

§ § §

Meanwhile, in Washington, Harold Harper had asked Paul to meet with him for an update. But Harold's most urgent need was to learn the name of the Russian who was suspected of complicity with the terrorists. He decided to be direct. "You told me two days ago there is suspicion that a highly placed Russian may be involved in all this, maybe as a supplier of the poisons. I would like to know who it is in case we intercept any intelligence from our own staff."

The logic of this escaped Paul, but he had no reason not to reply to his boss. "The Department of Defense believes that it may be Vassilly Rementrov, Chief Deputy for Security. I have not heard anything in the last twenty-four hours about this, however. Jeff did not ask us to keep this information confidential, but I assume we must do that."

Harold nodded vigorously. He certainly intended to do that, with the exception of sharing it with Svi. After Paul left his office, Harold pocketed his Blackberry, opened his office door and said to Simone, "I'm going out for about fifteen minutes. Just hold my calls." He walked outside the building. Fortunately, he was able to get through to Georges on the first try. Georges seemed especially pleased with the information. "This may be worth a bonus!" Harold thought, envisioning the Porsche he intended to buy very soon.

CHAPTER EIGHTY-FOUR

At 3:30 p.m., a Yellow Cab pulled up to the front of the Mayflower Hotel's cabstand, and two women wearing headscarves got in the back seat. Nania said to the driver, "We are ready." One of the most highly trained of the FBI's SWAT team then drove them twelve blocks to the Washington Monument. Instead of taking them to the vendors' stands, however, he drove slowly down Constitution Avenue, passing the Monument on their left, then turned at 24th Street NW making a circle to come back to the Monument. None of them saw anything unusual during this circuit, nor did any of the twenty additional agents who were positioned in cars, cabs and on the ground nearby.

"You know," said Saleeth, as they were about to get out of the cab, "I should have asked him how he looks now—maybe he has shaved or cut his hair and I won't recognize him!"

"We'll find him!" Nania said, and took Saleeth's hand. They began walking toward the food vendors, who were only some fifty feet away. They were looking for the vendor who sold coffee under the yellow and black-tented stand.

At the base of the Monument, watching yet another group of tourists enter the structure, was a man with short dark hair, clean-shaven, wearing a driving cap and tinted glasses. He carried a lightweight seersucker suit jacket over his left arm. In the breast pocket of the jacket was a Browning 9mm he hoped he would not have to use. He had been in front of the Monument for some twenty minutes, carefully observing the people walking around or parking their cars. He now saw a Yellow Cab discharge two women in pants suits and wearing head-scarves. The slightly taller one wore sunglasses. Her companion paid the cab driver, who slowly cruised on, obviously looking for his next fare. As the women approached the coffee vendor's stand, Ahmed began walking toward them.

The two women appeared to be studying the menu on the coffee stand and had their backs to him. When Ahmed was ten feet away, as if by instinct, Saleeth turned around. "Ahmed?" she said in as normal a voice as she could make it. He stopped and looked at her. She removed her sunglasses and he saw her eyes.

Smiling broadly, he said nothing but closed the remaining distance and took her in his arms. "Saleeth," he whispered through her headscarf, "Oh, Saleeth."

Saleeth felt the greatest conflict of emotions she had ever known. Her relief at seeing her brother was real, as much because it proved he was not dead as because this was part of her assignment. At one time they had been so close, and he had been her greatest friend and advocate. And yet, and yet… if everything she had been led to believe was true, her brother was a dedicated terrorist and a killer. He might be prepared to kill right now if he knew who she had become. She had rehearsed this meeting in her mind for so many hours, and now she had to play her part. "My brother," she whispered back to him, keeping her arms around him for a few more seconds.

Then she stepped back. Still smiling into his eyes, she said, "This is my friend, Nania. I have her and her family to thank that I can be with you today. She is going to walk behind us so we can talk. I hope that is all right."

Nania nodded at Ahmed but said nothing. He came to her and looked at her directly, smiling. "I am indeed grateful for all you have done for my sister. You and your family. Please permit us some time alone. I will try not to inconvenience you too long." Then, turning back to Saleeth, he said, "Shall I buy us all a cup of coffee and then we can walk?"

"Please!" replied Saleeth, and Ahmed made the purchases for all three of them. When they turned away from the vendor, Ahmed and Saleeth began walking along the mall to the west of the Monument. Children, teenagers and dogs were playing with Frisbees on the grass. It was a relaxing summer scene in Washington. Nania dropped about twenty feet behind them. Her short-range radio was activated.

Saleeth had her story well-rehearsed but her plan was to find out as much about him as he would tell. "You know, it must have seemed silly to you that I put ads in all the newspapers, but I did not know how to find you. I tried all your old numbers and they did not work! I was afraid to call anyone in the family—I think *he* knows most of them and may have told them I was sick or had run away and that he wanted to find me."

"I apologize for being hard to find. I have a very important job now with a multi-national corporation, and I have had to work under cover. I am so sorry about that as I have also looked hard for you!"

"What it is you do?" Saleeth asked, taking his arm and now squeezing it affectionately.

"I'm working with several governments who buy services from my company," Ahmed said, having also thought about what he would say and how he would explain his elusiveness. "I came to Washington to negotiate a very sensitive matter—I am not even traveling under my own name, so I am very glad you placed the ad. Can you tell me who your husband is?"

She had known this question was coming. "Dear brother, I would like to wait. Please understand that I have my reasons. Also, I don't want to put you in any danger. But what I would like to do is talk about whether you think you could get me out of the United States and back to our home without his finding out—because he has many friends in high places and they may be looking for me."

Ahmed stopped and faced her. They had strolled away from the larger crowds and he was sure no one could hear them. Nania was still a good twenty feet behind them. "Has he harmed you physically?" he asked, thinking, "And if he has, he will die for it as soon as I am finished with my other work here."

"He hit me once—that was right before I left, but he has threatened me many times. He has two more wives but they are not in this country. He also has a mistress. When we met, I did not know any of this. He promised me many things, including that he would let me work, that we would have children, that I could live a very free life. All were lies. I should have known something was wrong when he did not want me to contact you or any of our family when he wanted to marry me. But he told me he had had a feud with our father and that he loved me dearly. I have come to believe he is mentally deranged." Her lips trembled and she bit her tongue hard to force tears into her eyes.

Ahmed took her arm and held it tightly. "Before Allah, I will get you out. You must give me a few days. I will need time to arrange it, but because of my work, I have friends. We may need to get you out of this country by car or private aircraft in case this animal has people watching the major airports. Will you be safe for two or three more days with Nania?"

"Yes! We may need to find a new hotel since I am very nervous that he can track me down, but I can wait."

"Can you move to Nania's family home?"

"I do not want to put them in jeopardy, and besides, her mother is not well."

"Then I will call you tomorrow evening, but if you feel you need to move out of the Mayflower before that, then you must leave a message at the switchboard about how I can reach you. My cell phone is out of order, but I will find you. By tomorrow, I will have a plan." The look of relief and gratitude in her eyes could not be anything but genuine, he thought. Before turning to signal Nania to join them, she looked closely at Ahmed and asked, "My brother, will you be coming with me?"

For the first time, she saw a troubled look in his eyes. "Dear Saleeth, I will try, but I can only do that if my business here is finished. But you will be safe no matter what. I will not entrust you to anyone but to people I trust with my own life."

"Then, it is in Allah's hands," she said softly. They both turned and motioned for Nania to catch up with them. Then, very casually, the three of them walked back to the Monument. The two women took the first cab in line and Ahmed said he would be taking the subway back to his hotel. Ahmed and Saleeth parted with another embrace.

When the cab, again with an FBI driver, had gotten them one block away from the Monument, Saleeth let out a long sigh. "I think he believed me," she said, and with Nania's recording device turned on, Saleeth related the entire conversation into the little machine. They had agreed that Saleeth should not wear a wire in case Ahmed somehow discovered it.

Ahmed, meanwhile, was walking the five long blocks to the Metro Center subway station where he planned to board a train to return to his Maryland hotel. Despite his feeling that this had not been a trap, he had a plan to ensure that he would not be followed. He would get on the train, wait until it was near a station, pull the emergency cord, and escape in the ensuing confusion. He would have to time his actions correctly so that the train would be partially in a station. He doubted anyone would be able to catch up with him if he did this, but he could also tell if someone was deliberately following him.

But, as it happened, although three undercover FBI agents were following him closely as soon as he left the Monument grounds, luck was following him, too. When he walked down the steps into the Metro Center station and got to the Red Line platform, a fight broke out among several teenagers who, judging from their tee-shirts and hurled epithets, came from opposing local gangs. The fight escalated, the Metro security policy arrived, and people began to flee. Ahmed quietly exited the station, using a different stairway, hailed a cab, checked the traffic and decided he was not being followed.

The three FBI agents cursed, having lost him in the confusion at the station. Just to be sure, Ahmed exited the cab five blocks before it reached the Maryland border and walked the rest of the way back to his hotel. The weather was lovely, and he needed time to think. They had to get through Saturday's planned events, and he had to get Saleeth out of the country. And he was sure there was still a price on his own head. "But I have found her—I have found her!" he told himself over and over again. Knowing this gave him the courage for all the things he must do next.

CHAPTER EIGHTY-FIVE

Raul's flight got in to Dulles Airport at 9:45 p.m. on Thursday. Based on their arrangement, in fifteen minutes Saleeth would be trying to call him. He had to preempt that for the moment, so he sent her a short text message that said, "Tied up in a meeting—will call you on your cell later." Then, he took a taxi directly to the Mayflower Hotel. He had debated whether to dial her room directly, but he feared she might not answer herself if all this was part of a government operation. So he dialed her cell phone, just as he had said he would in his text message.

She answered it on the third ring and having recognized his number, said "Raul! I was afraid we were not going to talk tonight—thank you for calling."

"Sorry I was tied up earlier. I hope I'm not interrupting anything—are you back at your hotel?"

If only he knew! Saleeth thought to herself, but she said, "Yes, I'm in my room, trying to relax. We are making progress, I think, but I will be here a few more days."

"I'm sorry to hear that!" he said, trying to sound disappointed. Then, "Did you by any chance see *USA Today* today?"

"No," she said, sounding puzzled, "why?"

"Well, it's not so important but they did an article—with a picture—about one of my projects. The coverage was really very flattering, and I just thought perhaps if you hadn't seen it, I could ask you to go down to the gift shop in your hotel, buy a copy, and then call me back. I'd really like your opinion of the piece. But if that's inconvenient, we can talk about it when you get back to California."

"I'd love to see the article," Saleeth exclaimed, charmed, since Raul seldom talked about his work. Even though she now knew he was an agent, she also knew he was a very talented architect. "I'll tell you what—I'm still dressed and I was just going to make some tea, so I'll go down to the lobby, buy the paper— if they still have a copy—come back up and call you. Is that all right?"

"Perfect!" Raul replied. "I'll be waiting for your call." He sprinted out of his third-floor room and took the emergency exit stairs to the lobby two at a time. Then, he walked casually to the gift shop and moved to the back, pretending to be looking for a book.

Saleeth turned to Nania, who was sitting in an easy chair in the Saleeth's room. "I'm going down to the gift shop to buy *USA Today*. You don't need to come."

"All right," replied Nania, who was reading some reports. "We have two agents in the lobby, and I'll let them know you are on your way down and going to the gift shop."

Saleeth, without her headscarf, left the room and took the elevator to the first floor. She was half way across the lobby, having nodded to one of the agents she recognized, when she saw that there were a couple of people in the gift shop in addition to the African-American clerk. A blond woman with a large purse was browsing. A dark-haired man stood at the rear of the shop, near the book section. As Saleeth came up to the clerk, the blond lady left the shop. Saleeth asked, "Do you have any more copies of *USA Today?*"

Before the clerk could even answer, Raul turned and said, "You could borrow mine."

Saleeth stared. She had not anticipated that he would come and certainly not without telling her. Several thoughts went quickly through her mind. What would the agents in the lobby do if they saw her with someone? How could she persuade him to leave her and not interfere with the operation that he certainly knew nothing about—or did he? Had he become involved in the operation somehow? But that would mean he knew who she was!

She moved toward him. "Raul! What a pleasant surprise—you are looking for a book, I see, so let us look together." She took his arm and literally pushed him back to the rear of the shop where she was sure the agents could not see them.

Once they were back near the books, she kept her hand on his arm and said urgently, "You must leave here now. I am involved in something—something more than I have told you, and you may jeopardize it."

He turned to look at her directly. For a few seconds he said nothing, probing the look in her eyes. Then he said, "I know who you are, Saleeth. I do not know what this is all about, but I can guess most of it. I'm also with the Agency."

She let out an audible sigh. "How long have you known about me?"

"About who 'Judith Abrams' really is? Only since last night when a friend at the Agency told me about a legend that had been arranged for someone important. About why you are here, only since I saw the ad in the *Washington Post* this morning and figured out what you were doing."

"Oh, Raul, then I must tell you, I have known for several weeks that you are with the Agency, but I could not tell you about me—I could not. Please, please forgive me."

The smile spreading over his face told her all she needed to know about his willingness to forgive her. "But we must not let the agents in the lobby see you just now. They might think I am in danger."

"Of course, but may I come to your room—or you to mine?" He knew it was bold, but he wanted to hold her in his arms tonight and convince himself that they could be together forever.

"I must not come to yours. I am in a connecting room with another agent, a woman, Nania, and if you come to mine, she would need to know who you are." She paused slightly and then smiled. "But there is a lock on the door between the two rooms!"

"Then give me your room number and tell me when to come to you."

"It's 804. Come in 20 minutes. If there is anything wrong, I'll call you on your mobile before that."

"I'll be there."

"Let me leave the shop first," she said, and passing the clerk, she picked up and paid for an issue of *USA Today*. "Too bad there really isn't an article about him in it," she thought, "but much better to have him here in person." This would complicate everything, but just seeing him made her feel better.

In twenty minutes, Raul stood in front of Room 804. She had been waiting for him, and the door opened before he knocked. As soon as he walked in, he saw an older, dark-haired woman in a tan suit who now rose from her chair and moved forward to greet him. "You must be Raul!" she said, smiling. "I have called the Agency to check on you—you check out."

He shook her hand and produced his identification. "Just in case you get asked if I showed you this!" he said.

"Well, I think there is one too many agents in this room, so, Saleeth, I'll see you tomorrow. I'll still be taking all your calls, so I may have to interrupt you tonight if we hear from anyone that needs to talk with you."

"I understand, Nania, and I'll be ready for our 8 o'clock meeting with Andy and the others. Thank you for everything today." Nania disappeared behind the connecting door. They both heard her lock it from the other side, and Saleeth did the same from her side.

As soon as they were alone, Raul took her in his arms. For moments they stayed this way, not talking. Then he led her to a chair and gently pushed her into it. "I have missed you so much," he said, "and when I learned about all this, I was so afraid of losing you."

"They needed me here—and I wanted to help. I wish I could have told you."

"Has your brother made contact yet?"

"Yes," and she related the events from earlier in the day. "Now, we have to wait."

Raul stood moved toward the mini-bar. "Would you like something?" he asked, opening the door of the small refrigerator.

"Yes, I think a white wine would be good—will you have something also?"

"Jack Daniels!" Raul answered, with a short laugh. He seldom felt like he needed a drink, but he did now.

"Come and sit with me," he said, bringing their drinks to the low table in front of the overstuffed couch. She moved to him and they embraced for minutes before turning to their drinks. "How much does anyone know about what your brother has really been up to?" he asked.

"Not as much as we would like, but much of the evidence points to his involvement in the terrorists' plot. He seems to be have been the person who contacted CNN and is to some extent masterminding at least part of all this."

Raul took her hand. "My main objective is that you will remain safe. This is a brave thing you are doing, and I will stand by to be of any help I can." She smiled at him then, and he reached for the top button of her blouse. He had thought she might protest, especially with Nania in the next room, but she did not.

He led her to the bed and continued to undress her. At the same time, she loosened his tie and began to undo the buttons of his white shirt. The maid had turned down the bed. Raul gently caressed her for several minutes, drinking in her scent, her smile, her touch. He wanted to go slowly but was so aroused after several minutes that he let out a soft "please" and she rose to mount him. This time felt even better than the first. And, despite the feeling of urgency, they were able to prolong their climaxes and match each other's rhythm.

After the first time, she lay in his arms and said, "Now I'm not sleepy!" and laughed.

"I'll get the rest of our drinks," Raul said, rising and crossing the room. She admired him as he moved away from her—the long, strong legs, the tapering waist, the head of slightly unruly dark hair. She loved everything about him.

He returned with their glasses. Saleeth sat up. "You said you had something important you wanted to discuss with me when we talked the other night. I know that was before you knew who I really am, but can we still talk?" She was fully awake now.

Raul, still naked, knelt by the side of the bed and took her both of her hands in his. "Ms. Saleeth al-Kodari, I would be deeply honored if you would give me your hand in marriage!"

While it had occurred to her that this might be the subject, the events of the past 48 hours had all but wiped thoughts of such a future from her mind. Earlier, she had known she would have to tell him about who she really was, and she had not been sure how he would react. Now he knew, and he still wanted her! But would it be right for him, for them? Would her entanglements with her past and even with her brother make it impossible for her to ever be with Raul? As she looked at him, one thing became clear: she loved him.

She took his face in her hands and lightly kissed him. "I think I would love nothing more than to be your wife. Will you let me get through this week and then ask me again when it is over? I do not know what I may have to do or where I may have to go, but I will give you a final answer in a few days. In the meantime, please know that I love you and want you more than anything in the world."

It was enough for him. More, in fact, than he had expected. He got back into bed, kissed her and held her. After they finished their drinks, she began to stroke him and they both became quickly aroused. Afterwards, they turned the lights out and slept for several hours before the alarm went off. Raul showered, dressed quickly, kissed Saleeth, who was already up and in her robe making him coffee. "I'll go to my room—you have a meeting and probably a busy day. Can we have dinner, at least?"

"I don't know what is going to happen today, but I'd like to have dinner. Let me call you on your cell phone after six tonight if that's all right."

"It will have to be!" he said, giving her a long kiss, accepting the coffee and marveling at how good she looked in the morning without makeup and with her hair falling loose over her white robe. "I have things to do, too, you know. I think there is a very good jeweler or two along Connecticut Avenue, and I have a little shopping to do." He kissed her again and quietly let himself out.

Saleeth stood watching the closed door for a few minutes, and then she sat down to enjoy the rest of her coffee. "Mrs. Saleeth Caballero," she said aloud and then smiled. And then, she said softly, "Thank you, 'Judith Abrams'—thank you for helping me to find him."

CHAPTER EIGHTY-SIX
June 15, in Moscow

Pyotr knew that Elena was sleeping in the chair beside his bed in his Moscow hospital room. Daylight was creeping in under the window shade. She had come late the night before, carrying some clothes for him, which she told the guards that he would need as he began to walk around on the grounds. Some of her clothes were also in the suitcase. The guards privately doubted that they would be allowed to let their star patient do any strolling, but they were respectful. Shortly after she arrived for the visit and after the night nurse had left, Elena whispered the plan to Pyotr. Now, in the early morning, he thought to himself, "In a few hours, we will be in Germany." At 7:30 a nurse came in with breakfast for them both and Elena helped him dress.

At 8, the Russian official to whom the military guards reported came to tell them that at 9 they would be relieved of their posts, as Col. Pyotr Olenshinsky would be leaving the hospital in the company of two Americans from the Embassy. The guards were quite surprised but used to following orders.

At 9, two strapping Marines, now employed by the American Embassy as cultural attaches, entered Pyotr's room and introduced themselves to him and Elena. "Colonel, we are ready to leave when you are. We have an Embassy car waiting, and your airplane is ready at the airport."

When everything was packed, the two Marines helped Pyotr to his feet, escorting him through the door. No one challenged him, and the hospital administrator was at the front door to see them off. He fervently hoped the Colonel would give a good report on his stay at the hospital since it was very dependent on government funding.

The car sped to the airport and the four people riding in it were airborne within half an hour of boarding. The US aircraft was cleared for a direct route to Hamburg, Germany, where it landed safely six hours later. The first phone call Pyotr made when they were checked in to their hotel was to Maya's office, where he left a brief message with her personal assistant. It said, "Your old friend and his wife are now enjoying the scenery in Hamburg and want to thank you."

§ § §

It was before breakfast, Moscow time, when Vassilly received a call from Abu "This is early for you!" he exclaimed when he heard Abu's voice. "Are you in Paris?"

Abu ignored the question and plunged into the reason for his call. "We want to talk with you about the next opportunity, the purchase that we talked about some months ago. I do not want to do this over the telephone. Can you visit us soon?"

Clearly, Abu's organization must think things were going well to initiate what Vassilly was almost certain would be a discussion about buying weapons. "I'm available within reason—where and when?"

"I'll send you a message," Abu replied. "It will be in Europe. We would like to meet within the next week. I will come alone for this first meeting and I will expect you to do the same. But there is a condition that my council is imposing."

"And what is the condition?"

"We have respected all you have done, but my colleagues are worried that if anything should happen to you, we need to know the names of one or two of your closest associates with whom we can make contact. We are at a very delicate stage of our operation now, as you know, and we have never met any of your people, nor do we know if we would have the cooperation of your government without your being around."

Vassilly reflected on this request. While he fully intended to be the only contact with Abu and his people for the time being, he saw nothing wrong in sending them the name of one of his associates, retired from the Russian military, who not only had knowledge of where certain supplies were hidden within their vast country but who had been very instrumental in getting the anthrax spores spirited to Canada and Abu's people there.

"I will send you a message with a name and his contacts. He was very help-ful in your recent plan and he can be trusted." Vassilly made a mental note to let his associate, Mischa, know that his name had been revealed to Abu "But if he tries to go around me, he'll regret it," Vassilly said to himself, although he trusted Mischa—up to a point.

The fact that Abu and his people were likely looking for special weapons—possibly nuclear—now would mean he would have to brief President Lebrovny, or at least bring up the subject, since there was no way that he, Vassilly, working on his own could pull off this next deal. Selling the spores had been easy, and he had seen no reason to tell Lebrovny anything about that—especially if the plot had failed. But, it had not failed, and now he felt sure Lebrovny would be interested. After all, many in the government still looked on America as a potential enemy.

Of course, Lebrovny was harder to read—and, therefore, harder to work for—than some of his predecessors had been, particularly Putin. However, if Russia cooperated with Abu and the movement, it could not in the end do anything but weaken the Americans, and this was an old goal with Vassilly and with some of his compatriots.

"I'll look at your message and get back to you," he told Abu.

Ten minutes later, Vassilly had Abu's message, complete with the suggested date, which was the following Monday, plus the name of the village in Switzerland, the name of a private inn, and even driving directions. He replied just as swiftly that he would be there. He fully intended to go to the actual meeting alone but to bring one deputy with him who would stay nearby. He thought about asking Mischa but then rejected that. Better to have someone lower level at this point to whom he did not have to reveal much. Vassilly trusted Abu and his people only so far. "And, of course, *he* won't be traveling alone, either," Vassilly thought to himself.

"I think I'll wait until after this first meeting to brief Lebrovny fully," he decided. "All I'll tell him is that I have an important meeting in Switzerland that I must attend." The truth was that he wasn't sure how that meeting would go, and his hand would play better with the Russian President if he had a concrete proposal to offer, with a dollar figure attached, when he returned from the trip.

CHAPTER EIGHTY-SEVEN
June 15, in Washington, DC

On Friday at 8 a.m. in Washington, DC, President Bradley met in the Oval Office with Jeff Sanchez, Jimmy Buttero, Eileen Johnson, and Paul Blake. "Is Harold is still traveling?" he said, turning to Paul.

"He's on a plane to Cleveland to see how we can improve the security along the US-Canadian borders."

"I'd like to hear from each one of you," Elliott said, after they had helped themselves to coffee and tea. "Paul, what do we know about the origin of the anthrax?"

"We think that the anthrax spores had to have come from Russia, but we still have not traced their path here. They might have been smuggled in from Canada to a lab or labs here. We are working on that."

The President leaned back in his chair, "Based on my conversation with President Lebrovny, he, too, will be looking into that. As you know, we had good intelligence from Maya's source that the Chief Deputy for Security might have been involved in trying to get the GLONASS programming stopped, so he might be implicated. President Lebrovny has promised me more information when they have it."

Jimmy spoke next. "We haven't seen any special chatter to indicate any individuals or groups are up to anything, but we're monitoring a number of different sources. You know, of course, about the use of our agent who is the sister of al-Kodari, and that he made contact with her yesterday. She has told him she wants to leave the country, and we are working with our friends at the Bureau to ensure that we don't lose track of him the next time the two of them meet." Jimmy was still fuming about how the agents had lost the tail on Ahmed, but he and Eileen were collaborating on how to improve the surveillance.

Eileen had been looking intently at the screen of her cell phone. "I have some news," she said, raising her head. "Shortly after the DC police found the body on E Street that we were able to identity as Rafik Muhaimin, a cab driver came forward to tell the police he had agreed to leave his cab while two passengers had a conference. He had apparently also been paid to leave his keys in the cab so it could be moved, which it was. Our people have analyzed every inch of the cab and found some hairs not belonging to the cabbie or the victim. We asked Saleeth al-Kodari to give us tissue samples, and she complied. Our people have just reported finding a close match between her samples and the hair in the taxi. This might mean Ahmed al-Kodari was in that cab and killed Muhaimin. This could be a no honor among thieves thing or mean a real rift in their organization. We're continuing to pursue it."

President Bradley stood up. "We're making progress. I deeply appreciate everything that you are doing. I am going to keep on with my schedule as much as possible, but I am counting on Jeff to get us back together any time we need to talk. I don't think these people will sit by, and I don't think this is just about money."

Jeff decided to say something in front of the group that he had already said privately to Elliott Bradley. "Mr. President, I really wish that you would cut back on your public appearances just for a few days and cancel the state dinner tomorrow night. If they are going to try anything, the next target may be you." Jeff glanced around the small group and could see support in the eyes of the other three. But the President smiled and shook his head.

"Jeff, we've discussed this before, and I greatly value your advice as always, but I've told the American people that we are on top of this, and it would not be a good idea for their President to disappear right now. I have plenty of security, and I'm not planning any trips for the next few days—just some appearances locally. If we get any hard evidence that I need to be more careful, then I will be. We can always lock the Vice President in the swimming pool to keep her safe!" This was a joke, but they all had trouble mustering smiles. They all felt something was coming, and none of them knew what it would be.

CHAPTER EIGHTY-EIGHT

Ahmed wanted all the details for the weekend to be perfect. First, he called Luis who assured Ahmed he was ready. Then, Ahmed called Georges who agreed to meet him in the park near DuPont Circle at noon that day. Ahmed had a favor to ask Georges now, and he wanted to do it in person.

When they sat down on the park bench a few minutes after noon, Ahmed laid a copy of the *Washington Post* on the bench between them. Georges picked it up and casually opened it to the front page. On the top of the page, Ahmed had scrawled, "Luis is ready. I will make the call to get him out at 9 p.m. I will call you first. If you do not hear from me between 8:45 and 9, then you must make the call." Following that, Ahmed had written a local phone number.

Georges pretended to be reading an article. After a minute, he looked up at Ahmed and said, "Interesting article! I understand its point completely."

Ahmed looked around at the people near them. Most were eating lunch, reading messages on their mobile devices, or even napping. He moved closer on the bench to Georges. "I need to ask if you can arrange something. My plan was to leave the city soon after Saturday night. Now something personal has come up. I would like to use the corporate jet to get out of town, with a friend, and fly somewhere out of the country where I could get another flight to Europe. Can you see if the jet is available?"

Georges raised an eyebrow. It was true that he was in charge of such logistics, but he still might need to report to the "Travel Agency" if the Gulfstream was going to be flown out of the country, and he had not, as yet, admitted to his meetings with Ahmed. "I can try but I cannot promise anything. It would be better if we could fly you somewhere within the country where we could arrange for you to take another flight out of the country. Will that be satisfactory?"

Ahmed disliked the complication of an additional flight to get out of the US, "but better that, to get quickly away from Washington, and then make my way out of the country from another city," he thought to himself. "If that is the only possibility, yes."

"When do you need to know if this can be arranged?"

"As soon as possible—Saturday night or Sunday morning,"

"I may get questions when I ask for this," Georges continued. "What would you like me to say?"

"Tell them you may need to get Luis out. That could also be true, although he should be able to avoid any problems and take care of himself as we planned." Ahmed paused. He decided to trust Georges. "I have found my sister after two years. She has escaped an abusive relationship. She is in danger and wants to leave the country. I need to get her out. I would like to take her myself, but I know my own life is in danger. If she, at least, can be flown out on Saturday or Sunday, I could be at peace."

Georges remembered hearing about a missing sister. He also felt certain he could arrange for the jet without too many questions being asked, but he had, himself, been curious about Ahmed's reason. He sensed Ahmed was telling the truth. "And, if he goes back with her and they find him, they can do with him as they please," he thought. "It will be out of my hands." Georges had his own plans for the aftermath of Saturday night, and they did not involve flying anywhere on the "family's" corporate jet.

"Call me tonight between 6 p.m. and 7 p.m., and I will have an answer for you." Without looking at Ahmed, Georges arose with the *Washington Post* under one arm. He walked out of the park without looking back.

CHAPTER EIGHTY-NINE

By 3 p.m. on Friday, Harold Harper had concluded his meetings in Cleveland and was waiting to fly back to Washington, DC. His level of confidence in what they were doing to protect access to the US from Canadian waters was higher than it had been when he had left Washington. He was now thinking about how to get a call in to Svi Levi, since when they had met in Annapolis Svi had demonstrated a keen interest in how the US was guarding its borders against further attacks. In Annapolis, Svi had given him a new cell phone number, and much to Harold's annoyance, he realized that he had left the only copy of it in his office, carefully inserted in the back of a calendar that he was sure he had locked in his desk.

"Just have to wait until I get back," he thought. Instead of calling Svi, he used his iPhone to ring Simone, his secretary. "I'm coming back," he told her, "but if I'm not in the office by 5, you can leave. In fact, leave early if you want to. I'm going to work late. Just leave whatever has come in for me to look at and let Paul know I'll be back."

Simone appreciated Harold's thoughtfulness in calling her. She spent fifteen minutes organizing papers for Harold and also called Paul, who was in his office. "He says he may not make it here until after 5," she told Paul, "but he wanted you to know he would be in and probably working late. I'm leaving papers on his desk. If you won't be here after 5, just bring me anything you want him to see."

"Thanks, I will," Paul said, feeling some surprise that Harold would work late on a Friday but acknowledging that he had been around the office more than usual recently and had sincerely engaged in the issues surrounding the poison attacks.

Simone collected telephone notes and four folders Harold would want to read and went in to place them on his desk, which was, as usual, disorganized. She began straightening it up. Most of the papers scattered around were notes Harold had written for his own use later, and she merely tried to place them in orderly piles. In doing so, she moved a pad of paper with a note in Harold's hand. It simply read, "SVI. CALL BY FRIDAY, URGENT." The acronym "SVI" was new to her.

She was standing, puzzling over it, when Paul joined her. "Door was open," he said, setting down another folder on Harold's desk.

Simone looked up at him and smiled, then looked back down at the cryptic note. "Paul, do we deal with any organization called 'SVI'?"

Paul saw the piece of paper. "Not that I know of. Maybe something he's involved with personally?"

"I'm just concerned that if it was a call he was to have made today that perhaps he has forgotten it."

"I'll be here when he comes in, no matter what time that is, so I'll remind him," Paul said, and reached for the note. He left his folder next to the ones Simone had brought in, and both of them left Harold's office.

When Paul got back to his desk, he did a computer search for SVI and came up with two organizations, one a dance school in California, and one a marketing firm in Paris. He could not imagine Harold needing to call either one of these. He stared at the note for a few more seconds and then had a thought. Harold often printed in block capitals, so suppose "SVI" was really "Svi" and was a name or part of a name. He quickly ran a check against all names in the Homeland Security database and came up with no matches. Still with a nagging feeling about this, he called one of Jimmy Buttero's two top assistants, Bob Singh, at the CIA. He knew Bob was briefed in on Trial Run.

"Bob, can you have your people run a check for me on something? The name 'Svi' has turned up in something I'm working on. I'm not sure if it's a first name or a last name or maybe even just part of a name, but I'd like to know what you find."

"Sure thing." Bob said, not asking any further questions.

In fifteen minutes, Bob was calling back. "If it's a first name, we have eighteen matches. If it's a last name, we have only two. Do you want the entire list?"

"Please," said Paul, and within a few seconds they appeared on his computer. The two last names were both of people in Eastern European countries, both associated with universities. On the list of first name matches, there were three that could conceivably be people with whom Harold had some dealings. The one listed as number two was a low-level Canadian immigration official; the one listed as number ten was a retired minor government official in the UK; the one listed as number seventeen was an Israeli businessman. However, when Paul looked more closely at the notes associated with each name, he noted that the Israeli businessman had died two years previously. Also, the name had a flag next to it that Paul could not decipher.

He called Bob back. "Sorry to bother you, but one of the name matches, number seventeen, 'Svi Levi', has a flag next to it. What does that mean?"

"It means that we've had some indication that someone else might be using his name even though he's dead. Identity theft."

"Do your records show who that might be or whether it's been recent?" Paul asked.

"Let me check." Bob took another few seconds and then said, "I'll read what I'm looking at: "Three reports of use of the name, one in Canada and two in the US, within the past year. A Canadian rental car company reported the name. Hotels in Tahoe and Palm Springs also reported it. That's all I'm seeing on this one. Oh, wait: the car company and the hotels did provide phone numbers for 'Svi Levi.'"

Paul took a deep breath. "Bob, I need another favor, and I'd appreciate it you could just get the information and let me work on this after I get it."

"In other words, don't ask any questions?"

"Right. But I promise to tell you later, and it's probably nothing. What I need is to know if any calls have been made from Homeland Security headquarters— on any of our phones—to any of the phone numbers for the two names listed as numbers two and ten on the first name list. After you have that checked, I'd like to know if any calls have been made to any of these numbers from my cell phone or from Harold Harper's cell phone."

"That may take a little longer, but I'll get back to you as soon as possible," Bob said, concealing his surprise.

"Would the Bureau have anything more on this Svi Levi that you don't have?"

"Don't think so; we share these databases completely, but you could call Eileen. Sometimes things slip between the cracks or the coordination is less than instantaneous." Paul decided to do just that. However, when he called Eileen's office, she was out and not reachable, and he decided to wait for more information from Bob Singh before he pursued it further with the FBI.

This time, it took Bob half an hour to call Paul back. "No calls from any of your phones to any of the numbers we have for these two. Hope that helps! Do you want me to check any others?" Paul had anticipated the answer. "No and thanks." He hung up and sat thinking. Was he pursuing something utterly irrelevant and unimportant? "Let's review the bidding," he thought to himself.

"Harold has been getting increasingly interested in some details about the poison attacks. He goes on short trips and while we know where he goes, we know very little about why. He is talking about retiring in the Bahamas, maybe buying a boat there, but I don't know how he would have the money to do that—it may be all talk. Maybe I'm too caught up in what's been happening lately that I'm seeing demons where there aren't any."

Paul stood up and began pacing his office. "It would help to have a phone number for this 'Svi'," he thought, and realized that he should have asked Simone to look further through Harold's papers. He left his office and rushed down the hall. It was 4:20 p.m., and Simone was getting her purse out of her desk drawer. She looked up and smiled as Paul burst in, then frowned as she saw the look on his face.

"Is anything wrong?" she asked, worried.

"I don't know," Paul replied truthfully. "But I'm going to need access to Harold's office after you leave. I'll lock up if he isn't back when I leave here, and if he comes while I'm here, I'll explain what I'm doing."

"He isn't going to tell me," Simone thought, but with her profound respect for Paul, she was not about to deny him. "Yes, please, just lock up."

"Thank you, Simone," he said and held the office door open for her. He needed some time before Harold returned and time was growing short.

He sat down at Harold's desk and began to look through the stack of papers Simone had organized. While he did so, he played back in his mind the conversation with Bob Singh. And then it hit him—Bob had mentioned that the file on "Svi Levi" had shown three reports of that name being used in North America in the past year. Two times it had shown up at US hotels, and now Paul remembered that two of Harold's golf outings had, in fact, been in Palm Springs and Tahoe. He would have to get the exact dates from Bob and check his records on when Harold had traveled and where he had stayed.

Paul was making a mental note to do this when the office door flew open and a very surprised Head of Homeland Security found his chief deputy sitting at his desk. "What the hell?" Harold exclaimed, stopping to stare as Paul hastily got up. "What are you doing at my desk?"

CHAPTER NINETY

Paul rose to face his boss but he did move from behind the desk. He waited until Harold had walked across the room and stood looking belligerently at him. Then he said, "Harold, who is Svi Levi?"

Harold gripped the corner of his own desk and continued to stare at Paul. "I don't know what you mean!" he said angrily.

Paul still had not moved. "You had a note to call him urgently. There was an Israeli businessman by that name, but he died two years ago. His identity has been stolen. So, who is Svi Levi?"

Without taking his eyes off Paul, Harold slowly lowered himself into the nearest leather chair. "I don't know anyone by that name. What note are you talking about?"

Paul held up the piece of paper on which Harold had written himself the message. For a moment, Harold felt relieved since he had feared for a few seconds that he had inadvertently left Svi's new cell phone number out on his desk.

"Oh, I think you do know someone who is using that name. And I think you've been meeting him for your golf outings this past year, say in Palm Springs and Tahoe?" Paul was taking a chance now, since he had not had time to corroborate any data from the Agency. But it was too late to back out, and his accusation had the desired effect.

Harold sat back in the chair and closed his eyes. For a minute, neither man spoke. Then Harold opened his eyes and slowly sat forward. "He's an Israeli intelligence agent. I met him at a dinner more than a year ago. And, yes, he's paying me if that is what you are going to ask next, but we work with the Israelis all the time. I'm not doing anything that half a dozen other people in this town aren't doing. Sometimes our esteemed leaders don't give our friends in the Israeli government all the information they need, and they are among our best friends internationally. So I decided to help."

"And to line your own pockets," Paul thought, but he had to press Harold. "I'm going to make one phone call now," Paul said calmly, "and you are going to sit here and listen while I make it." He picked up the phone, put it on speaker, and dialed Bob Singh's number at the CIA. "Bob, I have one more favor to ask—can you run a check and see if by any chance there is an Israeli intelligence agent who has ever used or is now using the name 'Svi Levi'?"

"Let me get back to you—it should be pretty quick," Bob replied. "Do you want me to call you?"

"Yes, please call Harold's direct line." Paul gave him the number.

Harold got up and walked to the window of his office. The phone rang. Paul picked it up. "Paul here," he said.

"It's Bob," and Paul put the phone back on speaker. "We have absolutely no records of any Israeli agents—official or otherwise—ever called or going by the name 'Svi Levi'. That doesn't mean we might not have missed something, of course. The real Svi Levi was a clothing merchant; his company bought and sold fabrics and did custom sewing. He suffered from a heart condition and died two years ago."

"Do your files have a physical description of him?"

"Yes. He was five feet six inches, 195 pounds, receding hairline, brown eyes, pock-marked skin. That's about all I can get at this level. You want me to dig deeper?"

"No, thanks, that'll be useful for us for the time being. I'll get back to you."

"I suppose you still can't tell me what this is all about?"

"Not right now, but we will at some point. Just background for now."

Harold walked back to his desk. Paul had moved to the leather chair, and Harold sat down in his own swivel chair. His expression was tense. "He told me all the right things," he said, almost as if to himself. "He told me they wanted information on the terrorists' attack here so they could get ready if something happened in Israel—and so maybe they could also help us better." He looked over at Paul directly. "He may really be an agent—Singh said that they don't always know."

Paul said nothing. He wanted Harold to work out in his own mind what was happening. After a minute of silence, Paul said, "How does he contact you, or do you contact him?"

"I have cell phone numbers for him, usually at least two. He calls me if he wants a meeting, but I can call him at any time."

"Do you know where he lives? If he has a job that is his cover?"

"He lives in California. I don't have a home phone number for him."

"How do you get paid?" Paul could hardly keep the distaste from his tone.

"When we meet, or otherwise he mails me the money. I have a special post office box."

There was another pause. Then Harold looked directly at Paul. "Are you going to report this?"

"You know I have to. Can you tell anything about his nationality, other than that he might be Israeli?"

Harold closed his eyes, trying to bring to mind Georges' voice. "He has an accent. I always thought it sounded more French than anything else, but it isn't quite that, either. Israelis can be transplants from many places; I didn't think anything about his accent not being right."

"And you have a current phone number or numbers for him?"

"Yes. We met two days ago. He gave me a new cell phone number." Slowly, Harold unlocked the lower right-hand drawer of his desk and took out the small leather book calendar. He opened it and pulled out a sheet of paper with the number. He put the paper on the desk in front of him. "I was supposed to call him no later than today."

Paul walked behind the desk, almost standing over Harold. "Here is what we are going to do. You are going to call Bob Singh back and explain that you've been having contacts with someone you now think may not be who he says he is. That you want to bring the Agency and the Bureau into this. It's up to you if you want to admit you've been paid and how long this has been going on. I don't care about that. After the Agency and the Bureau get involved, it's also up to you what you do, although if I were in your place, I'd hand in my resignation. You may have endangered the lives of thousands of people."

Harold said nothing. His gaze seemed transfixed on the cell phone number he had thought belonged to a man named Svi Levi. Paul took out his own cell phone and dialed Bob Singh. "Bob, it's Paul again. We have a situation here. You may want to come in or send someone." Paul handed the phone to Harold.

CHAPTER NINETY-ONE

Forty-five minutes later, Bob Singh and Eileen Johnson's deputy, Al Bartle, were in Harold's office. Paul had made strong coffee for everyone, although Harold had not touched it. Harold's explanation took twenty minutes, during which Bob and Al took notes. At the end of the twenty minutes, Al spoke first.

"Mr. Harper, you may have committed a crime against your government. If you would prefer legal counsel at this point, please feel free to call someone."

Harold rose and walked back to the window, where he said nothing for two minutes. When he turned, his face looked ashen. "I don't need anyone right now. Is there anything I can do, any way I can cooperate that will help my situation?" Even now, Harold was thinking primarily of himself.

"If you cooperate, we will note that for the record, and it should help you. Bob and I need to confer." Al and Bob Singh got up and walked out to Harold's outer office.

"What do you think?" Al asked as soon as the door was closed.

Bob began to pace. "It's likely he's dealing with a foreign agent—and not one who is friendly. My guess is that it may be Georges Labadie, but it's hard to know. It may not be anyone connected with the recent poison attacks, but the man clearly isn't who he has told Harper that he is. I think we should set a trap, using Harper."

"Do you want him to set up a meeting?"

"Yes, and the sooner the better. Let's see if Harper can do that without arousing any suspicions on the part of our suspect."

"Suppose they have some kind of code so that Harper can say something to him to alert him?"

"From the look on Harper's face, I don't think he'd do that now. Of course, he's been a pretty fair actor so far, concealing this contact from everybody. I think we'll have to tell him what to say."

They worked on the strategy for a few more minutes, sitting at Simone's desk. When they returned to Harold's office, Al again took charge. "We want you to contact 'Svi' and tell him you have more information for him, just as you had told him you would. But tell him you must meet. Say that you want a payment during the meeting. That you are planning a trip and need a little something in advance. Set the meeting for tomorrow, Saturday, sometime around noon or the afternoon. If he cannot make it, say you must see him Sunday. Do you know if he is still in the DC area?"

Harold's complexion was still pale. "I think he is, but I don't know. He has the use of a jet and he moves around a lot, I think. But I'll try. If he asks about this new information, how much can I say? And where should I tell him I'll meet him?"

"Tell him that you have learned the names of two of the people the government suspects of having been involved in the poison attacks and that the government knows what they are going to do next. Can you use your friend's house in Annapolis again?"

"I'm not sure—my friend is coming home tomorrow, but I can offer to meet him in Annapolis, maybe at the waterfront. We could go out on a boat. He would probably think that would be a safe place to talk."

"How do you usually call him—from your home or from a cell phone?"

Harold reached into his suit jacket pocket and withdrew his mobile phone. "From this phone," he said. "Do I make the call now?"

"No, we need to arrange a trace. I think it's time for you to come over to the Bureau with us. You can make the call while we're there."

"Do you want me, too?" Paul asked.

"Yes, if you can make it. You've been part of the President's and Jeff's team—you need to know what is going on." Bob answered quickly.

"Then let me get my briefcase from my office. I'll meet you in the parking garage." He noted that Al was walking on one side of Harold, with Bob on the other. "No handcuffs—yet," he thought, "but, really, psychological handcuffs work just as well."

§ § §

Once in Al's office with the telephone trace set up, Harold made his call to "Svi." He did not really expect to reach him on the first try, but to his surprise Georges answered. Trying to make his voice sound normal, Harold said, "I've been out of town—just got back. Have some more information for you, especially names of people we think might be implicated—two of them in fact. Can we meet? I'd also like an advance when we do—more travel coming up."

Georges had expected Harold's call, but he was surprised at the request for a meeting. "He must really need the money," he thought, but there was no reason they could not arrange something. "Do you want to meet at your friend's house, as we did the other night?"

"No, he may be back, but that city is a good place. Down by the waterfront, at the dock where the tourist boats go out. Let's go for a boat ride around the harbor. Say tomorrow at noon?"

"Fine, and if something comes up, just give me a call."

"At this number?"

"Yes," Georges said, and rang off. He'd have to get some cash together for Harold, but it might be worth his while. "If he really does have names, we need to know that," he thought. Sooner or later he would have to cut Harold off; sources inevitably dried up or got into trouble. "But not yet," Georges thought, "not when things are going so well."

CHAPTER NINETY-TWO

Georges did not need anyone's permission to schedule the Gulfstream for a flight within the US, although after the fact he would have to report what he had done and why. He did call one of the two pilots they used, both US citizens but both loyal to the cause and completely trustworthy. The younger one was available any time on Saturday and Sunday. The aircraft was currently on the ground at the Winchester, Virginia Airport, and the pilot said he could make arrangements to fly it from there that weekend. "Let me get back to you about which day and time," Georges said, thanking him.

At 6 p.m., he called Ahmed. "Your plane can be scheduled as needed." He explained to Ahmed where the airport was. "You will have a domestic flight south and I will make additional arrangements for the next leg of your journey. What time do you want to leave?"

Ahmed had given this a great deal of thought. If anything went wrong on Saturday evening, he might need an escape plan early, but his main concern now was for Saleeth and getting her out safely. Sunday morning would be better for that, and perhaps he could join her after all. "I'd like to board the flight at 9 a.m. on Sunday. There will be two passengers, as of now." He suspected that Georges had told the pilot to fly them to Florida where they could get a flight to the Bahamas, or perhaps even board a boat. Georges would give him those details later.

Georges would later instruct the pilot that if only one person showed up for the flight that he had permission to take off if that person said no one else was coming. Georges did not intend to be at the airport himself—"too dangerous," he thought.

As a precaution, Ahmed had checked out of his Maryland hotel and moved across the state line into northwest DC, where he had found a small hotel that accepted his fake passport and cash payment for two nights without question.

At 6:15 p.m., Ahmed tried Saleeth's room at the Mayflower and again Nania answered. When he asked for Saleeth, Nania handed her the phone. "Please leave your room and call me from a pay phone or a cell phone," he said when he heard Saleeth's voice. He gave her the number of the phone he was using. "I have made all the arrangements. I will give you ten minutes to get to another location to call."

Saleeth and Nania immediately dialed Andy Shannon and the two other agents who were monitoring all calls to and from the hotel. "We have a trace on that call," Andy said, "but it's likely he used a pay phone or another disposable cell phone. Just wait ten minutes and use the safe cell phone to call him—stall him as long as you can and arrange to meet him again if you can."

Saleeth waited nine more minutes and then dialed Ahmed's number on the room phone. "Ahmed?" she said when he answered.

"Are you all right?" he asked, the anxiousness evident in his voice.

"Yes, my brother, I am safe and I am all right but eager to see you again. Shall we meet tonight?"

"No," he answered quickly, "I cannot do that, but I have a flight arranged for both of us on a private plane on Sunday morning. The people who own the plane are business associates of mine. We leave at 9 a.m., so we need to be at the Winchester, Virginia Airport no later than 8 on Sunday morning. You may bring as much luggage as you wish, but do not be late. Do you still have a passport?"

"Yes, and very little luggage—I left almost everything behind when I left *him*. It seems so long to wait until Sunday. Could we see each other tomorrow?" she asked, trying to prolong the conversation.

"I'm sorry, but I will be very busy in meetings right up until the time we leave. But you may call me at this number if you need me. Do you expect to stay at your hotel until Sunday?"

"I feel safe here, and Nania is staying with me. But I will call you if I am going to move. Are any of your meetings nearby? Perhaps we could just meet for coffee!"

Ahmed ached at having to say "no" to her again, but he was doing his best for her and that meant he could not see her until Sunday morning, if then. "I will meet you at the airport. Allah be praised that we will be together then."

Andy and the team had been able to trace the call to a location in Northwest Washington, but not to a specific location. "The problem is," Andy said when they had convened a conference call to discuss their next steps, "if he doesn't show up on Sunday, then we need to find a reason for you not to take that plane ride and make it plausible to him—assuming we are able to get you back in touch with him."

"Perhaps I could say that at the last minute I was afraid that my husband was behind all this and I did not want to get on the plane alone?"

"We can try that—and we'll think of some other alternatives between now and Sunday. We'll meet in your room Saturday at noon." They rang off.

Nania got up and stretched. "How do you feel about Indian food tonight?" she asked. "There's a great restaurant one block from the White House, and it's easy for us to walk, along with our armed guard, of course!"

"OK," said Saleeth, "but I need to call Raul and tell him what we are doing." He readily agreed to meet them in the lobby to walk to the restaurant, although she suspected he was disappointed that Nania would have to be included. "But only for dinner," Saleeth thought to herself, "only for dinner."

<h1 style="text-align:center">CHAPTER NINETY-THREE</h1>

June 16, in Annapolis, MD

Georges left himself enough time to drive to Annapolis and arrive at the waterfront an hour early. He parked his car in a free parking lot behind a clothing store, several blocks from the docks. He liked to do reconnaissance of a meeting site.

Two teams of CIA and FBI agents were also making their way to Annapolis. The Agency people by car, the Bureau people via helicopter. Harold traveled in the helicopter. He was wearing a wire. Paul had opted to drive his own car. Strictly speaking, he did not need to be there, but he had briefed Jeff Sanchez late on Friday night about Harold, and Jeff had asked Paul to go to Annapolis as an extra pair of eyes.

Eileen Johnson had gone in early to her office. Her administrative assistant had offered to come in to help her, and by 9:00 a.m., they were both at work.

By 11:30 in Annapolis, the tourists were ambling in and out of the shops. Georges, too, was strolling around. He had his eye on a small French restaurant for lunch—after the boat ride. The money for Harold was in a manila envelope in his sport jacket's inner pocket.

By 11:45, all the agents were deployed. Jeff had found a parking meter near the waterfront and sat for a while in his car. Harold had been let out of an unmarked car several blocks up the hill from the harbor and had walked to the dock. He disliked wearing the wire but knew it was their best shot at getting something incriminating from Georges. He spotted Georges looking at the various sailboats moored just beyond the harbor wall. The cruise boat office was just feet away.

Harold walked casually by Georges and said loudly enough to be heard. "Nice day for a boat ride—I think I'll try the *Miss Sally*."

Georges waited a few seconds and fell into step behind him. Both paid for tickets at the booth, and both boarded the boat, which was a two-decker rated for 66 passengers and holding about 30. The ride was scheduled to start at 12:15 p.m. and to last for 45 minutes.

At 12:16, with the safety briefing concluded, the captain backed *Miss Sally* out of her slip and slowly moved through the Annapolis harbor. They would cruise up the bay, go under the Memorial Bridge, turn south to the West River, and then return to Annapolis. Moving at a discrete distance from the *Miss Sally* were two private motor boats that had no distinctive markings and were populated by men in sports clothes who might or might not have been planning to fish. They did, however, have a catch in mind. Half of them were FBI; the others were CIA.

Georges and Harold had taken seats on the uncovered upper deck. They sat toward the back of the boat, and the two rows ahead of them were empty. The sun was bright, but on the water there was a breeze and the air felt pleasant. "Shall we have a coffee?" Georges asked politely, looking around to see who was on the upper deck.

"Too hot for me—but you go ahead. I'll wait here."

"I'll bring you a water then," and Georges departed for the lower deck and the bar. By the time he came back with their drinks, two young children were playing in the seats immediately in front of them, so Georges gestured toward the rail at the back of the deck, and Harold got up to join him there. The boat had moved out of the Annapolis harbor and was in the Chesapeake Bay. The captain was narrating and pointing out sites of historic interest, including the Naval Academy.

After opening his water bottle, Harold said, "Thanks for coming—sorry about the short notice."

"Quite all right," Georges replied. "And you have some news for me?" Harold was about to give his rehearsed answer, but his attention was diverted by a 22-year old hotshot who was driving his father's speedboat and had decided to show off to his date. The young boater was weaving in and out of vessels along the waterway and suddenly decided to cut in front of the *Miss Sally*. The little boat was on *Miss Sally's* starboard side but then sped ahead of her and swerved left just beyond her prow.

The captain of *Miss Sally*, who had operated powerboats for 26 years, swung the wheel hard to the right to avoid what looked to him like a sure collision. The boats missed each other, but *Miss Sally* rolled a few degrees to starboard before steadying herself. On the top deck, Harold lost his balance and fell against Georges, who had just put down his coffee and who caught Harold to prevent him from falling. In doing so, he felt something under Harold's sports jacket and shirt and suspected immediately that it was a wire.

"The barman forgot the cream for my coffee! Will you excuse me one more time?" Georges said with a broad smile, and without waiting for an answer, he headed toward the stairs at the middle of the top deck.

Harold was not quite sure what was happening, but the agents who could both hear and see what had happened all groaned. "He felt the wire!" the lead FBI agent said in his boat, and there were groans of assent. Still, at least they now had some good photographs of Georges.

After five minutes, Georges had not reappeared on the top deck. Five more minutes went by, and Harold decided to go to the lower deck. When he got there, he found Georges standing at the snack and drinks bar, having a conversation with the attendant.

"I was waiting for you. Do you want to go back upstairs?" he said, as soon as he got next to Georges.

Georges turned around and stared at Harold. "Do I know you?" he said, with a polite smile. Harold froze. Georges turned back to the attendant and resumed his conversation.

Harold sat down on the nearest bench seat and waited. After a few more minutes, Georges moved away from the snack bar, found a seat next to an elderly couple, and immediately began conversing with them. Harold climbed the stairs to the upper deck.

His wire was live so when he was safely at the back of the boat, away from all the other passengers, he spoke into it. "Something's happened—he's ignoring me. My cell phone is on if you want to call me. I'm on the upper deck and he's down below."

Within less than 20 seconds, his cell phone rang. The lead FBI agent was on the other end. "Stay where you are—he may come up. He may be testing you. But when you fell against him, he may have felt the wire. We're watching him."

The next twenty-five minutes felt like the longest in Harold's life. He knew he could not approach Georges, but if he didn't get evidence via the wire, his own career would be seriously in jeopardy. Finally, he made up his mind to do something. "I'm going to the lower deck—I have to use the restroom," he said into the wire.

The lead FBI agent was not happy. This was not going according to plan, and he did not trust Harold. "We'll try to intercept Labadie as he comes off the boat. Maybe we can hold him under the pretext that he is carrying cash to bribe a US government official," he broadcast via his own radio to the other agents.

On the lower deck, Harold saw Georges still in animated conversation with the elderly couple. He went up to him. "I need something from you," he said softly but firmly, grabbing Georges' left arm and literally lifting him out of the seat. Harold outweighed Georges by a good 30 pounds and he was strong.

Georges rose and moved a few feet down the center aisle of the boat. When they were back in front of the snack bar, where the attendant was closing out his cash register in anticipation of docking, Harold turned Georges toward him and stared at him. "You have something for me, and I have earned it!" he said in a somewhat louder voice.

Georges returned Harold's stare with a puzzled look. "My friend, I have no idea what you are talking about!" He pulled away from Harold's grasp.

People were staring at them now. Just then, the captain made the announcement, "We're docking in two minutes—in your seats, please."

Georges again sat down on the nearest bench seat, but there was no room for Harold, so he moved three rows back and sat, not taking his eyes off Georges.

The docking was quick and smooth; the dockhands had the gangplank locked in place within a minute of the boat's being tied up to the pier and stood ready to help people off. Passengers were queuing up, and Georges was the third one to disembark. "He's coming off the boat!" the lead FBI agent radioed to the others, and since they had agreed to detain him whether or not Harold had gotten anything incriminating via the wire, they began to move in.

Harold had just reached the gangplank and saw Georges already on the dock, when it happened. Georges suddenly reached into his jacket pocket and threw dozens of fifty-dollar bills into the air. They started to settle all over the dock, some of them going into the water. The dock was crowded, and people, especially the children, were quick to react. They ran after the airborne bills, grabbing at them, falling on them, and screaming. Two teenagers jumped into the water, one forgetting that he could not swim, and immediately hollering for help. In the few seconds it took for the agents to figure out what happened Georges simply vanished.

Harold, who had stopped just beyond the gangplank, thought he saw a figure that looked like Georges getting into a black and white taxi that was parked along with several other cabs a few feet from the wharf, but he couldn't be sure. Nevertheless, he spoke into the wire, "He may be in one of the taxis!" Two agents immediately sprinted toward the parked taxis but not before the first two had pulled out and driven up the main street, away from the pier.

All the agents assigned to the takedown had been posted on the two boats and by the docks. The agent who had been nearest to the taxis had binoculars, and he was able to get license numbers on both cabs, although he could not see that either of them was occupied. He called the special Annapolis police number that had been given for coordination and was rewarded two minutes later with the sound of sirens. By this time, the pandemonium on the dock had substantially subsided.

On a quiet street six blocks from the wharf, Georges had straightened up from his crouched position in the backseat and was paying the taxi driver, who thought he was letting off his passenger at a private residence. Georges got out. He had added dark glasses and a porkpie hat. He had removed his sports jacket. When the cab sped off, he walked behind the house and followed an alley to the parking lot where he had left his rental car. He put on a light-weight hooded golf jacket, removed his dark glasses and substituted a pair of tinted ones. Then he simply drove out of Annapolis, carefully following all the direction signs to Route 3, which took him by a circuitous route back to the Beltway around Washington and back to his hotel.

His plan paid off. By the time he was two miles out of Annapolis, all roads feeding into Highway 50, the usual route to DC, were blocked by the police and the FBI. The police had issued an APB for both the taxis that had left the dock when Georges was last seen. The surprised driver who had picked up Georges was stopped on the outskirts of Annapolis some ten minutes later. He readily described his passenger and where he had discharged him, but, of course, that was of no help to the police, the CIA or the FBI, who descended on a very indignant homeowner on a quiet residential street in Annapolis five minutes later.

Paul was on his cell phone to Jeff Sanchez. "It didn't work. Something went wrong. They didn't get anything, and he got away."

Jeff's tone was grim. "I'll tell the President."

CHAPTER NINETY-FOUR

June 16, in Washington, DC

Few Americans realize that Norway continues to be one of America's strongest allies. In terms of military cooperation, behind-the-scenes intervention in international trouble spots, and major cultural exchanges, Norway is a staunch friend. During the poison attacks, Norway's ambassador to the US and Norway's intelligence service had been kept fully informed. Norway's Prime Minister had promised all necessary support. So, the fact that President Bradley planned to host a dinner honoring the Norwegian Prime Minister's official visit to the US on Saturday, June 16, did not seem unusual. What might have seemed strange was that at a time of extremely tight security such a state dinner would go forward—but that was the President's decision. The Prime Minister had asked if he and his wife should postpone their visit, but Elliott Bradley had given a firm "no."

Beginning on Friday, Alan DeLong, the White House Chef, started actively reviewing plans for the Saturday evening state dinner. Trained in the best culinary traditions of France and the US, he prided himself on knowing the specific tastes not only of the President but also of visiting dignitaries. For Norway's Prime Minister, Arne Bjornstad, he would spare no effort—especially with regard to the fish courses, of which there would be two: lobster bisque and soft shell crabs to precede the roast prime rib. Alan ruled his staff with remarkable democracy; he had allowed debate about the soup course. In the end, the staff had concurred that lobster bisque, featuring the best of Maine lobsters, would set the right tone.

"Let's review the staffing," Alan said, ticking off agenda items at his all-hands meeting on Friday morning. His assistant read from a notebook. "We have four assistants coming in." He named them. "All have worked with us before. They will be checking in at 2 o'clock Saturday and receiving their assignments. They will be working on the soup course, the crabs and the fruit tart." Alan looked at his own list of items. "As of now, the dinner is for 30 people."

One of the sous-chefs raised her hand. "Alan, are we guaranteed shipment of the lobsters and crabs today? You remember the problem with the supplier we had last November."

"Yes, we are guaranteed. We are using Freshest Fish Market as they have always proved reliable."

With that, they turned to a discussion of the china to be used. "For the hors d'oeuvres course, we will be using the French provincial; for the main course, the Lincoln china." After clarifying that, Alan led them through a detailed discussion of the timetable for the dinner and their individual duties.

Alan also prided himself that he was a hands-on chef. At 2:10 p.m., on Saturday, he presided over his busy staff, sampling everything from the hors d'oeuvres to the soup to the chilled aspic. The four assistant sous chefs whom he had hired for the day had arrived promptly at 2:00. Alan was particularly glad to get Luis Jimenez, who had proved reliable for more than four years. Alan usually assigned Luis to the soup station, and this was where Luis was working at 4:00.

"First, I must give you your soup spice package for the special orders that came in with the fish you sent us." Alan handed Luis a small package with two bottles in it, and Luis thanked him. Then Alan said, "Luis, you remember the routine for the special orders?"

Luis looked up and smiled, "Yes, Alan, I remember. Everything will be ready on time."

At 5:16 p.m., the guards at the White House's back gate were inspecting the identifications of the first guests. The humidity had dropped slightly and the evening promised to be fair. At 5:20, Norway's Prime Minister, Arne Bjornstad and his wife Eva, left Blair House, just across the street from the White House, and with two Secret Service agents escorting them, walked to the White House.

"Mr. President!" Arne said, as soon as he saw Elliott Bradley waiting for them.

"Prime Minister Bjornstad, Mrs. Bjornstad!" Elliott said, shaking their hands. Elliott had no regular female hostess for these types of occasions, so tonight he had invited the director of the Smithsonian, Jessica O'Merrill, to sit on his right at dinner, and she was now waiting in the Blue Room to join Elliott, Arne and Eva for a drink before the formal cocktail hour began.

"This room is so lovely!" Eva exclaimed, as she looked around the Blue Room. "And the collection of china—may I just peek at all of it?"

"Of course, Eva, and if there is something you especially like, I'll have one of the attendants remove it from the case so you can have a better look!" Elliott smiled broadly. "In fact, take a look at the display in the hallway, too. I'm told there is a soup tureen there that Dolly Madison selected from France. Jessica is an expert—she can tell you all about everything here."

As Eva and Jessica moved toward the east side of the room, Elliott took Arne's arm and steered him toward to the tall windows that overlooked the sweeping back lawn of the White House. Earlier in the day, the President had expressed his personal thanks to the Norwegian government for their offer of help during the recent crisis. Now he said, "Some of my advisors thought I shouldn't have a formal dinner while we are still searching out the bad guys, but I'm grateful that you and Eva wanted to do this."

The Prime Minister, who was an inch taller than the President, turned to him with a twinkle in his bright blue eyes. "We wouldn't miss your hospitality for anything—and this is Eva's first time at a White House dinner, so I could not disappoint her."

"We have extra security measures everywhere—even at Blair House, as I'm sure you've noticed," Elliott went on in a low voice. "As I told you this afternoon, we're on the trail of two or three of the ring-leaders, and I'm confident we'll get them. Then maybe we can find out what is really behind all this."

As they spoke, other guests began to enter the Blue Room, and both men moved to greet them. From the President's cabinet, he had invited the Secretary of State and the Secretary of Health and Human Services and their spouses. The Vice President was away and several other cabinet members had had prior commitments. Jeff Sanchez was accompanying Maya. Other guests included Norway's Ambassador to the US, the head of the Friends of Norway organization, a sprinkling of people from the arts who had some connection to Norway including the conductor of the Dallas Symphony, which had just held an all-Norwegian music festival, and two retired journalists who had covered Norway early in their careers. It was a congenial group, and all of the guests looked forward to what they knew would be the excellent food from Chef DeLong's kitchen.

Just after the first round of drinks, Maya and Jeff approached the President and drew him to the side of the room for a few seconds. Maya was smiling. "I want to report that our friend Pyotr and his wife are now enjoying the comforts of Hamburg. I have talked with him personally. He is resting and grateful to you and our British friends for this very timely trip." Elliott returned her smile and reached out to shake her hand. "That's very good news. Thank you, Maya. I look forward to seeing him again one of these days."

At 7:50 p.m., the head butler announced that dinner would be served shortly. He and his assistants ushered the guests from the Blue Room to the Gold Room, where an elegant table had been set. The centerpiece, a china bowl given to

President Eisenhower by the Norwegian government, was filled with multi-colored irises and tulips. The Lincoln china shone on the table, complimented by the George Jensen silverware from Denmark. Small Norwegian and American flags were posted at each place.

The seating took a few minutes. The President sat at the head of the table, with Jessica O'Merrill on his right, Eva Bjornstad on his left, the Secretary of State on her left, and Arne Bjornstad next to Jessica.

The order of serving included a tomato aspic salad, followed by the lobster bisque. Then came the soft shell crabs, the prime rib with potatoes and asparagus, and finally a fruit tart. Coffee and after-dinner drinks would be served again in the Blue Room. White Chablis would accompany the aspic and fish courses, followed by a Pinot Noir with the beef. Elliott left the wine selection to Alan DeLong. Sometimes, when he dined alone, Elliott simply liked a very cold Budweiser.

While the aspic plates and freshly baked French bread were being served, the kitchen staff was at their busiest. Alan hovered over each station for a few minutes. The lobster bisque was being ladled into a tureen that had a warming device in the bottom so that it would be kept hot until served in the dining room.

"Do we have the special orders ready?" he asked Luis, who had been working over a small pot on the stove.

"Yes—they will go up in the smaller tureen."

Alan eyed the pot. In it swirled a rich tomato bisque but no lobster pieces. The Secretary of State and the conductor of the Dallas Symphony were allergic to shellfish. So, Alan planned to serve them the tomato bisque, well seasoned, followed by a mushroom tart instead of the soft shells. It was the kind of substitution the kitchen was very familiar with, and the trick was to make it as unobtrusive for the guests as possible. It was well known that the Secretary of State had allergies—shellfish and strawberries among them, but Alan made sure the requirements of every guest at every meal were known beforehand.

Alan walked away toward the ovens. Luis emptied the last of one small spice packet he had been concealing in an aspirin bottle inside his apron pocket into the tomato bisque. He stirred it some more. "Allah be praised," he said to himself, as he transferred the mix to the small tureen and walked it over to the food elevator. Two large tureens with the lobster bisque were being loaded; Luis added his tureen last.

"Special people again tonight, eh?" said one of the other assistant sous chefs. Luis smiled.

When the soup course was served, Arne Bjornstad beamed appreciatively at his host. "Wonderful lobster bisque!" he exclaimed.

Eva turned to her companion on her left, the Secretary of State. "Mr. Goldovsky, do you enjoy lobster often?" she asked in her lilting English.

"I'm afraid I'm allergic to all shellfish and several other things" he said apologetically, "but the chef here always takes care of me—whenever they serve soup, he always makes me a nice tomato one!" and with that, he lifted his soup spoon to his mouth.

CHAPTER NINETY-FIVE

hmed had questioned Luis closely about the timing of the courses at a state dinner. Early in the planning stages, he told Luis that the poison must be something simple and that they had to administer it so that it was clear they could focus on one victim. Luis told him that the soup course would be consumed between 8:15 and 8:30 p.m. This meant that Ahmed would have to make the phone call at a time that should get Luis out of the White House before anyone suspected him.

At 8:45 p.m., Ahmed called Georges' number. The phone was answered with a "yes?"

"I'm here and I will make the call," Ahmed said.

"I understand. Don't call this number again. I will find you," The line went dead. For a moment, Ahmed wondered if something had gone wrong that he should know about, but Georges had one of the two cell phone numbers Ahmed was keeping active so he assumed he would hear from Georges later.

This time, Ahmed planned to use one of the phones in the lobby of his hotel for the 9:00 p.m. call. He did not worry about a trace since he planned to leave the hotel soon after making the call. He would drive his newly acquired rental car to the Winchester Airport and either stay at a motel nearby or stay in the car, which would be uncomfortable but probably safe. His small bag was packed. He turned out the lights in his room and walked down to the lobby, where he located the phone booth near the men's room. Fortunately, it was the old-fashioned kind with a glass door that closed.

Ahmed dialed the special number of CNN's Washington Bureau. He bypassed the central switchboard and got immediately to the on-duty editor's desk. Getting this number had been surprisingly simple—it was on two web sites.

As soon as he heard the editor identify himself, Ahmed said, "Listen carefully. This is not a hoax. I am calling to tell you there is a bomb planted inside the White House and it is set to go off in fifteen minutes. I am the same person who spoke to your Mr. Blitzer several days ago, and my organization was responsible for the poison attacks in the US. Your government did not keep their word to us, and we said we would begin killing people. Tonight we are carrying out that promise. Mr. Blitzer's producer is Jean-Beth Reque. If you are recording this, she will recognize my voice, as will Mr. Blitzer. But if you do not wish to take note of this call, that is up to you. The bomb will explode in 14 minutes." Ahmed hung up.

§ § §

The serving staff at the White House had cleared the plates from the soup course and replaced them with the soft shell crabs, which drew appreciative murmurs. While clearing the plates, one of the butlers noticed that the conductor of the Dallas Symphony had not touched his soup. "Such a waste!" he thought, but he knew some people were finicky. What he did not know was that the conductor, who has specifically requested no shellfish, thought he had been served lobster bisque and was annoyed. Just at that moment, the Secretary of State pushed his chair back. Elliott looked up and saw that the man looked pale and had beads of perspiration on his forehead.

"Will you excuse me, Mr. President?" Secretary Goldovsky said, "I will be back quickly," and without waiting for an answer, he walked toward the dining room door nearest to the rest rooms, which were down the hall. Alarmed, Elliott signaled for the head butler.

"Jerome, I think Mr. Goldovsky may be indisposed. Will you check on him in a few minutes, please?" The head butler nodded and discretely left the room. Everyone else was enjoying the crabs, and the symphony conductor was happy with his mushroom tart.

In the formal dining room, the soft shell plates were being whisked away when President Bradley looked up to see his personal Secret Service agent running into the room, followed closely by Jerome. "Mr. President, we have a bomb scare! We need to evacuate you and your guests immediately—into the basement, sir."

The President rose. "Ladies and gentlemen, we have a bomb scare and must go to the basement bomb shelter. You will be perfectly safe there. Please follow me." As he started to leave the room, Jerome touched his arm, and Elliott turned around. "Mr. President," Jerome whispered, pale and shaking, "I have found the Secretary of State in the men's bathroom. He is unconscious, sir. We'll get him out."

In the kitchen, two agents were escorting the staff out. "If anyone wants to leave the premises, you may go. Otherwise, we need you in the basement bunker," the Secret Service agent in charge yelled before the terrified staff actually began moving. Luis quietly picked up his chef's bag and started to follow the crowd. At the last minute he froze: Secret Service agents were checking all the doors.

CHAPTER NINETY-SIX

Saleeth, Raul and Nania were having dinner in the Mayflower's dining room since the lead agent wanted them within telephone contact of the Mayflower's switchboard in case Ahmed called Saleeth at the hotel. They were just finishing coffee when Nania's cell phone rang. She listened for a minute, her face registering surprise and dismay. "We'll wait in the room," was all she said and closed the phone. "Something has happened, and it's urgent that we go up to the room," she said. Nania was silent on the elevator ride. When they got to the room, she immediately turned on CNN.

"So far, no bomb has been found on the White House grounds," the CNN reporter was saying, "but as we stand here in Lafayette Park, we can see at least a dozen law enforcement cars in the area. Tonight the President was hosting a dinner for the Prime Minister of Norway and his wife. It is not known if they are still in the White House. We have also learned that the Secretary of State, who was attending the dinner, has apparently fallen ill and been rushed to the George Washington University hospital just a few blocks from here. We will continue our coverage of these breaking news events here in our nation's capital in just a minute." The screen went to a commercial. Nania muted the sound.

"Two agents are on their way over here with a tape from CNN. There was a call to the CNN desk editor here in Washington, warning of a bomb at the White House. Saleeth, they think it may have been your brother who called. They are running a voice comparison with the tape from his call two weeks ago to CNN, but they want to know if you can identify the caller again this time."

Raul reached for Saleeth's hand. "Can we see what the other networks are saying?" Raul asked, and Nania handed him the remote. Everyone was reporting on the bomb threat. ABC was running a bulletin that Secretary of State Goldovsky's condition was listed as extremely critical.

"How long will they wait to see if there really is a bomb?" Saleeth asked Nania.

"I don't know. They'll search thoroughly. It may be that there isn't one or that if there is, it didn't explode on schedule."

They watched the television coverage for another ten minutes before one of the security men outside Saleeth's door called in to say that the agents with the voice tape had arrived. When they came in, they set up a playback machine and inserted the disc on which CNN had recorded the call. "The quality here is not the best," said the older agent, "but we would appreciate your assessment, Ms. al-Kodari."

Saleeth listened intently. "Please replay it," she requested and listened again. "I believe it is Ahmed. I cannot be one hundred percent sure, but I believe it is his voice." She looked from one agent to the other and then said, "But I don't understand—they don't seem to be finding a bomb. Did someone intercept it?"

"We don't know yet," the younger agent said, "but it's quite possible this was a hoax, although we don't know why."

Just then, the cell phone of the older agent buzzed. He took the call and was silent for a minute. Then he pocketed the phone. "The Secretary of State is dead. They believe it was cardiac arrest, but there will be an autopsy. If he didn't have a heart attack, he may have been killed, and the bomb threat may have been some kind of cover-up."

They all stared at one another, trying to figure out what had really happened. Finally Nania said, "We need to have a meeting about tomorrow morning, Saleeth. I'm going to call Andy Shannon." Saleeth nodded, confused about what all this meant for her and for the plan to capture Ahmed. "I can hardly think of him as my brother anymore," she said to herself and felt great sadness.

§ § §

At 4:15 a.m. Paris time, Abu was fully awake and watching CNN International. He was quite pleased with what he was seeing, "Although it might have been better if we had killed more than just their stupid Secretary of State and maybe there had been a real bomb," he confessed to himself. Nagging at him, too, was how much he could trust Ahmed who had, despite everything, apparently carried out his role again. His phone rang.

"I have two things to report," Georges began. He related in the briefest terms possible the Annapolis meeting, downplaying the danger he might have put himself—and the movement—in and emphasizing the success of the evening. Then he added, "I need to tell you something more. Yesterday, Ahmed asked for the use of the Gulfstream to get himself and possibly a female out of the country. I agreed since I knew you did not want him captured by anyone in their government. The plane is scheduled to leave from an airport near Washington at

9 in the morning tomorrow. Right now, the pilot has instructions to take them to Miami, Florida, where we have connections to get them out of the country."

"Who is the female?"

Georges decided to give Ahmed some cover. "He was not specific, but it may be his sister. He said that if he could not make the flight, he still wanted her to go."

"And is he planning to come back here or where?"

"The second flight I've arranged for him goes to the Bahamas. From there, I have told him he is on his own."

"This sister—if it is his sister—who is she? I mean, what does she do?"

"I don't know—he has only spoken of her to me a couple of times in the past, and I'm not sure that's who he wants to take with him. Is that important?"

"It may be. The reason I had ordered him 'returned' originally was because I had a tip that came from one of our trusted operatives that Ahmed had betrayed us to a relative working for the US Government. Is it possible she works for the government?"

This time, Georges paused, trying to think of the two brief conversations he had had with Ahmed about his sister, whose name he did not even re-member. "It's possible, but I would find it hard to believe. Ahmed is smart."

"Then here is what I want you to do. Keep the schedule for the plane that you have planned. But inform the pilot that he is to fly to the Fort Lauderdale Executive Airport and not to let his passengers off the plane until he has further word from you. I will tell you later which building he is to taxi to. We have a cell there with people I trust. I can make sure his passengers are taken off the plane and held. If it's only the woman, we have to find out who she is and what she knows. If it's him as well, I'll deal with that. Report back to me tonight after you have talked with the pilot. By then, I'll know what hangar the plane should go to."

Georges felt relieved. At least Abu had not dwelt on the events in Annapolis, and he had put Georges in control of what was happening next. Georges dialed the pilot's cell phone and gave him the altered instructions, which the pilot did not question.

CHAPTER NINETY-SEVEN

Just before 11 p.m. on Saturday, Saleeth, Nania, Raul, Andy Shannon, one other CIA agent and two FBI agents were meeting in Saleeth and Nania's suite. Raul offered to excuse himself, but they all asked him to stay. Andy Shannon had done so reluctantly, realizing that Raul and Saleeth were emotionally involved, but Andy was a professional. "I can sort all that out later," he told himself, for he had not given up on persuading Saleeth that he could offer her a better life than anyone else could.

"Let's go over the original plan," Andy began. "We'll have agents in the parking lot, inside the terminal, and in two aircraft on the tarmac. Also, two agents will be posing as mechanics, working on a plane that is tied down right outside the terminal. If Ahmed shows up, Saleeth will identify him by greeting him as 'my brother' as soon as he walks into the terminal building. It's also possible he may wait to enter the terminal until she is walking out to the plane. The normal security is minimal, and there is no metal detector. He could move very quickly from the parking lot through the front door to the desk and out the ramp door to the plane."

Saleeth took over the narrative. "Once I identify him, I move away quickly with the excuse that I need to use the restroom. The agents apprehend him. This could happen either inside the building or when we walk out to the plane. If he walks out to the plane alone, because I am already on it, I will disembark to wave at him and welcome him. That is how you will know it is him."

Andy continued, "My guess is that he will come in some kind of disguise—maybe good enough that you won't even recognize him, Saleeth, but unless he doesn't plan to go with you, he will eventually have to board the plane and we can get him then."

"What if he sends a decoy?" Nania asked.

"We'll have to trust Saleeth's judgment. If she doesn't signal that it's him, we won't move. But, Saleeth, if a stranger does board the plane, then you must get off. We can delay the take-off long enough for you to do that. Just say that you have forgotten some luggage and walk back into the terminal. You will be well protected."

"And if he does not come at all?" Nania asked, although she knew the plan.

"Saleeth will wait on the plane for fifteen minutes. Then she will disembark, saying she must call her companion, and we will take her away from the terminal while continuing to keep our agents on duty in case Ahmed and the pilot have some kind of arrangement. If necessary, we will apprehend the pilot and interrogate him, since he is likely someone connected with these people," Andy replied. "And, we'll have Saleeth try to make phone contact with Ahmed but by then he will probably have disappeared."

"Do you mind if I ask a question?" Raul asked. "What if Saleeth called him tonight or very early tomorrow and told him she was afraid to leave without him? That Nania's family had been contacted by her 'husband' and that she was fearful of getting on the plane alone?"

Andy stared at Raul for a minute. "It's a possibility," he finally said. "Saleeth, what do you think?"

"If I can reach him, I think it might help to get him there," she answered. "Unless he has come to suspect me, he really thinks he is helping me to escape."

"And what if he arrives earlier than we do and boards the plane?" Nania asked.

"He won't," Andy said with conviction. "He wants to help Saleeth more than himself. If he thinks she won't board without him, he'll wait for her."

"Unless he gets on the plane, sees me on the tarmac, comes to the steps of the plane and motions me in," Saleeth added. "Then what?"

"You don't board unless you are sure it's him and you still call out 'my brother'. At that point, we'll surround the plane and you do *not* continue to board. If you are half way up the steps, turn and run back toward the building," Andy answered, reinforcing a contingency they previously discussed.

"I think I should call him now," Saleeth said, looking around the small circle of agents. There were nods from most of them. "Should I do it on the hotel phone or my cell phone?"

"Use the phone here in the room; we have a trace on it and there is no reason he should not know you are still at the Mayflower. That might even seem more credible," Andy instructed.

Saleeth found the last cell phone number Ahmed had given her and made the call. "Ahmed!" she said, making her voice tremble when he answered. "I am so sorry to call you but today my husband made contact with a member of Nania's family and threatened that if they know where I am, they must turn me over to him. Ahmed, I am coming to meet you tomorrow, but I am afraid of what he might do. You said you might not be able to go with me, but I will not feel safe getting on the plane without you. He could have someone hiding on the plane to get me!"

Ahmed had been expecting a call from Georges with the final details of the second flight, and his heart sped up when he heard Saleeth. He had wondered up until that minute if he should accompany her or if she would be safer on her own, and he had been prepared to tell Georges that the plane would have only one passenger the next day, but now he knew what he must do.

"I will be there, my sister, I will not abandon you. You must not be afraid. Leave your hotel tonight and find another place to stay if that will make you feel safer. Is Nania still with you?"

"Yes, and she will not leave me until I am safely with you."

"That is good. I promise you I will be there. Now, I have some other business to take care of, but I will see you in the morning. Sleep well, and may Allah be with you."

After the call, Saleeth relaxed a little. "I think it worked," she said. "And if he isn't there, I think he will still try to stay in contact with me."

"Let's hope it works—this may be our best chance!" said the senior FBI agent. After this meeting, he was going to drive straight to Winchester to supervise getting his people in place and liaising with the CIA agents.

After all the agents had left and Nania had excused herself and closed the connecting door to her room, Raul took Saleeth's hands in his. "I want to come with you in the morning," he said.

"No, Raul, wait for me here. We've been through all this. If he shows up, they will capture him, and I will be back. If he does not, I will come back here anyway. I don't want you to be in any danger or to worry about me." She paused, touched at his concern. "I love you," she said simply.

Raul reached into his jacket pocket and pulled out a small box. "This is just about the least good moment I can think of to give you this," he said, handing her the box. "But please open it."

She did so, and inside sparkled a 2-carat, round-cut diamond ring. Saleeth looked up at him with glistening eyes. "I accept. Oh, Raul, I accept!"

CHAPTER NINETY-EIGHT
June 17

The drive from Washington, DC, to Winchester, Virginia, takes about two hours. Those agents who were going to appear by 7:30 a.m., left in their cars from several locations at 5:30. Other agents had arrived at the airport the night before and after checking out their positions, had had a short night's sleep at a local Days Inn. A CIA agent drove Saleeth and Nania in a car with a Mayflower Limousine Service sign on it. But it did not belong to the Mayflower, and it was armored.

At 1:00 a.m., Ahmed had a call from Georges who relayed the final instructions about the second flight. After his call to CNN, Ahmed had driven to Winchester and stayed in a Holiday Inn Express near the airport. At 5:00 a.m. he checked out and drove his rental car to an office building diagonally across the road from the airport. There, he had an excellent view of the airport, its parking lot, the terminal building and some of the aircraft tied down on the tarmac.

When he visited Winchester the previous day, he had entered the terminal briefly, noting the spacious waiting area to the left, the service desk to the right, the corridor to the pilot's lounge and rest rooms, the two small meeting rooms off the lobby, and the stairs leading to what looked like offices on the partial second floor.

There were no metal detectors, but the door leading out from the terminal to the tarmac was locked and had to be remotely unlocked behind the service desk. The entire airport was cordoned off with a high metal fence that had two gates—one to the right of the building to admit vehicle traffic onto the field, and one gate to the left, where traffic exited. The gates were controlled from the service desk inside. "I could get those gates open, if I needed to," Ahmed had thought to himself at the time, noting that sometimes a car would pull up, say something into the small speaker, and the gates would open. No visual ID was apparently required.

Ahmed counted only seven cars in the parking lot Sunday morning. He thought that at least two must belong to airport employees, and some to aircraft owners. One of them, an old SUV, had a coat of dust and looked like it had not been driven for some time.

Now, at 7:00 a.m., the first sign of life Ahmed saw was the arrival of a white van with red lettering on the side, which he could not read. A man dressed in lightweight coveralls got out on the driver's side. He went into the terminal and soon came back. The van started up and drove around to the entrance gate to the tarmac. The driver leaned out and spoke into the voice box; the gates opened long enough to let the van in, then closed. Ahmed saw the van drive to the side of a Lear Jet that was tied down near the hangar next to the terminal building. The driver and another man, also dressed in coveralls, got out and retrieved a box of tools from the back of the van. Both of them entered the plane. One of them came back out quickly and opened his toolbox under the left wing.

Ahmed could not see well enough to know exactly what repairs were being made. He did note that a Cessna Citation and a King Air jet were also on the field, but tied down and not showing any signs of life. Near the hangar next to the main building, he saw the Gulfstream with the "N" registration that Georges had described to him.

Ahmed's plan was to wait until he saw Saleeth arrive and go into the terminal. He wanted to observe carefully who might be with her or even following her. He expected Nania to be by her side. He would wait until a few minutes after 8 a.m., enter and find his pilot and then suggest that he and Saleeth board the Gulfstream. Georges had told him that the pilot would file a flight plan to leave at 9 a.m. but could probably get them out before that if necessary.

At 7:15, Ahmed saw a couple park their car in the airport lot and walk into the terminal. The man, who had bright red hair, was in a uniform. "Probably a pilot for one of the jets," Ahmed reasoned. The woman with him might well be an attendant; she had on a dark suit and high heels.

What Ahmed could not see was Andy Shannon and three other agents in the airport's upstairs office with the manager of the terminal, who had been both fascinated and terrified at the events that seemed about to unfold at his airport. "Wish I could take pictures of this for my grandson!" he had thought and then felt ashamed. "This is serious business," he said. He was sitting in front of the audio control panel that enabled him to talk to the front desk and broadcast out over the field if necessary.

Ahmed glanced at his watch: almost 7:30. He decided not to drive across the road to the terminal building until he saw Saleeth. But if she was late, he would drive the few hundred feet from where he was parked and leave his car at the farthest end of the airport terminal next to the dusty SUV. Then, just as he was beginning to wonder if she would come at all, he saw a large, dark car with lettering on the side pull up to the walkway in front of the terminal. Two women got out, both wearing headscarves. Even at this distance, he knew it was Saleeth and Nania. His heart began to beat faster, but he forced himself to wait. "It will be good to see who else arrives now," he said out loud and drew his black case that contained his two guns a little closer.

Within two minutes, his vigil was rewarded. A small compact car pulled into a parking space and a slightly built man got out, carrying a large brief case. He, too, was dressed in a uniform, and Ahmed could see a bright red band on either shoulder of the dark jacket, as well as a red symbol on the brief case. This was the clue that he was the Gulfstream pilot. Georges had told Ahmed only that "Mr. Arnold" would be flying them to Florida. Ahmed knew the name must be a cover, but he did not care. Ahmed started his engine and slowly eased his car out of its spot, heading toward the terminal.

§ § §

Raul waited until he had seen Saleeth's driver leave from in front of the Mayflower. They all agreed the night before that he should not go to Winchester. He was not part of the plan. Now, as he watched her leave, he thought, "but what harm can there be in my just being close by and observing?" He had been wrestling with this thought all night—a night he had spent in his own room alone—and he knew now what he must do. He took the elevator back up to his room, spent a few minutes there, and returned to the lobby. At the bell desk, he handed his car claim to the bellman on duty. "I would like my car brought around, please," he said. He had a Google map of the route. He calculated that at this hour of the day, the drive to the airport would take about two hours.

CHAPTER NINETY-NINE

Saleeth looked around the lobby of the terminal and turned to Nania. "I don't see him." They walked over to the lounge area. Saleeth placed her small suitcase on the floor and they both sat down. Saleeth had no wire or radio, but Nania had her 2-way radio. Calmly she spoke into the concealed lapel mike. "We don't see him yet."

Andy, who was waiting in the manager's office, had an almost unobstructed view of the main floor of the terminal. He spoke briefly into his own radio. "We've been in place for 90 minutes—if he's here, he's hiding! A young man in uniform went into the pilot's lounge about five minutes ago—that may be the pilot. Al and Anita are in there wearing flight uniforms. They can give us a head's up in a minute or two."

Just as he said this, Anita, the woman in the suit whom Ahmed had seen walking in earlier, came out of the pilot's lounge and went into the ladies' room. Immediately, she got on her phone. "Confirming Gulfstream pilot in the lounge. He's filed a flight plan and is checking weather to Florida." She came back out and went to the service desk, where she struck up a conversation with one of the two female employees.

Ahmed was out of his car and walking toward the front door of the terminal. He noticed a late-model Toyota Corolla parked at the opposite end of the parking lot from where he had left his rental car. It looked like someone was in the driver's seat, but he did not worry about it.

He took one last look around the grounds before opening the door to the terminal. Just as he did, the young pilot with the red shoulder stripes walked into the main lobby. Upon seeing Ahmed, who was wearing tinted glasses and no hat, the young man came over to him and offered his hand. "Are you Mr. Miller? I am Mr. Arnold—I will be flying you and your wife today."

Ahmed had now noticed Saleeth and Nania in the waiting area. He returned the pilot's greeting. "Thank you. We will be ready to leave as soon as you wish."

"I need to get out to the plane—give me about fifteen minutes to cool down the cabin, and then you can come out any time. Our flight plan gives us a 9 a.m. departure."

The pilot walked toward the door leading out of the terminal to the tarmac, and the desk attendant pressed the button to unlock it for him. Saleeth was on her feet and starting toward Ahmed, just as he began to walk toward her. Focused as he was on her, he noticed that Nania had gotten up but was not moving.

Just at the moment he was about to speak to Saleeth, the terminal intercom squawked loudly, and Ahmed heard the words, "There he…" The transmission stopped abruptly and a very embarrassed terminal manager, who had accidentally hit his transmit button on the console in front of him, turned to mouth an apology to Andy Shannon.

But in those few seconds Ahmed knew. He knew that this was a trap. He knew that whether Saleeth was a part of it willingly or unwillingly—the call last night, the meeting near the Monument two days before—all of it was a set up.

Ahmed unzipped his black bag and reached in. Saleeth was two feet away from him. "My brother!" she exclaimed and moved to embrace him. He let her come. Just as she reached her arms out, he raised his Glock to her head. Smiling, he said, "Don't worry, we will get out of here—together—just as we planned. And then we will talk later." He held the pistol so it was quite visible and began walking her toward the door leading to the tarmac.

"He's got a gun," Nania whispered into her radio, just as Andy Shannon relayed the same message. All the agents on the field readied their weapons. They did not have a clear view of what was happening inside the terminal building but they wanted to be ready if the action moved outside. They could see that the Gulfstream pilot had boarded his aircraft.

"Freeze the door lock!" Anita hissed to the desk attendant who knew something was wrong but could not see Ahmed's gun. She activated the lock on the door. Ahmed, holding Saleeth's right arm and keeping the gun at her head, tried the door twice before he turned to the desk.

"Unlock this door, or I will shoot my sister." When nothing happened, Ahmed momentarily moved the barrel of the gun from Saleeth's temple, pointed it at the desk attendant, and shot. The young woman fell over, unconscious and bleeding. "Now, unlock the door!" he said again, and the assistant receptionist, trembling and crying looked up at Anita.

"*Do it,*" she said, and the door was unlocked.

"Drop him if you can get a clear shot!" Andy said to the agents on the field, as he and all the agents in the terminal gathered near the door. "I'm going out—cover me." He opened the door. Anita was calling for medical assistance for the young receptionist. Her companion from the Bureau was close behind

Andy and now crouched just outside the terminal door, covering Andy. The other agents were taking up positions inside near the windows.

"He might double back and not go to the plane!" Anita said into her phone. "We're covering the terminal, but we need someone in the parking lot."

Nania ripped off her head-cover and ran to the front door of the terminal, her own gun pointed straight out.

Seeing Nania burst out of the front door was the first thing that alerted Raul to trouble. He saw Nania look around, then take a crouching position near the bushes that partly concealed the walkway to the parking lot. Within a minute, the red headed agent whom Raul also recognized had joined her. Raul leaped out of the Corolla and ran toward them. "Where is Saleeth? Where is she?" he yelled, his own gun now in his right hand.

Both agents were startled to see him. "She's on the field. Something tipped Ahmed. He has a gun to her head," Nania called to him as Raul ran toward them.

Without waiting for any more explanation, he ran into the terminal, saw the agents in position there, and headed for the door to the tarmac. In the background, he heard a siren but whether it was police or an ambulance, he did not know. He kept going.

On the tarmac, Ahmed and Saleeth had walked half the distance from the building to the Gulfstream. Ahmed noted grimly that the repairmen at the Lear jet were now pointing guns at him. He had no doubt that there were other agents concealed in some of the other aircraft on the field. They could shoot out the tires of the Gulfstream, and he and Saleeth would never get away. He stopped.

Without releasing his grip on Saleeth's arm, he turned toward the terminal where he judged most of the agents to be. "If you try to stop us, either now or when we are on the plane, I will kill her, the pilot, and as many of you as I can." He waited. No response. He noted that one more agent had come out of the door while he was speaking. One more gun pointed at him did not make much difference now. He turned back toward the Gulfstream. "Keep walking," he said to Saleeth, who was resisting his pull. He was practically dragging her now.

Then, in one of those clarifying moments that people in a crisis can have, a scene flashed into Saleeth's mind from a movie she had once seen. She pulled back from Ahmed's grip. He did not let her go, and he kept the gun at her head, but he turned to look at her. "You are not my brother—not after what you have done. And I am proud to be an American!" she said to him in a biting tone. When she saw the look of horror in his eyes, she felt some reward—and fell into a very convincing faint.

Andy, Raul and all the agents who had a clear view had seen her say something to Ahmed, but they had all assumed they would somehow have to get her away from him or disable the plane and then shoot him. Raul, however, had been repeating to himself for the last minute, "She is strong, she is smart, she will help us," when he saw her crumple. He had been aiming at Ahmed's head before she fell. Now, he shot.

Andy and the two Lear Jet agents also got off shots as Saleeth fell. Ahmed went down with four bullets in his skull and two in his chest, the last two courtesy of the agents on the Cessna and the King Air. As he fell, his body partially covered Saleeth's. With their guns still ready, all the agents ran toward the pair, just as Saleeth began to crawl slowly out from under Ahmed.

Raul and Andy reached her at the same time. She looked up at them both. "Raul!" she said, and reached her arms to him.

Andy Shannon realized that any hope of his winning her died at that moment. But he would never forget the elation of knowing that she would live. If his own impetuous scheme of anonymously getting word to Abu that Ahmed had betrayed his cause had ever implicated or threatened Saleeth, Andy would not have forgiven himself. "It's probably better this way," he told himself and, in time, he came to believe it.

Two of the CIA agents ran toward the Gulfstream. The pilot had heard the shots and came out to the boarding stairs. He had his own gun in his hand but did not raise it. When he saw two men with guns pointed at him, he dropped his weapon and raised his hands. He was badly frightened and did not know what he should do. Then a thought went through his mind: maybe the man called Georges would help him.

CHAPTER ONE HUNDRED

We have a line on who might have arranged the boat for the diamond drop," Eileen Johnson was saying over the phone to Jeff Sanchez several hours later on Sunday. The news of Ahmed's capture and shooting had, of course, made the rounds of the Trial Run team.

"When our agents went back to talk with people who own businesses and work along Water Street, a waiter at the restaurant next to the Freshest Fish Market said he had seen two men there carrying scuba gear out to a small tent on the market's dock a week ago. He thought that was interesting but he didn't make much of it. The owner of the Freshest Fish Market is Luis Jimenez. We interviewed him again, as well as all of his people. No one knew anything about scuba gear, of course. We're still trying to get a line on the boat itself and who might have owned or rented it. But Jeff, here's a really interesting note—Jimenez moonlights part time as an assistant chef at the White House. Guess where he was last night?"

"Eileen, the last report I had—you probably got it, too—is that the autopsy on the Secretary should be conclusive by later today. If it's poison, do you want to go after Jimenez or let him lead you to any others who might be involved?"

"I think we go after him and then grill him hard. Since it looks like al-Kodari may have been a ringleader and the dead man, Rafik, may have been in on the plot, we may have taken out two of the key people. Too bad about our not getting Georges Labadie in Annapolis. Harold is cooperating completely. I don't know how much more he can tell us, but we're still talking with him. Do you want a joint briefing from the Bureau and the Agency for the President tonight or tomorrow?"

"Tomorrow will be fine, Eileen. I've talked with the President twice this afternoon, and he's satisfied with everything that is being done. He'd like to meet Ms. al-Kodari at some point—to thank her, and I've relayed that to Jimmy and Bob. And he wants to thank our whole team when it looks like we have this wrapped up."

"Do we know anything more about the Russian connection?" Eileen asked.

"We are trying to find out where Vassilly Rementrov is. President Lebrovny has offered to have Vassilly arrested, but Elliott told him we would prefer to see where Vassilly turns up next, and who he might be dealing with. As of this afternoon, I don't have any more details. But, I'm about to call all the members of our team and ask for a conference call tomorrow at 10."

"I'd welcome that. We need to compare notes about some things. And, Jeff, I'm not convinced they didn't plan to deliver more poisons some other way. Remember what al-Kodari said to Wolf Blitzer? So far, they may have arranged the killing of our Secretary of State, but they could still be planning to attack one or more of our allies—or other cities in the US. And unless Jimmy and his people know for sure who was giving the orders to al-Kodari and Labadie, we don't even know who the real kingpin behind all this is, although we could make a pretty good guess."

"Were there any cell phones or other electronic devices with al-Kodari that you could use to trace his recent calls?"

"Jimmy's people are working on that, but I haven't heard any positive news. He likely was far too cautious to leave us much. Our best bet is probably still Labadie. The pilot doesn't seem to know much."

"Call me with anything you get," Jeff said, feeling very tired—he had been up nearly 24 hours.

§ § §

Two FBI agents sat in a black SUV outside Luis Jimenez's apartment in Southwest Washington, DC. Two others were stationed near the Freshest Fish Market on Water Street, even though the store was closed on Sunday.

At 2:55 p.m., a short but powerfully built, dark-skinned man emerged from the apartment building, carrying an overnight bag. "That's gotta be him," the senior agent said, quickly checking a set of photographs lying on the front seat.

"Let's go," the second agent said. They had clear instructions: pick up Jimenez, don't let him do anything foolish like commit suicide, and bring him in for questioning.

They both jumped out of the car. "Freeze, Mr. Jimenez, FBI!" the senior agent shouted as they went into a crouch position with guns aimed directly at the clearly startled man. He dropped the suitcase and held up his hands.

The first agent patted him down while the second agent kept his gun trained on him. They cuffed him and pulled his wallet out of his pocket. The senior agent opened it, then looked up at the suspect. "This says you are Marcos

Jimenez. Is that your name?" The man nodded, seemingly too frightened to speak. "We are looking for Luis Jimenez—do you use that name, too?"

The man held his now manacled wrists awkwardly behind him. He was not armed. "No," he finally said, in nearly a whisper. "I am his cousin. Please—what is this? I have done nothing wrong!"

The senior agent was on his phone. He listened for a minute and then said, "We're taking him in." To Marcos Jimenez he said, "Your cousin is under suspicion of having committed a federal crime. Is he in this building? Do you know where he is?"

The man shook his head from side to side several times. Finally, he said, "I don't know. He is not here. He called me earlier and asked me to come over. He asked me to go into his apartment and wait and then come out in two hours. That is all I know. He was not there. The apartment was open."

"We are taking you in for questioning as a possible accessory to a Federal crime," the first agent said, and both agents hustled Jimenez into the back seat of the SUV. The younger agent got in beside him.

"Mr. Jimenez, you had better think hard about where your cousin might be because if we cannot find him, we may have to keep you at FBI headquarters for quite a long time."

Marcos closed his eyes and rested his head on the back of the seat. He knew that he, himself, might be imprisoned. He had, after all, helped Luis with the pickup of the bags. But if he went to jail, so what? Luis was the important one in the family, the one they all looked up to, the one who protected them. Maybe now he could repay Luis by protecting him.

CHAPTER ONE HUNDRED ONE
June 17-18

Late on Sunday in Europe, Vassilly Rementrov made himself comfortable in a Zurich hotel. His colleague, a minor official in the Security Office, went to bed, but Vassilly stayed up for one last brandy. The more he thought about the possible negotiations he expected to have with Abu, the better he thought the prospects were for making some real money. Profit could come of this—for Russia and, of course, for Vassilly himself. The selling of the spores from the secret stash had proved very lucrative.

The sticking point would be to persuade President Lebrovny that such an alliance was a good idea, "but I can talk him into it," Vassilly thought. He had taken the opportunity to report to Lebrovny that he, Vassilly, was going on a trip that might prove valuable to the nation. He had told Lebrovny that he needed to take an assistant, and Lebrovny had suggested the very man Vassilly had in mind.

Now, early on Monday, he and his colleague drove their rental car to the village and inn designated by Abu. Vassilly's plan was to drop off his assistant about two miles from the meeting place, where the man would stay concealed for an hour, then make his way to the inn, disguised as a hiker. Vassilly did not discount the thought that he might need protection at some point, and his colleague knew how to use a gun. If all went well, they would meet at the same spot the next day and drive back to Zurich.

After Vassilly had checked himself into the inn, he found the small but picturesque dining room where Abu had suggested they begin their meeting. There appeared to be no one else at the inn—at least not in the dining room.

"Vassilly!" The voice came from behind him. Vassilly turned toward the patio door in time to see a tall, slender man in a loose shirt and trousers enter. He stood to shake hands with Abu "This is a quaint place you have chosen—and very private," he said approvingly to Abu.

Abu shrugged. "It belongs to a friend of the family, and the food is good. Let us have some lunch and then begin our serious discussions."

After Abu had signed for the meal, he said, "Come, let's go for a walk and start our talks. If all goes well, we can enjoy a good dinner after concluding our business."

Vassilly glanced toward the lobby and the patio several times during lunch, but aside from the proprietor and their waiter, he saw no one. He hoped that his assistant was now on the grounds. When both men got up from the table, Abu opened the door to the patio. The afternoon was balmy, with low humidity and an almost cloudless sky.

"There is a path we should take," Abu said, moving ahead of Vassilly. "It will give us a beautiful view and we can be sure no one will overhear." Without waiting for an answer, he led the way. After about ten minutes, during which the path became noticeably steeper, they came to a clearing. The view was, indeed, spectacular. Below them was a sharply dropping cliff that seemed to end in a thicket of trees some fifty feet below. Across the small canyon was another small mountain. "Sometimes, I have thought of moving to Switzerland," Abu said, smiling. "And now, what do you have to offer this time—or would you like me to tell you what we think we need?"

Vassilly had come prepared for either question, and he also had pictures of certain items that he wanted to show Abu, just to reinforce the point that Russia had some really interesting weapons for sale. He had slipped the documents into the small briefcase that he had been carrying, which he had laid on the ground as they came to the clearing. Now, he bent down to retrieve the case, and as he did so, he caught movement out of the corner of his eye.

The man who had posed as their waiter rushed straight out of the dense bushes to their left. Before Vassilly could even make a sound, he felt strong hands pushing him toward the edge of the cliff. He yelled then, as loudly as he could and reached out to grab his assailant. He was vaguely aware that Abu had moved back away from the edge. Losing his footing, Vassilly knew that he was going to be thrown over the cliff, and just at that second a shot rang out. Amazingly, it was not the waiter who fell but Abu. The second shot hit the waiter, but not before he had given a strong enough push to Vassilly to send his body flying out into space. Vassilly's final yell as he fell lasted for several seconds. Then there was silence.

The waiter and Abu were dead; a very calm Russian marksman swiftly took their pulses. Then he stepped up to the edge of the cliff to be sure Vassilly, too, was gone. His orders had been to finish Vassilly off, but he liked the idea of also getting two renegade al-Qaida—or whatever they were. President Lebrovny would be pleased, he thought.

As a precaution, he also retrieved Vassilly's briefcase. "And he was going to make a deal with these bastards!" he thought, shaking his head. He started back for the inn by an indirect route. He had a set of keys for the car, and he intended to get out of there as quickly as possible. "No sense running into more terrorists," he thought, adjusting his gun back into its concealed holster. He looked back briefly. It really was a beautiful view.

CHAPTER ONE HUNDRED TWO
June 19

And you believe the man who met with Rementrov was high-level al-Qaida?" President Bradley was saying on the secure phone to President Lebrovny. Jeff Sanchez sat across from the President.

"Mr. President, I am not proud of what Rementrov did, but, yes, I believe we may—as I think the English expression goes—have killed two birds with one stone." President Lebrovny chuckled at his own joke. "Apparently, they were both killed by one of the terrorist's body-guards—we don't know why." President Lebrovny felt this lie expedient. Even if the Americans suspected that he had a hand in the events, he was sure they would never ask.

"We have evidence that Rementrov was in touch with this man over some time. We are looking into what other negotiations they might have had. There is already some evidence that Rementrov sold them something of ours. I will let you know what we find out." President Lebrovny added in a more serious tone. "And I am happy to tell you that I have personally talked with Pyotr, and he is fine. We will have him stay in Germany for a few days until he is quite well and we are sure that his enemies went no further than Rementrov."

When the call was over, it was 1 p.m. The Trial Run team had teleconferenced earlier to compare notes. Jeff was making their report to President Bradley when President Lebrovny's call came through.

"Let's make a supposition," Elliott Bradley said. "Just suppose that the Russians, via this man Rementrov, sold anthrax spores to al-Qaida, and that those were the spores used in the attack on us. Do you think Lebrovny would ever admit that? I mean that they even have a stock-pile of spores and some went missing?"

"It's possible," Jeff said, leaning back in his chair. "He might admit it to you, unofficially. He has as many problems with terrorists and potential threats as we do, and he's been reasonably cooperative. The other thing is that we might ask Maya to talk with Pyotr about this, unofficially, of course. The military intelligence in Russia is still quite good. Pyotr might be able to find out more than the President!"

"Let's hope you are right!" the President answered. "But we interrupted your briefing from the team. What's the status of the traces on Luis Jimenez and Georges Labadie?"

"Jimenez apparently had bought a plane ticket several weeks ago for a flight this past Sunday in his own name—one way—from Reagan National to Ft. Lauderdale. We know there is a cell of the bad guys there, so we're going to try to trace him. Interestingly, the pilot who was to have flown al-Kodari and his sister has admitted that he was directed to file a flight plan to Miami but then divert to Ft. Lauderdale.

"As to Labadie, he seems to have vanished. The pilot had a cell phone number for him but the number is now out of service. The Agency file on him indicates that he's slippery. But, thanks to Harold, we have pictures of him and even a voice print. He'll turn up. We know his habits now: that he likes golf, expensive hotels, and good cigars. And he won't have his Gulfstream to travel on anymore. Incidentally, the Bureau is going over the plane with a fine tooth comb, although so far they haven't reported anything useful from their search.

"There is one other thing—the Bureau thinks they have found out where both labs are that probably put together the actual packages of poisons. Ahmed al-Kodari had some phone numbers on a piece of paper in his wallet, and one of them ties to a facility near Colorado Springs; the other is outside of Calgary. The Bureau and the Agency, with help from local authorities, have them under surveillance and will probably go ahead and make some arrests."

The President got up to retrieve coffee for both of them. "I've asked our press secretary to announce Harold's retirement later today, but to bury it in other announcements," Elliott said, picking up a paperweight and tossing it from hand to hand. "I think I'll appoint Paul to succeed him. What are your thoughts?"

"An excellent choice!"

"We'll have to charge Harold with something milder than treason and prosecute him, of course, but I'm asking that this be slow-rolled. First, we can reassure the nation that the attacks are over and the terrorists are not going to hurt us."

"I'm going to visit the hospitals in Cleveland, Boulder and Austin later this week," the President continued. "And I'd like to speak to the American people on the subject of the poison attacks one more time, but I think I should hold off until we have all the information we can get. But this afternoon in the press conference, I've authorized a statement about our having completely shut down the poison plot and anticipated subsequent actions that were threatened.

If someone asks—and you know they will—what 'subsequent actions' means, we will admit that the murder of our Secretary of State appears to have been masterminded by a terrorist who has been apprehended.

Later in the week, we'll release al-Kodari's name and pin most of the blame on him. If President Lebrovny can verify a connection between Rementrov and this man who was killed regarding the source of the poisons, we'll say that the anthrax was smuggled into North America illegally, apparently stolen from a Russian stockpile. But I'll give the Russian government credit for uncovering that connection. And I'll say—truthfully—that the leaders of this plot have all been apprehended or killed."

"The press will be hungry for more details," Jeff warned.

"I intend to emphasize all the good work our Homeland Security people and the CDC did, and how well our various agencies cooperated. We can turn this into an assurance for the American people that even though something bad happened, we got on top of it."

"Mr. President, I trust your judgment completely," Jeff said, amused that the President could read his thoughts.

In the end, the press conference went off surprisingly well, with most of the press asking questions about how health officials were coping in the aftermath of the poisons, how the balloon attack was masterminded, and about the details of the Secretary of State's death. A *New York Times* reporter probed for more information about how anthrax could have been smuggled out of Russia, to which the press secretary gave only a vague reply. Only one reporter, from the *Washington Post*, asked about the incident on Sunday at the airport in Winchester and got a short answer about an attempt to hijack a private company's plane.

The press secretary adroitly fielded all the questions, following the President's order to name no names but leaving a strong impression that things were returning to normal. No one asked about an incident in the mountains of Switzerland where three men died because no one knew about it. The next day, Russia's news agencies would have two lines about the death of their Chief Deputy for Security during an "unfortunate hiking accident" in Switzerland, but only two east coast papers picked up on the story. No one else bothered with it.

CHAPTER ONE HUNDRED THREE
June 20

Carmen Caballero took the red-eye from San Francisco to Dulles overnight on Tuesday, arriving at the Mayflower Wednesday morning, drowsy but eager to see her brother and meet her prospective sister-in-law. After a quick shower and change of clothes, she joined them in Saleeth's suite.

"So you are Raul's mysterious woman!" she said, smiling broadly, as she took both of Saleeth's hands.

Raul looked at the two of them with pride and love. There was a resemblance! His sister, slightly taller, had the same thick, glossy black hair pulled back from a wide brow, and they both had the same lilting voice. "They'll get on well," he thought to himself and smiled at them both.

"I think you may have been the one who got us more involved than we might otherwise have been," Saleeth said to Carmen when they were all enjoying scrambled eggs and coffee. She then related the conversation about "Mr. Miller" and how that had triggered her call to Andy Shannon.

"You'll meet Andy tonight," Raul added, "as we've asked him to join us for dinner. He's a bachelor!" He raised an eyebrow at Carmen, who laughed.

"But before that, we're going to the White House to meet the President," Saleeth added, sounding just a bit awed.

The visit to the White House included a private tour and fifteen minutes with President Bradley, who was at his most gracious. He insisted on hearing the story of Saleeth's coming to the US as a student and eventual recruitment by Andy. "Your loyalty and bravery may never be publicly acknowledged," he said, taking her hand at one point, "but I will never forget what you have done." Saleeth blushed deeply, while Carmen and Raul beamed. "And, I will expect an invitation to the wedding," the President said, looking very serious.

§ § §

The dinner party began at 7:00 p.m. at L'Auberge Chez Francois. The restaurant was the best Andy could think of. As it turned out he brought them news.

"They've captured Luis Jimenez, and with him some other suspected terrorists in Ft. Lauderdale. We've been suspicious for some time of a cell down there. Jimenez's presence gave the excuse we needed to go in and round up several of them. They're going to try to get a confession about the White House poisoning, at least, and maybe more. Hopefully, he arranged the diamond pick-up, too."

All four of them shared a celebratory bottle of Pouilly Fouse and put in their advance orders for dessert soufflés. Now, watching the evening clouds turn to pink, each of them had pleasant thoughts.

Carmen was delighted to be with her brother and his fiancée, and she found Andy pleasant enough—certainly good-looking. Saleeth was feeling deeply grateful for how this was all turning out, and she was able—for now—to put thoughts of Ahmed out of her mind. For the first time in two years, she had been able to communicate openly with her family in Jordan and Saudi Arabia, and this had given her great comfort. She and her cousin had both wept a little when they spoke—and then laughed when Saleeth confessed that she was engaged.

Raul was blissfully happy to have the two most important women in his life together, and was not unaware that he had bested a rival for Saleeth's affections. But he liked Andy, who continued to be deeply grateful that Saleeth was all right. Andy still felt pangs of anxiety over what might have happened— and over what he had lost, but he had to admit that Carmen Caballero was an attractive woman. He would have to arrange his assignments to get to San Francisco more often.

CHAPTER ONE HUNDRED FOUR
June 21

Traffic on Interstate 70 west of Kansas City was not heavy. The tow truck that had been called to assist a breakdown found the silver Buick and pulled over. The driver was standing by the car, sweat trickling down his forehead. "What seems to be the problem, sir?" the tow truck driver asked politely. He noted that the driver was dressed in what looked like expensive sports clothes and wore tinted glasses.

"Don't know. The engine just stopped. I was able to guide the car to the side of the road, and I called the rental car agency."

The tow truck driver did a preliminary check under the hood. "These advanced cars—it's almost always something with the computer—very hard to fix out here," he said straightening up. "What I'm authorized to do is to drive you back to Kansas City, towing your car, and when we get there the agency will have a replacement for you. Will that be all right?"

The driver gave an exaggerated sigh but then said, "It will have to be." Without saying anything more, he got into the passenger seat in the tow truck.

"Wonder if he's a foreigner," the tow truck driver thought to himself, for he had noted what he thought was a strange accent. On the drive back to Kansas City, there was not much conversation. When they arrived, the agency had a car waiting, and the driver, after completing some paperwork, sped away. "Not even a thank-you!" the tow truck driver remarked to no one in particular as he guided his truck and the disabled car to the garage.

The breakdown was, however, only a minor upset in Georges' plans, and it made him just two hours late arriving in Las Vegas where he planned to spend a couple of days before going on to Los Angeles. "Time to work up some new identities," he thought as he passed through the outskirts of Denver. Their plan had not gone as well as it should have but he, personally, had many options—and more than one possible employer. "I'll be back," he said out loud in the car, over the reggae playing on the radio.

§ § §

At 9:20 p.m., Eastern Time, the President was concluding his televised address to the nation. "We are confident that all the attacks using anthrax and Cryptosporidium have been completely contained. The laboratories in the US and Canada where the Cryptosporidium microorganisms were harvested and the poisons were packaged have been shut down. We believe the anthrax spores were taken illegally from a stockpile in Russia, without knowledge of the Russian government, and smuggled into North America. There are no more known sources of the spores in our country or our neighbor to the north. We have had full cooperation from President Lebrovny. While we deeply regret the many lives lost and the illness of many of our fellow citizens, the worst is over. The terrorists did not win. As I reported to you earlier, the ringleaders are dead, and their plot to blackmail the US and our allies has been completely foiled. They cannot hurt us now, from beyond the grave."

EPILOGUE
June 22

The haystack gleamed in the Wisconsin morning sun. Wesley Christianson had taken the two older boys into town with him. Ann Christianson was in the house, on the phone. Six-year old Zach wondered out to the barn, where he saw his dog, Melissa, doing something in the haystack. "Come here!" he called, but she did not come. He went over to the haystack. She was trying to burrow into it. He grabbed her collar to pull her back, then knelt and put his hand in to where her nose and paw had been. He felt his forgotten jacket that his brothers had thrown in there some time ago, and on top of it he felt something with slightly rough edges. Very carefully, he pulled it out. It was a white box made of material that he knew people sometimes used to pack things in. When he turned it over, he could see nine little flap doors at the bottom. Zach opened each of the flaps and saw what looked like nine light bulbs deeply recessed in the nine holes. He had no idea what it could be.

"I wonder how it got in our haystack?" Zach said to himself. He started to break into the Styrofoam. Suddenly he heard his mother calling him to come inside. What to do with the box? His closet had a shelf with extra space to store his treasures. He ran to his room and hid the box on the shelf. "I'll open it later and maybe I'll take it to school for show and tell in September." He closed the closet door.

APPENDIX ONE

The Report of the CIA's Directorate of Engineering

Dave Soltis was the head of the special electronics section in the CIA's Directorate of Engineering. Balloon number 101, which had fallen into the senator's back yard, had been picked up by a CIA airplane in Nashville at 3:00 p.m. on Wednesday, June 7. By 6:00 p.m., Dave had assembled a team of his best hardware and software engineers and they had begun work on the task of backward engineering the hardware and software of the balloon payload.

Ten hours later, they had completed their analysis and had finished writing a summary report for the DG. However, it took three hours to safely remove the glass light bulb contagion container vessel and send it to the CDC for analysis. Dave had already forwarded the preliminary report and promised to have a detailed formal report finished by midday. The CDC made their determination within one hour after opening the light bulb. This enabled Dave to send his full, formal report to the DG by 9 a.m., with an offer to have the engineers available for questions or to brief others as required.

The DG sent it on to Jeff Sanchez, who sent it to the President and to the team. The report that Jeff read and forwarded was the following:

CIA Summary Report on Balloon Electronics, Software code, and Materials

Our findings are divided into hardware and software. All of the hardware is commercially available off the shelf in many countries throughout the world. The software is straightforward code. Based on the hardware and software assembly, we have deduced the operational sequence and function of the system.

A block diagram of the hardware is shown below:

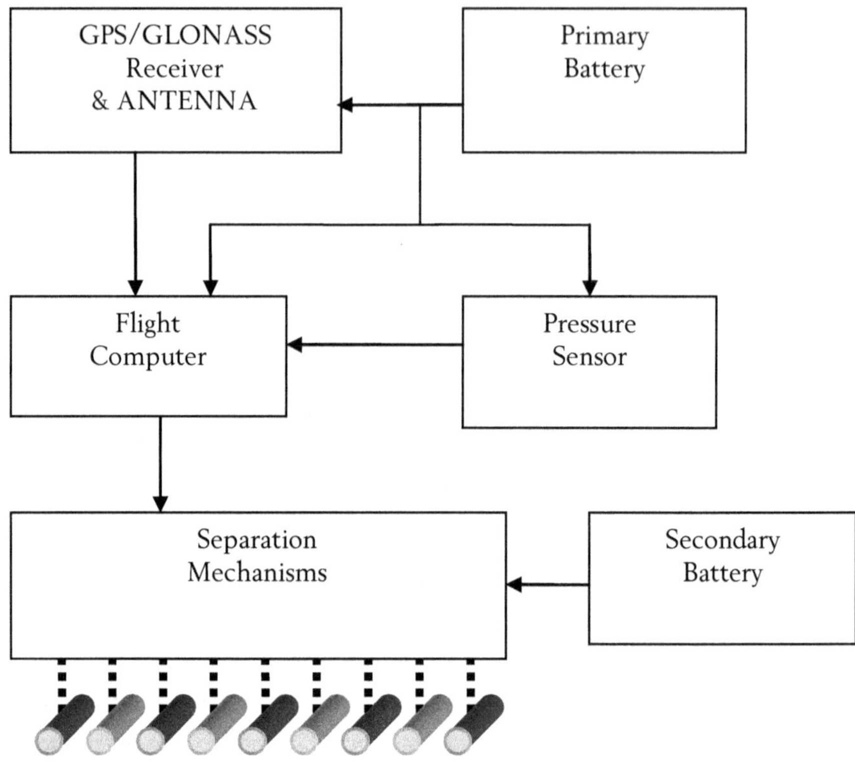

PAYLOAD CARRIER

The electronics shown above are housed in a box consisting of blocks of Styrofoam glued together in the shape of a cube about 14 inches on a side. It has thin fiberglass tape load spreading straps terminating at a plastic snap hook about 2 feet above the top of the box where it attached to another plastic ring at the bottom of the balloon net. The bottom of the box had nine equally spaced 2 ½ inch diameter holes about 8 inches deep. At the top of each of these holes is a short ¼ inch hole that leads to a 2 ½ inch diameter plastic plate that in turn houses a release mechanism. The container functions to provide a structural and thermal environment for the electronics and electro-mechanical mechanisms that constitute support and release for nine payloads.

One of the drop payloads had failed to release, was not damaged, and was subsequently removed and analyzed. The release mechanism consisted of a set of wax initiated pawls clamping a ball attached to the drop payload. There were no obvious wire or magnetic connections to the drop payload and x-rays clearly showed that the electronics for contagion release was self contained and designed to set off a pyrotechnic device based on a laser ground proximity sensor. An on/off switch was conveniently placed on the bottom of the drop payload cylinder. The unit was placed in a bomb proof enclosure and then extracted from the carrier without complications. Components inside the box and the drop payload were placed at angles to minimize radar cross section and very few metal parts were used.

Drop Payload Structure and Electronics

The drop payload is a cylinder designed to just fit into the cavity of the payload carrier. It has external fins to stabilize it during drop. It contains electronics, pressure sensor, laser altimeter, battery, a light bulb filled with contagion and a pyrotechnic charge to explode the bulb. The whole apparatus is mounted in foam inside a polypropylene shell.

The top of the cylinder has three stabilizing fins and a short ball end shaft for support and release. The bottom of the cylinder has an on/off switch, LED, and laser transmit and receive lens. On the side of the cylinder, near the bottom, there is a spring loaded arm switch that would arm the circuits upon drop assuming the on/ off switch was in the on position.

The electronics function to hold off all power until drop. The pressure sensor holds off the ground proximity sensor until 10,000 feet and the ground proximity sensor closes a pyrotechnic fire relay at 100 feet above ground. Preliminary estimates of accuracy of the proximity sensor are +/- 25 feet. The pyrotechnic device is referred to in the amateur rocket business as an electronic match. We have not tested this device but similar devices would blow the light bulb apart.

Light Bulb Contagion Carrier

The purpose of the carrier containers is to provide a structural and thermal environment for the electronics and electro-mechanical mechanisms that constituted the payload release device as well as support for the nine payloads that were attached. The interface between the payload carrier container and the balloon was a simple, mechanical quick-connect/disconnect clip.

A standard 100 watt light bulb has been modified by drilling two holes through the socket and sealing two glass tubes about ¼ inch outside diameter with epoxy. One of the tubes was clearly used to fill the bulb with contagion

Fugo

and flame sealed. The second tube was closed at the bottom and open at the top and extends almost to the end of the bulb. A pyrotechnic charge is inserted in this tube and the wires are sealed with epoxy at the top. The pyrotechnic wires lead directly to the fire relay.

Contagion Report

CDC just reported that the light bulb contained 25 cubic centimeters of Anthrax. They are now working on the source. If we are correct that all of the drop payloads are identical, and that all 600 balloons were launched, then it is possible that the system will deliver 198 pounds of anthrax and other toxins.

GPS/GLONASS Receiver

The GPS receiver's Patch Antenna and Low Noise Amplifier circuit cards were removed from their commercial package and mounted directly in the Styrofoam box. The cards are from a TF50 GPS & GLONASS unit available from Laipac Technology Inc.

Pressure Sensor

A Vaisala Barocap Barometer PTB110 configured to work with a 3.7-volt power supply was also mounted directly to a Styrofoam flat.

Batteries

The main battery pack consists of 3 packs of Lithium Ion batteries wired in parallel and the drop battery pack consists of a single pack of three batteries connected in series. These batteries are available from multiple commercial sources.

Flight Computer

A LP3500 low-power single-board computer featuring built-in analog and digital I/O was used. It consumes less than 20 mA when fully operational and less than 100 µA in its power-save mode. It is available from a company called Rabbit and has the following features:

Microprocessor:	Low-EMI Rabbit 3000T @ up to 7.4 MHz
Memory:	512K (2 x 256K) SRAM 512K
	Built in Real-Time Clock and Watchdog/Supervisor
Board Size:	3.65" × 2.60" × 0.45"

Interconnection Wiring

The components were connected with aerospace quality electrical wire. Connections to the circuit board revealed irregular and somewhat amateurish soldering techniques.

System Function

All of the electronics were found to be functioning when the package was received for analysis. GPS, GLONASS, and pressure sensor outputs were simulated and the computer system outputs were observed. It was straightforward to back out the code stored in computer memory.

The software programmed into the payload computer described above functions to command each of the nine payloads to drop. Payload location is always based on dead reckoning methods to account for temporary or permanent loss of either GPS and or GLONASS signals. This means that just shutting down GPS and GLONASS will not disable the drop commands. It will, however degrade the accuracy.

Drop decisions are based on calculating the payload's radial distance to pre-programmed target locations. We have found over 12,000 targets loaded into a target table.

Number	Latitude	Longitude	Radius	Payload
	(degrees)	*(degrees)*	*(Km)*	*(Type)*
1			5	A
2			5	A
3			2	B
***				
***				
***				
12354			2	B
12355			3	A

Each number in the first column is associated with a place. For example Number 1 may correspond with San Francisco. Number 12000 may correspond to Norfolk, Virginia. Numbers 11000 through 12355 defined the US coastline from Boston to Miami. These numbers in effect call for all remaining payloads to be dropped prior to passing into the Atlantic between these two cities.

Latitude and longitude are the center of the place to be attacked given in degrees to three decimal places. These coordinates appear to be selected upwind from the population center associated with the place based on statistical surface wind patterns for that location.

The radius of a target circle is a triggering range number that starts the computer to call a subroutine that make a more detailed set of calculations when the circle is entered. This radius number must be some kind of priority value associated with the target. We do note that these circles are adjusted downward from east to west. This may be associated with the larger number of targets in the east.

Most type A targets are associated with population centers, and there are only four payload drop mechanisms wired for this type. Conversely, there are 5 type B's and they are reserved for water targets.

Default drop commands will be issued to all payloads if the pressure altitude is sensed to be less than 10,000 feet.

The GPS/GLONASS receiver provides the payloads' current position. The pressure sensor provides information on low altitude abort situations. They are the only real time inputs to the system.

The software runs the hardware in a power saving mode based on time to target estimations. Mandatory wake up checks are built in at once per hour.

The electronics function in a normal mode and in a default mode should situations be experienced due to intervention or normal component failure.

Software Logic

The flight computer was probably powered up just prior to launch and the GPS would have initialized. The computer code start sequence synchronizes its internal clock with GPS and performs routine housekeeping checks on battery conditions and pressure sensor calibration against GPS altitude.

After a two-hour hold, the computer starts its dead reckoning routine followed by its payload release subroutine. This was probably included to give the balloon time to reach altitude with some margin to accommodate handling prior to launch.

The nominal routine and subroutine sequence follows:

Read GPS and housekeeping metrics. Store the GPS state vectors (latitude, longitude, altitude, time, velocity, and heading) and battery voltages and temperatures.

- Calculate and store dead reckoning vector (velocity and direction).
- Read entry # n from table.
- Using haversine equations to calculate range vector to target from last dead reckoning vector, calculate Range (c), and store in memory.
- Calculate Range from table R(t) divided by calculated Range(c), and time to target for target n table entry and repeat for n+j until j = end of table; i.e., until the table is exhausted.
- Store in memory: #n, range and time to target.
- Read memory and test each target for R(t)/R(c), and time to target.

At this point there are two possible outcomes that lead to separate subroutines that produce two distinct outcomes:

- Find largest R(t)/R(c).
- If greater than 1, enter refine for drop command subroutine.
- If less than 1, enter go to sleep and wake up later subroutine.

Refine for drop subroutine

If R(c) is less than R(t), the computer initiates a repetitive tracking of the particular target to determine if the range is converging or diverging. If the target range is converging, the calculations continue until they begin to diverge at which time a drop command is given for the next available payload of the appropriate A or B type. When a drop command has been given for a specific payload type, the computer automatically indexes forward to the next available payload of that type and puts a 2 hour hold on the just bombed target to allow time to drift off the target.

It is important to note that this process will continue independent of GPS being jammed or shut down. The decision will be based on the dead reckoning state vectors and therefore subject to large errors as time passes. However, if the GPS state vectors can be changed in such a way that the GPS position is deliberately skewed out of the US, then no drop commands would be given. This may be a weakness in the design.

"Go to sleep" and "wake up later" subroutine

If R(c) is greater than R(t) for all cases, the computer selects the smallest time to target from the set and uses this time (with margin added) as the maximum amount of sleep time available. The computer will then command both the GPS and the computer to sleep (low power) mode. A mandatory 1 hour maximum sleep time is programmed in. The computer will wake up and wake up the GPS when the sleep time has expired and start the whole process over.

Low altitude and or low voltage default subroutine

The computer will send an all payloads drop command if the pressure altitude corresponds to less than 10,000 feet and if drop battery voltage goes below all fire V(min).

The computer will not allow the low altitude command to execute until 2 hours after computer start in order to give the balloon time to climb well above the 10,000 feet level. This means that the payloads must be launched within 1 hour of payload turn-on.

Software code

The computer software was written in a code known as SPLAT. It is a popular in Australia and variants of it are used in several finite state machines.

Elizabeth Young

Elizabeth Young has worked in the telecommunications and satellite industries since starting her career in radio in Washington, DC. After serving as President of the Public Service Satellite Consortium, she joined COMSAT as VP and General Manager of Aeronautical Services and after a brief retirement spent teaching and writing, she became a General Manager SITA, the international company providing communications services to the aeronautical industry. She lectures frequently and maintains a consulting practice that includes clients in the US, Europe and Australia. She has held teaching appointments at The American University, The Ohio State University, Emerson College and Christopher Newport University. Her doctoral degree is from Columbia University.

http://www.EYoungbooks.com

Other books by Elizabeth Young

Do You See Him Now
(May 2011, Infinity Publishing)

Ellie Courtland has been haunted for thirty-three years by having witnessed the murder of her mother, an FBI agent. She has always hoped to remember more about the murderer. Suddenly, during one tumultuous week, she sees a picture that looks like him. She teams with the FBI to identify him. But he is looking for her, too, and her search tips him off. Everyone is a suspect – her mother's former partner, a friend's father, even her own long estranged father. While Ellie juggles the two men in her life, her teaching and her search, the murderer is closing in.

A Bother of Bodies
by A.J. Capper

Mabel Fuller and her brother are on the run because of Mabel's attempt to kill their mother fifteen years ago. But they're not worried about the law. Their main concern is the family that raised them, the McAllisters. Mabel and Dean manage to avoid the large Irish network with frequent moves and aliases. Or, so they thought. When dead bodies turn up in Dean's newly-purchased barn, the brother and sister fear the McAllisters have found them. Until they realize it's something worse...

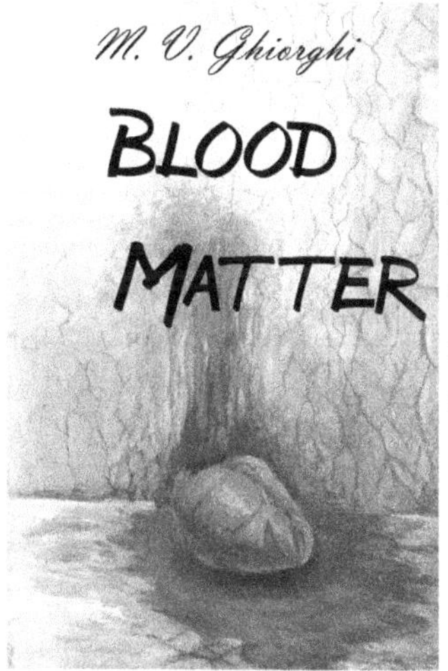

Blood Matter
by M.V. Ghiorghi

A broken hearted FBI Agent on the run from his demons... a sadistic genius with a penchant for vengeance... a beautiful forensic psychiatrist with a monstrous past...A doomed love triangle born of crime. Can Agent Vasquez survive the *Blood Matter?*

Visit Divertir Publishing at

http://www.divertirpublishing.com/